JUST FOR THE SUMMER

FAY KEENAN

Boldwood

First published in Great Britain in 2021 by Boldwood Books Ltd.

This paperback edition first published in 2022.

1

Every effort has been made to obtain the necessary permissions with reference to copyright material, both illustrative and quoted. We apologise for any omissions in this respect and will be pleased to make the appropriate acknowledgements in any future edition.

A CIP catalogue record for this book is available from the British Library.

Paperback ISBN: 978-1-80415-284-3

Ebook ISBN: 978-1-83889-104-6

Kindle ISBN: 978-1-83889-103-9

Audio CD ISBN: 978-1-83889-227-2

Digital audio download ISBN: 978-1-83889-101-5

Large Print ISBN: 978-1-80280-233-7

Boldwood Books Ltd.

23 Bowerdean Street, London, SW6 3TN

www.boldwoodbooks.com

This one's for my sister, Helen, and my brother, Luke, who tolerate my big-sisterness, and who I'd be more than happy to live next to. Thanks.

1

SOLD. The sight of the yellow and blue rectangular sign atop the post in the front garden of Kate Harris's home gave her a jolt. Though the sale had been confirmed some weeks ago, the estate agent had obviously amended the sign while she'd been dropping her three sons off at school. A neat but spacious detached property in the heart of one of Cambridgeshire's most attractive villages, it had been snapped up quickly a few weeks back by a young family desirous of more space.

Kate had been preparing herself, mentally and in more practical terms, for the ordeal of uprooting her sons and herself since the start of the year. It was only logical, now that the divorce had gone through and her ex-husband, Phil, had set up home with his new partner, that the house would have to be sold to release the equity and allow them both to start afresh. When the house had finally gone on the market in February, it had only been for sale for six weeks before an offer had been made and accepted. So now, in late March, knowing all of this, why did Kate's stomach turn at the sight of the sign? Why did her hand clench convulsively around her car keys as she pressed the key fob to lock it where it stood on the driveway? Why did her face feel hot, and her mind start to race?

Before she could take more than a deep breath, the phone in her other hand pinged. It was a WhatsApp from her friend and next-door neighbour, Lorna.

Saw the guy come to change the sign. Any news about when you have to get out?

Kate grinned. Trust Lorna to take the direct approach. She wasn't exactly renowned for her subtlety. That was probably why they got on so well, though. Kate, with three sons in the house, had discovered that subtle got her absolutely nowhere, especially when it came to getting them to complete their household chores. She valued directness in her friends, too. Turning sideways, she was unsurprised to see Lorna putting her recycling bins out, and obviously waiting to catch her for a chat, and check in.

'Fancy a coffee?' Kate called as Lorna set down the last of her green bins. 'I can fill you in on all of the gory specifics if you like.'

'Thought you'd never ask!' Lorna replied, hurrying over to the low fence that separated the front gardens and hopping over it. 'It's been a while since we had a proper catch-up.'

As Kate made two cups of coffee from the machine that would, most likely, end up in storage in the next few weeks, Lorna filled her in on the latest gossip from the Year 6 parents' WhatsApp group, to which Kate had resolutely refused to belong after she'd been passive aggressively reprimanded for dropping 'the f-bomb' on the forum, as one member had primly named it, with the caveat that, 'I'm sure I'm not the only one who checks her phone in sight of small eyes.' Kate, who had boys of thirteen and sixteen as well as her eleven-year-old, had merely rolled her eyes and refrained from pointing out that she was sure most modern parents had said a lot worse in front of their kids, and if they hadn't, then their siblings certainly had. She encouraged her sons not to swear in the house, but she was pretty sure that once the front door closed on them, all bets were off. Fortunately, Lorna, who had a higher tolerance for the playground pecking order, kept her up to date with anything of significance.

'I cannot wait to delete that bloody group from my phone, the second the gates close on the kids in the summer,' Lorna said. 'I mean, don't get me wrong, most of them are great but it's starting to feel more and more like some high school movie as the kids hit puberty. And it's only going to get worse.'

'You're a braver woman than I am for staying on there.' Kate laughed. 'And I'm grateful, so you can give me a heads-up on anything I'm likely to have forgotten for school.'

'Happy to take one for the team for a mate.' Lorna grinned. 'Inside, I'm counting the days, too. But enough of that crap. How's the packing coming?'

Kate sighed. 'Slowly. Much as I hate to admit it, Phil was right when he said that most of the stuff in this house is mine. He wasn't just being noble. I mean, apart from a hideous sideboard that I insisted he took with him when he buggered off, a wardrobe full of clothes and then the usual splitting of the CD and DVD collections and the pots and pans, the rest of it really does belong to me and the boys.' She shook her head. 'I never realised I was such a hoarder!'

'Well, you were married for sixteen years, and three kids will fill your house faster than teenage girls to the O2 Arena to watch Harry Styles, so it's hardly surprising.' Lorna took a sip of her coffee. 'So, when's the completion date?'

'The first Monday of May half term,' Kate replied.

'Jesus! That's about ten weeks away. You'd better get your act together, then.'

'You're not kidding.' Kate sat back on the padded bar seat that had been 'hers' for the duration of her marriage. Phil had been a creature of habit, and would never dream of sitting in it, far preferring the other side of the table. That rigid sense of routine was what had made his sudden declaration, just over two years ago, that he'd fallen in love with a fellow architect at his firm, all the more shocking. Within two weeks of telling her, he'd moved out of the family home and into his new love nest one village over, and set up home with alarming speed. While she couldn't complain about his financial support of her and the boys over the past two years, and he'd been more than helpful in terms of his access to the boys at weekends and in the school holidays, now that the time had come to actually move out of the family home, Kate's sadness and grief was creeping back up on her.

'It's all right to feel miserable, you know,' Lorna said, obviously sensing that behind the jokes about WhatsApp, Kate was struggling. 'You've been through so much over the past couple of years. And I know you don't like it when I call Phil "that shit of an ex-husband", but you didn't deserve any of it.'

'I'm fine.' Kate swallowed a mouthful of still scalding coffee to try to get rid of the lump in her throat. 'It's not like I didn't know this was coming.'

'Still doesn't make it any easier,' Lorna said stoutly. 'I know when Dan finally moved out, I kept finding his stuff for months afterwards. I couldn't look at the hook on the back of the bathroom door without imagining his dressing gown on it. It takes time.'

'Well, I've got a couple of months to pack everything up,' Kate said, 'and Mum's offered me the annexe at the bottom of her garden for the time being – although God knows how all four of us are going to fit in there – it's only got two bedrooms and a sofa bed in the lounge. Guess where I'll be sleeping!'

'Sounds like it'll be, er, *cosy*,' Lorna said. 'I'd offer you my spare rooms, but something tells me the last thing you'll need is to witness the new people setting up home in your old house.' She looked thoughtful for a moment. 'Although, now you come to mention it...'

'What?' Kate looked at her friend, who smiled enigmatically.

'Is the annexe your absolute last resort?' Lorna said. 'As in, if something better, but with a teeny, tiny string attached came along, you'd snap it up?'

'Yeah, I suppose,' Kate said. 'What are you thinking?'

'Leave it with me,' Lorna said, finishing up her coffee. 'It might not be what you want, but I'm pretty sure I can find you something better than the bottom of your mum's garden, for a few months at least.' She stood up. 'I'll text you later. Don't say yes to your mum just yet.'

'Okay,' Kate said dubiously. 'But you do know that I've got three sons, right? And they're often not the most careful of people. If what you've got in mind involves anywhere expensive, with breakables, it's a non-starter.'

'Oh, your lot aren't that bad,' Lorna said. 'I'll be in touch. Now get on with that packing. Or at least thinking about what to put in boxes first!'

Wondering, as she often had over the years that she'd known Lorna, whether her proposed 'solution' would actually lead to more complications, Kate still couldn't help feeling intrigued. Anything that meant she didn't have to squish into the annexe with her mum's beady, disappointed eye on her from the other end of the garden had, surely, to be a good thing. Didn't it?

2

Four weeks on, and Kate felt as though she was going to go bald, she'd torn so much of her hair out trying to get her sons to pack their stuff up ready for the move. Surely it wasn't essential to take every PlayStation game with them into their temporary accommodation? As it had turned out, Lorna's idea for a place to stay had materialised. She'd sorted out a charming cottage in a nearby village (thankfully not the same one where Phil and his new partner, Jennifer, were living), which belonged to a friend of hers. A holiday let, the 'teeny, weeny string' that came attached to the place was that the owner wanted it freshening up before offering it as an Airbnb for the summer season. Strapped for cash already, so needing the job done on the cheap, he'd offered it to Kate rent-free if she spent the next few weeks giving it a lick of paint. Because it was a holiday home, the redecoration needed to be neutral, and hard-wearing. Kate, who'd spoken to Lorna some time ago about *possibly* starting her own business as a painter and decorator, was initially thrown into a tailspin, until Lorna had reassured her that the owner 'couldn't care less what you do with the place, so long as it looks good in the photos'.

Kate had agreed to let the cottage become her first blank canvas, and was already excited to pick out some colours from the Farrow and Ball and Craig and Rose colour charts. With the boys at school all day, she hoped she could tackle the living areas and the three small bedrooms with minimal disruption to them. And with, in theory at least, as few possessions as possible, this shouldn't involve too much packing and repacking. As it was, the boys had moved most of their stuff that they wanted immediate access to Phil's house so that they could at least have it at weekends.

But there was still the mountain of other random stuff to sort out. She stared around the living room in exasperation. Initially, she'd been really good at packing things in boxes, marking them carefully with contents and rooms they should go in, and stacking the boxes in the conservatory. But as time went on and her frustration rose, she found herself grabbing the Sharpie and writing 'Random Crap – Living Room' and 'Rubbish Old Toys – Tom's Room' in rising exasperation.

And that was before she'd even tackled the loft. Logically, she knew she should have started there first, but she hated climbing about in the draughty, dark space at the best of times, and now without Phil there to hold the ladder, she was even more nervous about it. But, since the boys were all at school, and she'd hit a bit of dead end in terms of packing stuff the family still needed until they finally moved out, she supposed the time had come.

Struggling up the old aluminium retractable ladder a few minutes later, Kate looked around in rising despair. She'd *never* expected to move from this house, at least until all three of her sons were grown up and she and Phil no longer needed the space. After the initial shock of Phil's betrayal, she'd gone into a kind of long-term crisis mode; shutting out her own grief and anger in an attempt to keep her sons on an even keel, and only breaking down in private, in the middle of the night when they were sound asleep, or, in the early days, when she'd done the school runs and was safely behind the locked front door again. She'd got through it with the help of the friends who'd stuck by her, Lorna especially. Those who felt too awkward about taking sides, the 'couple' friends who couldn't quite come to terms with the new status quo, had drifted away, but the hardcore of mates she called her own had helped her through it. Nights spent drinking wine on the sofa, and putting the world to rights, and later, when she'd been up to it, nights out doing the same thing, had helped immensely. But the hard reality now was that she had to tackle this mountain of stuff in the attic, the stuff that had been put up here and out of mind, that neither of them really knew what to do with.

Bracing herself, she climbed the ladder, rung by careful rung, and then reached for the pull cord for the naked bulb hanging from the apex. Stepping up into the boarded space, she headed for the first in a series of plastic lidded boxes that were stashed in the eaves. The cool, spring breeze coiled around her like a waking serpent, and she shrugged deeper into her thick grey cardigan. She didn't want to spend too long up here.

Opening the first of the many boxes, she sighed in new exasperation. She remembered, now, why they'd been put up here. When her father had died, her mother, Selina, had downsized from the spacious family home to a smaller bungalow on the outskirts of the village, about a mile from Kate's current house. Even though her new property had an annexe, that same annexe that was waiting stoically for Kate and her sons, should she need it in later months, Selina had refused to store the seemingly endless stream of toys, games and books from both Kate's and her brothers, Aidan and Sam's, childhood in the annexe, as at the time it had a serious damp problem. Kate also knew that her mother had recently become a disciple of the Marie Kondo method, and so had been adamant that the old clutter just *had* to go. As a result, Kate had agreed to stash these in her attic, and even though her brothers, who both lived in Somerset, had come to visit since their mother's move to a smaller place, every time they'd left again Kate had slapped her forehead and remembered she'd forgotten to give them their share of the stuff.

Well, she thought as she surveyed the boxes, *there's no way all this is going into storage at my expense!* There were about ten plastic stackable boxes that contained toys, board games, old schoolwork, ancient audio cassettes, and each was packed to the brim. She wondered if Sam and Aidan would be able to pop across at some point before her house move and collect them, but then she had a better idea. The Easter holidays were coming up in a week's time, and she'd been itching to take the boys away for a change of scenery, just for a few days. She couldn't justify a full-on foreign holiday at this time of year, with the move coming up so soon, and her eldest son, Corey, about to take his GCSE exams, but perhaps a few days in Somerset might be a good halfway house? She could take her brothers' share of the stuff down with her, get a bit of fresh country air and unwind for a bit. If one of her brothers couldn't put her and the boys up, then she could book something last minute on the internet, she was sure.

They'd all spent a raucous family Christmas together, their mother included, last year, when Kate and her boys had squished themselves into Aidan's two spare rooms, and Selina had stayed with Sam and his wife, Florence. Family harmony had been helped by the fact that Sam and Aidan lived in two of the three terraced houses on Bay Tree Terrace in Willowbury, which meant that they could all hang out together over the festive period without worrying about how they were going to get home again, and their mother could head off to bed when she'd had enough. That Christmas had been, despite the cramped bedrooms, one of the best she'd had in ages, and the perfect tonic to a stressful period of her life. Even

Selina had defrosted a little once she'd had a few glasses of Somerset's finest mulled cider, and it had been a much better Christmas than the previous year when, still reeling from the separation, she'd spent Christmas Day alone as the boys had gone to stay with Phil.

That train of thought was just the distraction she needed to head back down the ladder for the moment. After all, she reasoned, dragging all of those heavy boxes down from the attic by herself was a risky business; she'd wait until her sons got home from school and then they could help her so she didn't break her neck going up and down from the loft. Grabbing her phone, she texted the family WhatsApp group and asked if either of her brothers would be able to offer a place to crash for a few days during the Easter holidays. Sam must have been off shift, as he responded straight away, and they swiftly arranged a date. Breathing a sigh of relief that now at least there would be ten fewer boxes to worry about when moving day eventually came, Kate looked once again around her living room and wondered where to start.

3

When the Easter holidays came, Kate was relieved that the house was already in a much better state than it had been. The attic had been sorted, and her sons had been surprisingly interested in all of the stuff that was soon going to be stored in Sam and Aidan's houses. They'd spent ages looking through the evidence of their uncles' childhoods, fascinated by the old schoolbooks and the mix tapes that, in one or two cases, appeared to have been gifted to Sam by girlfriends past, if the careful rounded handwriting on the inserts and the choices of songs had been any indication. Kate wondered what Florence, Sam's wife, would think of those, and then smiled – knowing Florence, she'd just laugh it off. Everyone had a past, after all. Even Kate, who'd met Phil aged eighteen, had had a boyfriend or two before that.

Tom, Kate's youngest son, had discovered Aidan's old board game Battleships and had set it up, and, to Kate's astonishment, night after night for a week, he'd challenged each of his brothers to a game. It had actually managed to displace the PS4 in their affections for a while. On a rather different note, Kate had discreetly removed a naked centrefold of 1990s model Claudia Schiffer from their curious eyes when she'd opened an old A4 exercise book of Sam's and found it.

The three boys had been pleased about a change of scenery for a few days of the holiday. They liked seeing their uncles, and Kate thought that, actually, a bit of time away from the house that was feeling less and less like their home by the day would do them all good. As she settled them in for the long drive west, she felt herself finally starting to relax.

'Are we nearly there yet, Mum?' Will, her middle son, joked as they pulled off the driveway.

'Nearly.' Kate grinned. Although, just getting away from the house was enough to make her feel lighter. Lorna waved from her kitchen window as they left the cul-de-sac. She, as ever, had promised to keep an eye on the place. Kate would miss having her next door when they moved into the Airbnb place during the next half term holiday.

Three hours later, and after watching the landscape changing from the flats of Cambridgeshire to the commuter belt and then the chalky landscape of Dorset, Kate finally made it to the Somerset border. The boys were getting restless, having swapped the front passenger seat between themselves when they'd stopped a couple of times on route, and Kate herself was looking forward to a cup of tea and unwinding at Sam's place.

As they headed over the Mendips and dropped down into the small town of Willowbury, Kate caught sight of Willowbury Hill, the ancient mound rising, green and stately out of the surrounding hills, and marvelled at what a beautiful place her brothers had found to live. There was something quaintly charming, too, about the sloping High Street, that, even though she'd been on the road for over three hours now, she took a detour to drive down. The shops that lined either side of the road were a delightful mix of the quaint and quirky; a health and well-being shop called ComIncense, with pastel coloured bunting strung up outside that matched the violas in the wooden tubs either side of the front door, the Cosy Coffee Shop, and a small gift shop, just before the Travellers' Rest pub, that stood on the corner of the High Street, sand coloured stone warm in the spring sunshine.

As ever, the mix of walkers on the pavements either side was as eclectic as the shops. Some were obviously tourists, down for the Easter break and wandering up and down the street with all the time in the world. Others looked more like locals, busily completing their shopping and meeting and greeting one another on the street. Willowbury was a draw all year round for those who wanted to spend some time in a picturesque Somerset town that had a feel and a spirit all of its own. Not for nothing was it known as the New Age capital of England. Kate smiled as she saw two little girls wearing lilac fairy wings skipping along the pavement. Her smile widened when she saw the man holding their hands was also wearing a pair, in the same vibrant colour. *That image is Willowbury, to a tee*, she thought, although there were plenty of people out and about who were more conventionally dressed, too. Her eye was caught, as she drove, by the bright, vibrant display of the local bookshop, Vale Volumes, which had been closed over the Christmas holiday when they'd last visited Tom and Aidan, but now appeared to be doing a brisk trade with tourists down for the Easter holidays.

'This place is *so* weird,' Tom said, from the back seat. 'But kind of cool, too.'

'It's certainly never dull!' Kate replied. She loved coming back to Willowbury, and at the moment, the place was just the tonic she needed to get away from the stresses of the house move. A few days in the Somerset countryside would hopefully recharge all of their batteries.

In a few more minutes they were pulling into the parking space to the side of the three houses on Bay Tree Terrace. Reassuringly conventional, they looked even more welcoming when Sam, Kate's brother, loped towards them from where he'd obviously been working in the garden at the back of the houses.

'Hey,' he said warmly, giving Kate a hug and a kiss on the cheek. 'You made great time.'

'Traffic wasn't too bad,' Kate replied, once Sam had released her. She looked him up and down. 'You look well.'

Sam grinned. 'Florence is taking eating for two to heart, so she's cooking massive portions of everything.'

'That's not what I meant!' Kate laughed. 'But now you come to mention it...' She poked Sam's non-existent gut. 'How's she feeling, otherwise?'

'Pretty good,' Sam said. 'Tired, but loving being pregnant. She's popped out to grab some bits and pieces for dinner tonight, but she'll be back soon.'

'I was going to suggest dinner at the pub,' Kate said. 'But maybe tomorrow night would be better.'

'Sounds good,' Sam replied. Catching sight of the boxes that were stacked high in the boot of Kate's Volvo, his eyes widened. 'Jeez. You weren't joking about the amount of crap from your loft, were you?'

Kate, who was making sure the boys all had their overnight bags, kept smiling. 'Afraid not. You can see now why I wanted rid of it all!' With a hint of mischief in her heart, she reached into her handbag and pulled out the centrefold she'd found in Sam's old school exercise book, which she'd thought better of binning in the end and passed it to him while the boys surged ahead towards the house. 'Thought this might bring back a few memories!'

Sam's jaw dropped, and then, as if he was the fourteen-year-old that Kate remembered having such a crush on Claudia Schiffer, he glanced around to make sure Florence, or worse, their brother, Aidan, wasn't about. 'You could have just chucked *this* out!'

'It was worth keeping it for the look on your face,' Kate teased. 'You were so nuts about Claudia, it was no wonder you never had a girlfriend!'

'That's what you think,' Sam shot back, grinning. 'You didn't know *everything*, Katie.'

'Sure,' Kate replied. 'But perhaps it's worth chucking that before your wife sees it. Even if she's cool with your teenage crushes, the pregnancy hormones can play havoc with your sense of proportion.'

'Noted,' Sam said. 'Although, it is a great picture...'

'On your head be it, little brother.' Kate smiled. 'Now, are you going to give me a hand with the rest of this stuff or not?'

Still grinning, Sam popped the boot and grabbed the first couple of boxes, proving, perhaps, that Florence's home cooking hadn't done too much damage to his fitness after all.

4

That evening, once the boys had settled into Sam and Florence's house, they were joined by Kate and Sam's other brother, Aidan, and his husband, Tom, from next door. Florence, true to her Yorkshire roots and her pregnancy cravings, was cooking up a storm, and after a couple of glasses of wine, Kate was feeling thoroughly relaxed. There was something so easy, these days, about just hanging out with her sons and her siblings. In the past, when her boys had been younger, she'd always been worried about what they were getting up to, but now, as they played an impromptu game of football on Sam and Florence's long stretch of lawn, she felt she could chill out and just let the evening wash over her.

'It's so peaceful,' Kate observed as she caught the sound of a nightingale carolling somewhere in the woods that backed onto the house. 'If I lived here, I think I'd just be in a permanent state of relaxation.'

Florence, who was off the booze but nonetheless seemed as chilled out as the other adults, smiled. 'The pace of life is a little slower here, although it's not quite the backwards rural idyll it used to be. Since the railway line got put back in, a lot of commuters have moved in. You can get to London in just over two hours these days.'

'So it's not just incense readers and organic risotto rice knitters any more, then?' Kate laughed. 'Shame.'

'Oh, there's plenty of that still, too,' Aidan chipped in. 'And if you want a neopagan blessing for your newborn baby, or an aura reading before you agree to marry the love of your life, that's all still available, too.'

Kate raised an inquisitive eyebrow. 'Is that what you two did, then?' she said, grinning at Aidan's husband, Tom, who'd just grabbed himself a beer and was returning to the garden table on the patio.

Aidan laughed. 'Nah. I knew he was a keeper without Mariad O'Flaherty telling me what colour his aura was!'

Kate laughed too, then glanced to make sure none of her sons were in earshot. 'Perhaps I should have dragged Phil here sixteen years ago and consulted a fortune teller!'

Aidan gave her a quick look, and Kate knew he was checking that she wasn't hiding a deeper meaning in the remark. Reassuringly, all she felt was the humour, this time. It hadn't always been that way, in the aftermath of Phil's departure.

'If he comes anywhere near this place, I'll shove his aura where the sun doesn't shine,' Aidan said. 'He might be the father of your kids, Kate, but he's still a lying twat.'

'Oh, come on,' Kate admonished her youngest brother gently, 'it's water under the bridge.'

'Really?'

'Really.' She took a sip of her wine. 'It's all about the future, now. I mean, the house has been sold and I've had the best clear out I've had in years. It's time to move on.'

Aidan shook his head. 'And moving on means redecorating this cottage you've been lent, does it?'

Kate grinned. 'Well, it's a start. I can't afford to buy a new house anything like what I had when I was married to Phil, and I don't want to rush into something I might regret, so the cottage will be a chance to catch my breath, to think about what I really want to do now, and what's best for me and the boys. It's weird, after all these years, to be thinking like that, but I'm getting used to it.'

'You always did have a good eye for design,' Aidan said. 'I remember, when we were teenagers, you spending the Easter holidays one year redecorating your bedroom. Mum nearly had a heart attack when you suggested it, but you got stuck in and even she liked it by the end.'

Kate grimaced. 'Although, to be fair, those light purple walls and lilac curtains were definitely of their time.'

'Purple's out for this Airbnb job, then?'

'Definitely!'

Aidan glanced at Tom, who, Kate noticed, gave a slight smile and a nod.

'What?' she said, as two pairs of eyes swivelled in her direction.

'Well,' Aidan said. 'We were wondering...'

'About what?'

'If you've got nothing better to do for the summer... how about moving into our place and slapping a bit of paint on the walls?'

Kate nearly spat out her drink. 'What?'

'The place needs a bit of a facelift, and I figured, if you weren't up to anything else, you might do it for us. We'll pay you, of course.' Aidan grabbed a handful of crisps from the bowl on the garden table.

'Can't Sam help you with that?' Kate asked. 'After all, it's not like he's got a long way to go.'

'Well, yeah, but I wouldn't trust Sam to paint by numbers, let alone my living room walls. Would you?'

'Oi!' Sam, who had hitherto been kicking the football around with his nephews, looked affronted. 'I'll have you know that I've got great taste.'

'That's why Florence made you take back the diarrhoea yellow you picked for the baby's nursery, is it?' Aidan countered lightly as Sam sank into a garden chair, breathing a little more heavily than he should have been after a casual kick about.

'I hate to point out the obvious flaw in your plan,' Kate said, 'but the boys and I barely fit into the spare rooms at Sam's as it is. And your house is even smaller. How am I supposed to decorate around you, and them?'

'Well, here's the thing,' Aidan said. 'Tom and I have booked a little holiday. Kind of the honeymoon we couldn't have because Tom was in that thing at the Bath Theatre Royal straight after the wedding.'

'My biggest role to date,' Tom interjected. 'I mean, I wasn't going to turn down a crack at *Godot*, was I?'

'Of course not,' Aidan soothed, obviously sensing ruffled feathers. 'But since Tom's got a bit of a break before rehearsals start for his next project, we thought we'd push off for a few weeks in the summer, see a bit of Europe and take the honeymoon then. So you and the boys will have the house to yourselves, if you fancy it.'

'And while I'm here, I get to spend some time redecorating your gaff?' Kate grinned.

'Well, yeah. Unless you've got other plans.' Aidan raised an eyebrow.

Kate shook her head sardonically. 'Obviously not. Except, of course, finding a house I can call my own, but, you know, I'll put that on hold for you, little bro.'

'So you'll do it, then?' Aidan, seemingly unaware of the ironic tone in Kate's voice, asked.

Glancing down the garden, where the boys were still kicking the ball about, Kate thought about how lovely it would be to move into this beautiful, calm terrace for the summer. It would certainly take the pressure off having to find somewhere else to live, for the moment, and meant another six weeks where she wouldn't have to consider her mother's garden annexe as home. That was something she definitely didn't want to think too much about, unless it became unavoidable.

'If the boys are okay with coming over for the summer, then I'll do it,' she said, turning back to Aidan. 'But only if they're happy.'

'Fair enough,' Aidan said. 'And I'll even make sure there's a bottle or two of the local cider in the fridge for you, if you like.'

'How kind.' Kate grinned. As they argued idly over what the job was worth, Kate feeling distinctly awkward about haggling over prices with her brother, she felt a sense of relief. Okay, so being itinerant for the next few months wasn't ideal, especially with three sons in tow, but she loved being in Willowbury, and, since it was the summer holiday, the boys wouldn't be missing any school. With Phil sharing custody, she was sure they could arrange the time between them so the boys were happy. Sitting back in her garden chair, breathing the scent of freshly cut grass and feeling the warmth, still in the air, she felt a real sense of belonging, for the first time in a long time. It felt odd to be so far from home but, she supposed, she was with her brothers, and, in reality, her house in Cambridge wouldn't be her home for much longer.

Just as she was contemplating all this, her youngest son, Tom, came back up the garden and collapsed dramatically onto the wooden bench near the table. 'I'm starving,' he announced, wiping an exaggerated hand over his brow. 'Can I have some crisps?'

'You're just about to have your dinner,' Kate admonished, sighing as he reached out a sweaty paw and grabbed a handful of the crisps on the garden table, stuffing them into his mouth. Well, she supposed, they were on holiday, after all. Tom, stoical, stocky and cheeky to the last, grinned at his mother and kept chewing.

'You're an oik,' Kate admonished, but she could hear the affection in her own voice. She slapped his hand playfully as he reached for more snacks. 'Wait until your dinner.'

Just at that moment, Florence called through from the kitchen diner, and Sam sprang to his feet to help her.

'Go and make yourself useful to Aunt Florence,' Kate said to Tom.

Tom rolled his eyes and shuffled off in Sam's wake. Shortly afterwards, having obviously caught sight of the chocolate cake Florence had made for pudding, Tom's exclamation of delight was audible from the patio.

'I think at least one of them's not going to have a problem living here for the summer if Florence can be persuaded to cook for them,' the older Tom of the group said wryly.

'You may be right, there,' Kate said. She called to her two other sons, who came jogging back up the garden, more than ready for their dinner. She'd discuss the potential project with them over the next couple of days. Hopefully, Phil would also be on board with the idea.

5

Fortunately, after a few days in Willowbury, which had included more of Florence's brilliant cooking, several walks up to Willowbury Hill to burn it all off and many, many more games of football in the garden with their uncles, the boys seemed on board to spend at least some of their summer holiday in the town. The laid-back atmosphere of Willowbury was having an effect on them all, and after a particularly enjoyable afternoon spent drinking Pimm's in the courtyard garden of the Travellers' Rest, Kate was deciding that she would be more than happy to move into Aidan and Tom's place for the summer holidays.

On her return to Cambridge, Kate then had to contend with the dual worries of actually moving out of the house, moving into the Airbnb cottage for a couple of months and arranging what the heck was going to happen to the boys for the long summer vacation. At eleven, thirteen and sixteen, the boys were too old for her to simply make decisions above their heads; it was important to Kate, as it had been throughout the separation and divorce, that they had a say in their situation. She'd always prided herself on putting them first, and this situation was no different. Now that she had to make more and more decisions on her own, it was doubly important that she got these right. Phil tended to concur with her on most things, which, given the circumstances of their split, wasn't surprising. He seemed desperate not to rock the boat.

Kate, moving into the Airbnb cottage during May half term, was enthused to be using it as her first real blank canvas. Having the project also kept her thoughts away from the sadness of moving out of the house she'd shared with Phil, giving her a new focus, and something she could really get her teeth into. She loved transforming the place into something that would make tourists sigh with pleasure, and the rent-free existence insulated her from the more pragmatic concerns about what was going to happen with her living arrangements when the autumn came. Her sons, happy to have the relative continuity of their dad's house, spent most weekends with him, giving Kate plenty of time to scour Pinterest for colour ideas for the bigger project of Tom and Aidan's house over the summer. It was a project she was beginning to feel really excited about. Aidan, true to form, had told her to 'just pick some colours and get it done before we get back'. Tom, who was rather more attuned to all things design, had made some suggestions, and sent Kate several pictures of the new sofa they'd bought, and the flooring they were considering, to help her to narrow things down a bit. Between the three of them, they'd come up with a broad canvas, and Kate couldn't wait to get started. It would be tricky with three boys in tow, and Tom and Aidan's black cat Lucifer to keep away from the wet paint, but Kate was confident that she could manage it. After all, she'd masterminded clearing her own house, moving herself and the three boys out of it and settling them into temporary accommodation without any major catastrophes, so painting a few walls in six weeks should be child's play in comparison.

Of course, just as she was beginning to put the plans in place for the summer, Phil decided to drop in a complication. Kate, who'd gone to Cambridge city centre for a trawl around the shops on Saturday afternoon with Lorna, was miffed to receive a text from him, asking for the boys' passport details. She frowned. Phil hadn't mentioned anything about taking the boys abroad, and it was really something he should have raised with her earlier than a few weeks before the summer holidays began. Texting a swift reply, she waited, sipping her latte, for a response.

'What's he up to this time?' Lorna asked, obviously clocking the familiar frown on Kate's face.

'I'm not sure yet,' Kate replied. 'I thought he was staying put for the summer, but he's just asked me for the boys' passport numbers.'

'Last-minute deal?' Lorna said.

'Maybe,' Kate said. 'He never bothered taking the initiative and booking anything for us when I was still married to him, though.' She knew she sounded a little bitter, but she couldn't help it. Phil had always left big ticket things like holidays to her to sort out, all the time they were together, and while they'd had some lovely trips to France and Germany, it had been her who'd had to do the logistics for them.

Swiftly, the response from Phil came back. Kate felt a lurch of annoyance and something like jealousy as it did. 'Florida,' she said softly, as Lorna raised a questioning eyebrow. 'Three weeks. Leaving two days after school breaks up. If it's okay with me, of course.'

'Well...' Lorna said, giving her an encouraging smile. 'At least you won't have to worry about the boys for the first three weeks of the summer hols, and you can get stuck into the decorating without their huge feet treading emulsion everywhere.'

'Yes, true, but it still stings, you know. We'd talked about taking the kids to Disney World when they were younger, and always said it would be better to do when they were old enough to really appreciate it, and now he's doing it, but instead of me, he's taking

Jennifer.' She shook her head. 'I know it shouldn't hurt... but it does. I mean, why wasn't I worth the trip and she is?'

Lorna reached out and gave Kate's hand a squeeze. 'Would you still want to be married to him? Just for the sake of a trip to see that ridiculous mouse and his gurning "have a nice day" entourage?'

Kate smiled slightly at Lorna's turn of phrase. 'No, of course not. But it still makes me a bit sick.'

'Look at it this way,' Lorna said stoically. 'You don't need to worry about the kids for half of the summer holiday, and you get to spend the summer hanging out rent-free in your brother's house. From what you've told me about Willowbury, too, it's not like you're stuck in the arse end of beyond. Willowbury has more than enough to keep you entertained, and, unlike Disney World, it's authentic. Go and enjoy it. And bugger the mouse. So to speak!'

Kate laughed, despite herself. 'Nicely put, as ever.'

They finished their coffee and headed back out onto the High Street. Determined not to show Phil that any of this holiday business bothered her, Kate sent a neutral text back to him saying that she'd send him the boys' passport details when she got home. Then, putting it out of her mind as best she could, she focused on enjoying the luxury of a child-free afternoon's shopping.

6

Some weeks later, with the Airbnb cottage nearing completion, and still not having found anything on the market nearby that she really felt she could buy, Kate broke the habit of a lifetime and decided to focus only on the short term. Always a planner, never a 'see where life takes you' kind of person, she'd spent most of her life, before and during her marriage, making sure everything and everyone had been where they needed to be, had what they needed to have and knew what they needed to know, almost to a fault. Now that the boys were sorted out for the first three weeks of the summer holiday, she was at liberty to focus on what she was going to do with her time in Willowbury, when she got there. It was an odd feeling, and the thought of returning to her mother's annexe in September still filled her with dread, but she was determined not to rush into anything. After all, co-parenting with Phil did give her a certain amount of leeway, and even if she did end up in the annexe, at least the boys would have their rooms in Phil's spacious new house to escape to if it all became too much. Of course, she dearly hoped it wouldn't come to that, so she was keeping half an eye on Rightmove, in case that elusive perfect house within her budget suddenly appeared. Having the annexe as a fallback was a useful option, though, and meant that the pressure was off, to a certain extent. She knew she and the boys couldn't live there forever, but at least they would have a roof over their heads, however small that roof was.

On the day before the boys left for Florida, having mediated between the three of them over which socks, pants and jeans really belonged to which child, Kate eventually managed to get all of their stuff into the car and get them over to Phil's place. An elegant five-bedroomed house in a village on the outskirts of Cambridge, it was a markedly different proposition to the place he'd shared with her. *But then*, Kate thought, *Jennifer's salary as a full-time architect must have certainly helped out to buy it.*

As she parked the car, Corey, her eldest son, turned to her from the passenger seat. His two brothers had already flung open the rear doors of the Volvo and were impatiently waiting for her to pop the boot so they could grab their stuff.

'Are you going to be all right, Mum?' Corey said, his face a picture of concern.

Kate, quailing a bit inwardly, but determined to put on a brave face, painted on her brightest smile and nodded. 'I'll be fine,' she said. 'You just focus on having a brilliant time in Florida.'

'I'm looking forward to seeing Epcot and Universal Studios,' Corey said, and Kate smiled back.

'Just remember to text me occasionally and let me know how you're getting on.'

'I will.'

As they got out of the car and sorted out the luggage, the three boys strode ahead of her up the generous pathway to the front door of the house. They'd rung the doorbell before she'd even made it halfway up. The door opened, and Phil beamed brightly at his three sons, clapping Corey on the back heartily, reaching out and squeezing Will's shoulder and then ruffling Tom's already unruly hair.

'All right, lads? Dump your stuff in the dining room, except what you need for tonight. We've got an early getaway tomorrow morning.'

They moved past him into the house, and for a moment, Kate and Phil were alone on the doorstep. Kate noticed that Phil's hair was thinning on top, and that the bags under his eyes were more pronounced than they had been. New jeans, in a more form fitting cut than he usually wore, looked good, though, as did the salmon-coloured polo shirt, which she also didn't recognise. Jennifer's influence, presumably.

'What time's the flight?' Kate asked.

'Seven o'clock tomorrow morning,' Phil replied. 'Taxi's coming early.'

'Well, here's all of their documentation,' she said, handing over the passports. 'Corey wanted to keep them but I thought it would be safer to give them straight to you.'

'Thanks,' Phil said. He paused, before adding, 'You're looking well. Will told me that the house you've been redecorating looks great.'

'It was a good project,' Kate said. 'I needed something to keep me busy.'

'And Aidan's got you doing his house now, hasn't he?'

Kate smiled, knowing that they'd already discussed all this on the phone, but realising that Phil was trying to keep the conversation flowing. It felt so strange to be making small talk with the man she'd shared so much of her life with but, for the sake of family harmony, she went with it. She was about to open her mouth to ask a little more about the itinerary of the holiday, when Jennifer appeared from a room off the generous hallway. To Kate's eyes, she looked a little peaky; perfectly well groomed, as ever, but a certainly a bit pale. She wondered if they'd both had a bug or something. The boys often brought things home from school, and summer flu season was approaching.

'Hi, Kate,' Jennifer said brightly. 'How are you?'

'Fine, thanks,' Kate replied. After two years, the three of them had reached a kind of amicable existence, but they'd never be down the pub drinking together. It was enough. 'I think the boys have got everything they need. They're all pretty excited.'

'So am I,' Phil said. 'It'll be great to get away before...' he trailed off, glancing at Jennifer, who cut in a little too quickly.

'Before work kicks off again in September,' Jennifer said. 'We've both got a lot on at the moment with that new development getting the go ahead over at Strensham Mead.'

'Well, have a lovely time,' Kate said. 'And keep in touch.' She looked past Phil to where the boys were coming back out of the dining room, having dumped their bags as instructed.

'Be good, boys,' she said as they came back to her briefly to say goodbye. 'And text me lots of pictures.'

Suddenly, the reality of her three sons flying four thousand odd miles away for three weeks hit her, and she swallowed back a lump in her throat. She pulled her middle son, Will, close to her in a fierce bear hug, and before he could wriggle away, she planted a huge kiss on his forehead. 'Text me lots.'

Will wriggled away and exaggeratedly wiped a hand across his forehead. 'Okay, okay. Bye, Mum.'

As she bid her goodbyes to them all, and made her escape, Kate couldn't help another pang of something that felt like jealousy mixed with a rather dangerous nostalgia. *No,* she thought quickly, *there's no going back. And I wouldn't want to, anyway.* Driving back to the cottage, where she still had a few things to pack away before her own trip to Willowbury, she tried to focus on the future.

7

Seventy-two hours after saying goodbye to her sons, and safe in the knowledge that they'd landed safely in Florida, Kate looked despairingly at the peeling wallpaper of Aidan and Tom's living room and sighed. From the corner, Lucifer, the black-haired, green-eyed cat who inhabited the house, looked at her with an equivalent level of disdain.

'Why the hell did I agree to this?' Kate said to the walls and the cat. Unsurprisingly, there was no answer, from either of them. 'I must have been having a perimenopausal moment when I let them talk me into it.'

Glancing at the screen of her mobile phone, which had lit up briefly with *yet another* message detailing just what a wonderful time the homeowners were having on their six-week tour of southern Europe, Kate had a good mind to text them back and tell them the bloody deal was off. She didn't need a place to live, she hadn't just accepted the job because she was strapped for ready cash, and in no way had she taken it on because she knew they felt sorry for her. No. No way any of that was true. Honestly.

'I know they're paying me for this, but I should have quoted to include danger money!' Kate addressed the cat as, having put out a hand to stroke him, he lashed out at her with his left front paw. Putting aside any thought of an amicable relationship with her reluctant housemate, she turned back to the peeling wallpaper, which dispiritingly revealed itself to be just another layer underneath which at least two more layers had been put over the years. The previous owners had slapped a bit of gloss paint over the top, a textured example of particularly hideous seventies décor, in the hope that it would spruce up the living room a bit, and as a result, removing the stuff had been hellish. That had taken the best part of a day, and now she was grimly steaming the last of the backing paper, trying to see if the walls were actually any good underneath.

Yet again, Kate wondered at the wisdom of taking this job. 'Really,' she addressed her remarks to Lucifer, who looked at her unapologetically from the back of the dust sheet-covered settee, 'it wasn't as if I had a great deal of choice in the matter.' The cat stared at her blankly, nonplussed that he had, to all intents and purposes, become Kate's confidant over the past few days since she'd moved in. Kate had a yen for dark, mysterious and brooding males, but having been married to a man who'd successfully managed to keep his other woman a mystery for the past few years, she now appreciated a bit of honesty. *At least Lucifer makes no secret of his disdain*, she thought. That was progress.

Grabbing her wallpaper scraper, she attacked the remnants of the backing paper with a little more gusto. Six weeks had seemed ample time when she'd quoted for the job, but now she wasn't so sure. She'd need to patch plaster any spots and cracks in the walls before she got a watered-down undercoat onto them. Then there were the numerous other jobs; repainting the skirting boards, a coat on the living room door, waiting for the professional plasterer to skim the hall ceiling so that she could then paint it... the list went on.

But this was what she'd chosen to do, she reminded herself, and it wasn't as if the owners of the house could nitpick too much; she was related to one of them, after all. As if on cue, yet another message came through on the 'Grand Tour Life Goals' WhatsApp group of a lake in Tuscany, obscured slightly by the duo in question gurning a selfie in front of it. Between that and the messages from her sons, who were having a whale of a time in Florida, she was starting to feel like Cinderella.

Kate tried to extinguish the flicker of irritation that flared within her at the picture. She should be happy for them all, and she was, really she was, but it was difficult to feel anything other than sorry for herself when she was the one, at age thirty-nine, without a permanent home, without a life partner and without, at the moment, any form of steady income. Although the terms of the divorce and the house sale had left her reasonably comfortably off, there was still the future to consider.

As the third photo came through on WhatsApp, she debated sending something rude back by way of response, but then decided that a coffee from the High Street might be a better option for her sanity. Ensuring the steamer was turned off at the wall, she cleared away her wallpaper tools and wriggled out of her white painter's overalls. Willowbury was what you might charitably call a laid-back place to live, but even she drew the line at striding out covered in paint. Her confidence might have taken a knock in the process of her divorce, but she wasn't going to let it derail her pride in her own appearance. Despite the fact that, even in her overalls, she was still likely to look less odd than some of Willowbury's more eccentric residents, she couldn't quite bring herself to let it all hang out just yet. With another five and a half weeks left living in the town, though, who knew how she might feel at the end of her stay?

She closed the front door of the terraced house behind her, booting the recalcitrant Lucifer out before she did, and felt a bit lighter. She never thought she'd be the live-in painter and decorator for her little brother, Aidan, and his new husband, Tom, but then life had a habit of throwing her curve balls when she least expected it. Perhaps a summer in Willowbury was just what the doctor ordered.

8

If he looked back over his life, Harry Sinclair had never dreamed he'd end up here, in this town, running this business. A year ago, when he'd taken over Vale Volumes, the bookshop on Willowbury High Street, it had been a ramshackle mess of random reads, transcendental how-to guides and the odd, moth-eaten Agatha Christie that made his eyes hurt every time he'd tried to sort it all out. True to the spirit and flavour of the New Age town of Willowbury, he'd retained many of the spiritual tomes, but over time he'd gradually introduced more mainstream titles, in the hope that this would encourage his customers, who were, more often than not, tourists, not to just stare at the shelves before backing out of the shop again, having bought precisely nothing. Pagans and New Age followers were all very well, but they could only buy so many books.

Harry had widened the reach of the bookshop, setting up a website to advertise some of his more unusual stock, but also focusing on developing an additional regional theme, bringing in more local authors as well as stocking some national and international bestsellers. The eclectic mix seemed to be going down well. As he walked around the store during a quiet spell, he also allowed himself a moment of satisfaction that in a year he'd turned around what had been a failing business into something far more successful. Sure, takings still weren't quite where he'd like them to be, but they were definitely on the up, and he could feel proud of himself for that.

Now that he'd truly settled into his new life as a bookseller, he could also start to think about where next to take the business, and the premises. There was no doubt that the place was looking a bit shabby, and not in that lovely, upmarket way that every interior decorator seemed to favour these days. The historic leak in the main ceiling of the shop, while now dry, had left a nasty stain, and the walls were once cream but had seen better days. Only the thought of having to empty his beloved bookshelves had stopped Harry from repainting when he'd moved in; he'd been more concerned with getting the business going, and any delay to that would have cost him money. However, there was no avoiding the fact that the place could do with a lick of paint and bit of an over-haul. If things had worked out better with his last girlfriend, he might have been able to go to her for advice; she always had such a good eye for colour and design, but, sadly, the commute from where she still lived in Islington to the West Country had proved too much. In the end she was too happy in her career to consider giving it up to help him to run a shabby, independent, initially at least, loss-making bookstore. They hadn't parted friends, after Harry had declared his intentions to chuck in London life and up sticks to Somerset, but, in the end, he reflected, that had been for the best. A clean break from all aspects of London life was what he'd needed, and he'd certainly got that in Willowbury.

Alas, though, there was no doubt that the bookstore was getting shabbier. Now that he didn't have to panic over every penny earned and spent, perhaps it was time to redecorate. He might even be able to afford to employ someone to do it for him, so that he could keep focusing on the business of selling books. There must be plenty of painters and decorators around Willowbury who'd be only too happy to give him a quote for the job. Resolving to put this on his 'to-do' list for after the weekend, he decided, while it was quiet, to pop down to Jack Winter's Cosy Coffee Shop just a bit further up the High Street and treat himself to a cheeky cappuccino. He knew he really should just buy some decent coffee, but he justified the takeaway by saying to himself that he was supporting another local business. He and Jack had struck up a bit of a friendship since he'd moved to Willowbury; both were expats to the West Country from London, and even though they'd had different professions in their past lives, they had bonded over their shared reminiscences of the city.

Flipping the sign on the front door to 'Gone for a coffee – back in ten minutes', he headed up the High Street. He smiled as he caught sight of the sign on the door of Mariad O'Flaherty, the local reader of auras. It merely read: 'Cat needed walking, back in fifteen minutes'. He'd obviously picked a popular break time. He smiled as he saw the lady herself come floating back down the street. She was a vision of purple and pink scarves and flowing skirts, her greying dark hair in one plait over her left shoulder. Harry didn't pretend to understand exactly what it was Mariad did in her shop; her services, as well as aura reading, included Tarot, runes and seances, but he had been ridiculously reassured when she'd caught him one day and remarked on the health and vitality of his aura. The move to Willowbury had obviously done him good spiritually.

'Morning, Mariad!' he called as she passed him, and he was rewarded with a beatific smile.

'Morning to you too, Mister Bookseller,' Mariad replied, her gentle, soft Irish brogue music to Harry's ears. He could listen to her for hours, even if she regularly called him *Mister Bookseller* because she was hopeless with names. She'd joked, soon after she'd introduced herself, that she remembered people by the colour of the light that surrounded them rather than their names, which Harry thought quaint, and also a damned good excuse for not having to try to remember.

'Beautiful day.' Harry peered up the High Street to Willowbury Hill, the ancient, grass covered mound that rose impressively out of the Somerset landscape and loomed over the top of the High Street.

'That it is,' Mariad replied. 'Off for your habitual at Jack's?'

'Yup,' Harry said. 'Any recommendations?'

'The organic Madagascan is just the ticket if you fancy something different,' Mariad replied.

'Thanks, I might give it a go,' Harry said, although he'd probably end up just going for something bog standard and less exotic; his taste in coffee was alarmingly pedestrian. *Much like my life, these days*, he thought. Moving to Willowbury a year ago had been exciting, and opening the bookshop had been a good challenge, if tiring, but for the past couple of months he'd been settling into a homely routine. He didn't mind that, but he did wonder what else life might have in store for him at times.

'Have a good day,' Mariad said, by way of parting, and swept past him in a rainbow of skirts and scarves.

'You too,' Harry replied, raising a hand. As he glanced back up again at Willowbury Hill, which was beautifully backlit by the strong summer sun, he felt a wave of appreciation for this strange town which had given him a life and a living. But he still could feel a slight sense of... what? Stagnation? Routines becoming habits? In his previous life as an investment banker, no two days were ever the same, but as a bookshop owner in a small town, sometimes he felt like Bill Murray in *Groundhog Day*. He shook his head. Perhaps he should organise getting the shop redecorated; that, at least, would shake things up a bit. Entering the domain of Jack's Cosy Coffee Shop, he thought that he just might try that Madagascan organic blend, too.

9

Kate looked up as the door to the Cosy Coffee Shop opened to admit its latest customer. She was enjoying the break from the wallpaper nightmare, and the latte she'd chosen was creamy but had enough of a caffeine kick to power her through until lunchtime. The slice of carrot cake was an indulgence but, she figured, she'd be working the calories off just getting the last of the wallpaper down. Her back and shoulders already ached from the physical labour, and she hoped that, the more work she got, the sooner her joints and muscles would toughen up. For the past thirteen years she'd worked part-time in an estate agent's office, but since she'd split from Phil, she'd had a bit of a renaissance with this painting and decorating business. Although it was a lot harder physically than desk work, she was finding it rewarding. She hoped that Aidan and Tom would enjoy the final result, too.

As if on cue, her mobile pinged. Expecting *yet another* 'we're having an amazing time and look at this beautiful view' WhatsApp from the happy couple, she was perturbed to find it was a message from her eldest son, Corey:

Hope you're having a great time at Uncle Aidan's. Just wanted to let you
know that I miss you. But don't tell Tom and Will I said that! Here's a
picture of Mickey Mouse for you x

Kate smiled. It was unlike Corey to be so open about his feelings
with her, despite her best efforts over the years as a mother to three
boys. He'd been born independent, she often joked, and very rarely
let her into his life these days. At sixteen, he'd just finished his
GCSEs and was rapidly heading towards adulthood. He was
growing into a handsome and articulate young man, and while
Kate felt a stab of sadness for the baby and the child he used to be,
she also felt an incredible sense of pride and love that, despite his
parents' initially less-than-amicable divorce, he'd seemingly taken
it all in his stride. He'd been a shoulder for her to lean on during
the darker times last year, and in his silent understanding way, he'd
given her a great deal of strength to pick up the pieces and move on
from her marriage.

I miss you too (and your brothers, of course!). Hope you're having a
good time! Say hi to Mickey Mouse for me! xxx

'Can I get you another coffee?' Jack, the proprietor of the Cosy
Coffee Shop, called from behind the counter.

'Oh, what the heck, the wallpaper's not going anywhere!' Kate
smiled back at Jack. 'Yes, please.'

As Jack busied himself with preparing another latte, Kate
looked around the coffee shop, which was pleasantly busy, but not
overcrowded. She liked the high stools by the counter, which gave
that part of it an American diner feel, while there were lower tables
on the main floor of the café and near the window. Kate assumed
that, given the nature of Willowbury, Jack must have his 'regulars'
who sat at the counter and passed the time, much as people would

have done at a bar in older generations. *Coffee shops are the new pubs these days*, she thought.

Standing to come and get her drink, ignoring Jack's 'it's all right, I'll bring it over to you', Kate ambled over to the counter.

'You're new around here, aren't you?' Jack asked as he handed over her exquisitely patterned latte. 'I mean, you don't look like a tourist.'

Kate nodded and took a sip of her drink before replying. 'Yes, I'm staying at my brother's house for a few weeks while he's on a trip.'

'House-sitting, then?' Jack said.

Kate laughed. 'Cat-sitting is part of it, except the cat doesn't like me! To be fair, I'm not that fond of him, either, but then I suppose he's got more reason to dislike me than I have him.'

'How so?' Jack wiped down the counter where he'd spilled some of the milk he'd steamed.

'I'm earning my board by redecorating the house while my brother is away,' Kate said. 'Cats are creatures of habit, I guess, and he's not keen on having mouldy wallpaper dropped on his head!'

'Can't say I blame him, then,' Jack smiled. Kate thought, for a moment, just how attractive he was. With his sandy hair and blue eyes that crinkled at the corners, he looked a little bit like Chris Hemsworth in the right light. She'd barely looked at another man all the time she'd been married to Phil; *for all of the good that did me*, she thought, her mind darkening for a moment.

'Everything all right?' Jack was looking at her curiously, and she realised that she'd been staring blankly back at him.

'Sorry.' Kate mentally shook herself. 'I was miles away. My sons are on holiday in Florida with my ex-husband and I was wondering what they were up to.' It wouldn't do to admit to eyeing up the barista.

'How many do you have?' Jack asked. 'Sons, I mean!'

'Three,' Kate replied. 'All growing fast, and generally eating anything that's not nailed down.'

'Well, if they come and visit, send them my way,' Jack laughed. 'I'm always happy to slip an extra pastry to a hungry boy at the end of the day!'

'Thanks,' Kate smiled at him. Really, he was very attractive, even allowing for divorcee bias. 'Can I have one to go with the coffee? Stripping wallpaper seems to have given me an appetite.' She'd just have to work extra hard to burn off that, as well as the carrot cake.

'Sure thing.' Jack picked a delicious looking Danish from the pile on the cake stand in front of him and popped it on a plate. As Kate reached for her bank card to pay, he waved it away. 'This one's on the house. Call it a welcome to Willowbury.'

Kate thanked him again, and decided to take the coffee and cake back to her chair at the table by the window. She turned, with a full latte glass in one hand and the pastry plate in the other, and, too late to do anything about it, collided with the tall figure who was standing behind her, spilling half her replenished latte down the arm of his jacket.

'Shit!' She took a step back, cursing inwardly and outwardly that she'd not even sensed anyone behind her while she was talking to Jack. Where the hell had this guy come from? And what was he doing standing so close to her?

'Sorry,' the man said apologetically. 'I left my glasses in the shop and I was just trying to read the specials board. I didn't mean to startle you.'

Kate shook her head. 'Next time, maybe wait for the person in front of you to make a clean getaway before you go sneaking up behind them.' Her tone was a bit more impatient than it should have been, given that she'd been the one to spill the latte on him, but she had been looking forward to that second coffee, and now he was wearing most of it. Realising that she might have sounded harsher than she'd intended, she grabbed a handful of paper napkins from the dispenser on the counter and rather ineffectually tried to sponge the coffee from the man's sodden arm.

'It's all right,' he replied, not without an understandable trace of impatience himself. 'Leave it. I can take it off.'

Face flaming with embarrassment, Kate stepped away as he shrugged out of his jacket and put it on the bar stool next to him. She looked down at her half empty latte glass and swallowed back a sigh. It was about time she got back to stripping the walls, anyway.

'Can I get you another coffee?' the man asked, as if to try to counter the previous irritation in his voice.

Kate shook her head. 'No, thank you. I'd best get back to what I was doing.' She knocked back the rest of the rapidly cooling latte and put the glass down on the table, taking a couple of napkins and wrapping up the Danish pastry to have later. As she glanced back up at the stranger in front of her, quite a long way up, actually, as he was a fair bit taller than her, she forced a smile of apology. 'I really am sorry about the jacket.' She noticed that he'd tactfully rolled up the sleeves of his white shirt while her attention had been elsewhere, presumably to disguise the latte stain that had seeped through the summer weight fabric of his dark blue jacket. His forearms were lightly tanned and he had large, capable-looking hands.

'Honestly, it was my fault,' he replied. 'I should learn to remember my glasses!'

There was a pause as both seemed to be wondering what else to say, and Kate pondered how to make a dignified exit.

'Well, goodbye then,' she settled for finally. God, she was out of practise with her small talk! Although, she reflected as she stepped away from the counter and turned towards the door, she'd made easy enough conversation with Jack. But then Jack was a barista, and, presumably accustomed to chatting to people all day long as they ordered their coffee. Aloof at the best of times, Kate had realised long ago that it took her a long time to warm up and chat to people.

'Bye,' the man replied, and Jack also called out a cheery farewell as she opened the coffee shop's door and stepped back out onto Willowbury High Street. Kate found, as she walked back down the busy road, that her heart was racing after the incident. But, really, apart from the jacket, there was no harm done; the accident had been six of one and half a dozen of the other, as her father used to say. Swallowing back a rush of sadness that he was no longer around to talk to, as she'd really felt his loss in the weeks and months after her separation from Phil, she tried to focus back on the job in hand. Vowing to try to bond a little bit more with that damned cat Lucifer as well, she headed back to Bay Tree Terrace.

10

'Smooth!' Jack laughed as Harry sat at the bar stool next to his wet jacket. 'Oh, er, get me, Mr Bumbling Bookseller who can't even remember to put on his glasses!'

'I normally wear contacts, as you well know,' Harry muttered, 'but I ran out yesterday and I left my glasses on the shop counter. They make my head hurt if I read in them for too long.'

'You sound like a grumpy teenager.' Jack poured Harry's requested cappuccino and slid it over the counter to him. 'Perhaps try to make sure you leave at least three feet between you and any customers in future, even if you haven't forgotten your specs!'

'Fair point,' Harry conceded. 'I really should know better, but years of buying coffee in crowded London coffee shops sort of gets you in the habit of standing closer than you should. I forget that normal people outside the capital have personal boundaries when it comes to existing in public spaces together.'

'You're not wrong,' Jack replied, breaking his own rule and pouring himself a coffee. 'Once you've spent years pressed up against someone's armpit on the Tube every morning and evening, personal space doesn't seem such an issue.'

'And she spilt the coffee on *me*, remember?' Jack said. He glanced at his jacket. 'Looks like a job for the dry cleaner if it's to have any hope of being salvaged.'

'Well, if you will go in for fancy threads, even now you're in the countryside, what can you expect?' Jack said. 'Although, having said that, your fashion sense is pretty tame compared to a lot of my clientele who wear cloaks or, at the very least, crushed velvet trousers.'

'That's not strictly true any more though.' Harry took a sip of his coffee. 'Willowbury might be a spiritual soup, but it attracts as many people who are just observing the madness these days. If it didn't, I wouldn't get half the business I do!'

'Are you suggesting Willowbury is becoming, horrors, mainstream?' Jack asked, eyes wide in mock astonishment. 'Don't let Alan Somerville or the druids hear you saying that! Our local rockstar-in-chief still credits Willowbury for his, er, spiritual inspiration in the latter years of his career, and the druids will claim they've as many members as the local Jedi Order these days.'

'Jedi? Seriously?' Harry nearly spat out his coffee. 'I'd better get some copies of the film novelisations in, then, if that's definitely a thing around here.'

'You'd better believe it,' Jack said, although Harry wasn't sure if Jack was just pulling his leg. He'd fallen victim to Jack's offbeat sense of humour before. I mean, being a *Star Wars* fan was one thing, but did people around here really strut down the High Street wielding lightsabres and muttering about the Dark Side? Willowbury wasn't known as the New Age capital of England for nothing.

'So, who was that woman, anyway?' Harry asked as he reached the bottom of his coffee. 'I don't think I've seen her around here before?' It was tourist season, which meant there were a lot of temporary visitors to the town, but she hadn't had the laid-back bearing of a tourist, from the limited time he'd had to interact with her.

'She's staying in the village for the summer, redecorating some house or other,' Jack said. 'Seemed a bit...' he paused tantalisingly, as only Jack could. The Cosy Coffee Shop was known to be a hive of gossip, and Jack himself was a major contributor to that reputation.

'A bit what?' Harry's eyebrows perked up, although he was aware he was being led.

'Oh, I don't know.' Jack topped up Harry's black coffee with some foamy milk to make the cappuccino. 'A bit lonely, I suppose. She is clearly missing her children, who are spending the summer away from her.'

'Stands to reason,' Harry said.

'Who knows, she might even pop into your gaff if the telly gets boring and she fancies something to read,' Jack said, a teasing glint in his eye. 'Then you can introduce yourself to her properly, rather than having coffee chucked all over you.'

'At least it'll give us an icebreaker,' Harry grinned, although he didn't provide Jack with any more ammunition. Jack had been teasing him about his single status pretty much daily since they'd become friends, even though Jack himself was also unmarried, having been divorced some years ago. Jack and his ex-wife shared custody of their twelve-year-old daughter, who came to stay in Willowbury with him at weekends and in the school holidays. She was due, in fact, any day now, by Harry's reckoning.

'Oh, I meant to say,' he continued, after taking another sip of his latte. 'That Jacqueline Wilson collection you wanted me to order for Gracie has arrived. Thinking about it, I probably should have brought it along with me.'

'Great,' Jack said. 'She's coming down tomorrow evening. She moans enough about being away from her *real* house and her friends when she comes down here. At least the books'll give her something to focus on.' For a moment Jack looked desolate, and Harry tried to think of a few words of comfort, but, unfortunately, his experience of tweenagers was even less than his experience of small children, so he was at a bit of a loss. 'Well, why don't you pop down when she's arrived and I'll put them behind the counter for you?' he said, eventually, feeling frustrated that he didn't know what else to say.

'Thanks,' Jack said, and then, obviously making an effort to brighten his own mood, he grinned. 'How are the preparations for that other great author's visit going?'

It was Harry's turn to look downcast. 'How do you think? I mean, most authors I've dealt with are easy-going to a fault and seem genuinely pleased to be given time and space to speak. This guy, however...'

'I've heard he can be a bit of a diva,' Jack replied. 'If you can even call a bloke a diva, that is. His Twitter feed reads like the Burn Book from that Lindsey Lohan film that Gracie loves so much. What was it? *Mean Girls*? I don't think he's keen to make friends.'

'His agent only told him to do a bookshop gig in his hometown because of the positive, rather than the negative publicity, I reckon.' Harry drank the dregs from his coffee cup. 'So you can tell from that just how excited he is to be back here.'

'Ah, well,' Jack said. 'On the bright side, it'll bring in a few punters and you should sell a shedload of books. You might even be able to afford to get the place redecorated!'

'Steady on.' Harry grinned back. Jack gestured to Harry's empty cup. 'Another for the road?'

'Thanks, but I'd best get back,' Harry replied. 'The lunchtime rush is about to start.'

'For you or me?' Jack asked. 'Do you fancy a quick drink tomorrow evening before I meet Gracie off the train?'

'Sounds good,' Jack replied. As he hopped off the bar stool and walked out into the summer sunshine and bustle of Willowbury High Street, his mind went back to the woman he'd met. Despite the embarrassment and irritation about spilling her coffee, she was still very attractive. But did she have brown eyes or blue? And was her hair tied back or around her shoulders? Cursing his inattentive nature, he concluded that it didn't really matter. Unless their paths crossed in the coffee shop or his bookshop, he was unlikely to see her again, anyway.

11

That evening, Kate received a text from Sam and Florence inviting her to dinner. Initially, when Sam and Aidan had come to Willowbury, they'd shared the house that Aidan had bought with his settlement from the army after he'd been discharged for physical and psychological injuries following a tour of duty in Afghanistan. The house share had largely been a success, but when Sam had fallen in love with Florence, the teacher who lived on the other side of the party wall, he'd moved next door once things had turned serious.

The relationship, in its early stages, had not been without its issues, including having to act opposite each other in the town's Christmas production and the well-meaning but misguided antics of a group of their friends in trying to get them together more quickly. But all had, eventually, ended well and they'd been very happily married for nearly a year, and now had a baby on the way, too. Even after what had happened with her own marriage, Kate was thrilled that Sam, the older of her two brothers, had found someone as lovely as Florence to spend his life with. Sam had always been cautious about falling in love, but Florence had gradually broken down his natural reserve and Kate knew from the conversations she'd had with both of them that they were blissfully happy together. The news of Florence's pregnancy, coming so soon after they'd married, had been a surprise, but a wonderful one, and she knew that, while having a baby would present its own challenges, they would rise to them.

As a helicopter pilot working for the Somerset Air Ambulance, Sam's job was pretty intense, but no more so than his previous career, when he'd flown Lynx helicopters for the Royal Navy. Coming out of the Navy had been a wrench, but one Kate knew Sam had gradually accepted, and now, forging this new life in Willowbury with Florence, who was a secondary school teacher, she knew he'd finally felt able to put down some real roots.

So it was that Kate found herself sitting at the wooden table in Florence and Sam's cosy kitchen, eating a hearty supper, which was exactly what she needed after the hard work of stripping wallpaper all day.

'This is fabulous, Florence, thank you so much,' Kate said as she tucked into the most delectable home-made lasagne, garlic bread and salad. 'I know I've said this before, but my brother fell on his feet when he married you!'

'He's not such a bad cook himself,' Florence replied, glancing over at Sam and smiling. 'He wooed me with his deep-fried breaded Camembert, many moons ago!'

'Sadly, that's off the menu for now,' Sam said, reaching over and placing a hand on Florence's burgeoning baby bump.

'Although the doctor did say that a little bit of what I fancied would do me good from time to time in the last trimester,' Florence countered gently. She reached for Sam's glass of red wine but he put his hand over it.

'Not on my watch,' he said.

'Spoilsport,' Florence grumbled good-naturedly.

'How long have you got to go?' Kate took a bite of her garlic bread and then a good slug from her own glass of red.

'Eight weeks,' Florence replied. 'Although maternity leave starts in six, thank goodness.'

'Cracking timing,' Kate said. 'Five more weeks of summer holiday, a week of the new term and then you get to leave for a year. You couldn't have planned it better if you'd tried!'

'I know.' Florence rolled her eyes. 'It wasn't deliberate, believe me! Had I known we'd get pregnant so quickly, we could have taken our time.'

Kate tried not to cringe at the 'we', as well as the thought of her brother making babies – somehow, she still viewed him as a twelve-year-old, even though he was in his mid-thirties. 'Well, make the most of the time before the baby comes; there won't be a lot of sleep afterwards!'

'I always kind of hoped that being a teacher would prepare me for having children of my own, but to be honest the only thing it's prepared me for is choosing the names,' Florence said. 'There are so many names I've had to strike off the list because I've taught naughty or rude kids that have them! It's a wonder we've agreed on any at all.'

'I don't think we have, have we?' Sam said. 'I mean, when all you can bring to the table are names that any kid in the playground would get beaten up for...'

'Like what?' Kate asked. 'I mean, I got away with naming all three of my boys after actors from eighties films, and Phil was none the wiser, so I don't think I can judge you on anything!'

Just as Sam was about to enlighten her about some of Florence's more suspect name choices, all three of their mobiles pinged with WhatsApp messages.

'Jeez, do they have to take and send photographs of *everything*?' Sam grumbled. 'I mean, I really don't need to see any more photos of their bloody food or hear about how amazing another frigging lake is.'

'Let them enjoy it,' Kate said mildly, forgetting that she, too, had been having exactly the same thoughts that afternoon. 'After all, it's great to see Aidan so happy. We can allow him a few hundred photographs.'

'So long as he and Tom don't make us sit through them all when they do get their arses back here, too,' Sam said. 'And, knowing Tom, I wouldn't put it past him!' Tom, as an actor, relished an audience, in whatever form it took.

'Hopefully I'll be back home by then,' Kate said, although she felt a pang as she said that. Home was a moveable feast right now.

As if he'd read her mind, Sam asked, 'So, are you any closer to finding a place to live, Katie?'

Kate shook her head. 'I just don't know what I want, that's the problem.'

'It must be hard, having to find somewhere for the four of you,' Florence said, her face sympathetic. 'Especially after everything that's happened.'

Kate nodded. 'It really is, but to be honest, there are plenty of new builds near to where our old house is that I could afford, and with the money Phil'll be paying for the kids, the mortgage won't be a problem for a few years. The problem is that I'm not sure I want to move in somewhere so close to where he is, knowing that all of our old friends will still be around us, and feel like I'm constantly reliving the old times. There's a bit of me that just wants to up sticks and get the hell out of there.'

'That's understandable,' Florence said. 'But what about the boys? Moving schools and areas can be tough.'

'Corey's about to start his A Levels and was making noises about going to the local college instead of staying on at school, Will is going into Year 10 and about to start his GCSEs and Tom is starting secondary school, so in a sense they're all transitioning to the next phase of their education. It wouldn't be easy, but I wonder how long it would take for them to adjust.' Kate, half talking to herself, felt her mind starting to race. This strange life she was living for the summer certainly wasn't typical of how the rest of her life had panned out up until now, but then she hadn't expected to be divorced at thirty-nine and painting houses to earn money, either. Perhaps now was the time to take risks.

'You're not seriously thinking about moving away from Cambridge, are you?' Sam asked, brow creasing.

'I know what you're thinking!' Kate tossed her head. 'I've been keeping an eye on Mum for years, and she's not getting any younger. But I can't keep living my life on everyone else's terms. I'm still young enough to make a fresh start – I mean, let's face it, Phil's ensured that I don't have much of a choice in one area of my life, so why not go the whole hog and move somewhere new, too?'

'I just don't want you to make hasty decisions that you might regret later off the back of the divorce,' Sam said. 'You've always been a bit all or nothing in your approach. Sometimes it's better just to take stock.'

'Sam,' Kate said patiently, 'my cheating ex-husband saw to it that I can't stay in the family home, he's set up house with his new squeeze and my boys are all getting older. If not now, then when?'

'I get it, really I do, Katie,' Sam said. 'And I hope that spending the summer here might give you a bit of relief from the shit that Phil's put you through. I just don't want to see you leaping from one thing to another without having properly thought through the implications of those decisions.'

'I'm homeless and pretty much jobless, Sam,' Kate said, and a shiver went through her. 'Okay, so there's money in the bank from the house sale and Phil's settlement and ongoing payments for the kids are enough to keep me afloat for a bit, but for the first time in a very long time, I have the space to make some new choices.'

'Well, if it helps, Willowbury Academy is a great school,' Florence replied. 'It's still quite new, and we've had a lot of students moving into the area recently, because it's got such a good reputation. And the head of Year 7, Josie Sellars, is a mate of mine. She'll look after Tom, I'm sure.'

'I know it would be a wrench to move to a new place, but the boys could catch up with their old mates during the weekends that they're staying with their dad.' Kate continued the thought that Florence had started, and felt a flicker of excitement. 'For the first time in a long time, I'm free to make some independent decisions, and you know what? I think I'm going to like doing it.' Triumphantly, she knocked back the rest of her glass of red, and in her haste she spilled half of it down her top.

'Well, let's hope you're better at decision-making than drinking,' Sam quipped. 'You know where we are if you need us, though, Katie.'

'I know,' Kate said. 'And I appreciate that, Sam, I really do.' Stretching her arms above her head, she glanced at the clock on the wall of Florence and Sam's cosy kitchen. 'I'd better get back next door,' she said. 'I need an early night if I'm to get two coats of paint on the lounge walls tomorrow, and it looks like I have to get out of this top.' She rose from the table and, giving Florence a hug, she walked to the front door with Sam.

'You're welcome to move in with us if you need to get away from the decorating,' Sam said. 'It can't be much fun waking up to it all and going to bed with it, too.'

'It's fine, honestly,' Kate replied. 'Because I'm living on site, I can start and finish when I like, so it suits me. If I wanted to paint until midnight without disturbing anyone, I could.'

'Fair enough.' Sam paused. 'But I meant what I said before,' he added as they said their goodbyes. 'You're not alone in this. If you'd let me a year ago, I'd have punched Phil's lights out for what he's done to you and the boys. But I'm kind of glad you didn't.'

'A year has given me a lot more perspective too,' Kate said quietly, mindful that she was talking to the relatively newly married. 'By the end of our marriage, Phil and I really didn't have anything in common except the kids. Yes, he was a twat for carrying on before we'd gone our separate ways, but there wasn't a lot to stay for, to be honest. It's for the best, I promise.'

Sam shook his head. 'I hope you're not just putting a brave face on it. You don't have to with me, you know.'

'I know.' Kate smiled. 'I'm telling the truth, honestly. Now get back in there and do the washing up so your wife can put her feet up.' Hugging her brother, she pulled open the front door. As she stepped out into the warm dusk of a Somerset summer evening, she breathed the sweet scent of freshly cut grass and the honeysuckle in the nearby gardens and smiled. Things might be a bit uncertain right now, but she had been telling the truth to her brother. Even with the uncertainly over where she was going to live, she felt a real sense of optimism for the first time in a long time.

12

The next evening, Harry was meandering around the store, straightening shelves and noting where the gaps were, ready to order in new stock where he needed it. Harry liked to keep the bookshop open until six o'clock each evening, so as to catch any commuters coming back down the hill from the railway station on their way home. The platform at Willowbury was literally just a slab of concrete and a weather shelter, and he wanted to try to catch the passing trade of train users either before or after their commute, since not everyone liked to read on a phone, and a fair proportion of his trade did come from those who wanted a 'proper' book to tuck under their arm in the morning. It was always a nice time, that hour or so between five and six p.m., when people, tired from a day's work in Bristol or Taunton, strolled back home and, if he was lucky, popped in for a natter and a new book.

As he was straightening up the books in the Historical Fiction section, he was momentarily distracted by the sight of Gracie, Jack's young daughter, running down the street towards the shop.

'Have you got them?' she gasped as she burst through the door of the shop, causing the slightly knackered office worker who'd popped in for the latest Lee Child novel to glance up in surprise.

'And hello to you too, Gracie!' Harry grinned at her. 'Good trip?'

'Fine.' Gracie rolled her eyes. 'Dad insisted I call him when I got on the train, and every half an hour after that so he knew I was okay. It was, like, totes lame.'

'He worries about you, doing the trip from your mum's to here,' Harry said reasonably. 'It's a long way for a, erm, for someone your age.' He had been about to say *little girl*, but he was pretty certain that moniker would have earned another eye-roll from Gracie.

'It's not like I haven't done it before,' Gracie replied. 'Ever since I turned twelve I've been allowed to catch the train here by myself. Dad worries too much.'

'That's his job,' Harry said consolingly. Turning back to the counter, where the Jacqueline Wilson box set lay waiting to be collected, he got out a brown paper carrier bag and popped the books inside.

'That'll be twenty pounds, please,' he said as Gracie hovered impatiently by the counter. She handed over the cash and he handed over the box set. 'Enjoy.'

'I will.' Gracie beamed at him and in her excitement to get her hands on the books she suddenly looked much younger than she was.

'And when you've finished all those, I've got some recommendations for you. Pop back in and we'll see what we can find.'

'Thanks, Harry,' Gracie called over her shoulder. She was already halfway across the shop. 'See you around.'

'Bye, Gracie, say hi to your dad for me.'

'I will.' And she was gone, racing back up the High Street to meet Jack at the coffee shop.

'Nice to see a child who's not glued to her mobile phone all the time,' the seeker of Lee Child observed as she handed over a small pile of the author's Jack Reacher books, some new, some second-hand.

'I'm sure she's pretty keen on her phone as well as her books,' Harry said, 'but you're right, it is lovely to see such enthusiasm, long may it last.' He tapped in the prices of the books to his till and took the proffered bank card. 'Some good choices here,' he continued. 'Let me know what the new one's like. I haven't had the chance to read it yet.'

'I will.' Taking her purchases, the customer glanced at the walls as she left. 'Do you have any plans to refurbish the shop? I don't think it's had a lick of paint since the previous owner retired.'

'I know,' sighed Harry. 'I've spent the past year putting it off, but I suppose I ought to just pull my finger out and get someone in to sort it out.'

'Wouldn't take long,' the customer said. 'Bit of a bugger moving all the bookshelves, though.'

Harry laughed. 'I'd be tempted just to paint around them!'

'Then you definitely need to get a professional in!' And with that, she, too, mooched out onto the High Street.

Harry gave it another half an hour or so, and then, content that the commuters had all headed home for the evening, he began the process of cashing up. *Not a bad day's takings*, he thought, *for an independent bookshop in a sleepy Somerset town*. Willowbury was attracting its fair share of tourists since the ruined Priory in the centre of the town had become a National Trust site, and his takings were definitely benefitting.

Just as he was finishing up, his phone pinged with an email notification. Noticing it was from Artemis Bane's publisher, his heart sank. Artemis was doing his book launch in a couple of weeks at Harry's shop, and, while Harry was initially over the moon to have scooped such a big name author away from larger venues, the logistics were proving complicated. He'd already swapped several

emails with them, recommending a hotel and other things for the
author's visit; what did they want now?

Dear Harry,

Sorry to trouble you again, but Artemis has asked if it is possible to
provide an armchair for him to sit in during his talk. He would particularly
appreciate one with a sprung back. I hope this will not cause too much
of an issue?

Best regards

Eloise Padgett

Publishing Assistant

Harry sighed. It looked like tomorrow he'd end up blowing
some of his takings on an armchair for Artemis, then. If the man
hadn't been such a huge draw, he wouldn't have bothered, but
Harry knew he'd end up selling treble figures of the latest Artemis
Bane novel as a consequence of the author's visit, so he'd have to
suck it up. He'd heard so many horror stories about Artemis Bane,
he wondered just how much of an ordeal this session was going to
end up being. At least he had a couple of weeks to get prepared for
it. Perhaps there might even be time to get the walls painted before
the World's Greatest Urban Fantasy Author (self-proclaimed)
descended for the signing. Flipping the sign on the shop door to
closed, he headed upstairs to his flat above the shop.

It was only when he got through his front door that he remembered he'd agreed to meet Jack in the Travellers' Rest pub for a
drink after they'd both closed up. Then he realised that Gracie
must have been on an earlier train. Sure enough, as he swiped to
his texts, he saw a message from Jack sending apologies and asking
for a rain check. He felt a slight pang of something he couldn't quite
identify as he thought about Jack and Gracie's relationship. Father
and daughter might live miles apart during the week, but their joy

at being together was wonderful to behold. Harry felt sad for Jack that he was living so far away from his daughter, but at least with the rail links reinstalled to the West Country she was only a train ride away in one of the leafier Bristol suburbs.

He wondered whether, if fate had had different things in store for him, he'd be changing nappies and taking toddlers to the playground now instead of working six days a week in his own bookshop. There was definitely a part of him that increasingly wondered what he'd missed out on. He'd just have to focus on the far bigger part of him that thought, actually, if he could avoid all the baby stuff and skip to the parts where children could read, he wouldn't have minded having some of his own. He liked older kids and got on well with the teenagers who occasionally visited the shop looking for copies of the Harry Potter novels or some set text or other for school on the cheap. Pulling the door between flat and shop shut for the evening, he went into his kitchen to begin making dinner.

13

Having slept the sleep of the physically exhausted after another day of decorating, Kate woke feeling refreshed enough to consider taking a quick walk into the centre of Willowbury before she began putting the first coat of paint on the living room walls. If she was feeling particularly energised, she might even head up Willowbury Hill and really blow away the dust and paper particles that she was sure were still clinging to her, despite a bath last night.

Locking the front door behind her, she smiled as she saw Sam coming back from the direction of the town. He looked harassed.

'Everything okay?' she asked as she headed down the path from the front door.

'Yes, ish,' Sam said. 'I was just grabbing some Haribo for Florence – she's got these ridiculous cravings for those really sour ones at the moment – and I got a call from base. Mathias, our other pilot, has gone off sick, so they want me to get over there as soon as I can. They're going to use the relief rota for the night shift, but I was looking forward to a bit of downtime today. I was meant to start nights tonight, but since I'm covering until seven p.m., the rotas have shifted a bit.'

'That's a bugger,' Kate said. 'I was going to ask if you fancied giving me a hand sloshing some paint on Aidan and Tom's living room today.'

Sam laughed. 'Even if I was around, I'd have turned you down! Florence and I were going to have a crack at putting the nursery furniture together.' He sighed. 'Guess that'll have to wait.'

'I can give her a hand if you like, in between coats of paint,' Kate said. 'I'm a dab hand with a flat-pack.'

'That would be great, actually,' Sam replied. 'She's been in fine health for most of this pregnancy, but the doctor warned her against doing too much now. If you could give her a bit of hand, that would help a lot.'

'Consider it done,' Kate said. 'It's been ages since I've thought about baby stuff, so it'll be fun.'

'Only you could see assembling Ikea furniture as fun!' Sam grinned at her. 'But each to their own, I suppose.'

'What time do you have to leave?'

'Pretty much now, actually. I'll just let Florence know and then I'll get off.'

'Okay. Tell her I'm having a quick walk, then I'll do some painting and I'll be with her after lunch.'

'Will do.' Sam paused. 'I know this wasn't exactly where you thought you'd be ending up at this point, Katie, but it's brilliant to have you close again. Even if it is only for a few weeks.'

'Thanks.' Kate felt a warm glow of pleasure. She and Sam hadn't been close as children; as the older sister she'd always been on the sidelines when the two brothers teamed up, but she was pleased that, as adults, they'd discovered they liked spending time together. 'I'll see you later, okay?'

As Sam went into the house to break the news to Florence of his unexpected work shift, Kate reconsidered heading up Willowbury Hill. If she had to paint and then put furniture together, she may well need all the energy she could muster. That didn't mean she didn't want to stretch her legs a little bit first, though. Perhaps a walk up the High Street and a takeaway coffee from the Cosy Coffee Shop was in order. There was a bit of her that quite fancied seeing Jack again, but she'd try not to spill coffee on anyone today. She felt her face flushing as she remembered the embarrassment of that encounter – hopefully the guy was just a tourist and she wouldn't have the horror of seeing *him* again.

Willowbury in the summer was a picturesque and unique sight. Bunting was hanging from most of the shopfronts, and incense wafted from the shop doorways every time someone walked in or out. It wasn't unusual, Kate was rapidly finding out, to see people sporting fairy wings or cloaks as they ambled up and down, with patchwork jackets and dresses also a bit of a regular thing. Bare feet in the summer seemed to be an acceptable fashion choice, too, but one Kate wouldn't be adopting any time soon. Of course, there were enough more conventionally dressed tourists and locals wandering about, but there was a gentle air of acceptance, and no one seemed to bat an eyelid even at the more outlandishly attired people.

As she continued up the street, she passed the charming looking bookshop that she'd driven past when she and the boys had come down for the Easter holidays. At that time, she'd been too preoccupied with other things to linger in a bookshop, but now she had a free half hour or so, she thought she'd take a look.

The outside was a little shabby; its pale blue paintwork definitely needed a bit of a touch-up, but the large windows were spotlessly clean, and the window display of 'Holiday Reads' caught her eye instantly. There was a string of brightly coloured bunting draped across the top of the window, a deckchair in one corner with a copy of a *Sunday Times* bestselling author's most recent hardback sitting decorously atop it, and actual sand had been scattered across the plinth behind the window, with other headlining fiction titles poked into the top of sand filled plastic buckets, their spades leaning at jaunty angles. Gratifyingly, Kate also noticed that between the more famous authors' creations there were also titles with which she was less familiar that seemed to be from writers local to the area. *Whoever owns the bookshop obviously has a creative streak*, she thought as she looked through the window display into the shop itself. Glancing at her watch, she decided to take a quick look inside; perhaps she'd find a book to read while she was drinking coffee at Jack's place.

Kate pushed open the shop's door and was immediately assailed by that wonderful, slightly musty old book smell that pervades places like this. However, she was pleased to see that it wasn't just second-hand books, but also brand-new titles that could be found here. Arranged by genre, Crime and Thrillers were just to her right, Relationship Fiction to her left, and, at the back, in its own little area, was a Children's section. The middle aisles were marked 'General' and at the front, just behind the window display, there was even a section for 'Local'. The shelves were all dark wood and gleaming, not a speck of dust in sight, and the coloured spines of the books gave the place a warm and cheerful air, although Kate couldn't help but notice, with her decorator's eye, a large damp patch on the ceiling above the Children's section and quite a few marks on the walls. The owner had done everything to distract from them with his or her displays and shelves, but the whole place could definitely do with a lick of paint.

Kate had loved visiting bookshops and libraries as a child, and she felt the familiar tingle of excitement running down her spine as she spotted at least six titles she'd like to buy. Like most shoppers, most of her books came from Amazon these days, and she had a Kindle for convenience, but there was something about a real bookshop that still appealed to the bookish child in her; the girl who loved to read under the bedclothes until late into the night with a torch stolen out of one of her brothers' rooms. Gratifyingly, she could see a couple of kids browsing the section at the back. She felt a pang as she thought about how much Corey, her eldest child, would love this place. He was as bookish as she had been, and she used to have to drag him out of places like this on the weekend shopping trips to Cambridge.

'Morning!' a cheerful voice called from the counter, which, as she turned, she realised was tucked just out of the way at the back of the shop.

'Morning,' she called back absently. The newest release from one of her favourite authors had caught her eye, and she'd reached for it just as the voice had called to her. Opening the book, she only just managed to restrain herself from taking a deep sniff of the new, crisp pages. The first paragraph grabbed her instantly, and she decided that this would be her companion for coffee this morning. She'd have to be careful not to get too sucked into it, though – she was being paid to do a job at Aidan and Tom's house, after all.

Browsing the shelves for a little longer, she also found a copy of *Antony and Cleopatra*, which she knew was one of Corey's set texts for A Level in September, so thought she'd buy it for him, along with a fantasy novel that was on offer from one of the many tables positioned around the store. If she was wrong, she could always keep either, or both, for herself. She'd loved studying the play at school and was long overdue a reread. Finally, glancing into the children's section, she found the latest David Walliams for Will, and then a Tom Gates novel for Tom.

As she approached the counter, still looking at her book choices, it wasn't until she was at the desk that she looked up. Right into the smiling face of the man she'd spilled coffee on yesterday.

'Hi,' the man said.

Face flaming, Kate muttered a slightly less than friendly sounding greeting in return. Obviously noting the tone of her voice, the man paused before reaching out a hand for her purchases.

'Some good choices here,' he observed as he took them from her. 'If you're a fan of this guy, perhaps you'd think about coming to our book signing for Artemis Bane in a couple of weeks' time?' He was looking at the fantasy novel Kate had chosen.

Kate, who'd been digging around in her purse for her bank card looked up briefly. 'Artemis Bane is coming *here*?' Was she imagining it, or did the guy behind the counter look faintly affronted at her tone?

'Well, yes,' he said. 'He's a local, raised a few streets away from here, in fact, so his publisher thought it would be nice to include this place on his book tour. We do quite a good trade, you know.'

Now he sounded defensive as well.

'I'm sure you do.' Kate smiled. Then, by way of mitigation, she added, 'You've got a great range here – I love that you sell old and new alongside each other. And that seaside window display is great.'

He seemed to thaw slightly at the compliment. 'Thanks. I really enjoy putting the displays together. Although we're a little way from the coast, here, I think the holiday reads theme still works.'

'It certainly does.' Kate nodded as he offered her a brown paper carrier bag with the name of the bookshop printed on it. 'It got me in here, for a start! I'll definitely be back in for another read before the end of the summer.'

'Great,' the man smiled, and then, as if realising who she was for the first time, added, 'although if you're holding a cup of coffee, I might give you a wide berth!'

Kate tried to look cross, but as she looked into the bookseller's sincere, open face, with its slightly prominent nose and deep, dark blue eyes, she couldn't muster up the emotion, so she laughed guiltily.

'I'm sorry about that,' she said. 'Did the jacket clean up all right?'

'Whipped it straight into the dry cleaners when I left Jack's yesterday,' he said. 'They seemed to reckon they could do something with it.'

'I'm happy to foot the bill,' Kate said. 'Let me have it when I come back for a new book.'

'No, honestly, it's fine.' He regarded her again for a moment, before adding, 'I'm Harry, by the way.'

'Kate.' She held out the hand that wasn't clutching the brown bag of books. 'It's nice to meet you without having to throw coffee your way to do it.'

'The same.' Harry's hand was dry, and warm, and as their palms touched, Kate felt a distinct flutter in her chest. Putting it down to embarrassment, she released the handshake first.

'Well, I'll see you around,' she said as she turned towards the door.

As Harry bade her goodbye, she again couldn't help but notice the shabby walls and the damp ceiling of the bookshop.

'I'm a painter and decorator, by the way,' she said suddenly. 'If you need someone to sort out that damp stain and give the walls a lick of something new, I'm going to be around for a few weeks this summer. I'd be happy to quote for the job.'

Harry looked surprised. 'Well, er, thank you,' he said. 'I'm not quite sure what my plans are yet, but I'll certainly keep that in mind if I do decide to, er, touch the place up.'

'Great.' Kate swiftly left the bookshop. As she came back out into the light of the sunny High Street, she kicked herself a little. Had she sounded too critical by pointing out that this man's shop needed redecorating? She had to work hard to be tactful, at times;

she'd always had her mother's very direct, no-nonsense nature, but over the years she'd learned to temper it. Unfortunately, being the mother of three growing boys had eroded much of her learned diplomacy; perhaps she needed to think about her approach with people a little more now she was rebuilding her life after her divorce.

14

After passing a pleasant half hour engrossed in the book she'd bought and a latte, Kate headed down the High Street and back to the first coat of paint on Aidan and Tom's living room. Nearing the row of terraced houses that was currently home, she felt again the pleasure of knowing that both of her brothers were happy and settled now. It had been a touch and go few years for them all. When Aidan had been injured in Helmand Province, his life had changed irrevocably. Years of physical and psychological therapy had created a new normal for him, and now he was in a settled, long-term relationship with Tom, the final piece of the puzzle seemed to have fallen into place. As she approached Bay Tree Terrace, she saw Florence was coming out of the front door of number two.

'Hey,' Kate called out when she reached their adjacent garden paths. 'How are you doing?'

Florence looked blank for a moment, and then, much to Kate's shock and concern, she burst into tears. Hurrying to Florence's side, she put an arm around her. 'What's wrong?' Rummaging in her jeans pocket, she pulled out a tissue. 'Don't worry, it was fresh this morning.'

'Thanks.' Florence blew her nose noisily and allowed Kate to lead her to the front door of number one. Slipping the key in the lock, Kate hurried Florence through to the kitchen and sat her down on one of the spindle-backed wooden chairs while she filled the kettle and flipped the switch.

'Whatever's the matter?' Kate asked as she sat down in the nearest chair, waiting for the kettle to boil.

Florence shook her head. 'It's stupid, really, just hormones.'

Kate smiled. 'Tell me. I've had three babies. There's not a lot I didn't go through when I was pregnant with the boys.' *And for quite a while afterwards*, she added silently. Grabbing another tissue from the box on the kitchen table, she then just decided to pass Florence the whole box. Pregnancy tears were usually fat, wet and required whole loo rolls to mop them up.

Taking a deep breath, Florence looked up at Kate and smiled. 'It's all so stupid, really, and I'm ashamed of myself for breaking down like this. It's just... what if this baby comes and I don't know what to do with it? What if it doesn't like me? What if I don't like it? I've seen so many kids over the years who've been irreparably damaged by their parents, sometimes even from before they were even born. What makes me think I'm going to do any better?' She put her head in her hands again.

Kate reached out and put a gentle arm around Florence's heaving shoulders and let her cry for a few more moments. When her sobs had subsided a little, she gave Florence's shoulders a little squeeze.

'I promise you, every parent in the world goes through this kind of thing at least once,' she said gently. 'And, being a teacher, I bet seeing the whole spectrum of children doesn't help at all.'

Florence sniffed. 'That's exactly what my friend, Josie, said the last time I started having a meltdown.'

'Well, she's right,' Kate said. 'We all go through it, and we all come out the other side. This childbirth thing is probably one of the hardest things you will go through, but you'll get there; you *will* get through it. And you'll have Sam by your side when you do. I know how much he loves you, and anyone can see how excited he is about this baby. I've never seen him like this over anything before. He's always been so reserved, so private about everything; but with you, and now the baby, he's finally starting to open up.'

'What was he like, you know, when he was younger?' Florence asked. 'He doesn't really say a lot about his childhood.'

Kate grinned. 'Well, I wish I could tell you he was different, but in reality, he was just shorter. He was always such a reserved kid, and navy life only enhanced that ability to be self-reliant.' She paused and smiled at Florence again. 'If it's any consolation, our dad was exactly the same. In the end, Mum just gave up trying to get him to open up to her – but she isn't exactly demonstrative, either.'

'It's a wonder you all turned out so well,' Florence said, then blushed. 'Sorry, that's a bit rude, isn't it?'

Kate grinned broadly. 'You're family now – you're allowed to criticise your in-laws!' She paused, and a thoughtful expression came over her face. 'Don't get me wrong, Florence, we always felt looked after as kids, but Mum and Dad were both pretty emotionally remote. That kind of thing is difficult to shake after a lifetime.' She stood up, remembering that she had put the kettle on to boil for tea. 'Seeing Sam with you now, it's a revelation for me. He's so much more open, so much more affectionate than he's ever been. When he knew you loved him, it was more than just about him and you; my relationship with him seemed to get better, closer, somehow, too. I have a lot to thank you for.'

Florence smiled back. 'That's really lovely to know. And, for the record, I've loved being welcomed into the family – with Mum and Dad up north still, and my brother in Australia, it's nice to have Aidan next door, and now you.'

Kate brought over two mugs of tea and set them down on the table. Feeling the need to remind Florence of a time when she perhaps felt a little less emotional turmoil, she reminisced a little on the wedding that they'd had.

'I remember walking down Willowbury High Street and wondering just what the hell you'd both got yourselves into!' she said. 'It being the summer, do you remember the amount of bunting there was outside the shops? And the smell of incense was overwhelming. The church had more flowers outside than I've ever seen in my life, and I remember that eccentric pagan couple who kept handing out posies to every guest as they went through the gates. They weren't anything to do with the official wedding party, were they?'

'Nope,' Florence replied. 'The vicar told me that they were likely to rock up to spread their blessings and goodwill, as they do for every wedding in the town's church, and not to be alarmed by them. They mean well.'

'Yes, but then contrast that with Sam's ex-Navy mates doing the guard of honour, and your teacher friends all throwing confetti made from the pages of vintage romance novels and I think it was probably the most memorable wedding I've ever been to, and I count my own in that, too!'

Florence laughed. 'Teachers are the biggest troublemakers at parties. We have to keep so buttoned up in our day to day lives that we just cut loose whenever we get the excuse. My friend, Josie, especially. How she made it home after the reception, I've no idea. Even three days afterwards she was recovering from an excess of Prosecco!'

'I know the feeling,' Kate said. She remembered, to this day, the thumping headache she'd woken up with the morning after, and how Corey, Tom and Will had dragged her up Willowbury Hill to 'blow away the cobwebs'. She also distinctly remembered throwing up behind an elderflower bush when the boys had gone on ahead, and swearing off Prosecco for life. *That, like her marriage, was an oath that had gone by the wayside*, she thought ruefully.

'I hadn't imagined I'd fall pregnant so quickly,' Florence said. 'Not that I'm complaining,' she added hastily. 'Plenty of people I know end up trying for years. It just all feels as though it's happening really fast now. One day I'm taking a test and the next I'm about to stop work.' She shook her head. 'And I've worked full-time since I qualified out of university. How am I going to cope with the change of pace?'

'I'm not going to lie; it'll probably freak you out,' Kate said. 'And it will take you a while to get used to all of the changes. But I promise you, Florence, you will cope. There will be good days and bad days, but you'll get through them. And you'll have loads of people around to help you through the trickier times. Sam, especially.'

Florence blew her nose noisily. 'Thanks, Kate. I know it's just the hormones getting to me, but it all feels so huge at the moment.' She glanced down at her baby bump. 'As am I.'

'You look fabulous,' Kate said, and she wasn't just saying it to make Florence feel better. Despite the puffy eyes and the tears, pregnancy really did suit her.

'Thank you.' Florence gave a brighter smile. 'All these worries must seem so daft to you, when you've been through it three times.'

'Not at all,' Kate said, taking a sip of her tea. 'I carried all three of my boys differently, but with all of them the worry was there that I wouldn't take to them. Especially after the miscarriage I had between Will and Tom.' She shook her head. 'I was so worried after that, that even when Tom got past the twelve-week mark I couldn't relax. Poor Phil had his work cut out, night after night, trying to keep me calm.'

'I'm sorry,' Florence said, 'I didn't mean to remind you of a difficult time.'

Kate shook her head. 'It's fine, honestly. This divorce wasn't just because he found someone else – the marriage was over long before Jennifer came on the scene. We just couldn't admit to it.'

'You seem very reasonable about it all,' Florence said in surprise. 'Doesn't it hurt?'

'Of course,' Kate said. 'But I had to do a lot of soul-searching when the bomb dropped. Phil and I had been together since school; there'd never been anyone else for us. When things started to wane, and all we had left in common was the kids, it was kind of inevitable that one of us would end it. He met Jennifer and he couldn't help it; I can't blame him for that.'

'And the boys? How are they about it all?'

'Confused at first, and obviously the end was a wrench for everyone. But the thing about having undemonstrative parents is that you don't approach things with all guns blazing. Mum and Dad taught me to hold back, to keep my emotions wrapped up and deal with things pragmatically. Some people might call that cold, but for me, in the end, it was self-preservation. Phil cried when he left our family home for the last time; but I couldn't.' Kate shrugged. 'We all put the walls up to protect ourselves, I guess.'

Florence sipped her tea thoughtfully. 'So, what next?'

'Find a house, move in, try to get this decorating business off the ground,' Kate said. 'No point dragging my feet about it. Plenty of people want a woman for a decorating job, and I think I'm good at it. Work shouldn't be hard to find, if people are willing to take the risk on a new venture.'

'Especially if you take some shots of what you end up doing

with this place,' Florence said. 'I mean, getting that wallpaper off was impressive enough!'

Kate grimaced. 'I can still feel the stuff under my fingernails, it was so thick!' She glanced at the clock on the back wall behind Florence, which Florence immediately noticed.

'Sorry, I should let you get on.' Rising slightly awkwardly from the chair, she made to walk out of the kitchen.

'I'll see you in a couple of hours next door, anyway,' Kate said. 'Sam said you've got some flat-packed nursery furniture for me to have a crack at.'

'It would be great if you could help,' Florence said. 'Sam was going to do it, but there's no telling when he'll be back tonight.'

'I'll pop round when I've got the first coat on the living room walls,' Kate said, walking Florence back to the front door. She paused for a moment, uncertain whether or not she should reach out and hug Florence again. *That was another consequence of having a natural, ingrained reserve cultivated by years of emotionally distant parenting*, she thought; *you just never know when a hug is the right thing to do*. Even having had three children of her own, whom she hugged ferociously and regularly, as often as she could get away with, she still felt unsure about the etiquette of hugging outside her own immediate family. Settling in the end for a quick squeeze of Florence's arm, she bade her goodbye.

As Kate headed back towards the living room and the trestle table she'd set up with her paint pots, trays, rollers and brushes, she thought again about the change in her brother, Sam, since he'd met Florence. *Perhaps love really does give people the chance to embrace new things*, she thought. Maybe, despite years of habit with Phil, she too might find someone who'd awaken her own hopes and desires again.

15

After a good morning's painting, where she began, finally, to see what the room was going to look like once it was finished, Kate headed next door to help Florence with the nursery furniture. Florence had been told by her midwife to take things as easily as she could in the last weeks of her pregnancy. Although the midwife had stopped short of advising Florence to stop work early, she had to be mindful of that. Thankfully, by the time the summer holidays were over, she'd only have a few weeks left in the classroom before she went on leave, so she and Sam were confident she'd make it through.

In a couple of hours, the nursery furniture had been assembled to their mutual satisfaction, and just as they were sliding the changing table into place against one wall of what was to be the nursery, they heard the front door opening and Sam calling a cheery greeting up the stairs.

'We're up here,' Kate called down. 'Your timing, as ever, is perfect. We've literally just put in the last screw!'

Sam poked his head around the nursery door. 'Lovely job, it

looks great.' He grinned. 'How about dinner at the pub as a thank you?'

'Sure,' Kate said. 'If you're up to it, that is, Florence?'

'Try and keep me away,' Florence said. 'I could do with a walk.' Stretching out her arms to the ceiling, she grimaced and then clutched her left side between ribcage and baby bump.

'You okay?' Sam, all concern, moved towards her.

'Fine,' Florence said. 'No one tells you about the exquisite double-edged sword that is a tiny foot in your ribs!'

'Or the midnight kick to the bladder!' Kate laughed. 'Corey, in particular, was a real one for doing that. I don't think I slept at all in the late stages with him.' Suddenly overwhelmed with longing to find out how her children were getting on in Florida, she resolved to give them a call later. The pictures they'd been sending her were fantastic, but she had a yearning to hear their voices.

As they walked down to the Travellers' Rest pub, in the heart of Willowbury High Street, talk hopped about from new baby plans, to the horrors of Aidan and Tom's walls, to updates on Kate's three boys, and then, eventually, to Kate's future. Kate still hadn't seen anything on Rightmove that she wanted to take a closer look at, so it looked as though her mother's annexe was going to have to be home when she returned to Cambridge, for a few months at least.

Sam got the drinks in and they settled outside on one of the tables that looked over the High Street. It was a lovely evening, with the waning sun still casting a warm glow over the honey-coloured stonework of the pub and its neighbouring buildings, and Kate breathed in the fresh, warm air, and felt the knots of tension created both by the hard work of decorating and the thought of her sons being so far away from her slip, albeit temporarily, away from her.

She sipped her pint of cider thoughtfully as Sam and Florence bantered amiably about babies' names and then more thought-fully about the cases Sam had flown that day in the air ambulance. Kate was content to let it wash over her. *There's a couple who will go the distance*, she thought, although she was sure that she could remember a time when she and Phil had only had eyes for each other; when the prospect of ever being apart seemed unthinkable. How time could change things! But there was no point dwelling on that. They'd created three beautiful boys between them, after all; the marriage hadn't been bad until the end.

'You okay?' Sam asked, obviously clocking the faraway look in Kate's eyes.

'Fine,' Kate said, snapping back to the moment. She took another sip of her pint, and then felt her face start to flush as she realised that Harry, the man who owned the bookshop, was right in her eyeline where she was staring up the High Street. He had a satchel with him, and, glancing at her watch, she realised that he must have shut up shop for the night. She shifted a little uneasily in her seat, remembering the coffee incident, and also the forthright way she'd told him his shop looked a bit shabby so soon after she'd complimented him on his window display.

Florence, who had a keen eye for shifts in body language, after so many years of being in the classroom, glanced at Kate curiously. 'What's caught your attention?'

'Nothing,' Kate muttered, feeling embarrassed to have been caught out.

'Really?' Florence raised an eyebrow and grinned as she caught sight of Harry. 'Oh, hang on a minute...' she trailed off tantalisingly. 'Was he the guy you were telling me about? The one you threw coffee over?'

'Yup,' Kate confirmed. There seemed to be little point denying it, since she'd told Florence the story when they'd been putting the nursery furniture together.

'Should we ask him to join us, by way of a peace offering?' Sam teased. 'I'm sure he wouldn't say no to a pint, especially if you promise not to throw yours over him again!'

'No!' Kate hissed, but it was too late as Sam turned around and smiled at Harry as he reached their table. Inwardly cursing her brother's ability to put her on the spot, she was mollified slightly when Harry caught sight of her and gave a really rather lovely smile.

'Hi,' Harry said, pausing to acknowledge them. Sam hadn't even said anything, just grinned in the man's direction but it seemed to be enough to make Harry pause. 'Beautiful evening, isn't it?'

'Lovely,' Florence agreed. 'And this is a great spot to appreciate it.'

'Certainly is.' Harry seemed a little bit nervous and out of place now he'd actually stopped, and Kate wished she had something she could say to continue the small talk. She felt completely out of practise when it came to talking to new people; she'd been so entrenched in her comfort zone in Cambridge, being out of it felt nerve-wracking. Before she could try to come up with something to contribute about the niceness of the summer weather, Harry had spoken again.

'I'm glad I've run into you again,' he said, looking over at Kate. 'I was hoping to catch you at some point in the next week or so.'

'Oh, have you got your dry-cleaning bill?' Kate said. 'Let me have it, and I'm more than happy to reimburse you, as I said.'

Harry looked vaguely discomfited. 'No, no, it's not that at all,' he said. 'I did say there was no need to worry about that.'

'Oh, okay,' Kate said. 'What was it, then?'

'Well,' Harry said, taken aback by her directness, it seemed. 'You know you mentioned about being a painter and decorator when you came into the shop? I was wondering if you'd be able to give me a quote for a fast touch-up.'

Kate burst out laughing. 'I'm sure you didn't mean that *quite* as it sounded.' Her laughter and Harry's *double entendre* finally seemed to break the awkwardness, and as Sam and Florence joined in the laughter, they all seemed to relax.

'Not exactly,' Harry conceded, grinning.

'Have a seat, mate, and tell Kate all about it while I get some more drinks in,' Sam said. 'Florence, can you give me a hand?'

'Sure,' Florence stood up, surprisingly light-footed for a heavily pregnant woman. 'Same again, Kate?' she asked.

'Please,' Kate replied.

Sam took the drink requests and he and Florence headed off to the bar.

A slightly uncomfortable silence descended between Kate and Harry as they both seemed to be contemplating what the hell to say next. *Why am I finding this so difficult?* Kate thought. Years of making small talk with people she barely knew on the school run should have prepared her for talking to a man over a pub table in the sun, but she found herself struggling to think about what to say.

'So, what was it you wanted me to, er, touch-up?' she eventually blurted out.

Harry smiled, and something inside Kate fluttered. She tried to ignore it. There was no way she was ready for any kind of *fluttering* to occur.

'The bookshop, of course.' He smiled more broadly. 'You said you might have time to quote while you were in the area, and I was wondering if you would have time to actually do the job before the blessed Artemis Bane descends for his book signing. He's coming in two weeks' time, and I really want to make the place look as good as it can for such a prestigious event.'

'Even working every evening between now and then, it'll be tight,' Kate said, then grinned. 'You don't ask for much, do you?'

Harry sighed. 'It's too good a gig for me and the shop to pass up.

He'll bring in more in one night than I usually take in a month, so it's more than worth the effort.'

'I guess,' Kate said dubiously. 'But I might need you to muck in a bit. I'm just a one man, er woman, band at the moment.'

Harry smiled. 'I'm more than happy to help. Does that mean you'll come and take a look?'

Kate smiled. 'Of course. You do know I'm just starting out, though? You could probably get someone local who'd do it faster.'

'Are you trying to do yourself out of a job?' Harry asked. His eyes crinkled a little at the edges.

'Well, no,' Kate said, 'I'm just trying to put you in the picture. This is a new career choice for me, and while I've painted a lot of houses for friends and relatives, your shop would be my first professional job.'

'Honestly, I really don't mind that,' Harry said. 'I don't have a clue about colour, and I just want it to look tidier than it currently does.' He looked a little foxed, suddenly. 'Also, I don't have that much of a budget for it...'

'... so my lack of previous client testimonials might be good for you, in terms of what I'm likely to charge,' Kate said wryly.

'Well, something like that, yes.'

There was a pause between them, but this time Kate didn't feel awkward. Something about Harry's open face and attractive smile put her at ease. Just for a moment, she felt as though she really was on holiday, and as the faint scent of the blossom from the rambling roses on the pub's walls reached her, that sense of relaxation intensified. She felt lighter, somehow, and definitely happier.

As Sam and Florence returned to the table with fresh drinks, though, Kate came back to Harry's proposition. 'Well, how about we do a deal, then? I'm up to my eyes in paint for my brother Aidan's house. If you think you could muck in on your Sunday afternoon when the shop's closed, I'll try to get it done in good time for

Artemis Bane's visit. I can come in after you close of an evening and do an hour or two each night, and whatever I don't manage to finish by next Sunday, you can help me finish off then. That way, I can keep costs down and you won't have to close while I'm doing the work.'

'If you're okay with that, it sounds great,' Harry said. 'And, of course, I'm more than happy to help out where I can.'

'It's a deal.' Kate stuck out her hand, and Harry shook it. 'How about I come over tomorrow evening and you can show me what you want, and the colours?'

'Sounds great,' Harry said. He took a long gulp of the pint of cider Sam had bought him. 'And how much will it cost?'

'I can measure up tomorrow and give you a figure for my labour, and then it's just a case of adding in the paint on top of that, unless you've already bought that?'

Harry laughed. 'I wasn't even thinking about repainting it until I got the email from Artemis's publisher asking me to host the event, so colours haven't crossed my mind!'

'Well, we can take a look tomorrow and perhaps I can make some suggestions,' Kate said.

'Now that really does sound like a good idea.' Harry took another sip of his pint. 'I'm not very adventurous when it comes to colour, and my inclination is to paint it all magnolia, but I'm sure you can come up with something a little more creative.'

'Definitely,' Kate said.

As Sam and Harry chatted, Kate was content just to sit and listen. For the first time since she'd moved into Aidan and Tom's house, she felt the stress lifting. Long may it last.

16

After Harry had left them to it, and the three of them had enjoyed some wonderful food at the pub, Kate said goodnight to Florence and Sam. She'd enjoyed seeing them, and it had been nice to chat to Harry as well. She took a long, hot bath, trying to unknot some of the muscles she'd been using since she started redecorating.

Just as she was getting out, her mobile rang. Suppressing a flash of irritation that it always happened when she needed to relax, she smiled when she saw Corey's name appearing on screen. She'd intended to call her sons before she went to bed, as the time difference meant that they'd be well into their day.

'Hey,' she said as she swiped the phone and held it to her ear.

'Hey, Mum,' Corey replied.

Immediately, Kate's mum radar (her mum-tenna as she'd often joked to Phil in the old days) perked up. There was something, even in those two words, in Corey's voice, that immediately concerned her.

'Have you had a good day?' Kate asked. She was tempted to jump right in and ask him what the matter was, but despite what she'd learned about having three boys in the house, with Corey it was often better to tread carefully as he tended to clam up if she blundered on in too soon.

'Not bad.' Another pause.

Kate imagined her son, still in the lanky stage of his adolescence, legs too long and feet too big, sprawled, perhaps, over a sofa or a bed. His blonde hair, which was the same as hers and Sam's, needed cutting before the school holidays ended.

'What have you been up to?'

'Nothing much.'

'What, with all of the Everglades to explore? You must have been up to something.' God, this was going to be harder than she'd thought. She tried another tack. 'How are your brothers?'

'Annoying.'

No change there, then. 'Was there something you wanted?'

'Not really.'

'Just to hear your mum nagging you from a few thousand miles away, then?'

There was a laugh, or it could have been a sob, at the other end of the phone. 'Something like that.'

Kate's heart ached, and she wished she could just jump in the car and go and see her eldest son face to face. After what felt like an eternity, Corey spoke again.

'Look, Mum... it's not working out.'

Kate's aching heart sank even further. 'In what way, lovely? Aren't you enjoying the holiday?'

'I don't want to talk about it over the phone. Can I come and stay with you when we get back?'

'Oh, Corey...' Kate sighed. 'I know this is all really odd, but give it a bit of time, okay? Dad feels like he's missed out on a lot because of what happened, and he really wants to spend some time with you this summer to make up for that.'

'Yeah, right.'

'Have you spoken to him about how you're feeling?'

'No way, Mum. He doesn't give a toss.'

'I'm sure that's not true.' Kate felt a real stirring of unease at Corey's words, and the urge to see him face to face hit her again. 'Why do you think that?'

'Because he's too wrapped up in Jennifer and the new baby to even remember that I exist.'

Kate nearly dropped the phone. 'The new *what*?'

'Oh, shit. Mum, I'm so sorry.' Corey's voice was absolutely mortified. 'I wasn't supposed to tell you until it was official.'

'When's it due?' Kate asked numbly.

'I dunno,' Corey replied, with characteristic teenage boy ignorance of the actual details. 'Some time in February, I think.'

Despite the divorce, despite the fact that she and Phil had been growing apart for years, and that she'd agreed without a struggle to separate, it still hurt. Emotions, it seemed, were not so easy to walk away from, even with that amount of water under the bridge. A lump rose in her throat and the wild mushroom risotto she'd eaten at the pub was threatening to make a reappearance. Struggling to stay in the moment for Corey, not wanting to burden him with her own feelings when he was obviously having a hard time himself, she forced herself to speak. *So that was why Jennifer had been looking so peaky when I dropped the boys off*, Kate thought.

'I'll give Dad a ring in the morning,' Kate said, glad that, to her ears at least, her voice sounded normal. 'See if he's happy, when you all get back home, to send you over to me for a few days.' Then, she had a thought. 'What about your brothers?'

'They're okay,' Corey said. 'They love it out here, and they've stuffed themselves stupid on junk food and Coke every day.'

Nothing new there, then, Kate thought. Corey, as the eldest, always took things harder than his siblings.

'Let me talk to Dad in the morning, and I'll see what I can do.'

'Thanks, Mum.' Another pause. 'Love you.'

Kate flushed with pleasure at her son's uncharacteristic admission of affection. 'Love you too. Goodnight, Corey Dorey.'

She heard a laugh on the other end of the line, which made her heart flip with love and relief. 'Don't call me that.'

As they ended the call, Kate remained sitting on the side of the bath, where she'd sank when Corey had revealed the news about Jennifer's pregnancy. It hurt more than it should have. Such obvious evidence of her ex-husband's new life stung, even though she wouldn't change what had happened, not now anyway. Feeling a wave of self-pity washing over her, she thought for a moment about going next door to share the news with Sam and Florence, but then decided against it. They had enough on their minds at the moment; they didn't need her adding to it. She'd never found it easy to confide in people, anyway, and needed some time to mull this new information over before she spoke about it. Not to mention that she felt even more worried about Corey, now. He was obviously taking the news hard, and she wished she was there to reassure him. She'd definitely ring Phil in the morning when she'd had some time to think and had slept on it. She didn't want to be the kind of hysterical ex-wife who spent her time haranguing and screaming about everything that happened. A new baby was a big deal, though, and she was pretty pissed off that Phil hadn't told her the news himself; that she'd had to find out second-hand from Corey, who was obviously struggling. This was more than just a conversation about paying for school shoes.

As she fell into bed a little time later, she wondered, not for the first time, about the shift in emotional dynamics a divorce brought. Years of marriage, of knowing each other's moods, reactions and triggers, counted for very little when it was over, it seemed. Or maybe it was just her marriage. Drifting, later, into sleep, she welcomed the temporary relief from her buzzing thoughts.

17

The next evening, having managed, finally, to get hold of Phil on the phone and have a brief conversation about Corey's state of mind, Kate felt somewhat better. Phil had promised to keep an eye on their eldest son, and to try to spend some more time with him while they were all under the one roof in Florida. He hadn't mentioned Jennifer's pregnancy, though, which left Kate feeling as though things were a little unfinished. Why would he have told the boys, but not said anything to her? He must know that one of them would eventually let it slip to her. Perhaps it was a conversation he'd broach when they were back on the same continent. The omission unsettled her, but she was far more concerned about the children she had, rather than any new additions.

More cheeringly, after another day of hefting furniture back into place from where she'd moved it yesterday, Kate looked back and surveyed her efforts in the living room. *It's gone surprisingly well*, she thought as she looked at the walls, now the mellow shade of Farrow and Ball's Purbeck Stone, a beautiful colour reminiscent of the rocks of the Jurassic Coast. When Aidan and Tom had shown her their colour choices for the house, she'd been secretly relieved;

the thought of painting the whole place magnolia, or, at the other extreme, a series of outrageous 'statement' colours for each separate wall, had filled her with dread. But while Aidan would have been more than happy for her to paint it beige everywhere, Tom had taken a more elegant view, and she had to admit, he had an eye for colour. If the acting work ever dried up, perhaps she could take him on as an interior design consultant. She smiled at the thought; she was barely even up and running as a painter and decorator herself: she certainly shouldn't be thinking about a business partner just yet.

She was just slumping down onto the squashy pale grey sofa, and thinking fondly that when Sam and Florence's baby came along Tom and Aidan might have cause to regret that choice of colour, when she remembered she was supposed to be going to see Harry and give him a quote for painting the bookshop. Springing up again, she dashed upstairs and checked herself over in the bathroom mirror to make sure the Purbeck Stone hadn't crept under her decorator's overalls, squirted a bit of deodorant and ran a brush through her thick shoulder-length blonde hair. She also gave her teeth a quick brush, just in case the raw onion in the salad she'd had for lunch still lingered. Since she hadn't given Harry a precise time to come over, she hoped it wasn't too late and he'd have shut up shop for the day.

Taking a brisk walk towards the High Street, she again noticed the quirkiness of Willowbury. It made her smile that her strait-laced brother Sam had found a home here, not to mention Aidan. As she passed an archway that led into a small alcove of shops behind the High Street, she noticed a beautiful mural of a woman, bathed in moonlight, heading down to a lake. Amused, as well as impressed, she wondered if it was ever warm enough in Somerset to go skinny dipping. If there was ever a place to do it, she figured, Willowbury would be it.

Harry's shop, she reflected as she drew closer, was hardly the archetype of a Willowbury 'woo woo' establishment, though. Vale Volumes, and its owner had both looked reassuringly normal on the occasions she'd encountered them. In her mind's eye, before she got to the front door of the shop, she pictured Harry's dark hair that was running to grey, and she remembered with a small flutter the turned down, deep blue eyes that crinkled up at the sides when he smiled. A moment later, as she entered Vale Volumes' cool, welcoming space, she almost had cause to reconsider that thought. There, standing behind the counter, wearing what looked like the helmet of a medieval knight's costume, combined with a rather startling red and black striped jersey, Harry looked like a cross between Denis the Menace and King Arthur, complete with a large replica Excalibur in his hand.

Kate couldn't help but laugh as she drew closer and said what she hoped was a businesslike but brisk 'Hello!'

Harry, obviously unaware that someone had walked in, owing to the lack of visibility from the helmet, jumped a mile and dropped the sword. It landed with a clatter on the varnished oak floorboards.

'Sorry to startle you,' Kate continued, smiling as Harry whipped off the helmet before ducking down to retrieve his dropped weapon. 'I've just popped over to measure up and give you a quote for the painting.'

Harry smiled apologetically as he straightened back up. 'Sorry about the strange get-up,' he said as he put Excalibur onto the counter and then pulled the jersey over his head. His hair stuck up in all directions as he emerged, which he tried to remedy by rubbing a hand through it. 'I was just trying out some of the props that I ordered for Artemis Bane's book signing. Much as I loathe fancy dress, Bane's publisher suggested I get some bits and bobs in to set the scene for when he does his reading. I'm hoping that it'll be a scorcher that night and I'll just be able to get away with placing them strategically around the shop, rather than actually having to wear them myself.'

'That's a pretty weird combination, though,' Kate said, mulling over the items now on Harry's counter. 'I guess I should have paid more attention to my eldest son when he was reading the first two novels to find out what the significance of that costume is!' She'd read the first book in the series herself, but couldn't remember why those particular props were so important.

'Honestly, I'm not completely sure there is one,' Harry replied. 'Urban fantasy isn't really my thing, though, so I could be missing something.'

'It all looks very intriguing, anyway,' Kate replied. She glanced up at the ceiling of the shop and then, seeing the damp patch, and aware that Harry might be waiting to close up, got back to business. 'So, do you want to talk me through what you'd like me to do?'

'Absolutely.' Harry came out from behind the counter, and Kate couldn't help noticing that under that geeky costume pullover and despite the dishevelled hair, he looked far too suave to be a bookseller, who she'd always imagined as tweed-clad and rather shabby in their appearance.

'If you've got the time for the project, I'd like a light colour on the walls, and a bright white on the ceiling, to cover the age spots and give the place a real lift. The shelving's dark, so I want something that won't make it feel smaller or claustrophobic, and will offset the bookshelves without upstaging them.'

'Any thoughts on the actual colour?' Kate looked around at the space.

'Not really, although a shade of yellow might be nice.'

Kate tried not to wince. 'I'm not sure yellow would work in this space with the very dark shelving,' she said. 'It might end up looking like the inside of a 1970s pub!'

Harry laughed. 'I told you I was no good with colour. What would you suggest?'

Kate thought for a moment. 'There's this really nice shade from a company called Craig and Rose called Porcelain Blue,' she said. 'I've got a colour card at home that I brought with me to do my brother's place. I could order a tester pot if you like, see what you think.'

'Sounds good,' Harry replied. 'I'm impressed you can remember the names off the colour charts just like that.'

'Ah, but I bet if I asked you if you had a particular book, and you had it in stock, you'd know exactly where to find it, even if you had it in the stockroom out the back,' Kate replied.

'Well, you've got me there.' Harry nodded. 'Why? Is there something in particular you're looking for?'

'The collected poems of Christina Rossetti,' Kate said.

'To your left, third shelf down, dark blue cloth binding,' Harry replied immediately.

Kate headed over to where Harry had indicated, paused, and then pulled the exact book from the shelf. 'Impressive.' She felt the silky blue binding of the book's covers, and the sensation of the rough cut pages against the tip of her fingers. 'What about a copy of Atwood's *Oryx and Crake*?'

'Other side of the room, fiction, top shelf, halfway across.'

Again, Kate found the book. 'See? And you think it's cool that I remember the names of colours?'

'Well, it is.' Harry smiled. Kate found herself smiling back, and a lovely heartbeat's pause elapsed before Harry cleared his throat again. 'Do you need a hand measuring up?'

'Sure.' She pulled a tape measure from where she'd hooked it over the belt on her jeans and passed him the other end. 'I assume I'm painting behind the shelves and not just around them?'

'Yes please,' Harry said. 'They can all be shifted about, or so I was led to believe by the previous owner.'

As they set to measuring the shop, Kate found herself starting to relax a little. She felt as though she could really do a good job for Harry, and although it would mean even more work than she'd taken on with Tom and Aidan's house, she looked forward to the challenge. For the first time in a long time, she felt excited, and like this really could be the start of a new career.

18

Over the next week or so, Kate found herself getting into a bit of a groove. The living room of Tom and Aidan's place was coming along nicely, and she was beginning to get physically more able to cope with the demands of a painting and decorating job. Florence popped in most days, and while Kate wouldn't let her help out with the actual work, it was nice to have the company and to chat over a cuppa. She'd clear up at about four o'clock, grab a bite to eat and then head down the road with her painting stuff in the boot of her Volvo to crack on with Harry's shop.

At first, he'd tried to stay out of the way, apart from helping her to shift the bookshelves before she started each part of the room, or if she needed to ask him something, and Kate was initially glad for that. She suspected there was nothing worse than having a client hovering over your every move, and, as early as she was in this new venture, she was more than happy to be left to her own devices. However, after the first couple of evenings, Harry had been a bit more present, rather than just letting her into the shop and then scurrying into the back, or up the rickety stairs to his flat, and eventually the cups of tea he made her stretched into longer chats while she worked.

Kate, not being a natural confider in people, had been more than happy to let him lead the conversations. She found him easy to talk to, though, and before long they were discovering a shared love of bad mid-eighties stadium rock music and early morning walks, and very, very dark chocolate. She wasn't sure if she could be totally on board with his desire to drink whisky from a granite tumbler at the peak of Ben Nevis, but she thought she'd probably settle for cider at the top of Cheddar Gorge as a compromise. He didn't shirk when she suggested he picked up a brush, either, and was soon happily edging the walls while she made brisk work with the paint roller. They were getting on so well, in fact, that after a few evenings, their conversation had turned more personal; to Kate, it felt as though a friendship was beginning to bloom.

'So, what's the best thing about living and working in Willowbury?' Kate asked, apropos of nothing.

Harry laughed. 'Good question! I think it's that I never know what to expect when I open the front door to the shop of a morning. This morning, for example, it was a bare-footed pagan in a purple cloak, and yesterday a nun asked to use my loo. I mean, how can you refuse an envoy of the Lord?'

Kate found herself laughing along with Harry. 'I guess you will have scored points in heaven for that one!'

'And then there are the cosplayers,' Harry said, getting into his stride. 'I used to think I was pretty switched on with the current trends in that market but there has been such an explosion of different texts and fandoms since all of the streaming platforms launched, and I don't recognise half of the characters who come into the shop these days. Of course, I know a good Harry Potter when I see one, and ever since Artemis Bane hit the big time, I see a lot of the characters from his novels wandering up and down

Willowbury High Street in search of the locations that he includes in his books.'

'That's the guy who's coming to speak at the shop?'

'Yup.' Harry smiled ruefully. 'By hosting him, I'll make more money in one night than I do in a month, but my Christ he's got a long list of demands!'

Harry proceeded to fill Kate in on the long, frequent emails he'd received and by the end of it she was shaking with laughter.

'I'd just get him some lemons from the Co-op,' she said, 'and see if he really can tell the difference!'

'You're joking, aren't you?' Harry joined in with laughter. 'Apparently the last time he didn't get what he wanted at a book signing, he tipped his jug of water over the books that he was meant to be signing. The poor bookshop owner had already paid for them and could barely give them away after that. It's really not worth the financial risk.'

'Sounds like someone needs to bring him down a peg or two,' Kate said. 'My son Corey loves his books. I wonder if he would if he knew what a diva he was.'

'I've still got some tickets left for the event next week if you fancy bringing him along,' Harry said. 'Happy to save you a seat if you think you can stomach it.'

'Thanks,' Kate replied. 'They've just got home from a trip to Florida with their dad, but I'll see what he's up to and if he feels up to coming to stay for a night or two. I have been a bit reluctant to invite them down to stay with me as they all get really jealous of each other and I can't be seen, as their mother, to be playing favourites and choosing one over the others. However, Corey sounded a bit down on the phone recently. He seemed better the last time we talked, and I asked my ex-husband to keep an eye on him, but perhaps it would do him good to come and stay with me for a day or two.' Realising she was half speaking to herself, thinking out loud, she picked up her roller again.

'It must be hard being away from them,' Harry said.

Kate shrugged unconvincingly. 'They're getting older now. They like to think they don't need us, me and Phil, but it's amazing how quickly they come back to us when they want something!'

'Are they close to their dad?'

'Yes,' Kate said, although she knew that with Corey that wasn't entirely true. 'It hit them hard when we split up. Especially Corey, who always seems to feel things that much more than the other two. He is my eldest, but I find myself worrying about him so much more than Will and Tom. They just seem that much more street-wise, you know?'

Harry's slight hesitation to reply drew Kate's attention. 'Sorry,' she said, feeling as though she'd been banging on. 'I didn't mean to overshare. I know how tedious it is when you don't have kids to hear other people wittering on about their own.'

'Not at all,' Harry said. 'It's nice to hear you talking about them. I'm interested, really I am.'

'I would have thought you were more the footloose and fancy-free type!' Kate joked.

'Appearances can be deceptive.' Harry turned away and began painting a line by the skirting board again.

Kate, suddenly aware that she might have touched a nerve, felt in a quandary. Was it something she'd said? To be fair, she'd meant it as a compliment; Harry dressed entirely too well, all the time, to be a parent. It was only now that she actually had the time to take better care of herself, and her boys were almost fully grown.

As if reading her thoughts, Harry turned back to her. 'Sorry,' he said. 'I didn't mean to be quite so abrupt. I found out that father-hood wasn't going to be on the cards for me a long time ago. It's not something that I usually spend a lot of time thinking about these days.'

Kate's slow methodical strokes with the roller became even more so. 'You don't have to tell me if you don't want to, but may I ask why, Harry?'

'Well, the thing is that children the conventional way was never really going to be an option,' Harry said. He suddenly seemed to find the section of wall he was helping to paint incredibly interesting.

'In what way?' Kate asked.

'I, well, I found out I was infertile when I was in my twenties,' Harry said, still methodically rolling up and down the wall.

'Christ, Harry, I'm so sorry,' said Kate, giving him her full attention now, as she put her own roller carefully down in the tray. 'What a thing to discover.'

'I made peace with it a long time ago.' Harry turned back to her. 'And, the way things have turned out, perhaps it's for the best. I'm rather too set in my ways to start a family now, anyway.'

'But to have the possibility taken from you is awful.' Kate couldn't imagine what that would have been like; most of her twenties and thirties had been taken up with raising her three sons; the thought of being without them was unimaginable.

'I had a lot of therapy when the diagnosis came,' Harry said. 'And there were always other routes to having children; it just didn't work out that way, in the end. To be honest, now I'm here, I don't feel that much of a loss.'

Kate shook her head. 'I can't imagine what you must have been through.' She paused, searching around desperately for something to say that didn't sound trite or clichéd. She struggled, and in the end settled on complimenting him on the bookshop. 'This place is such a project, though – does it help to, I don't know, come to terms with it?'

Harry laughed. 'It's all right, honestly. I've had a fair few conversations like this over the years, and it's perfectly fine not to know what to say. No one can fix it, it is what it is, and I've learned to accept it.'

Kate put her roller back down in the paint tray and stretched her aching back. She reached over to the shelf where she had rested a cup of tea that Harry had made some minutes previously. Taking it, she glanced at him. 'So, did the move to Willowbury have something to do with... you know?'

'Yes, definitely,' Harry said quietly. 'That's really what my moving here was all about. There was someone who I thought might end up changing things, back in London, but... it wasn't to be. In the end, I just needed to come somewhere completely different, to feel things that were different. This place seemed to be the answer.'

'I can see why,' said Kate, putting down her teacup. 'Willowbury is certainly different.'

'It really is.' Harry smiled, but there was a sudden, deeper sadness in his dark, denim-blue eyes. Kate paused, wondering if she should push him to elucidate on this change of mood or not. When Harry then put the paint can down on the counter, and leaned up against it to drink his tea, Kate saw he was in the mood to talk.

'So, what happened?' Kate asked. 'If you don't mind my asking.'

'I did think I was going to settle down and have a family once, despite my diagnosis, but sadly it didn't work out.'

'I don't want to pry,' Kate said gently. 'But if you want to tell me, I'd like to know.'

Harry focused on his mug of tea. 'Some things can't be negotiated, and there were a couple of definite non-negotiables in the end.'

'From her side or yours?' Kate asked as she continued to paint. 'Sorry. It's none of my business, really.' They might be getting on well, but she still needed to curb that urge to ask the most direct questions.

'No, it's okay,' Harry replied. 'It's not really that interesting a story.'

'Oh?' Kate replied, even more intrigued.

Harry paused and smiled back at Kate. 'It's been a long time since I've discussed it. In fact, I'm not even sure that I've told anyone in Willowbury. Not even Jack! But somehow I feel I can talk to you. It must be doing all this manual labour that's making me a bit more relaxed.'

'Manual labour?' Kate snorted. 'I'd hardly call painting a few lines around the skirting board manual labour!'

Harry laughed. 'Maybe you're right, but it is for me!' There was another pause, and he seemed to be collecting his thoughts. 'Nicola and I were together for five years,' Harry said, between sips of his tea. 'And for a long time we were very, very happy. We worked in similar fields, had a good group of friends... you know the stuff. She'd always known I couldn't have my own children naturally, that there would be issues with conceiving if we decided to go down that route.' He paused, and Kate waited for him to pick back up. Although this had clearly all happened a while ago, she could see from the tension in the hand that gripped his mug that he wasn't in the habit of talking regularly about it.

'Well, we did decide, after we'd bought a house and reached a decent stage in our careers, that we would try for a baby, using a donor, and then after that, maybe get married. Nicola went into the whole thing with her eyes open. She loved me, and I loved her.' Harry swallowed. 'The problems came, of course, after a couple of rounds of treatment. She was badly physically affected by the treatment, and I felt so unable to help. Despite the doctors' best efforts, and all of our hopes, she just couldn't conceive.' Harry shook his head. 'I couldn't help thinking how much better off she'd be with someone different. Someone who *worked*.' He gave a short, humour-less laugh. 'She, of course, wouldn't have any of it; insisted that it didn't matter, but in the end, I knew it did.'

'I'm so sorry, Harry,' Kate said softly. 'It must be like a bereave-ment, in a sense.'

Harry nodded. 'After the last failed round, we decided to call it a day. We were both so tired of it all, and it seemed to take over every-thing else in our lives. After that, we talked about adoption, but I think something like that either unites or destroys a couple. For us, it meant we just didn't have anything left to give each other. We limped on for a while, but in the end, we called it a day. It was a mutual decision by the end, and to be honest I just felt huge relief that it was all over. That must sound cold, but we'd been through so much, and all I had left was self-preservation.'

'I can understand that,' Kate said. 'It must have just got to a point when you'd forgotten what it was you wanted in the first place, and just got immersed in the process.' She was reminded of the last months of her own marriage; how she and Phil had become two people who talked about their kids and nothing else, really. All common ground had gone by the end. Perhaps that situation wasn't so different to Harry's experiences of trying to have children in the first place; both were all consuming, if poles apart.

Harry nodded, swallowed hard and, as if to distract himself, took another gulp of his tea. 'All the counselling in the world can only get you so far. Eventually, you just need to make a decision. Nicola and I made ours, and the rest, as they say, is history.' He gazed down into his now empty mug.

Kate stepped forward and gently placed a hand on Harry's fore-arm. 'I'm so sorry, Harry. It can't be easy, I'm sure, coming to the realisation that children aren't going to be a part of your life. I'm sorry that it meant your relationship ended, too.'

Harry looked up at her after a moment or two and gave a smile.

'To be honest, I think we'd probably have gone our separate ways sooner or later. We just sped up the process. Looking back on it, it was for the best. After all, if we hadn't been through what we had, I'd probably still be doing eighty-hour weeks in the City, working myself into the ground for investors who couldn't give a shit. At least, this way, I'm in charge of my life, now. And the shop has been great therapy in itself.'

'You seem very settled here,' Kate said. 'And the place is a real sanctuary. I've heard so many people talking about it when I've been out and about in the town.'

Harry smiled more broadly. 'That's good to know.' He put his mug back on the shop counter. 'I suppose I'd better stop baring my soul and get back to painting the skirting boards.'

Kate still wanted to linger, to show just how touched she was that Harry had chosen to confide in her, but the moment for that had passed, it seemed. Putting her own mug down on the counter, too, she walked back to her paint tray and carried on. Her heart was still thumping, but as she began to cover the walls with regular strokes from the roller, she felt herself calming once more. Painting, for her, was turning into a kind of therapy.

'You said you were missing your sons?' Harry asked. He was obviously keen to deflect attention from the conversation they'd just had.

Kate took a deep breath. 'If I'm being honest... yes, I am, terribly. I also can't help wondering if coming back to live with me after three weeks in Florida is going to be one huge let down. You know, back to the rules and routines. I've always been the one who's the "fun police" in the relationship, and I think that's not going to change any time soon now Phil and I are divorced.'

'I'm sure that's not true,' Harry said, smiling at her. Kate felt something inside her flutter when he did. He did have a lovely and infectious smile. 'You seem, er, pretty fun to me.'

'You need to get out more!' Kate laughed. 'You've been spending too much time in this place.'

'Tricky not to, as a business owner in the high season,' Harry said. 'You're kind of chained to a place when the sun shines so you can make it through the leaner winter months.'

'You open six days a week?'

'And Sunday mornings in tourist season.'

'Being self-employed is a bit of a slog,' Kate agreed, 'and I've only been doing it for a couple of weeks!'

'But your work is much more physical than mine,' Harry said. 'Which reminds me, I can't believe I haven't asked before now, but what did you do before you decided to paint walls for a living?'

'Nothing like this!' Kate laughed. 'I worked in an estate agent's office. Admin and writing the copy for the houses mainly. That wasn't so physically demanding, but looking after the needs of three feral boys is pretty hard work at times, physically and mentally. Especially dragging the washing up and down stairs.'

'I can imagine!' Harry said. 'I was one of three boys, too. At least that means with me out of the child rearing picture, the family name continues with them.' For a second, he sounded desolate, but then moved swiftly on. 'Now, what do we have left to do?'

'Another coat tomorrow morning and it should be perfect,' Kate said. She stepped back and looked appraisingly at the much fresher wall in front of her. 'Though I say so myself, this blue was such a lovely choice,' she said thoughtfully. 'It's going to look like your wonderful mahogany shelves are resting on an endless sky.'

'You're right,' Harry said. He put down his brush and stepped back so that he was right next to her where she stood, admiring their efforts. 'It's the perfect colour.'

The silence that descended between them was companionable but laced with something else that Kate couldn't quite identify. She suddenly felt very aware of Harry standing next to her, of his slightly more rapid breathing and raised body temperature from painting, and his paint-splattered but lightly tanned arms in the tatty polo shirt and shorts that he'd changed into to help her finish the walls in time for Artemis Bane's visit. Glancing sideways, she also saw that he had paint flecks in his hair.

'You really ought to have put a cap on to paint,' she said, turning fully towards him with a smile. 'It's going to take a while to get that colour washed out of your hair.' Unthinkingly, she reached out a hand and touched one of the larger flecks of blue paint that had settled on the side of his head. As her fingertips made contact, she felt an incredible urge to slide her hand upwards, and to run it through his hair.

Kate could feel Harry's hair tickling her palm as he leaned, seemingly instinctively, into her touch. It was a touch that suddenly felt much more like a caress as she ran her hand through his dark hair which was flecked with strands of grey as well as the blue paint. 'You're going to need to give it a good wash tonight,' she said, her voice breathier than she'd expected it to be.

'Right,' Harry murmured. Kate's heart skipped in her chest as she felt him raise a hand to cover hers. 'I'll be sure to do that.' As if he didn't want to frighten her off, he slowly drew her closer to him, until her hand was resting on the nape of his neck.

'You've got a few splatters of blue yourself,' he said softly. He raised his other hand to her forehead. 'Here,' he murmured, brushing a thumb over the laughter lines at the side of her eyes. 'And here,' this time along the curve of her cheekbone, 'and here,' as he traced a fingertip under her chin, raising her eyes to his until she felt her gaze melting into his intense expression.

'Harry...' she whispered. 'What are we doing?'

'Checking very thoroughly for paint stains,' he said. And then he kissed her.

19

'Oh God, Kate, I'm so sorry.' Harry broke away from her gently, a few moments later. 'I don't know what came over me.' He gave a very nervous laugh and looked down at his paint-splattered hands.

Kate, her lips still tingling from a most unexpected kiss that she hadn't exactly ducked away from, gave an equally nervous smile. 'No harm done,' she said, trying to inject a brisk note into her voice as though she hadn't responded to him with all of the enthusiasm of a water-starved marathon runner. 'I never knew that painting a wall could be so seductive!' She glanced at the oversized clock on the far wall of the shop. It was past eight o'clock and she suddenly felt as though every bone in her body ached. Realising that between Tom and Aidan's house and the bookshop she'd effectively worked a twelve-hour day, she wasn't surprised.

'Well, I think I really ought to call it a night anyway,' she said. She reached for the plastic bag that would keep her roller and brush in decent condition until the next time and gestured for Harry to hand her his paintbrush. As their hands touched, she felt another fizzing tingle. This time, though, she was determined to ignore it. As far as she was concerned, it was entirely too soon to be feeling *those* kinds of feelings for anyone else. Especially not someone who lived on the other side of the country to where she knew she had to return. She'd never been one for holiday romances.

'Er, same time tomorrow?' she said as she moved her painting equipment and dust sheets to the back room of the shop.

'If that's all right,' Harry said, appearing to make himself busy with collecting up their mugs. 'Look, Kate... do we need to talk about what just happened?'

'Honestly, Harry, I think it's better that we just move on and I finish this job ready for your world-famous author to come and trash the place again, don't you?'

Harry, to his credit, after looking momentarily chagrined, clearly thought it was better to agree. 'Absolutely,' he replied. 'I mean, it's important that we gave Artemis a fresh canvas to ruin, if his reputation is anything to go by!'

As Kate left the shop, she couldn't entirely ignore the thump of her heart when she relived the incredibly exciting and definitely pleasurable sensation of Harry's lips upon hers. But to go down that route, even for a moment more, would take her to places that she definitely wasn't ready to go to, no matter what her heart and her tingling mouth were telling her.

Returning to Tom and Aidan's house, she suddenly remembered that she had left her phone on the kitchen table, rather than having taken it to Harry's shop. As she tapped the button, she was shocked to see nine missed calls from her ex-husband, Phil, and a series of increasingly concerned sounding WhatsApp messages. Swiping the screen, eyes urgently scanning the messages, her heart began to beat hard and frantically in her chest for an entirely different reason than it had when Harry had kissed her. As soon as she had got herself up to speed, she made a call.

'Phil? Yeah, sorry, I left my phone at home when I went out to do another decorating job. Have you managed to track him down yet? Have you checked with Kieron's parents? What about Joe's? Okay, okay, I didn't mean to teach you how to suck eggs. When was the last time you saw him? No, I spoke to him last night, but he didn't say he had any plans with anyone else today.'

For a moment, Kate paused as she remembered how distraught her eldest son had been on the phone when he'd still been in Florida. Although she'd spoken to him since they'd all got home a couple of days ago, and he'd seemed better, a horrible sick feeling started in the pit of her stomach and worked its way up her throat. She swallowed hard in an attempt to quell the rising nausea. What if...? No. That was stupid thinking; Corey had been upset but surely she'd have known, as his mother if he was considering doing something... drastic. She shook her head and tried to zone back into what Phil was saying.

'Yes, of course I'll let you know if he phones me,' she said. 'Make sure that you keep me posted as well. Do Will and Tom know that we're concerned? Okay, it's probably a good thing that you haven't mentioned anything to them as yet. But if he's not home by ten o'clock I think we need to call the police.'

With a trembling hand, Kate pressed the end call button and, finding that her knees would no longer hold her up, she sank down onto one of the kitchen chairs. All the aches and pains that she had been feeling as a result of so much painting and decorating now came a sharp second to the fear and panic that was coursing through her veins. Corey, her least streetwise, kind, quiet, sensitive sixteen-year-old son hadn't come home and neither she nor his father had any clue where he might be.

The sharp ping of her phone signalling a new message made her heart beat even faster. Slumping back in disappointment when she realised it was a message from Harry, rather than Corey, she was at least glad for the slight distraction for a few seconds.

Again, so sorry for how things ended tonight. Just wanted to make sure
you made it home all right.

Kate dithered about sending Harry a reply to fill him in on the
situation with Corey, but decided it wasn't really something she
could share with him. After all, they might be developing a friendship (kiss notwithstanding), but she didn't really want to inflict her
parental woes on him. Especially not after he'd disclosed to her
what he had that evening about his own inability to have children.
Anyway, with a bit of luck Corey would be home safe and sound in
his own bed by ten o'clock and she could stop worrying.

Although the last thing on her mind was food, it did occur to
her that she hadn't eaten since a very early lunch. Mindlessly
throwing together a cheese and pickle sandwich, she spent the next
half an hour ringing through to Corey's phone and cursing each
time she got voicemail. Corey was terrible at answering his phone
at the best of times, joking that it was only his mother who bothered to ring him anyway and everybody else just sent him a Whats-
App. She supposed he was probably right, but it just irritated her
that even though he knew this, he still refused to pick up.

It wasn't often now that Kate missed her marriage; but sitting
here at a kitchen table in a house that wasn't her own, completely in
the dark as to the whereabouts of her eldest son, she suddenly
desperately wanted to feel safe, reassuring arms around her. She
wasn't one for crying, but as the possibilities of what might have
happened to Corey raced unfiltered through her mind, she felt the
unwelcome prickle of tears.

Shit. Why had he been so stupid? Harry felt a hot flush of absolute mortification spreading not only over his cheeks but also through his entire body. He felt like a hormone-crazed sixteen-year-old who'd just had his face slapped at a party for coming on too strong. Just kissing a woman like that had never been his style, and he couldn't quite get his head around why he'd done it. It must have been something about his perceived sense of intimacy in that moment – he and Kate had discussed so many things in the time they'd spent painting the shop's walls; it was a situation where, not needing to make eye contact, the conversation had just seemed to flow easily between them. He'd been lulled into a familiarity that, perhaps, wasn't really there.

And yet, Harry thought, *she* did *kiss me back*. Admittedly for only a few moments before she'd broken away, but she *had* responded to him, her lips parting in the soft, tentative way of nearly all first kisses. Kisses that were wanted, desired, craved. His presumption hadn't been undesired or overly forceful, he was sure of that. It was just that way they'd left things, as if both of them couldn't quite believe what had just happened. But was that so surprising, under the circumstances? Perhaps it was because Harry knew that Kate was only in Willowbury for the length of the summer that he'd taken the risk. Should she have rejected him outright, he'd only have had to have seen her again for the duration of the decorating job, and then she'd be out of his life, out of Willowbury and back in Cambridgeshire. Gone from his life as quickly as she'd entered it. But there was a part of him that kicked against that notion, now they'd got to know each other. His natural sense of pragmatism made his head tell him that a long-distance relationship was no good, at his time of life, that it would be unworkable to try to pursue anything other than a friendship, but his heart, even after that one soft kiss, was suggesting exactly the opposite.

He chided himself gently as he loaded the two mugs into the dishwasher in his flat. It had been a few decent conversations and a single kiss; hardly a secure basis upon which to start making future plans. He'd obviously been on his own too long; celibacy didn't agree with him, that was for sure, if he could massively overthink one little kiss to this extent. He'd better ring Jack and suggest both of them have a night out in Stavenham, or, even better to purge this romantic malaise, head up to Bristol for a proper session. Cricket, beers and bars was definitely the way to go to purge all thoughts of romance. Not for the first time, he felt lucky that he didn't have any long-term ties to anyone else; after all, he could just up and go out if he wanted to; he was a free agent. Sometimes, caught up in the sleepy, quirky atmosphere of Willowbury, he forgot that. The fact that this train of thought was completely the opposite path to the easy intimacy that had sprung up between himself and Kate was something that didn't even occur to him as he texted Jack, suggesting a drink sometime next week when Gracie had gone back to her mother.

But it was no good, even once he'd firmed up a night out with Jack, his mind kept drifting back to the kiss. And what it would have been like to have properly taken Kate in his arms, whisked her upstairs, out of the paint-splattered overalls and into his bed. He couldn't deny that the attraction he felt for her was a strong one. Talking to her, and kissing her, felt so different to anything he'd ever felt before; the women he'd had relationships with in the past had been mostly in the same field of work, as driven and successful as him, carefully versed in the world of high City finance and perfectly poised in all things. He'd always been more of a fancier of the Natashas of this world than the Bridget Joneses, a lover of order, elegance and financial and emotional restraint. Kate, while certainly guarded and arguably emotionally restrained after her experiences of marriage and divorce, had a braveness about her that he found intriguing. A mother of three boys, throwing caution to the winds to start a new business and find a new home, even though there were huge odds against her, made him curious, made him feel an attraction that stirred him more than anything had in a long, long time.

But there was no point in thinking that way, he reminded himself *again*; Kate would be gone when September arrived, and he just didn't have it in him to commute back east once in a blue moon to see her. The shop, while running well, couldn't stretch to another full-time member of staff just yet, although he had a wonderful lady called Joan who covered a couple of afternoons a week so he could do his accounts and order stock in peace, so he was needed here for the foreseeable future. Cursing himself for overthinking everything, he settled down in front of the television to catch up on the latest episodes of the crime drama he'd got addicted to. Something about the emotionally remote detective in the snows of Sweden appealed to him, right now. Had he known the turmoil that Kate was going through, sat alone on the other side of Willowbury, as she waited for news of her eldest son, he might have been compelled to rethink his options.

It seemed an age that Kate sat there, alone at the kitchen table, willing her phone to ring. With every passing moment, the urge to just get in the car and drive back to Cambridgeshire intensified; that pull of the invisible umbilical cord growing stronger and stronger as the moments ticked by with still no word from Corey. She'd rung Lorna shortly after speaking to Phil, just in case Corey had headed back for a look at the old house. Lorna hadn't seen him, but promised to keep her eyes open, and offered to go out and look for him, if he didn't turn up soon. Kate felt hugely grateful to have a friend in her corner.

The clock on the kitchen wall ticked the seconds loudly; the sandwich she'd made still lay half eaten on her plate. This inertia, this inability to actually do anything constructive, was worsening as the time passed.

At ten forty-five, she grabbed her car keys and decided that, fuck it, even if she had to drive all night, she'd get back to Cambridgeshire and look for Corey herself. After all, she was his mother; wasn't there some unwritten rule about maternal instinct that meant that, if she just listened to her heart, she'd be led straight to him? Then she thought of all the mothers who'd waited, with hope and then without it, when their children had disappeared, and bodies had been discovered. What about instinct, then?

She'd phoned Phil, and then Tom and Will, a couple of times, but none of them could shed any light. Phil had been out driving the lanes of their village, and those two and three settlements over, just in case Corey had been caught out and was walking home from somewhere, and he had nearly crashed the car when he'd answered the call from her. Kate couldn't help thinking that if Phil hadn't even been able to find his own matching socks in the laundry basket without her assistance when they'd been married, he had bugger all chance of finding their eldest son, but, she conceded, at least he was in the same county. Tom and Will had been worried, obviously, but in their own ways had tried to reassure their mother. *He's probably just with a mate*, Tom had said. *Don't sweat it, Mum.*

All very well for him to say, Kate thought, but that did precisely nothing to calm her from four counties and three and a half hours away. She thought about nipping next door to see Sam and Florence, but they'd been at the hospital all afternoon after Florence had had an unexpected bleed and she didn't want to burden them with this, yet. Although they'd texted and said Florence was fine, Kate knew what unbearable fear this kind of thing could cause and resolved to keep Corey's disappearance to herself for as long as she could; after all, chances were he'd be back with Phil soon enough anyway.

She didn't even bother to pack a bag; she just wanted to get going, and she'd drive straight back once she knew Corey was safe. Much as she trusted Phil, even now, after everything, she needed to be out there looking for her son herself.

Grabbing the house keys from the bowl by the door, she was just double-checking she had her phone in her handbag when the loud chime of the doorbell made her jump out of her skin. Not even bothering to look through the spyhole that was inset into the heavy wood of the door, she threw it open, heedless of the lateness of the hour.

There, standing in front of her, swaying with what she hoped was exhaustion, hair dishevelled and greasy and hanging in front of his red-rimmed eyes, was Corey.

22

'Corey, thank God!' Kate reached forward and pulled her lanky, knackered-looking son into her arms. Instead of shrugging her off, as he did more and more these days, he responded, hugging her back so that she could feel his body trembling. When she was satisfied that he was, in fact, real, and not some longed-for illusion, she released him.

'Where the heck have you been?' Reluctant to break contact with him even for a second, she grabbed his hand and pulled him through the door. 'Your dad and I have been worried sick.'

'Yeah, right,' Corey muttered. 'Like Dad even gives a shit where I am.'

Kate decided not to dignify that with a response, just yet, although she was pleased Corey hadn't included her in the *not-giving-a-shit* category.

'We'd better call him and let him know where you've ended up.' Leading Corey through to the living room, she plonked herself down on the sofa, dragging him down to sit next to her. 'How on earth did you get here?'

Corey averted his gaze from her searching one. 'My mate Jake's uncle was running a lorry to Bristol so I went in the cab with him. Had enough money to get the buses from there to here. Took about ten hours, though.'

Kate's stomach went through the floor at roughly the speed that her heart accelerated. 'You mean you hitched a lift with someone you barely know? Without telling anyone?'

'Jake knew,' Corey replied, then added sheepishly, 'but I told him not to say anything.'

'And your dad, being Dad, didn't think to probe too deeply, I bet,' Kate said. Phil had never been great at dealing with teenagers other than his own. He seemed to lack the ability to interact with them in particularly useful ways. This hadn't really mattered until they'd divorced, but now Kate realised that, in situations like this, it really *did* matter. She shuddered inwardly to think of what might have happened if Corey had got out of the lorry at the multitude of motorway service stations or truck stops between Willowbury and Cambridge; if he'd been stupid enough to try to hitch another lift with someone he didn't know. Not that Jake's uncle was someone he, or she, was particularly familiar with in the first place. Feeling the sense of post-worrying panic washing over her, she pulled her son close again.

'Don't you ever, *ever* do something like that again!' she muttered into his shoulder, trying to swallow back the tears and make it anger instead. 'I've been worried sick about you since Dad called. Anything could have happened to you.'

Corey didn't respond for a moment, and when Kate felt him start to tremble against her, she held him more tightly, realising that the tears she was holding back, he had no such reserve about. Rocking him back and forth in her arms, as she had so many times when he was younger, her heart ached for her eldest son.

'I'm sorry, Mum,' he said quietly, when the tears had somewhat subsided. 'I just needed to get away for a bit. Dad and Jennifer are basically at work all day, so the three of us are left on our own a lot.'

'I thought your dad was meant to be taking the rest of the summer off?' Kate asked. 'What happened to that idea?'

'After we got back from Florida, he got called in to some mega crisis with the new housing development at Strensham Mead,' Corey said. 'So he's not really been around as much as he said he'd be. Not that I care,' he added defiantly, obviously trying to make up some ground after the tears. 'I mean, he didn't really worry about us when he was living with us, so why should he care now?'

Kate was unsettled by the bitterness in her son's voice. True, Phil had never been what you might call overly attentive to his sons; though she could remember him kicking a football around in the garden from time to time when Will and Tom were younger, Corey had never been interested in doing that sort of thing, so Phil had just left him alone, until they had ended up existing alongside each other in the house but never really spending one-on-one time together. As the years had gone by and Corey had developed into an academic, bookish young man, more interested in escaping into the covers of a George R. R. Martin novel than going to watch a Saturday local league football game with his dad and two younger brothers, so the gap between father and son had widened. Throwing them all back together in a house with Phil's new partner, even for just six weeks, didn't, on reflection, seem like the best course of action for her eldest, at least. She felt a surge of guilt about making the decision to leave them for the summer.

'How are your brothers handling things?' Kate asked.

Corey shook his head irritably. 'You know Tom and Will; so long as Dad keeps buying them new Xbox games and Fortnite skins, they're happy.'

'Really?'

'Don't worry about them, Mum, honestly. You know I've always been the *odd* one, as Dad and Gran would put it.' He managed a wry smile. 'You could have moved to Mars for the summer and those two would have been fine.'

'Thanks,' Kate said dryly. 'What a thing to say to your mother.'

'You know what I mean.' Corey gave a better smile this time, and despite the tired eyes, the lank hair and the general air of dejection, Kate saw a reassuring resurgence of the son she loved so dearly. She also saw a lot of his Uncle Sam in him – the quiet, reserved boy who had, when they were kids, kept everything locked up, never let on about how he was feeling until he exploded in tears or rage. She herself had been a pretty self-sufficient child, but she'd always appreciated her son's vulnerability; at least compared to his rather more rambunctious younger brothers.

'You look shattered,' she said, determined to focus on the here and now to stop them both from spiralling downwards into unwelcome introspection. 'Why don't I make you a sandwich, and then you can grab a shower and get your head down. I'm sure Uncle Aidan won't mind you borrowing some of his pyjamas if you want them.'

'Does Uncle Aidan even wear pyjamas?' Corey asked, grinning a little more widely. 'I never saw him as the type.'

'Well, just throw me your clothes and I'll put them through the wash while you're asleep,' Kate said. 'And I need to phone Dad, too; let him know you've finally turned up.'

'Like he'll fucking care,' Corey muttered mutinously.

'Corey Philip Harris…' Kate warned.

'Sorry,' Corey replied, grinning slightly. 'Can you just put it down to spending too much time sitting beside a trucker?'

In truth, it wasn't the swearing that worried her the most; it was the erosion of the relationship between father and son that would need sorting. Kate wondered just how she was supposed to fix that, given that she and Phil were now divorced. With a huge pang of guilt that nearly knocked her sideways, she realised, rightly or wrongly, that perhaps that should have concerned her more while she'd actually been married to the guy. But then, with three sons close in age, as a mother she had had her work cut out for her. Surely, on reflection, his relationships with his sons should have been his job to fix, and not hers? Phil had always been one to pass things on to her. Why should this situation be any different?

23

The next morning, Kate woke early. For a blissful moment, that split second between sleep and waking, she forgot the events of the previous night, but as consciousness fully returned, so did the memories and emotions. Relief had been uppermost in her mind when she'd poked her head around the spare room door to wish Corey goodnight (he was far too old, of course, to be officially tucked into bed by his mother), only to find he was already asleep. Unable to resist the urge to stroke his blonde hair, still wet from the shower, she'd gazed at him for a moment, before quietly shutting the door. She hoped his sleep would bring him a little bit of peace.

Unfortunately, the conversation she then had instigated with Phil had been less than peaceful. She'd tried to keep things matter of fact, God knows she'd tried, but the combination of her own guilt at not having seen this coming, and her irritation that Phil had apparently done so little to head it off at the pass had got to her in the end. It had been a mercifully short, but undeniably terse exchange, and as she'd put the phone down on her ex-husband, she still didn't feel as though much had been resolved. But, for now, her priority had to be the sleeping boy upstairs. She'd agreed with Phil that Corey would stay with her for the next few days, and then she'd put him back on the train to Cambridgeshire once she'd had the chance to talk things through, set things straight. In truth, Kate relished having the company. Her eldest son was, normally at least, no trouble, and generally had his head in a book. Perhaps he'd like to spend some time helping her paint the rest of the bookshop? After the slightly awkward kiss with Harry, it might be a good idea to have Corey as a buffer between them. She had no intention of mentioning *that* particular exchange to Corey; the wounds of the divorce were still too raw for him, she knew, despite his strained relationship with his father.

As Kate got herself and the hallway ready for the first coat of paint, she heard the floorboards creaking upstairs, and Corey emerged from his bedroom.

'Morning,' she called as the boy padded down the stairs and into sight.

'Hey,' he responded.

Kate breathed an inward sigh of relief to see that he looked, and seemed, a little more like his old self after a shower and a long, peaceful sleep. His eyes were brighter, his hair clean from the shower, and his clothes looked a lot better after a quick turn through the wash the night before. He'd obviously been into Aidan's wardrobe as well and found a checked shirt to throw on over his black T-shirt.

'Want some breakfast?' She gestured to the kitchen. 'There's plenty of bread for toast and even a jar of Marmite somewhere?'

'Nah, I'm good thanks,' Corey said. 'I thought I might go for a walk actually. Clear my head a bit.'

'You're not planning on taking off again, are you?' Kate laughed nervously, but her stomach turned at the prospect of Corey going off radar again.

Corey smiled. 'Don't worry, Mum. I'm just gonna go and check out what's new on the High Street. We didn't get to see a lot of it when we were here at Easter.'

'Can you stop by the Co-op and grab a pint of milk on your way back then, please?' she asked as he made to go out of the door. Grabbing her purse, she shoved a ten-pound note at him. 'Consider it a bit of going out money,' she said. 'Keep the change.'

'Thanks, Mum.' Corey smiled. 'I, er might need to buy a couple of T-shirts if I'm staying for a bit. I didn't really bring much with me.'

'We'll cross that bridge when we come to it,' Kate said. 'Although your dad's happy for you to spend the next few days with me here. You'll have to earn your keep, though.'

'Oh yeah?' Corey raised a wary eyebrow. 'How?'

'Plenty of painting to do if we're going to get it all done before Uncle Aidan and Tom get back from their holiday.'

Corey groaned. 'When's the next train back home?'

'See you in a bit,' Kate said, poking him playfully with the bristles of her paintbrush. 'Call me if you need anything.'

'Will do. Bye, Mum.'

As Corey sauntered out of the door on the hunt for what Willowbury had to offer, Kate smiled. Despite this rather dramatic blip, Corey was a sensible boy, and she knew he'd enjoy exploring the historic town for an hour or two. Perhaps she should have mentioned Harry's bookshop as a good place to visit, but, knowing Corey, he'd find it sooner or later. She felt a flutter of nerves as she thought about having to go back to the shop that afternoon and carry on with the painting, but swiftly shushed the butterflies in her stomach. She and Harry were both adults, and she had a job to do. What was the worst that could happen?

24

Harry was just putting out a pile of Artemis Bane's novels on the front table of the shop when the bell above the door rang, and in walked a rangy, good-looking lad of about sixteen. The boy's eyes lit up as he surveyed the long aisles of shelves, and Harry was pleased when his smile of welcome was returned.

'Hi,' he said as the lad approached. 'Welcome to Vale Volumes. Is there anything in particular you were looking for today?'

The boy shook his head, eyes still tracking the tall shelves like any other child would do in the proverbial sweet shop. 'I'm good, thanks. Just browsing. Although...' His eyes drifted to the pile of novels that Harry had been arranging. 'I don't suppose you've got any copies of his new book yet?'

Harry smiled. 'The release date's not for another few days, I'm afraid.' He looked at the boy, who, on closer inspection, looked awfully familiar. 'Are you here on holiday?'

'Sort of. I'm here for a few days and I didn't pack anything to read.'

'Well, if you like Artemis Bane, I can definitely recommend a few other authors to try to pass the time while you're here,' Harry said. He gestured to the shelves on the right-hand side of the shop. 'Would you like me to show you?'

'Okay,' the boy replied, smiling. 'I've not got a lot of cash on me, though.'

'Oh, I'm sure we can find you something that won't break the bank!' Harry smiled encouragingly. As they strolled towards the Fantasy section of the shelves, with the sub-section of Urban Fantasy in their sights, Harry couldn't help but mention it. 'That guy, Artemis Bane, is actually coming here next week to launch his new book, if you were interested in buying a ticket for it.'

'Artemis Bane's coming *here?*' the boy replied, a note of incredulity in his voice.

Harry tried not to be put out. After all, a semi-rural bookshop in the deepest part of Somerset was hardly the buzzing metropolis of Waterstone's Piccadilly, where all of the big names tended to do their launches.

'Yes,' Harry said. 'He was born and raised in the town. He's a local boy made good story. Do you think you might want a ticket? I can put your name down on the reserve list if you'd like.'

'Oh, man, I'd love to,' the boy said. 'My name's Corey, by the way. But I don't know if I'll still be here next week.' A cloud crossed his features. Harry wondered if he should ask, but he didn't want to probe.

'It's nice to meet you,' Harry said, introducing himself, too. 'And if you find that you will be around, let me know and I can always put one aside for you,' he said, as they reached the Urban Fantasy shelves. 'In the meantime, I can definitely recommend any of these authors to keep you busy before the new Bane hits the shelves.'

'Thanks,' Corey said, getting stuck in and pulling out a few titles to peruse.

'Just let me know if you need any help,' Harry said, returning to his pile of Bane books. As he was putting them out in what he hoped was the most enticing way possible, he glanced back at the boy, who seemed engrossed in the work of, to Harry's mind, one of the better writers of the urban fantasy genre. 'She's great,' he called across, breaking his usual golden rule of not interrupting a browsing customer. 'A cut above even the great Artemis Bane, in my humble opinion.'

Corey looked up and smiled back at Harry. 'Thanks,' he said. Again, Harry was struck with a sense of familiarity. Who did the boy remind him of?

After a short time, Corey approached the counter where Harry was now bustling about and rearranging a few bits of stationery that he'd recently decided would be a good 'last-minute purchase' incentive for the shop. Harry was gratified to see that Corey had taken his advice and had three books by the author he'd recommended.

'Let me know what you think of them,' Harry said as he took the books from Corey to ring them through the till. 'She's due to bring another one out at the end of the year.'

Totting up Corey's purchases, Harry realised that, with one brand-new and two second-hand books in his choice, the seven pounds fifty in change that Corey had in his hand was going to be a little short. But Harry could never refuse an avid reader a much longed-for purchase. Thinking rapidly, he smiled. 'You're in luck. The used books are buy one get one half price today, so in total that comes to seven pounds fifty exactly.'

'Really?' Corey raised a sceptical eyebrow. 'Isn't that a bit of a coincidence?'

'Never look a gift book in the spine, young man,' Harry replied, embarrassed by how hearty his voice had suddenly become. 'And if you get the chance, pop back in and let me know what you think of them.'

'I will.' Corey smiled broadly. 'And thanks.'

'You're welcome. Have a good day. And let me know if you want me to reserve a ticket for Artemis Bane's visit, too.'

As Corey left, Harry reflected, not for the first time, on how much nicer it was to be a rural bookseller than chained to his desk in the City. Even if he'd just done himself out of a couple of quid, the light in the boy's eyes at his new purchases had definitely been worth the price of a cup of coffee. With that in mind, he decided it was time to nip out and grab one from the Cosy Coffee Shop. He was overdue a chat with Jack, and if anyone could put his kiss with Kate Harris in perspective, it would be his friend. Flipping the sign on the bookshop door to 'Gone for a coffee – back in ten minutes', he headed out and up the High Street, which was looking particularly lovely in the strong summer sunlight.

25

A couple of hours later, having got sidetracked by the wide range of independent shops that Willowbury High Street had to offer, Corey returned with the milk and a fresh loaf of bread and he and Kate sat in the kitchen, plates of hot buttered toast and fresh coffee between them.

'So you like the look of Willowbury, then?' she asked between bites.

'Yeah, it's all right,' Corey replied. 'Some of the shops are a bit weird, but the bookshop is cool.'

Kate stopped chewing. She'd expected Corey to make a beeline for Vale Volumes as soon as he'd seen it, of course, but with her recent encounter with its owner very much on her mind, as well as the fact that she was heading back there this evening to, hopefully, finish the painting and no longer have a reason to be in Harry's space, her stomach started to fizz. On a mouthful of hot buttered toast, this wasn't an entirely pleasant sensation.

'Did you buy anything?' she enquired, trying to keep her tone casual.

'Three books,' Corey said, reaching for another piece of doorstep toast. 'The guy in there was really helpful. He said Artemis Bane's coming to do a book launch there next week.'

'So I've heard,' Kate said. Taking a deep breath, she continued, 'In fact, I'm helping the owner, Harry, to redecorate the shop for Artemis's visit.'

'Cool!' Corey said after he'd demolished the toast. 'Can I help?'

'I was hoping you'd say that.' Kate took the last slice of toast before Corey could pinch it. 'I'm working on the shop in the evenings after closing time. Moonlighting from this place, if you like. An extra pair of hands would be great.'

'Will you pay me?' Corey asked, a cheeky glint in his eye.

Kate snorted. 'I can barely afford to pay myself until Uncle Aidan coughs up for this place, but I'm sure I can stretch to something.'

'It's a deal, then,' Corey said. 'And Mum...'

'Yes?'

'Any chance I can stay here a bit longer and go to Artemis Bane's book launch? The bookshop guy said he'd reserve me a ticket if I fancied it.'

Thanks, Harry, Kate thought. But then she smiled. 'If your dad says it's okay for you to stay, and your brothers don't mind, then I'm okay with it too.'

'Cool!' Corey gave a broad smile. 'After all, when else am I going to get to see Artemis Bane in person?'

Given what Harry had said about Artemis's diva demands, Kate wondered what her quiet, sensitive son would make of his literary idol in person. But, she figured, she could hardly say no and send him packing back to his father's now he knew Bane was coming here, could she? And a break from his brothers might do him good. Furthermore, some time alone with her eldest son might be just what she needed, too, to get everything into perspective. She could always see if her other sons wanted to come down after Bane's visit for a few days, too. She'd have more time to take them out and about once the bookshop was painted. It would be lovely to have them all under the same roof again, however cramped it might be.

'Will you ring Dad later and check he's okay with it?' Suddenly Corey sounded like the adorable ten-year-old he used to be, when he always succeeded to wheedle things out of her.

'Sure,' Kate smiled, 'but I'm sure he won't have a problem with it.'

'Of course he won't,' Corey replied, his mood shifting again with lightning speed. 'He doesn't care where I am.'

'You know that's not true,' Kate admonished her son gently. 'But it seems a shame to send you back just for the sake of it. Perhaps a little break here will do you good.'

'Cool. Thanks, Mum.' And just like that, he was smiling again.

As Corey got up from the table, saying he was going to go and catch up with some reading, Kate wondered again about the roller-coaster of emotions that could happen inside teenagers. One minute the sun was shining, the next, it was all storm clouds. Adolescence, she reflected, could be an absolute arse kicker, regardless of whether it was you or your children going through it.

* * *

That evening, after a heavy day painting the hallway and the walls of the stairs, Kate stretched her back out and wondered if she really had anything left, energy-wise, to devote to Vale Volumes. Although she knew she was gradually getting stronger, due to the repeated physical activity, her bones and muscles kept reminding her that she was pushing forty and really hadn't taken great care of herself. She could blame birthing three children for some of it, she supposed, and she was definitely feeling her age that evening.

'We're heading to the bookshop in a few minutes,' she said to Corey as he emerged from his room. She hadn't seen him all afternoon, but that was usually the way when he got stuck into a new book. She knew she should be grateful; she'd had enough conversations with friends who had children the same age to know that they were more likely to be glued to their smartphones or games consoles than actual books. And although Corey did spend his fair share of time on both of those other options, he, much like his younger brothers, still had a genuine love for reading that she'd discovered and encouraged in them from when they were little.

'Great,' Corey said. 'I've nearly finished this book, and I thought I might swap it in for another one.'

'Harry's not running a library!' Kate laughed. 'I'm not sure if a book exchange is part of what he does.'

'Ah, but you and him are mates, aren't you? I'm sure you can talk him into it,' Corey replied, smiling broadly.

'We'll see,' Kate replied. She wasn't sure quite where her relationship with Harry stood right now. He was definitely a client, and possibly a friend, but was there still going to be an undercurrent of something else, after twenty-four hours to think about it? She didn't know whether she was looking forward to finding out or dreading it.

A few minutes later, they walked through the shop door, which Harry had left open for them, despite flipping the 'Closed' sign to dissuade last-minute customers.

'Hello?' Kate called as she closed the door behind herself and Corey.

'Hi,' Harry's voice drifted from the back of the shop. 'I'm just making a coffee. Do you want one?'

Reassured by the casual tone of his voice, Kate called back that yes, she would, then turned back to Corey. 'So, if you can just grab the dust sheets from the store cupboard at the back of the shop, we can get going.'

'Sure.' Corey smiled. He loped off towards the back of the shop, just as Harry was emerging with two mugs of coffee and a plate of oat and raisin cookies on a tray.

'Oh, sorry,' Harry said as he caught sight of Corey, 'we're actually closed for the evening.'

'Oh, er, no, I'm...' Corey stammered, his innate shyness seeming to get the better of him.

'This is my son, Corey,' Kate intercepted swiftly. 'He's come to stay with me for a bit, and I thought he could help out tonight, if that's all right with you?'

'Ah, yes, we met earlier,' Harry said. 'I thought you looked familiar when you walked in. All hands on deck seems like a good idea, if we're going to get this place up to Artemis Bane's standards before he visits. Can I, er, get you a drink? There are some cans of Coke in the fridge if you don't fancy a coffee.'

Corey smiled back, obviously relieved to be out of the spotlight again. 'Thanks, that would be great.'

'Help yourself to what you want,' Harry said. Then, turning back to Kate. 'Now, where would you like me to start?' As Corey went out to the back kitchen, Harry moved closer to her and she caught a tantalising waft of cologne that he'd obviously been wearing all day. Its musky scent mixed with the warm fragrance of his body, doing battle with the odour of the paint that she'd just removed the lid from. She felt her own body growing a little warmer, waking up once again, despite a hard day working on Aidan's house.

'You're the client, remember?' she laughed nervously. 'I can't get you working too hard.'

'Don't be daft.' Harry laughed too, a surprisingly low, attractive rumble. 'I know you're not charging me the going rate, and even if you were, I'd still be happy to muck in.'

'Well,' Kate said, trying to steady her thumping heart, 'you can put a second coat on the skirting board with me, if you like. I think the colour's set well enough on the walls and the ceiling now. We should get away with one coat on the exposed woodwork and then it's done.'

A look of what might have been regret seemed to pass over Harry's face as Kate confirmed that the job was nearly over. 'It looks great,' he said. 'And I'm sure it'll pass muster with Artemis and his fans.'

'I hope so!' Kate laughed again. She realised, with some surprise, that she'd laughed more in the past few weeks living in Willowbury than it felt like she had in years.

As they cracked on with the last of the painting, conversation flowed easily once more. Whether this was because Corey was there to provide a buffer, Kate wasn't sure, but she was glad that there didn't seem to be any awkwardness. In no time they were putting the lids back on the paint tins and clearing up for the last time.

'Well, that ought to do it,' Kate said as she straightened up from where she'd been kneeling on the floor. Her back ached terribly, and all she wanted to do now was sink into a deep, lavender scented bath.

Corey, from his position on the sofa in the Children's section, glanced up. 'See? You didn't need my help after all, Mum.'

'Good thing, too,' Kate said wryly. 'Since you've had your nose in that book all evening.'

'Yeah, but I'm starving now,' Corey replied. 'Can we get a take-away on the way home?'

Kate smiled. 'Because you've worked so hard, you mean?'

Corey rolled his eyes. 'Whatever. Can we?'

Kate walked over to where her handbag lay on the shop counter. 'Sure, okay. I could do with a bite to eat.' She thrust a twenty-pound note at her son. 'Go and pick what you want from the High Street, and I'll meet you back at Uncle Aidan's when I've cleared up.'

'Cool. Thanks, Mum!' Corey said his goodbyes to Kate and Harry and strolled out of the door.

'He's a good lad,' Harry said as Corey left. 'Seems quite level-headed.'

'You would say that, since he's a good customer,' Kate quipped as she picked up the dust sheet and folded it carefully.

'I see enough of them causing trouble around here to know the difference,' Harry replied lightly. He bent down to get the skirting board paint from where he'd left it on the floor, and when he passed it to Kate, there was a jolt as their hands brushed.

'Look, er, about last night...' he said, slightly gruffly. 'I'm sorry if I jumped in and it wasn't welcome.'

Kate's face started to flame as she remembered just how good Harry's lips had felt when they'd met hers, but also how discombobulated she'd been at the contact.

'It's... complicated,' she said softly, looking up into eyes that were kind, understanding and looking back at her with more than a little heat. 'I've had literally no practise at kissing anyone else in over two decades. I think I've almost forgotten how to do it.'

Harry smiled. 'From where I was standing, you did absolutely fine.' He drew a little closer to her, but just as he did so, the handle of the paint tin snapped in half. The tin crashed to the wooden floor, spilling its contents all over the parquet floor.

'Shit!' Harry exclaimed, dropping quickly to his knees. 'I hadn't noticed it was broken.'

Swiftly, Kate went to her box of supplies and grabbed some paper towels. 'Can you grab a bowl of hot soapy water?' she said as Harry scrabbled back to his feet with the paint can in his hands. 'It's only water-based paint, thank God, not gloss, so it won't stain if we get it up quickly.'

Harry hurried off and Kate began to soak up the thick residue of the paint. She couldn't work out if she was relieved or disappointed to have had the moment broken.

26

'Harry fancies you,' Corey said, without preamble, when he and Kate were both sat at the kitchen table eating the pizza he'd chosen for their dinner.

'Don't be daft,' Kate replied, hoping that the big bite her son had just taken would spare her any interrogation. 'I'm just doing a job for him. He's got to be nice.'

'Nah,' Corey said, giving Kate a knowing look. 'He was way too friendly for it to be all about the job.' He paused, and then looked searchingly at her. 'Have you snogged him yet?'

'Corey! Even if I had, I wouldn't tell you.' Well, it hadn't exactly been a snog, she rationalised.

'He's cool, though,' Corey said. 'I mean, if you *wanted* to go out with him... I'd be okay with that.'

'Give over,' Kate said. 'I'm not in the market for another relationship, and I'm not discussing my love life with my sixteen-year-old son.'

'Yuck!' Corey wrinkled his nose. 'I don't need, like, intimate details or anything.'

'I'm beginning to regret saying you could spend a few more days here,' Kate muttered mutinously, but with a twinkle in her eye. Corey knew she wouldn't send him packing when she'd said he could stay. 'Although, starting tomorrow, you're going to be my decorator's assistant, so no sloping off to your room to read for hours. You can earn your keep.'

'Fair enough,' Corey said, biting into the last slice of pizza. 'But I'm right, you know. About Harry.'

A warning look from Kate put an end to that particular conversation. She didn't think she'd ever be comfortable discussing her love life (not that she even really had one) with her son. *Surely*, she thought, *it should be the other way around?* But Corey hadn't shown the remotest interest in girls, boys or anything other than his books for all the time he'd been a teenager, that she'd known of, anyway. She knew teenagers all matured at different rates, but she also didn't want to pry. She hoped Corey would come to her in his own time, when he found someone he liked and wanted to share it. Even after all the disruption of the divorce, she hoped that would be the case.

'Right, well, I'm going run a bath and then get an early night,' Kate said as she grabbed the pizza box off the table and went towards the back door to put it out with the recycling. 'Is there anything else you need?'

'Nah, I'm good,' Corey replied. 'I might get stuck into the next book in that series Harry recommended.'

'Well, don't stay up too late,' Kate said. 'Remember, it's all hands on deck tomorrow.'

'When *are* Uncle Aidan and Tom getting back, anyway?' Corey asked. 'They've been gone ages.'

Not really; it just feels that way, Kate thought, remembering ruefully the thousands of WhatsApp messages the couple had been sending since they embarked on their Grand Tour. Out loud she merely said. 'The third week of August.'

'Well, you'll need all the help you can get, then,' Corey replied, loping from the room towards the stairs. 'I'd better sort out a pay deal.'

'We'll talk about that in the morning,' Kate said. 'Bearing in mind the pizza and books I've shelled out for since you descended on me.'

Corey grinned back over his shoulder. 'I'm sure you won't mind me visiting Harry's shop a little more while I'm here,' he said. 'I'm right, you know – he *does* fancy you!'

'Goodnight, Corey.' Kate tried her hardest stare on her eldest son. Unfortunately, that hadn't really worked since he was six. 'See you in the morning.'

'Night, Mum,' Corey replied cheerfully.

At least, Kate observed, Corey was looking a whole lot happier than he had when he'd descended on her yesterday. She still felt sick every time she thought of him hitching a lift in the cab of a truck, but, in the end, no harm had been done. And now he was here, where she could keep an eye on him, perhaps she could help him to see his relationship with Phil in a slightly more positive light. Smiling dully at the irony of this; Phil did have a lot of ground to make up with all of his sons after resigning from their marriage and finding someone else, after all. She headed off to a Neal's Yard bath and hopefully a good night's sleep.

Just as she was turning in for the night, her phone pinged. Swiping the screen, she felt her face flaming as she saw it was a message from Harry.

Sorry again about nearly spilling paint all over you. I guess that's worse than coffee! Artemis will love it, I'm sure. Can I tempt you and Corey to lunch to thank you for all of your hard work on the shop? 2pm at The Travellers' Rest on Sunday? Not to worry if not – H xx

The peace and relaxation she'd felt lying in a scented lavender bath suddenly dissipated. Harry obviously hadn't been put off at all by her rather nonplussed reaction to his kiss. The question was, did she want to pursue this, and him, further? Having said that, he'd extended the invitation to Corey, too, which was sweet of him. Perhaps she was reading too much into it, and he really did just want to say thank you for a job well done.

She waited ten minutes before texting back that she and Corey would love to meet him for lunch. With Corey there as a buffer, she hoped to feel less out of her depth. After all, dragging your teenage son along to lunch meant it couldn't be a date, didn't it?

27

Kate spent the next few days, with Corey as an assistant, breaking the back of the rest of the work on the house. At least, now the bookshop was finished, she could knock off at five o'clock, grab some food and relax in the evenings, although she did miss Harry's company, she had to admit. Their lunch together at the pub on the Sunday after the painting was finished had been pleasant, and she'd felt relieved and happy that Corey seemed to get on so well with her friend. It turned out that Corey and Harry had a lot in common, from shared favourite books to liking the same subjects at school, and Kate had been content to listen to them as they got to know each other. The three of them had parted happily. She knew she'd see him again for Artemis Bane's visit, as she'd texted Harry to reserve two tickets for her and Corey as a treat for her son.

The morning of Artemis's visit to Vale Volumes, Kate woke early. She found herself wondering how Harry was feeling, knowing that, in a few hours' time, he was going to be playing host to one of the most gifted, but notoriously difficult, authors in the country. She knew that she'd done her best to make the shop look great; the rest was up to Harry. Still in a quandary over her feelings for him, she just felt so rusty when it came to actually connecting with someone romantically, she wondered if she ought to pop into the shop and offer an extra pair of hands on the big day.

Corey was still in bed, but she poked her head around his bedroom door anyway.

'Are you awake?' she said softly.

'Yup.' Corey yawned. 'Whassup?'

'I'm going to grab a coffee and some breakfast at the Cosy Coffee Shop. Do you want to come?'

'Nah, I'm good,' Corey replied. Then, added, 'But can you bring me back a bacon roll?'

'If you promise to be out of bed and ready to get to work by the time I get back.' Kate grinned.

'Deal.' Corey rolled back over in bed. 'Don't rush.'

Still smiling, Kate pulled the bedroom door shut again and headed down towards the front door. She would go to the coffee shop for breakfast, and perhaps she'd take Harry a coffee, too; see how he was getting on.

A short time later, having grabbed a takeaway latte for Harry, she pushed open the door of Vale Volumes and headed towards the counter. Glancing to her left, she noted with approval that the paint seemed to have dried without any streaks, before focusing her attention on Harry, who appeared to be reading something. His gaze was focused on the counter in front of him, head bowed so she couldn't see his expression.

'Hi,' she said as she approached. 'I thought you might need some caffeine to see you through the rest of the day.'

Harry didn't respond for a moment, but when he did, he raised his gaze very, very slowly.

'Are you okay?' Kate looked, *really* looked, at Harry as she handed him his coffee, and already knew the answer as he shook his head. There was a sheen of sweat on his forehead, and his hand shook as he took his reusable coffee cup from her. 'Christ, you look terrible.'

'Thanks.' Harry looked clammily affronted by her words. 'But I haven't got time to be ill today. His majesty is due in five hours and I've still got loads to sort out.'

As if on cue, Harry's mobile pinged with a text from Eloise Padgett, confirming that she and Artemis were on route from London and expected to be checked in at the Travellers' Rest Inn by two o'clock. Suddenly, Harry's hands began to tremble and to Kate he looked increasingly like he was going to faint.

'I think you'd better get back upstairs,' Kate said. 'Looks to me like you've caught a dose of that nasty summer flu that's been doing the rounds.'

'Joan, my assistant, who works here a couple of days a week, has been laid up with it all week,' Harry said. 'I guess she was still contagious before she took the time off and passed it to me.' Harry shook his head, and the dizziness seemed to sweep over him. Staggering back from the counter, he leaned against the small table to the left-hand side of the cash desk, forgetting that it had a pile of the latest bestselling epic fantasy novel stacked up on it. They all went crashing to the floor, where, but for Kate dashing to his side, Harry would have ended up as well.

'I'm all right,' he said weakly, trying to right himself with Kate's help. But even as he said it, Kate knew he lacked conviction. 'What the hell am I going to do?' he groaned, pushing his dark framed glasses back up the bridge of his nose. 'Bane is due in five hours. I'd better take a ton of painkillers and get on with it.'

'No, you won't,' Kate insisted. She slipped an arm around him and began to lead him to the back of the shop where the door upstairs to his flat was. She felt him relax as she touched him, but being so close to him so suddenly was confusing, especially as the heat coming from his body, although it came from fever, was doing strange things to Kate's senses. *Get a grip*, she mentally chided herself. Somehow, they made it upstairs together, with Kate's arm still protectively around Harry's waist.

'Where's the bedroom?' Kate asked.

'Last on the left,' Harry mumbled. Staggering through the door, Kate led him to his large bed, where his knees sagged and he leaned back against the pillows.

'Why didn't you call me when you woke up, if you were feeling this bad?' Kate's voice, coming through the fog in his brain, chided him. 'You could have postponed Artemis Bane's talk until you felt better.'

'He'd never have put up with that,' Harry muttered. 'And a part of me just wants it over and done with, anyway. The sooner Bane arrives the sooner he can bugger off again.' He paused. 'Besides, I didn't think I knew you well enough to ring you and beg you to play Florence Nightingale.'

'Don't be daft,' Kate replied. 'Now, where's your thermometer?'

'In the cabinet in the bathroom,' Harry replied. 'Can you get me a bucket of paracetamol as well?'

* * *

As Kate disappeared on the hunt for medical supplies, Harry allowed his eyes to close again. Christ, he felt rough. But what could he do? The fans were already camping outside the shop. Earlier, he'd taken the pair of students who'd rocked up last night and spent the night in their sleeping bags on the doorstep a cup of tea and a bacon sandwich each, and allowed them to nip in to use his bathroom. He'd been feeling hot and shivery then, but nowhere near as bad as he did now.

In what seemed like just moments, Kate was back again. 'Open your mouth,' she said, and before he had time to reply, she'd shoved the thermometer under his tongue. He waited for a few moments until she removed it again and frowned.

'What does it say?' Harry asked.

'I don't think it's right,' Kate replied. 'It's awfully high. Higher than I'd have thought, even looking the way you do.' She shook her head. 'I've got one of those brilliant forehead scanning digital ones that I bought when the boys were small. Shame it's back home in Cambridge. I wonder if the local chemist has one?'

'Honestly, Kate, don't worry about it,' Harry said. 'Give me the paracetamol and I'll be as right as rain in an hour or so.'

'I don't think so,' Kate said darkly. 'There's no way you can handle Artemis Bane's event in this state.'

She reached over and placed a cool hand on his forehead. 'You're really hot.' She grinned briefly. 'And I don't mean that in a good way!'

'Thanks.' Harry tried to smile wryly but it came out as more of a grimace. Her hand felt good on his forehead, though. He wanted her to keep it there.

'Don't talk back,' Kate admonished gently. 'Now, you stay here and I'll ring Eloise Padgett and tell her she'll have to take Artemis home again.'

'We can't do that,' Harry said. 'He's fully booked for the rest of this year. We've got local and national press coming and the fans outside will never forgive me. I've got to get things sorted.' He tried to get up off the bed but was floored by another dizzy spell. He groaned. There was no way he was going to be able to stand up for five minutes, let alone entertain a shop full of customers and an eccentric author.

'Well, there's only one thing for it then,' Kate said firmly. 'Joan and I will have to handle it.'

'Joan's still laid up with the flu, too,' Harry groaned. 'And I can't ask you to step in. You don't know anything about this event.'

Kate smiled. 'I did a few cheese and wine evenings at the estate agents when I worked there. How different can this be?'

'But he's a complete pain in the arse,' Harry said. 'I can't ask you to just take over.'

'You didn't. I offered.' Kate, obviously well used to going into crisis mode, was already standing back up.

'But you don't know where anything is,' Harry replied.

Kate rolled her eyes at him. 'It's a bookshop, Harry, not the Bank of England. I'll manage. And Corey's an Artemis Bane superfan, so I'm sure if I need more information about the guy and his books, he'll be more than able to assist me.'

'Aren't you up to your eyeballs in paint?'

'Nothing that can't be put aside for one day,' Kate said. 'And you're in no state to go anywhere except to sleep, so don't even try to argue.'

Harry knew she was right, but that didn't make it any easier to agree. Artemis and his customers wouldn't thank him for passing on this bug, whatever it was. He just wasn't used to letting go of the reins.

Finally, closing his eyes again, he let out a long sigh. 'Okay. But please check anything you're unsure of with me. There's a folder of stuff for the visit under the shop counter, including the questions that I was intending to ask him for the interview part of the signing. His chair's already down there, and the water and lemons are in the fridge out the back. I'll keep my phone on as well, just in case you need me.'

'I'll nip out and get you some cold and flu remedy and a decent thermometer from the chemist,' Kate replied. 'And you'd better strip off and get into something more comfortable to sleep in.' She eyed his brown cords and button-down shirt. 'After I've gone, of course, unless you need a hand?'

Harry gave a wry, weak smile. 'I think I can manage.'

As Kate squeezed his hand and got up from the side of the bed where she'd been sitting, Harry struggled to sit up as another dizzy spell seared through his addled brain. As Kate left, Harry couldn't help but think that perhaps it would have been nice to have asked her to help with his buttons.

28

As soon as she left Harry's flat, Kate took several deep breaths. Her heart was thumping out of control, and her palms felt suddenly sweaty. She knew nothing about the logistics of organising an author event, and though she was confident that Harry had planned everything down to the last detail, she also had a sneaking sense that a lot of it had taken place in Harry's head. He was a gifted bookseller, but she got the feeling that organisation wasn't exactly his strong point.

Walking back into the shop, she went straight behind the counter and was relieved to see a folder of stuff to do with the visit tucked away on a shelf under the till. Hopefully Harry had left enough information in there for her to get on with things. It was mostly copies of the emails from Eloise Padgett, with Bane's requests highlighted so Harry didn't get any of them wrong. Kate glanced towards the front window of the shop, where the camped-out students were already being joined by other eager fans of Artemis Bane. 'So, what do we need to do?' she said out loud, trying to get to grips with the task ahead of her. If only Joan wasn't sick, too! She suddenly felt very, very out of her depth, and like she'd bitten off far more than she could chew.

Harry wanted Artemis to be in his armchair at the back of the shop, according to the notes. The centre reading tables had already been cleared away, and a stack of chairs for the audience were tucked away by the stockroom. She needed to get the armchair and the side table in place, but that wouldn't take long. The caterer was coming with the nibbles and booze at four, and then doors opened at five thirty for kick-off at six. Hopefully by then, Artemis would be in a talkative mood and the audience would just lap it up.

As if on cue, Kate's mobile rang. 'Hello?'

Kate could hear Harry coughing at the other end of the line.

'Yes, I'm still here, obviously. No, don't even think about it. I've got it all under control. Yes, I'll make sure it's all sorted out. Yes, I know where the hardbacks are. Go back to sleep. Bye.'

As Kate hung up the phone once more, she reflected that keeping Harry out of things and in his bed was going to be far trickier than handling Artemis Bane.

29

Later that day, having conceded that she couldn't keep the shop open all day alone, and then come back and run the event, Kate had popped up and told Harry that she was going to close the place early and get herself ready for the evening. As she was letting herself into Tom and Aidan's house, it occurred to Kate that she had absolutely nothing to wear for the event itself. She hadn't expected to be doing anything remotely sociable, apart from the odd visit to the pub, so hadn't bothered packing anything dressy. She didn't have time to go trawling around the shops this late in the day, but she didn't think paint-splattered jeans and a stripy top were going to cut it, either. Checking her paint brushes were soaking in some white spirit, she wondered if Florence could help.

Florence, thankfully, had just got back from an antenatal yoga class, and was sitting with her feet up on the sofa when Kate hopped over the wall that divided the pathways up to the terraced houses front doors.

'Come in,' Florence called through the open sash window. 'I left it on the latch.'

Kate opened the front door and joined Florence in the lounge.

'I've got a bit of a wardrobe emergency,' she said without preamble.

'Oh yes?' Florence raised a speculative eyebrow. 'What would that be, then?'

'I'm going to the Artemis Bane book event this evening, and whereas yesterday I thought I'd just be sitting at the back with Corey, minding my own business, instead, Harry's sick so I've have agreed to run the thing.'

'Yikes!' Florence exclaimed. 'That's one hell of an ask for someone you've only just met.'

'I know,' Kate said, 'but when I popped in to see him earlier, he looked so rough, I couldn't just leave him to it. He's got a raging temperature and I'm pretty sure he's caught that flu that's been doing the rounds. I didn't have much choice but to step in. And I've always been pretty good at crisis management, having raised three sons.'

'Well, he'll certainly owe you one, if not several, after tonight.' Florence grinned. 'But back to business. You'll need to borrow a frock.'

'Exactly.' Kate grinned back. 'I figured you might have a few that you're not using at the moment, and I wondered if I could be cheeky and raid your wardrobe.'

'You're lucky,' Florence said, rising from the sofa with some difficulty. 'I was going to fling everything in bags in the attic until next summer, but I'm suffering from a serious dose of pregnancy can't-be-arsed at the moment, so all the stuff I can't wear right now is still in my wardrobe. Come on up.'

Kate followed Florence up the steep stairs to the first floor, and then, at Florence's invitation, sat herself down on the end of the king-sized bed that dominated the room. Watching as Florence threw open the doors to the built-in wardrobes, she grimaced slightly as she saw the riot of colour that was Florence's clothing.

She'd rather hoped that she could snag a little black dress from her sister-in-law and have done with it, but it seemed that Florence's taste was a little more vibrant.

'So, I've got quite a lot of summer dresses.' Florence perused her rails for a few moments before pulling out a few options. 'What do you reckon?'

Glancing at the selection of dresses that Florence brought to the bed, Kate tried to feign enthusiasm. Colour wasn't really her thing but determined not to upset a very, very pregnant woman she decided to at least give Florence's dresses a go.

'Let's start with this one,' Florence said, thrusting a pink and purple maxi dress at Kate.

'I'm older than you,' Kate replied. 'And I'm a bit worried about my bingo wings!'

'Don't be daft!' Florence replied. 'With all that painting over the past few weeks, you must have triceps like Joe Wicks.'

'All the same, can we try something a little less, er, vibrant?'

Florence grinned. 'Okay, but the pink and purple will really make you stand out against the crowd.'

'Believe me, the last thing I want to do is to stand out tonight. Artemis is the guest of honour and from what his publishing rep Eloise has told Harry, he really doesn't like being upstaged.'

'But you *are* hosting the book signing,' countered Florence. 'And I'm sure that Artemis will expect you to make some kind of an effort sartorially.' She wrinkled her brow. 'From what I've read about him, he likes a bit of pomp and ceremony and to be made to feel as if he is worth the effort.'

Kate burst out laughing. 'I'm not sure that Harry would put it that way, given the amount of emails he has had from Eloise Padgett about this bloody visit. And now the stupid bugger has got the flu, he doesn't even have the energy to see the flipping thing through!'

'Well, you'd better make sure that you do Harry proud then.'

Florence threw a slightly less garish dress at Kate, which thankfully had a more subtle colour palette. 'Try this one then.'

Briskly, Kate stripped off her jeans and her paint-splattered T-shirt, thanking her lucky stars she was wearing a decent bra and knickers. Sliding the forest green and rose pink dress over her head and wriggling into it, the sensation of the luxurious material slithering over her torso made a tingle run down her spine that wasn't just to do with nerves. As Florence drew closer and zipped up the back of the dress for her, Kate tried to remember the last time she'd got dressed up in something like this. She was pretty sure that it had been way before her divorce, and that the night had probably ended badly one way or the other. Vague memories of a friend's wedding reception, too much Prosecco and Phil looking at her in exasperated disdain drifted through her mind.

'Yup,' Florence said approvingly. 'That'll do.' She headed back to her wardrobe. 'What shoe size are you?'

'Eight,' Kate said.

'These are a seven, but they're sandals so you'll get away with them,' Florence said, bringing out a box from the top shelf.

Kate, taking the box, wished *she* was the kind of person who kept her own shoes in the original boxes they came in, but three children pretty much put a stop to any notions of that level of care of her own possessions. Perhaps, when she got a place of her own, she'd make more of an effort.

As she opened the shoe box, she felt relieved that the sandals had a chunky heel, so with a bit of luck she wouldn't go arse over tit on Harry's wooden floors. 'These look great. If you're sure you don't mind?'

'I'm hardly likely to be wearing them for the next few months,' Florence said. 'I used to teach for eight hours a day in stiletto heels. I don't think I'll be needing anything more adventurous than a pair of Converse until the baby's born!'

'And probably for quite a while afterwards, I'm afraid to say,' Kate said wryly. She glanced at the shoes again. 'About fifteen years, in my case.'

'Go on then,' Florence said. 'Better make sure they do fit.'

Kate sat on the edge of the bed and slipped on the sandals, struggling a little with the first buckle. Although they were a little small, they looked pretty good, all things considered.

'Fab!' Florence exclaimed as Kate stood back up to look at herself again in the mirror. 'You'll knock them dead.'

Kate grinned. 'I just want to make sure Harry doesn't take one look at me and insist on getting back out of bed to do this evening himself!'

'You and Harry have been spending a bit of time together lately, haven't you?' Florence raised a speculative eyebrow. 'Holiday romance?'

Kate snorted, and plonked herself down on the bed. Ducking down to hide her face while she unbuckled the sandals, she shook her head. 'No! Absolutely not! I'm *so* not ready for anything like that at the moment.'

Immediately, Florence looked contrite. 'I'm sorry,' she said. 'I didn't mean to touch a nerve.'

Kate, who'd shed the dress, and slipped back into her jeans. 'Don't worry,' she said as she put her T-shirt over her head. 'You haven't. It's just that, even though the decree absolute came through six months ago, I still can't quite get used to being single again. Don't get me wrong, I don't want Phil back; we're better as we are, now. I just seem to have completely forgotten what it's like to interact with blokes that I'm not related to. Even on a friendship level.'

'It's no wonder you feel a bit rusty,' Florence said. 'I mean, this is new territory, isn't it?'

'But if I *was* looking...' Kate grinned, 'I could do a lot worse than

Harry. He is cute in that clever, bookish, Ben Willbond kind of way.' Kate had loved watching *Horrible Histories* as much as her sons had, and had harboured a bit of a crush on the actor.

'But you're not?' Florence grinned back.

'Nope,' Kate replied firmly. 'Holiday flings aren't my style, and in case you've forgotten, I live on the other side of the country. It's a no go.'

'Well, you'd best just enjoy tonight then,' Florence said. 'And I'll be there to keep an eye on you, anyway.'

'You bought a ticket?'

'Yup. Sam's on shift from seven o'clock so I thought I might as well head on down and see if Artemis Bane's all he's cracked up to be. I *am* an English teacher, after all.'

'He's hardly likely to end up on the National Curriculum, writing his kind of mass market fantasy,' Kate observed.

'But he should be entertaining, one way or the other.'

'Or a complete pain in the arse,' Kate replied. She hadn't filled Florence in on what Harry had told her about Artemis Bane's requests and demands, and didn't really have time to now, if she was going to get a bite to eat before implementing them. Gathering up the dress and shoes and thanking goodness that she had actually had the foresight to pack her make-up bag when she'd moved in next door, she said goodbye to Florence, thanking her again for her help.

'See you later,' Florence replied. 'Shall we walk down to the bookshop together?'

'I've got to be there about an hour before kick-off,' Kate said. 'Is that okay?'

'No worries,' Florence smiled, 'I'm sure I can amuse myself in a bookshop for an hour or so.'

Heading back next door, Kate checked her phone to see if Harry had texted her with any last-minute panics or instructions, but there was nothing from him. She did notice a text from her middle son, Will, though. Smiling as she thought of him, chunky, stoical and endlessly cheerful even in the face of such upheaval, she texted him back, and resolved to call him after tonight was over. Her younger boys knew the broad strokes about what had happened with Corey, but she hadn't gone into specifics. She still wasn't sure whether to be relieved or offended that neither Will nor Tom had expressed any desire to come over to Willowbury and spend time with her, but then from what Corey had said, they were more than happy with Xboxes and football. She hoped that was true and that they really were having a good time with Phil. Despite it all, she didn't want her former issues with their father to sabotage their relationship with him. What was done was done, after all. And, regardless of how attached they were to their games consoles, she was going to get them across to Somerset for some of the summer holiday; she missed them terribly.

After she'd stowed the dress and shoes out of the way upstairs, so they weren't damaged by the paint, she decided to grab a quick bite to eat and then have a shower. She wanted to spend a little time on her appearance before going back to the bookshop. She'd slobbed around in jeans and overalls for so long, it actually felt like a real treat to be getting out and about for the evening. She just wished poor Harry was well enough to be there – not least because she felt nervous about having to coordinate the evening by herself. She also hoped that Artemis ended up being a lot less demanding than his reputation suggested.

'You look great!' Florence said when she opened the door to Kate a couple of hours later. 'I was right about that dress.'

'Thanks,' Kate replied. 'You look pretty good yourself.'

'Yeah, you both scrub up quite well,' Corey said from his place beside Kate on the doorstep. He'd nipped round to Florence and Sam's earlier as well, to borrow a clean shirt and a better pair of jeans. At sixteen, he was already taller than his Uncle Aidan and so couldn't quite fit into all of the clothes in his wardrobe. Thankfully, Sam had plenty of smart things to choose from, and Kate had yet again marvelled at the resemblance between her son and her brother; they shared much of the same rangy, blonde elegance.

Florence grinned and gestured to the Isabella Olivier maternity dress in violet that she was wearing. 'My friend Josie from work lent me all of her maternity clothes – she's got better taste than me and spent far more than I was prepared to when she was pregnant with her son. If it was up to me I'd be mooching around in maternity jeans and T-shirts all day, but thankfully she gave me a few really decent things.'

Kate had fond memories of her own maternity jeans; in fact,

she'd worn them long after she'd given birth to each one of her children. She decided not to share that particular piece of information with Florence right now, though, who'd already expressed her determination to be back in her pre-pregnancy jeans in as little time as possible.

'Well, we've got plenty of time to wander down to the shop.' Kate looked at her watch. 'I wanted to make sure I had a moment to pop in and check on Harry before the guests get through the door.'

As Kate, Corey and Florence ambled along towards the High Street, Kate realised that she was seeing Willowbury at its most beautiful. The summer sunshine was still beaming over the town, and the half-barrel flower tubs that adorned the High Street at regular intervals were absolutely bursting over with blooms in a riot of colours. These contrasted wonderfully with the honey-coloured stone of buildings like the Travellers' Rest, where late afternoon drinkers, mainly tourists from the looks of them, were enjoying a lazy pint at the wooden tables out front. Kate remembered her first proper chat with Harry a few weeks ago, where she'd agreed to take on the decorating job in the shop, and how awkward she'd felt at the start of that conversation. Who would have thought, such a short time later, that she'd be putting the guy to bed and taking charge of the biggest book signing and launch the shop had ever seen?

'Penny for them.' Florence smiled.

Kate snapped back to reality, and Willowbury's picturesque High Street that sprawled upwards in a gentle incline towards the hill overlooking the town. 'I was just thinking about how much has changed over the past year. I never thought I'd be doing something like this, for a start! I feel a fair bit out of my comfort zone.'

Florence threw her a sympathetic look. 'I can't imagine how it must feel, but I can empathise a bit – moving to Willowbury was a bit of a culture shock for me, I can tell you.' Florence had inherited the house next door to Aidan and Sam's a couple of years back, so had upped sticks from Yorkshire to renovate it and make it her own. Falling in love with Sam hadn't been part of the plan, but after a fair few ups and downs, they'd both settled into life in Willowbury and now were pleased to call it home.

'Well, it's not as if I'm going to be here for very long,' Kate conceded. 'Although I can see why you and Sam, and Aidan and Tom, love it. Especially on a day like this.' As they headed towards Harry's bookshop, it became clear that there was going to be a full house for Artemis Bane's signing. The queue now snaked down the road, past the bakery next door and the florist, and looked to be getting longer by the minute. 'I bet a book launch in Waterstones Piccadilly would have dragged in even more punters, though. I wonder why Artemis decided to hold it here?'

'Often the quirkier places make better publicity I suppose,' Florence replied. 'I once went to a book launch in the vat rooms of the local cider farm – locations like that can really add to the atmosphere.'

'True,' Kate replied, feeling a sudden flutter of nerves in her stomach. 'I just wish Harry was still masterminding it, and all I had to worry about was swigging Prosecco and enjoying myself!'

'You'll be fine,' Florence soothed as they got closer to the front entrance of the bookshop. 'You've raised three sons – surely that's more scary than shepherding some fans of Artemis Bane through an evening.' She touched her burgeoning baby bump reflectively. 'Although, I've been teaching teenagers for years, but the prospect of parenthood fills me with terror!'

'Then let's just say we'll both be fine,' Kate replied. She took a deep breath and walked purposefully past the queue of eager Artemis Bane fans, many of whom were wearing T-shirts emblazoned with catchphrases from his bestselling series of urban fantasy novels, and chattering excitedly, awaiting the guest of honour. Grabbing the key to the front door, which she'd borrowed from Harry before she left to get changed, she swiftly let Corey, Florence and herself in, and then locked it again firmly behind them.

'How long until showtime?' Florence asked.

Kate glanced at her watch. 'Just over an hour and a half. Artemis is meant to be here ten minutes before the start. According to the efficient Eloise, he doesn't like to rock up any earlier than that as apparently he suffers from pretty bad stage fright.'

'Well, I'll just amuse myself and have a browse, then,' Florence said. 'Unless you need me to do anything?'

'I'm just going to pop up and see how Harry is, so feel free to have a wander and relax. But can you keep an eye out for the caterer – they're meant to be delivering the nibbles any time now.'

'Will do,' Florence said. Calling across to Corey, who was browsing the Transportation section of the bookshop, she smiled. Corey had been as in love with trains as his Uncle Sam had with planes and helicopters, for as long as she could remember, and was always on the lookout for new facts and figures. 'Any chance of making me a cuppa?'

Corey grinned. 'Coming right up, Aunt Florence.'

Kate was amazed, even with an hour and a half to go that she could hear a chant beginning outside among the assembled audience. The dulcet tones of 'We want Artemis... we want Artemis!' made her pulse race. This guy, evidently, had a vociferous fanbase. Trying to put them out of her mind, she hurried to the back of the shop and up the stairs to Harry's flat. She'd asked Harry if it was okay to leave the door on the latch, so she could check in on him when she returned, and Kate pushed it open softly, mindful of the fact that Harry might be sleeping.

Tiptoeing through the hallway of the flat, which extended through the entire reach of the shop, giving it a lovely sense of space, she tried to remember which door led to Harry's bedroom. 'Hello?' She called softly as she went. 'Harry, it's only me.'

As she reached the door to his room, which was ajar, she noticed for the first time how cool it was in the flat. *These old stone buildings are certainly worth the money*, she thought. And given how high Harry's temperature had been when she'd left that afternoon, a little bit of cool air on his brow would be just what he needed.

Pushing open the door, she could see Harry was turned away, and appeared to be sleeping. He'd managed to close the curtains against the bright light of the summer sunshine, so the room was gently lit by dissipated light seeping through. Kate crept towards the bed, not wanting to disturb him if he was in a deep sleep. He didn't stir, but she was reassured to see his breathing was regular and not laboured – obviously the cold and flu remedy had worked and helped him to get some rest. As she drew closer, she saw his tousled hair on the back of his neck, and the length of thigh outlined under the bedsheet. He'd kicked off the duvet, and, much like she would have done with her sons when they were ill, she pulled it up from the bottom of the bed and gently tucked it around him in case the fever made him chilly once it subsided. As she leaned in to tuck it over his shoulders, his warm, sleepy scent, the traces of deodorant and cologne, made her heart beat a little faster, and her own breathing quicken.

He still seemed sound asleep, and Kate knew she should head back downstairs, to make the final preparations for Artemis's visit. He'd be arriving soon, and she knew from everything Harry had said, that the shop had to be perfect. Should she wake Harry first, just to make sure he was okay? Leaning over him to grab the empty water glass that was on his bedside table, she jumped as, at that very moment, Harry rolled over and she found herself nose to nose with him.

'Hi,' he said, a little huskily. If he was surprised to see her there, he didn't show it.

'Hey,' she replied softly. 'Sorry... I just wanted to make sure you had something to drink if you woke up.'

Harry smiled, and Kate's heart flipped again. 'Thanks.'

For another long moment they remained, Kate alternately wondering how to get the glass without smashing it, and also feeling the warmth of Harry's T-shirt clad torso beneath, and altogether too close to her for comfort. Almost with a mind of its own, her left hand retreated from its journey to get the glass, and instead found itself resting on Harry's forehead as she hovered above him.

'You seem a bit cooler,' she said.

'I feel a bit better,' Harry said softly. 'Perhaps I could...'

'Nope,' Kate cut him off before he could suggest staggering downstairs and taking back control of the evening's festivities. 'Believe it or not, Corey, my sister-in-law, Florence, and I have got it all under control. You just get your head down and see how you are in the morning.'

Harry shook his head. 'You're right, I suppose. I feel like I've been hit by a truck. I don't think I'd be much good to anyone like this.'

'Is there anything I can get you before I get back downstairs?' she asked, trying to focus on the fact that he was ill, and therefore not someone to lust over. At least not right now.

'Just that glass of water, if that's okay?' Harry replied. 'I've got plenty of cold and flu remedy in the bedside drawer, and I suppose I should just get my head back down.'

'No problem.' Kate reached for the glass again, but as she did, she forgot that she wasn't wholly supporting herself on her other arm, and before she could stop herself, the momentum of the fall pushed her lips to Harry's.

Time stood still. His lips were warm, and soft, and, surprisingly, he didn't tense as she landed. For a delicious, safe moment, Kate stayed where she was, eyes closing in pleasure as the touching lips became a kiss, before she regained her senses and pushed herself up on her right arm again.

'Sorry. Didn't mean to do that,' she said quickly, the blush unstoppable as it spread over her cheeks, and, she knew, down her neck as well, which was more than visible in the silk sundress she'd borrowed from Florence.

'No harm done,' Harry replied, a note of surprise in his voice. 'Unless you catch this bloody flu, of course!'

'I'll get your water,' Kate said, grabbing the glass firmly and then standing up as quickly and gracefully as she could. She saw Harry opening his mouth to say something else, but she hurried out of the bedroom before he got the chance. Whatever it was, she definitely didn't want to hear it right now.

'Here you go,' she said, a few moments later when she returned to the bedroom. But this time Harry was nowhere to be seen. Hearing the flush of the loo in the en suite, she decided to make a break for it, before she had to come face to face with Harry once more. 'I'll see you when it's all over,' she called through the bathroom door, before dashing down the hallway and back out of his front door.

Shit. What was she thinking? Okay, the kiss had been an accident, but so much for what she'd said to Florence that afternoon about there being nothing between her and Harry. The way her heart, and the rest of her body, had reacted to him when her lips had collided with his had been enough to prove her wrong there. But now was not the time to be thinking about that; she had Artemis Bane's book launch to orchestrate. Taking a deep breath, she pushed open the door back to the shop and tried to get a grip.

31

The large white-faced wooden clock on the back wall of the bookshop edged towards the hour as Kate, Florence and Corey put the finishing touches on the preparations for Artemis Bane's arrival. Bane was due to arrive via the back entrance to the shop ten minutes before the event started, to avoid him being mobbed. Eloise had called the shop a few minutes ago to say that they were on their way from the King Arthur Suite of the Travellers' Rest, where Artemis had the room for the night.

The armchair was in situ, a small table beside it with a bottle of sparkling water and a glass with ice and a slice of unwaxed lemon, as requested. Copies of Bane's latest novel, already a best-seller from the pre-orders alone, were stacked on another table to the left of the armchair, ready to be signed. All around the shop were props and items that featured in the multi-million selling novelist's books: a longbow propped up against the Hobbies section, a giant red and white spotted teapot on the shop counter next to the till, and a picture of the St Mary Redcliffe church in Bristol that played such a huge part in the early stages of the new novel. Bane, despite his caprice and diva-like demands, was one of the most skilled storytellers of his age, as well as being one of the most accessible, and even Kate, who was not a huge fan of urban fantasy as a genre, had to admit that the first book in the series he was currently promoting had been a gripping read. She'd pinched it off Corey's shelf when she'd been suffering a bout of divorce-related insomnia, and had found herself drawn into Bane's perfectly crafted world of magical realism, Shakespearean riffs and dry humour. Kate had studied Hamlet for GCSE, and the twisted family dynamics in Bane's work really resonated.

'I think we're good to go,' Florence said as she passed Kate on the way to the back office to go to the loo. She gestured to the table that was set up in the far corner of the shop, where various bottles of wine and non-alcoholic drinks were in regimented lines alongside a fair few glasses. The tickets for this evening had been reasonably expensive, so the refreshment options were a step up from the usual indifferent mass catering options Kate had experienced at other dos. She was tempted to have a quick glass of white to ease her own nerves, especially after that close encounter with Harry, but figured she should probably try to keep her wits about her in case Artemis had any other requirements, or the place wasn't up to his standards.

She had to admit, though, that the shop was looking fantastic. She'd outdone herself on the paintwork; you'd never know how bad that historic damp stain on the ceiling above the Children's section was now. The walls, as dusky blue in colour as a starling's egg, offset the brilliant white of the ceiling perfectly, and added even more lustre to the heavy mahogany shelves. She felt a flush of pleasure at a job well done. Harry should be rightly proud of his beautiful shop, and she felt sad that he was upstairs, languishing in bed, missing his big moment.

A loud cheer outside on the High Street brought Kate's mind

back from the patient upstairs to the shop floor. She turned to Corey and Florence in confusion.

'I thought he'd arranged to come in the back way,' she said, brow furrowing.

'Looks like he was keen to meet his public after all,' Florence replied, ambling over to the shop's locked front door. Sure enough, as Kate hurried over to join her, she could see the tall, skinny, black jeans and T-shirt-clad Artemis Bane ambling up the High Street, looking relaxed and at ease and not at all suffering from the stage fright she'd been led to believe he found crippling. Trotting alongside him, and looking far more nervous, was a woman who Kate assumed to be Eloise Padgett. She was on his right-hand side, having interposed herself between him and the line of guests who were waiting to get into the bookshop. As they drew nearer, Kate saw her shake her head vigorously when a student thrust out a copy of Bane's previous novel for an autograph. Clearly, she didn't want any distractions for him before he got into the shop itself. Bane looked straight ahead, staring up towards the looming majesty to Willowbury Hill at the top of the town, not acknowledging any of the cheers and whoops that were getting progressively louder.

Tosser, Kate thought as he came into clearer view. What would it cost him to stop and have a chat with some of those people who'd been queuing outside all day, and in some cases, overnight, too? Clearly fame had gone to his head, local boy done good or not. And what was the point of arriving so publicly if he wasn't going to even crack a smile at the crowd?

Finally, Eloise and Artemis reached the bookshop. Waiting until the very last moment, but mindful that the great author might not respond well to being kept on the doorstep, Kate pulled open the door and welcomed them into the shop.

Kate, took a deep breath. 'Hi,' she said, sounding more confident than she felt. 'Welcome to Vale Volumes.'

Artemis, to his credit, looked a little taken aback. 'You don't look like the Harry I was expecting.'

'I did mention to you on the way over that Harry Sinclair had been taken ill,' Eloise explained patiently, clearly used to having to remind her famous client of these things on a regular basis. 'And that Kate would be taking over the running of tonight's event.'

'Oh, yeah, right,' Artemis said vaguely. 'Well, I hope you know what you're doing. This is some high-level publicity shit, you know.' Before Kate could respond, and obviously used to being in control of any situation, Artemis's attention had already been drawn by the props and décor of the shop floor. With a brief smile at Kate, and ignoring her outstretched hand, he wandered off to take a look around.

'I'm sorry,' Eloise said in an undertone. 'He gets awfully uptight before a gig like this. He might not seem it, but getting him to retain anything before showtime is an impossible task. He's absolutely focused on what's coming.' She smiled briefly and shook Kate's hand. 'It's nice to meet you. And it's a real shame that Harry's so ill.'

Kate nodded and smiled back at Eloise, who obviously had her hands full with her client, although she seemed to know him very well. Eloise, while still speaking with Kate to check out a few things, had her eyes firmly fixed on Artemis as he made his way around the shop, almost as if he was a hunting hound, intent on following his nose to his prey. Kate figured it was an expression of nerves, and tried not to take it personally when Artemis picked up the longbow that was resting against one of the shelves and put it back at a slightly different angle. Corey, clearly overwhelmed to be in such close proximity to his literary idol, was hanging back behind her, mouth slightly open, just watching Artemis. Corey had burned through Artemis's recent urban fantasy novels, and had been obsessed with its main character, Malcolm, for weeks. She knew Corey was desperate to get a signed copy of Bane's latest tonight.

'Right, well, if you'd like to make yourselves comfortable, we can let the audience in and get started,' Kate said, directing her comments to Artemis's turned back, and then looking to Eloise for confirmation.

'Absolutely,' Eloise replied. 'Come on, Artemis, let's get going.'

At the sound of her voice, Artemis seemed to come back to the shop floor from wherever in his head he'd been. Turning back to them, he gave a smile that, had Kate been a fan, would have melted her into a puddle all over Harry's oak floorboards. 'Of course,' he said, in a voice that was low and, it seemed to Kate, ever so slightly over-emphasised his Somerset roots. 'Let's not keep anyone waiting.' Lithe and loose as an Irish Wolfhound, he ambled over to where the striped armchair and the occasional table had been set up.

'Everything okay?' Kate asked.

Artemis glanced up at her and smiled again, this time really seeming to see her. 'Absolutely. And thank you for stepping in at such short notice.'

'No problem.' Kate smiled back. *So far, so good*, she thought. Artemis had been on time and appeared to be behaving himself. She couldn't help noticing that Eloise was still quivering with tension, though, as if she expected something to kick off at any moment. Was Artemis lulling Kate into a false sense of security?

Shrugging aside that thought, she headed back to the shop door to start letting in the crowd. *This is it*, she thought. It was all down to Artemis now to keep the show on the road. She hoped he'd make his audience happy.

32

Meanwhile, feeling utterly exhausted but equally unable to sleep, knowing what was going on directly below him, Harry tossed and turned. His temperature was coming down, and he didn't feel as shivery and feverish as he had done, but his legs still felt like jelly, even when he was lying down.

Harry hated being ill. It took him back, every time, to having a bout of gastroenteritis as a child, when his mother, patience worn thin because everyone in the house had gone down with it at the same time, had screamed at him for vomiting all over his bedroom carpet, and then virtually thrown the bowl of hot water at him to clear it up himself. Since that incident, he'd learned to battle through illness, never letting it get to him.

And now here he was, struck down with this deeply unseasonal flu bug and unable to oversee the biggest event his shop had ever hosted. Not just that, but he'd dragged in a woman he barely knew to mastermind the evening, whom he'd ended up in another clinch with, and now he couldn't stop thinking about. The feel, however fleeting, of her lips brushing his as she'd stumbled was enough to make the sweat break out on his brow again. Not even the coolness of his cotton sheets could help with that.

Turning over in bed again to reach for the glass of water that Kate had refilled before she'd gone downstairs, he cursed as it slipped from his fingers and smashed onto the uneven varnished floorboards of his room. The thirst was driving him mad, though, so he had no choice but to get up and get another one. Perhaps a plastic bottle would have been better, he reflected, all too late. Rolling over to the other side of the bed, to avoid the shards of glass, he slapped his feet down and took a deep breath before trying his weight by standing up. As his head started to spin, he breathed out, trying to regain a sense of equilibrium.

'Come on, you twat,' he muttered. 'You're a grown man. Get on with it.' Swaying on his feet, he was caught off guard by a hammering of applause coming from downstairs. Artemis had obviously started, and, thankfully, from the sounds of the sustained clapping, seemed to have been well received. Putting one foot in front of the other, he made it to the kitchen, and grabbed his reusable drinks bottle from the draining board, filling it with water and gulping the first lot down thirstily. Refilling it, he staggered back towards his bedroom, but before he got there he was distracted by another round of applause and a roar of laughter. Artemis was clearly captivating his audience now. He felt a flash of irritation that he wasn't down there listening to it himself. But Kate had taken one look at him and told him to stay put, and, looking in the bathroom mirror earlier, he couldn't blame her. Artemis and his adoring audience wouldn't thank him at all for spreading this to them.

Staggering back to his bed, he lay back down on top of his duvet as, even with a reducing fever, he still felt hot. When he was feeling better, he'd bloody well take Kate out for a proper drink, or perhaps even dinner, to thank her for stepping in at such short notice. There was something between them after those kisses; of that he was sure. And he wanted to know what.

But perhaps when he was feeling better. For the moment, all he could do was lie back, close his eyes and wait for this bloody fever to pass.

33

Kate was amazed to see how quickly Artemis slipped into role in front of an audience. She hadn't realised just how much authors had to become 'personalities' to sell books these days, but with the market becoming ever more competitive, perhaps this was the way of things now. And there was no doubt that Artemis knew this and did it extremely well. Languid and seemingly relaxed, he lounged in the armchair at the back of the store, his appreciative audience hanging on his every word. As he reached out a lazy hand to grab his glass of water flavoured, of course, with those Sicilian unwaxed lemons, Kate glanced at Eloise, who, in contrast, was quivering like a greyhound in a trap. Perhaps this air of relaxation, this calm detachment, was an act on his part, and he was prone to dropping the odd howler when he chilled out?

'So, that was the time I ended up stark bollock naked outside my hotel room in Singapore,' he was now saying. 'And after that I decided I wasn't ever going to be taking any drug that involved sticking something up my arse, ever again!'

The audience, lapping it up, laughed and clapped. Kate saw Eloise glancing around yet again, and then gesture frantically at

Artemis to tone things down a little, since there were a fair few older teens there who, while enjoying the stories, were a little too young for that kind of content.

'All right, Mum!' Artemis smiled gamely in Eloise's direction. 'She's telling me I need to keep the anecdotes a little more PG-rated if I'm to survive this evening unscathed.'

Kate suddenly realised that she wouldn't have swapped places with Eloise Padgett for all the money in the world. Artemis, while undoubtedly charismatic and charming, had a tendency to be a loose cannon that clearly it was Eloise's job to diffuse when it got too explosive.

'But that brings me, of course, to the inspiration for this latest, and last volume of the Redcliffe Trilogy.' A groan of disappointment rose up from the audience at the confirmation that this would, in fact, be the last one.

'Yes, I'm afraid so.' Artemis laughed heartily. 'It's on to pastures new for me, and finally some sense of closure for Malcolm, who, I'm sure, if he were real, would be just as sick of me as I am of him.'

Another warning look from Eloise made Artemis hastily revise that statement. 'I mean, not that I'm sick of him, of course, but it's time to give him what he really needs.'

And he was off again, charming, entertaining and ensuring that not one single person in the audience was going to leave without buying the newest book.

At last it was time for Artemis to finish talking, having answered Harry's list of questions with aplomb. Kate, who was doing the asking, felt a sense of relief that she'd pulled it off. He wound up his final anecdote, prompted by the last question of the evening, and prepared to sign books. Kate, off to one side, felt her shoulders relax at last. It had gone without a hitch. Now she just had to get him out of the shop without incident, and her job was done.

People were starting to leave, and as she collected glasses and plates from where they'd been abandoned, she realised that Corey, who had been chatting animatedly to a tall, fair-haired girl who looked about his age, was bidding her goodbye, after seemingly swapping phone numbers. He then edged up to Artemis with his own copy of the latest book in his hand. Looking up at him, realising he was the last one in the queue, Artemis started to chat with him. Kate watched Corey's face light up as Artemis asked him a few questions, and nod enthusiastically, taking the book gratefully when Artemis had finished chatting to him. As Corey turned away again towards her, Kate could see the excitement in his eyes at having met his favourite author.

'Okay?' she murmured as he came up to her to show her what Artemis had written.

Corey nodded, obviously still too starstruck to speak.

'Well, that went well,' Artemis said as he unfolded himself from behind the table where he'd been signing books. 'It's nice to be back in the old place.'

'Harry said you grew up here,' Kate replied. 'Do you come back often?'

'Christ, no.' Artemis shuddered, and then laughed. 'Not if I can help it, but my publisher thought it would be a good publicity move to be seen to support an independent bookshop rather than do this one in London.'

'Oh, right,' Kate replied. Corey was hanging back from her again, still overawed by Bane's illustrious presence. 'Well, it seemed to go well, anyway,' she added. 'But I'd better get on with clearing up now.' She turned to Corey. 'Can you go and load the rest of the glasses into the dishwasher for me?'

'Okay,' Corey said, clearly reluctant to be taken away from Artemis for a second. He took the tray that Kate gave him and ambled off to the back of the shop.

'If you're not doing anything later, why don't you join me for a drink?' Artemis edged closer to Kate once Corey was out of earshot. 'Considering you stepped in at such short notice, I think you deserve a night out to celebrate. We could have a drink and go from there.'

Kate's eyes grew a little wider at the unspoken implication. Was Artemis really hitting on her? Once again, she cursed her lack of practise at reading signals from men. It would be just like her to misread the situation, though, and assume he was making a move when he wasn't.

'That is one sexy dress, Kate.' Artemis lowered his voice suggestively, and suddenly Kate was in no doubt as to his intentions. 'It'd be a shame to waste it by going home alone so early.'

Christ, Kate thought, *you really are used to getting what you want, aren't you?*

Out loud she merely said. 'After such a busy day, I'm shattered. And there's Corey to think about, of course.'

'Ditch the kid,' Artemis said with the air of a man who had never had to worry about his own children. 'He's old enough to see himself home, surely.'

Kate bristled at the imperative. She remembered what Harry had told her about Artemis's liking for post-show groupies, and felt affronted that Artemis seemed to think she fell into that category. 'No can do,' she said briskly. 'Perhaps you'd better go and find someone else to share a drink with.'

'Oh, come on.' Artemis drew even closer to Kate, so that he really was invading her personal space. Unlike when Harry had done so, when they'd kissed, this felt distinctly unpleasant. 'You're not going to refuse a world-famous author a night of your company, are you? After all, I've just made sure your mate, Harry, can pay the bills on his shop for at least the next six months, and all in one night. Isn't that worth a drink or three with me?' Artemis raised a hand so that his fingertips traced Kate's bare skin from the inside of her elbow upwards, brushing over the side of her breast on its journey.

Kate jumped back, feeling a sense of revulsion that this man, however famous and loved by his readers, could be so entitled.

'I don't think so, Mr Bane,' she said firmly. 'I'm sure there are plenty of others out there on the High Street who'd love to spend the night, er, *evening*, with you. But I'm afraid I'm just not one of them.'

'Everything all right?' As she stepped away from Artemis, who seemed about to respond with yet another persuasive gambit, Harry's voice came from the bottom of the stairs that led back up to his flat above the shop.

Kate took the opportunity to put some much-needed space between herself and her harasser. She turned her head and saw Harry standing at the bottom of the stairs. He'd thrown on a pair of dark blue jeans and a black T-shirt, seemingly for the sake of decency, but he was still sweaty, dishevelled and distinctly feverish, if the flush to his cheeks was anything to go by.

'Everything's fine, Harry,' she said, smiling brightly in his direction. 'Artemis was just leaving. It's been a successful night; you'll be pleased to know.'

'Glad to hear it.' Harry walked towards Kate and Artemis, but paused within about five feet. 'I would shake your hand, Mr Bane, but I'd hate to give you the flu. Perhaps it'd be best if you headed back to where you're staying. You don't want to catch it.'

Artemis's eyes flashed with irritation as Harry's tone of voice made his real meaning clear. He was obviously someone who wasn't used to being turned down, and, on a high from the signing, was reluctant to let this go.

At that moment, Corey and Eloise, who had offered to help him, returned from loading the glasses into the dishwasher, and that was when Artemis obviously decided he was beaten.

'Well, thank you for hosting such a great night,' Artemis said. 'I'll be at the bar in the pub if you change your mind.'

Kate inclined her head slightly, unwilling to out Artemis as a pest in front of her son, who hadn't, thankfully, clocked any of the previous conversation.

'It was nice to meet you,' Corey said as Artemis departed.

'You too, Colin.'

'It's, er, Corey.'

'Right.'

As the shop door shut behind him, with Eloise not far behind, having quickly said her goodbyes, Kate took a deep breath and tried to stop the shakes that were running through her body as the adrenaline from the encounter subsided.

'You okay, Mum?' Corey asked, obviously noticing how pale she'd suddenly become.

Kate smiled. 'I'm fine. Why don't you go and grab us a pizza?' She crossed to the counter and handed him a twenty-pound note from her purse. 'I'll be back home in a bit, when I've finished clearing up. And then you can tell me all about that girl you were talking to before you got your book signed.'

As Corey left the shop, muttering good-naturedly about nosy mothers, Kate turned back to where Harry was still standing.

'Are you *really* okay?' Harry asked gently, approaching the counter where she was still standing.

Kate shook her head, suddenly unable to speak. She'd been on such a rollercoaster over the past couple of days, what with Corey's sudden absence and reappearance in Willowbury, being taken completely out of her comfort zone by having to step into running this evening, Artemis's most unwelcome pass at her and Harry's kiss, which had been more than welcome, she wasn't sure which way was up any more.

Harry, obviously mindful that he himself wasn't in the best

shape, paused before he made his next move. 'I know you've said you're not a hugger, but would that help in this instance?'

Kate looked up at him, took in the dishevelled hair, the glasses behind which the deep blue eyes looked tender and concerned, the black T-shirt and dark navy jeans and the fact that he clearly wasn't on top form himself, and, considering in that split second that she'd spent enough time in his sick room to probably have caught the flu herself already, she stepped forward and into his arms. As she did, she felt the tension draining out of her, and the unsettling encounter with Artemis seemed to sail away on a tide of calm.

Kate found herself relaxing and responding to the sensation of Harry's admittedly rather too warm from fever body, she breathed out. 'He might have been a money-spinning guest for you, but Artemis Bane is also a class one, grade A twat!'

'I rather feared that he would be.' Harry sighed. 'But booksellers can't be choosers sometimes. However, that said, I don't think I'll be agreeing to any return visits in the near future. I can't have him hitting on the staff, even if you were only here for an evening.'

'Staff?' Kate snorted. 'Who are you calling staff? I quit.'

'Good,' Harry said huskily. 'I wouldn't want to be accused of doing the same myself.'

Before she could think of a suitable retort, Kate found herself leaning up to kiss Harry hard on the mouth. 'Who's hitting on who?' she said softly as they both came back up for air.

Harry, to his credit, managed to stay upright during the kiss, despite the fact he hadn't eaten for twenty-four hours and was now even more wobbly than he had been when he'd come down the back stairs.

'Wow,' he murmured. 'I wasn't expecting that.'

Kate smiled. 'Let's just say I've had a bit of time to think about the other night, and I've decided to stop worrying so much. There are plenty of other things to worry about at the moment; I don't need to add angsting about kissing you to the list.'

'Fair enough.' Harry smiled back down at her. Then, regretfully, he shook his head. 'I wish I could make good on all of the promise that kissing you has just unleashed, but if I don't get horizontal again soon, alone, I think you're probably going to have to carry me back upstairs!'

Kate noticed again how shuddery Harry still was, and her heart stirred. She stepped out of Harry's arms. 'So, would you like me to help you to bed, then? And not in the exciting way?'

Harry grinned weakly. 'I can't believe I'm saying this, but yes please.' Turning back to the stairs, he limped up them, Kate not far behind.

'Probably just as well, anyway,' Kate said. 'Corey'll never let me hear the end of it if I disappear for too long.'

'I might need a bit of a hand here next week,' Harry said as they headed down the passageway back to his bedroom. 'Do you reckon Corey might like some work experience in this place? I'd pay him minimum wage, of course. Bit of pocket money for while he's staying here.'

Kate laughed. 'Well, he was supposed to be going home in a day or two, but I'm sure he'd jump at the chance of staying if he could work here. If you're sure you want my sixteen-year-old son hanging around the place.'

'He's a good lad, from what I've seen of him.' Harry sounded breathless as they reached his bedroom. Unfortunately, Kate realised it probably had more to do with the flu than excitement that she was there. 'If you think it might keep him out of trouble, and you're okay with it, that is.'

'He'd love it,' Kate said as she pushed Harry's bedroom door open. 'I have a feeling he'd be hanging out in Vale Volumes for free, anyway!'

'Damn,' Harry joked. 'I should have kept my mouth shut about paying him!'

There was a pause as Kate wondered whether she should now leave Harry to it. 'Is there anything else you need?'

'I think I can make it to my bed alone,' Harry said wryly. 'And all I really want to do is crash out.'

Kate smiled. 'I'll let myself out, then.'

Harry returned the smile. 'Kate... thank you. You went above and beyond today, for me and the shop. I really appreciate everything you've done.'

'It was fun, honestly,' Kate said, conveniently forgetting the nerves she'd felt about hosting the evening. 'Even if Artemis did live up to his reputation in the end.'

'I wonder how Eloise Padgett puts up with him,' Harry mused. 'If he behaves like that every time he's let loose, I think I'd have resigned ages ago!'

'I bet she's paid enough to look the other way,' Kate replied. 'And besides, he's about ninety-five per cent ego. I never felt under any particular threat from him. I'm sure there are plenty of his fans who'd have loved to have been where I was just now.'

'Well, I for one am glad you aren't one of them,' Harry said, rubbing his eyes.

'Call me if you need anything.' Kate decided now was the best time to leave Harry alone to recover. 'And hopefully, when you're feeling better...' she trailed off, suddenly too nervous to end that sentence. In truth, she really wasn't sure *how* to end it, anyway.

Thankfully, Harry didn't seem to notice. 'I will. And thanks again, Kate. I owe you at least another lunch.'

'When you're up to it,' Kate said. Leaning forward, she kissed his cheek, and felt a familiar tingle as her body responded to the warmth of his skin under her lips.

'Oh, God,' Harry groaned. 'I hate the flu!'

'See you soon,' Kate said.

'Kate? Are you there?' Florence's voice came drifting up the stairs. She'd been tidying up the back kitchen during the exchange with Artemis, and had only just emerged, having missed Kate and Harry's cuddle, thankfully. Kate knew she'd never hear the end of it if Florence had seen *that*.

'I'm here,' Kate called back. 'Just checking in on Harry.'

'Okay, I'm ready when you are.'

'I'd better go,' Kate said. 'But call me if you need anything.'

'I will.' Harry smiled. 'And thanks again, Kate.'

And with that, Kate headed back down the stairs and out of the front door of Vale Volumes with Florence. She breathed a sigh of relief that the evening, at last, was over.

34

As predicted, Corey was over the moon on Saturday morning when Kate told him Harry had offered him a job for a week or two. Partially fuelled by relief that he wouldn't have to paint walls to earn a wage, and mostly by the fact that he thought it would 'give him time to do some reading' while at work, Kate gave him all the standard warnings about minding his Ps and Qs, asking questions if he was unsure of anything, and not slacking off, to the point where her eldest son just rolled his eyes and asked her if she realised he wasn't nine any more.

'I just want you to make a good impression,' Kate said as she cleared away their plates and put them in the dishwasher. 'After all, if you do this well, you can always ask Harry for a reference for another job when you need one.'

'I'm sure he'd give me one anyway, he's so keen on you.'

Kate shook her head. 'This isn't about me.'

'Sure. You mean he just decided to give me a job out of the kindness of his heart?' Corey grinned at her and Kate was compelled to throw the dishcloth she was using to wipe the table at him.

'Well, whatever it was, he wants you there bright and early on Monday morning.'

'I'll be there.' Corey smiled. 'And don't worry, Mum, I'll do a good job.'

'I know you will.' Kate smiled back. 'If it was one of your brothers, I'd be more worried about them accidentally burning the shop down, but I think I can trust you not to let me down.'

'Absolutely,' Corey said, and sidled off to his room.

Armed with Corey's enthusiastic response, Kate phoned Phil and let him know that Corey was going to stay a bit longer. As soon as she was in a position to have her other two sons join her, she assured him, she'd make sure they did. For a few more days, though, she needed to properly break the back of the painting in Aidan's house, without too many interruptions.

* * *

A couple of days later, on the Monday after Artemis's appearance at the bookshop, Corey started his first shift at Vale Volumes. After crashing out all weekend, Harry was feeling considerably better, and Kate was charmed to receive a large bunch of freesias and lilies via the local florist on the High Street as a thank you for stepping in to run Artemis's evening. Attached to these was a card which read:

You saved my bacon, so how about joining me for dinner at the Black Swan Bistro in Stavenham on Friday evening? Corey, if he's free, is welcome too.

Harry x

Kate smiled. Harry was a hard man to resist, she was finding. Especially when he seemed intent on including Corey in things. Texting back a quick thank you, she walked back to the hallway that she'd almost finished painting and then nearly dropped the phone again as it pinged with another text, this time from Corey.

Harry's just told me he's invited you and me to dinner. I think it would be a bit lame to have your son tagging along and I totes don't want to be a gooseberry. Are you OK to go alone?

Kate grinned. She could see his point, made articulately by text and complete with gooseberry emoji, and she was sure he'd far rather get some gaming time in on the PS4 with Sam, if Florence was happy to let Corey hang out with Sam for the evening, and her brother wasn't on shift, of course. Texting back that yes, she was 'totes' okay with Corey not coming out to dinner, she tried not to think about what the outcome of that evening might be. Was it merely just a thank you for a job well done, or were there more kisses to come? She was surprised that she felt so keen for it to be the latter. Who'd have thought a summer fling was really what she wanted? Then she stilled that thought. Even without Corey sharing dinner with them, he'd still be here to come home to at the end of the night, and she couldn't exactly pretend to be fancy free and spend the night with Harry, even if she wanted to. Did she want to? The thought of sleeping with someone new for the first time since Phil was enough to make her back out of dinner altogether.

Relax, she told herself. *It's only dinner*. She didn't have to do anything she didn't want to. Her encounter with Artemis Bane was enough of a reminder of that. Dinner with Harry would be nice, but she wasn't going to get in over her head; especially on a first proper date.

So it was that Friday night arrived, and Kate was nervously pacing the hallway of the house, trying not to go off a cliff with nerves. Corey had gone next door for his gaming night with Sam, and Florence had texted her a picture of them both already ensconced on the living room sofa with yet more pizza and a big bottle of Coca Cola to keep them going as they tackled zombie Nazis on the latest *Call of Duty* incarnation on the PS4. From the sounds of it, they wouldn't be moving for some time, and Florence had suggested that Corey crash out on the living room sofa if it looked like they were going to make an all-nighter of it, rather than frightening the life out of Kate by coming through the front door at whatever-o'clock. Kate tried not to let her thoughts drift to what might happen with Harry, now that she'd have the house to herself.

As she saw Harry's VW Golf drawing up to the kerbside outside the houses, she stepped back into the hall, glancing in the mirror by the front door to check she didn't have lipstick on her teeth and her hair wasn't flying in all directions. To her relief, she looked calmer than she felt. She'd borrowed a patterned top and a pair of skinny jeans from Florence, and teamed them with the same sandals she'd worn for the book launch, and even she had to admit, she'd scrubbed up pretty well again.

Opening the door before Harry even had the chance to knock, she caught him in the slightly absurd position of raising his hand to the brass knocker. His look of surprise immediately put Kate at ease.

'Sorry!' she said as he stepped back from the door and she stepped out, closing it firmly behind her. 'Sam and Corey gave me the "don't stay out too late" speech earlier and I was beginning to feel like my own teenage son!'

'Better get out of here, in that case,' Harry said.

As they walked to the car, Kate noticed that Harry looked a lot better than he had a few days back. 'You've shrugged off the worst of the flu, then?' she said as she opened the passenger side of Harry's car.

'Yes, thank goodness,' Harry replied. 'Owning your own business is great until you are sick. I couldn't really afford to lounge around in bed, so I've been taking it a bit easier this week and I've actually been using that blessed armchair that Artemis Bane wanted for his talk to take the weight off in the quiet spells. You'll be delighted to know that Corey's been an absolute godsend and has been doing a fair bit of the heavy lifting. He's a quick learner, and seems really keen to impress me with his efficiency. I found myself having to invent things to keep him busy at times!'

'I'm really pleased to hear that,' Kate said. 'He's a good kid, but I did tell him to make himself as useful as he could while he was with you.'

'Well, he certainly has.' Harry paused. 'It's nice to get to know him a bit better, even it is just for a couple of weeks.' He glanced at Kate briefly then put his eyes back to the road. 'Kind of makes me realise what I've missed out on.'

Kate's heart went out to the man in the driving seat. Harry had been very matter of fact about his childlessness, when they'd spoken about it while painting the shop, but that didn't mean it didn't affect him, she understood that.

As if sensing her hesitation to reply, in case she said the wrong thing, Harry glanced back at her and smiled. 'Sorry,' he said. 'Being out of commission for a few days has made me maudlin. It gave me too much time to think about things I really shouldn't be thinking about. What a way to start what's meant to be a nice evening!'

'It's fine, Harry,' Kate said gently. 'I'm glad you can talk to me. And I'm glad you asked me to dinner. It'll be good to get out of the house, and Willowbury, for the evening. I haven't had the chance to visit Stavenham yet.'

'To continue the theme of our conversation, it's kind of like the big brother to Willowbury's irresponsible younger child,' Harry said, grinning this time. 'Willowbury's all experimentation and alternative living, and Stavenham is the upright, uptight, responsible, mortgage-paying stalwart. But no less beautiful in its own way, of course.'

'That's what I love the most about this part of the world,' Kate murmured, looking out of the passenger window as the fields, burned green gold by the summer sunshine, gave way to the honey-coloured stone buildings of Stavenham. 'There's so much contrast and variety. You're close to the sea, but there's plenty of countryside, there's history and tradition but also modernity and fresher thinking. And now my brothers have settled here, too, I can really see the appeal.'

'You sound like you might be hanging around a little longer than the summer,' Harry said. He paused again before adding quietly, 'I'd like it if you did.'

Kate felt a warm glow of pleasure wash over her at his words. There was no doubting the chemistry between them, but even after a few kisses she wasn't sure if he just saw her as a summer fling to pass the time. It was nice, if a little nerve-wracking, to know that he might be thinking of her in more serious terms. Then she stopped herself. This was exactly the kind of thinking she *didn't* need. She was, after all, only meant to be in Willowbury for the summer. It wouldn't do to get too attached. To anything. Or anyone.

All the same, as Harry's car ate up the few miles between Willowbury and Stavenham, Kate couldn't help wondering if this might not be just for the summer.

35

The Black Swan Bistro was at the top of Stavenham High Street, just before the entrance to the Bishop's Palace, which was the main tourist draw to the medieval city. That and the cathedral ensured that the place was kept busy all year round. As they were ushered into a private alcove that allowed Kate a view of the evening tourists and diners lazily ambling up and down the High Street, Kate had to congratulate Harry on his choice of venue.

'We're a bit spoiled for choice here,' Harry said. 'But I've heard this place being talked about by a lot of the customers who come into Vale Volumes, so I thought I'd give it a go.'

'You mean you're not a regular?' Kate asked wryly.

Harry grinned and took a sip from the glass of water he'd poured from the jug on the table. 'Much as Jack Winter likes to try to drag me out on the town, be that here or Bristol, I'm afraid I rather live up to my reputation as a dowdy old bookseller these days. So, no, in answer to your question, I'm not a regular.'

'Then I'm very pleased you've brought me here.' Kate's smile softened. 'Thank you, Harry.'

There was a pause between them again that ran the risk of

becoming awkward. 'Not that it's any of my business,' Harry began again, 'but have you, er, dated much since... you know?'

'Since my divorce?' Kate filled in for him. 'It's all right, you can mention the D-word. I'm long past dissolving into tears at the thought of it.'

'Much like me and the other thing,' Harry said, smiling. 'I'm sorry. I didn't mean to skirt around it.'

'And in answer to your question, no, not a lot. With the boys, my life's been pretty full anyway. I had a couple of dates with a friend of a friend, but I just wasn't ready for what he was hoping for. In the end, it seemed simpler to be happily single.' *Not to mention the near constant feeling of being too rusty at the game to keep trying to play*, she thought. She was still rather amazed she'd said yes to Harry. And yet here they were.

'I can imagine it's pretty full-on, being a mother to three of them.'

'It is,' Kate said. And then she suddenly thought that she didn't want to spend the whole night talking about her sons, and mother-hood, and the reasons why she'd ended up in Willowbury painting her brother's house. But how to get away from it? She coughed nervously, took a sip of her white wine and grinned. 'Seen any good rock bands lately?'

And they were off, bantering about their shared musical shames.

'For me, you can't get better or hairier than Foreigner.' Kate laughed. 'I mean, when it comes to a power ballad, there's none finer.'

'Oh, I don't know,' Harry countered. 'Bon Jovi are pretty much the epitome of eighties bad hair and power ballads, aren't they? I saw them in Milton Keynes in 1996 with a girlfriend, and I've never forgotten how amazing "Always" sounds belted out across a green field on a summer night.'

'I blame eighties movies,' Kate said. 'I mean, how many montages were there to terrible soft rock?'

Harry laughed. 'Which was your favourite, then?'

Kate thought for a moment. 'You'll probably be expecting me to say something girly like *Dirty Dancing*, but, much as I love the wiggle of Patrick Swayze's hips, I have to admit to a guiltier pleasure.'

'Oh yes?' Harry raised an eyebrow. 'And what would that be?'

'Promise not to laugh?'

'I solemnly swear.' Harry grinned.

'Okay. I had a real thing for *The Karate Kid*.'

Harry looked surprised. 'Well, I wasn't expecting that.'

'I even got away with showing it to the boys a couple of years ago,' Kate continued. 'Phil didn't like it at all; said it was a pile of sentimental nonsense, but for a while it was the boys' favourite film, too.'

Harry smiled. 'That's sweet.' A look passed over his face that Kate just caught before he assumed his usual pleasant expression. The question must have registered on her face because he immediately answered. 'If I'd had children, I always imagined sharing things that I loved with them.'

'It can be a bit of a risky strategy,' Kate said. 'I mean, they already know I named them after eighties movie stars, and they find that a bit embarrassing when someone twigs, but they can also be quite critical and unforgiving if they think something's, er, "lame".'

'So did you and your husband—'

'*Ex*-husband,' Kate corrected, but without rancour.

'Sorry,' Harry replied. 'Ex-husband – did you agree straight away on the names for your children?'

Kate laughed. 'Not exactly! We went through about a hundred

different names before we agreed on the three we actually ended up choosing.'

'I had enough trouble naming the bookshop,' Harry said, 'I can't imagine being responsible for giving someone their name for their lifetime, let along doing it three times.'

'You're such a dork,' Kate said. 'Don't tell me it's just a female thing to think up the names for your kids, even before you're in a position to have them?'

'Well, I didn't exactly spend hours and hours thinking about combinations,' Harry said. 'And after I got the infertility diagnosis, I kind of stopped thinking about it altogether.'

Kate felt her heart lurch again. 'Of course. Sorry, I didn't think.'

'Don't worry about it,' Harry said, his tone gentle. 'I asked you first, remember? And you haven't answered the question yet!' he grinned. 'So how did your boys get their names?'

Kate's smile broadened. 'You're going to laugh.'

'Try me.'

'Well,' Kate began, 'I was a bit of a fan of a certain type of movie when I was growing up. You know, those films about American teenagers in high schools, where each one was a massive stereotype but it all worked out okay in the end.'

'Yes, I remember seeing a fair few of them.' Harry grinned. 'And you've told me your favourite one, but you didn't name any of your sons after the lead actor in that film, so where did their names come from?'

'Not even I could call a son born in the twenty-first century Ralph!' Kate laughed. '*Karate Kid* notwithstanding, Judy Blume's book *Forever* put me off the name for life!' The moment she said that, she blushed. What if Harry didn't get the reference? Thankfully, he laughed along with her.

'I'm sure I've got a copy of that book stashed away in the Young

Adult section,' he said. 'Something tells me I'd better look it out if I'm going to fully understand.'

'I'll let you discover that one for yourself,' Kate said.

'So... the names?'

Kate grinned, relieved to be away from *that* particular conversational cul-de-sac. 'So, as well as the *Karate Kid* obsession, I loved *The Lost Boys* and *Stand By Me*,' Kate smiled. 'Then when it came to having kids... well, let's just say that Corey and Will still don't really know who they're named after!'

Harry grinned. 'Fair enough. Are you going to enlighten them one day? And which one was Corey named after, Feldman or Haim?'

'That would be telling,' Kate smiled back. 'Although if I told you I had a thing for one of the Frogg brothers...'

Harry's bark of laughter was sudden, but it made Kate smile more broadly. 'And don't even get me started on what they think of my taste in music!'

'So I take it you haven't been blasting their eardrums with Foreigner albums on a regular basis, then?'

'Definitely not!'

Harry leaned forward in his seat. 'Can I let you into a secret?' His dark blue eyes, warmed by the setting sun, twinkled mysteriously and the crows' feet at the corners made Kate's stomach flutter as she suddenly had to suppress an urge to touch them.

'If you like,' she said softly.

'I've got a Spotify playlist on my phone that's purely eighties hair rock, but I wasn't brave enough to put it on during the drive over. Shall I risk it on the way home?'

'I think you can take the chance.' Kate laughed. 'I won't think any less of you.'

'That's good to know.'

A companionable silence descended between them, that was

broken a few moments later by the waiter coming over with their main course choices. Kate, thinking that she'd be far too nervous to eat, actually felt ravenous as she looked down at the exquisitely presented pork tenderloin and Bramley apple puree, with a side order of vibrantly coloured young broccoli.

The rest of the meal was equally delicious, and as Harry gestured for the bill, Kate reflected that, *for a first date, this has been a pretty good experience.* Glancing at her watch, she was surprised to see that it was still quite early; not even half past nine. She wondered if there was any way to make the evening last a little longer, but she was at a loss for ideas.

As if reading her thoughts, as they headed out of the restaurant and back onto the High Street, Harry cleared his throat. 'If you like, we could have a walk on Cathedral Green before we head home.'

'I'd like that,' Kate said. 'I can't believe I haven't come to Stavenham and I've been living in Willowbury for nearly four weeks. It'd be nice to see a bit more of it.'

As they walked across the cobbled stones to the other side of the High Street and towards the archway that led to the green, Kate found herself drifting closer to Harry until her left hand brushed his as they walked. Feeling the jolt of electricity, her heart thumped faster when he carefully took her hand in his, so gently that it felt as though he was tacitly asking permission. Suddenly she felt like a teenager on her first date, and not a nearly-forty-year-old mother of three. Harry's hand was warm and dry, and instinctively felt right. They slowed their pace a little as they went under the archway and Harry steered them so they were in front of the cathedral.

'It's beautiful when the stone is lit up by the sunset, isn't it?' he said as they stopped to admire Stavenham Cathedral. There were a few people enjoying a late supper on the green, and the burble of chatter from those on picnic rugs gave the atmosphere a pleasingly continental flavour. The scents emanating from the other restaurants that backed onto Cathedral Green drifted through the air, mingling with the smell of cut grass from the generous lawns. Bordering the green, on the flagstones, were tubs and tubs of lavender, the scent of which reminded Kate of France in the summertime, and created even more of a summer holiday atmosphere.

'It really is,' Kate replied. She moved closer to Harry as they stood looking at the cathedral, and she could feel the heat from his body as her arm brushed his, her hand still clasped in his. 'This evening's been perfect. Thank you.' Looking up, she couldn't help but be drawn to the sight of Harry's mouth, smiling gently in the dying light, and his eyes, almost black in that same, sultry summer evening hue, looking down at her with undisguised affection.

'I think there's one thing that could make it more perfect for me,' Harry said softly, as he drew Kate towards him so that they were facing each other.

'And what would that be?' Kate murmured, pulse jumping at the sensation of being so close to Harry in this achingly romantic setting.

'This,' he replied gently, dipping his head and sliding his free arm around her waist until their torsos were touching, and, a moment after, their lips. 'And this time,' he said as they came up for air, 'I don't have a temperature, you don't have to apologise for slipping and I won't drop a paint can at your feet!'

'Sounds good to me,' Kate said and, with great enthusiasm, kissed him back.

36

The tension was palpable as Kate and Harry drove back to Willowbury. Something had shifted between them on the green outside the cathedral, and safe in the knowledge that Corey was spending the night at Florence and Sam's place, Kate felt a sense of reckless liberation that she'd not experienced in a very long time. Kate smiled, despite her tension, as, on Harry's car stereo, Foreigner implored them to know what love was. She laughed in the soft darkness at their shared love of bad rock music.

Harry drew up outside Aidan's house, and Kate turned to him. Feeling ridiculously brave and not at all like herself, she said, 'Would you like to come in for a coffee?'

Harry nodded. 'That would be lovely.' He parked the car and they walked up to the front door, Kate breaking free from Harry's protective arm which was around her to scrabble for her keys.

'Go through to the living room if you like,' she said. 'I won't be a tick with the coffee.'

Harry nodded and ambled off, and Kate took a moment to consider what she was about to do. She and Harry were in a holiday romance situation, that was all. Although painting houses was hardly a holiday for her, Willowbury *had* been a change of scene. And wasn't part of the holiday romance narrative that it gave you the chance to fling off real life, throw caution to the wind, and do things you wouldn't normally do? She was sure that was right, even if her sixteen-year-old son was in the house next door.

With slightly shaking hands Kate made a cafetière of coffee, arranged two mugs on a tray and brought it through to the living room, where Harry was ensconced on the sofa waiting.

'I promise not to spill this on you!' Kate said nervously as she carefully placed the tray on the coffee table in front of them.

'Glad to hear it.' Harry laughed softly, a sound that sent a flicker of desire through Kate. Suddenly, in this light, after a wonderful meal and that kiss on the green, she knew exactly what she wanted.

'Sod the coffee,' she murmured, moving closer to Harry until she felt his jeans-clad thigh brushing her own. 'I'd rather kiss you again, if that's all right.'

'No complaints here,' Harry murmured as Kate brought her lips to his, luxuriating in the taste and warmth of him.

A little while later, when the coffee had cooled and Kate was feeling like the teenager on holiday she'd remembered being all those years ago, she and Harry broke apart.

'We are very good at that,' Kate murmured. 'But the problem is, I have absolutely no idea what I'm supposed to do next.'

Harry smiled down at her. 'You're not supposed to do anything that you don't want to do.' He brushed a strand of hair out of her eyes. 'And I'm not in the habit of putting pressure on, so we can do whatever you want.'

'Now I really do feel like a teenager,' Kate replied. 'And the problem is, I feel like I've got the raging libido of a sixteen-year-old, too. What I'm worried about is that it's going to lead me into some very wild choices if we're not careful.'

Harry, in answer, pulled Kate towards him and onto his lap,

where she could feel an enticing hardness in his jeans. She wriggled provocatively and felt his hips thrust towards her reflexively. 'Keep doing that and I'm going to be following very close behind you in those wild choices.' His right hand tangled through her hair and stroked the back of her neck before he pulled her towards him for another kiss, into which he groaned.

'Would it be too shocking for me to admit that I basically want to drag you off to bed right now?' Kate said breathlessly.

'I promise not to be shocked,' Harry replied. 'But I have to warn you, I'm feeling a little rusty. It's been a while.'

Kate laughed. 'I'm so glad you said that. You're basically my first since...' she trailed off, then grinned. 'So, no pressure, then.'

Harry looked reflective for a moment. 'I promise not to judge if you don't. And we don't have to... you know. Let's see how it goes.'

'Agreed,' Kate replied. 'Although the way I'm feeling right now, don't be surprised if we end up swinging from the chandeliers!'

Harry looked wary. 'Are you sure they'll take our weight?'

'I'm willing to try if you are.' Reluctantly, but knowing she couldn't face the prospect of making love on Tom and Aidan's sofa and look them in the eye afterwards, she climbed off Harry's lap and took him by the hand to pull him up with her. 'Shall we?'

Without needing any further prompting, Harry followed Kate out of the room, leaving the coffee to stew gently in the cafetière, completely forgotten.

As Kate pushed open the door to the room where she'd been staying, Harry burst out laughing. 'A single bed? Seriously? It'll be like being a student again!'

Kate laughed, too. 'I know, but this room's so small, you'd never get anything bigger in here. It'll be cosy all right.'

'That it will,' Harry said, a husky note in his voice. 'But since I've got to open the shop in the morning, I probably shouldn't stay too long anyway.'

'You're going to love me and leave me, are you?' Kate said, then mentally kicked herself. 'Sorry. Rusty at this, as I said.'

In answer, Harry gathered her up in his arms and kicked the bedroom door shut behind him. 'Just keep doing what you were doing downstairs and we'll see how we go, shall we?'

They tumbled down onto the patchwork bedspread that adorned Kate's single bed, which was, thankfully, pushed up against the inside wall of the room. 'At least we're not in too much danger of falling out on that side,' Harry said.

Realising that the two of them were far from teenager sized, it soon became apparent that, in order to be comfortable, they'd have to press very close together. This wasn't really a problem; Kate found herself wanting to feel every inch of Harry against her, and there was no doubt, from what she could feel of Harry's body, that he felt the same way. But how far were they willing to go?

'Look, Harry,' Kate breathed as they began a slow, leisurely necking session on top of her bedspread. 'I was only half joking about being rusty.' She propped herself up on one elbow and looked down at him. His hair was dishevelled from her fingers running through it, and his face was flushed, eyes heavy with desire. She felt a warmth running through her core, just looking at him; the desire to know this man intimately was overwhelming.

'Kate,' Harry said softly. 'If I left it to my body to make the decisions right now, I'd be ripping your clothes off and making love until the sun came back up. But my head, not my cock, is in charge, if only by a fraction. You are under no obligation to put any part of you near any part of me. I'm happy to just kiss you on this ridiculous single bed until you throw me out. And if you do decide you want more... we can stop at any point.'

'Where were you twenty years ago?' Kate replied, touched beyond belief at his measured response to her indecision.

'I'm here now,' he whispered. 'So let's make the most of it, shall we?' He pulled her down on top of him so she could feel his whole length beneath her, and that sensation of being a teenager in a forbidden situation was shooting white hot bolts of lightning through her. She felt the throbbing, pulsing sense of arousal between her thighs. They hadn't even removed any of their clothes and she was ready to shag him senseless.

'Oh God, Harry,' Kate murmured. 'I think I'm ready to make some terribly bad choices.' She reached down Harry's body to cup the prominent bulge in his jeans.

'Glad to hear it,' Harry's voice was suddenly gruff with desire, and Kate knew at that moment that she was going to make the most of this time they had.

Just as she was unzipping his flies, and preparing to sneak an inquisitive hand into Harry's boxer shorts, the sound of the front door slamming made her jump out of her skin.

'Mum? Are you home?' Corey's voice came drifting up the stairs.

In a panic, Kate whipped her hand out of Harry's jeans and sat up hurriedly. 'Yeah,' she said, trying to make her voice sound as if she hadn't just been about to begin making love to her date. 'Everything okay? I thought you were pulling an all-nighter with Sam on *Call of Duty*.'

'That was the plan,' Corey said, 'but something came up.'

'If only,' Kate muttered, grinning apologetically at Harry, who was hastily doing up his flies.

'What was that, then?' Kate called, creeping towards the bedroom door. She motioned to Harry to stay put, mindful that, despite his evident liking for Harry, her son might not take too kindly to the prospect that his mother had been about to have sex on her first proper date in years. 'Give me a sec,' she whispered. 'I'll sneak you out in a minute.' Pulling open the door, stepping out swiftly and closing it behind her with an apologetic glance at Harry, she padded down the landing to the top of the stairs.

Corey was standing at the bottom of the stairs, snacking on the remains of the pizza that Sam had obviously sent home with him. Waiting until he'd finished his mouthful, he looked up at her. 'Florence has gone into labour, so they've headed over to the hospital. Sam figured I'd be better off sleeping back here tonight.'

'Oh my goodness,' Kate said, all thoughts of Harry forgotten. 'But she's not due for another two and a bit weeks.'

'Well, the baby must have had other ideas,' Corey said. As if noticing his mother's dishevelled appearance for the first time, he continued. 'Did you have a nice time? Were you in bed?'

'Er, yes, I did, thanks.' Kate knew she was blushing. 'I got in and must have nodded off.' She felt bad for lying to Corey, but the boy had been through so much over the past couple of years, she didn't want to freak him out by admitting that she wasn't alone. 'Look, er, why don't you head off to bed? I'll put the pizza box in the recycling. It's nearly midnight, after all, and I should probably phone Sam, see if everything's okay. You can use the bathroom first, if you want.'

'Okay.' Corey didn't seem to suspect anything was amiss. 'I'll see you in the morning. Do you think you might see Harry again? You know, have another date?'

Kate couldn't help the grin that spread across her face, both at Corey's innocent question and the thought of Harry himself stewing in her bedroom and, horrors, the cafetière and two untouched cups stewing in the living room, which would be a dead giveaway that she hadn't come home alone, too.

'I might,' she said, injecting a teasing note into her voice. 'Now get yourself off to bed.'

'Okay, okay,' Corey said. 'Night, Mum.'

'Goodnight, darling,' Kate replied. She waited until her son had passed her on the landing and she'd heard him lock the bathroom door behind himself before scampering back to her room.

'Quick,' she whispered, barely able to disguise her laughter as she saw Harry sitting on her bed like a teenager, flipping through his phone while he waited for her to come back. 'He's in the bathroom. You'll have to sneak out.'

Harry grinned. 'How exciting. Although not quite as exciting as what we were doing before Corey came home.' He stood up, strode over to where she was standing in the doorway and pulled her to him. 'You are the best kisser.'

'You're not so bad yourself,' Kate said, surrendering to another kiss before remembering that Harry was supposed to be leaving. 'Now, quick, get out before we both have some awkward questions to answer.'

Harry reluctantly disentangled himself and padded behind her down the stairs and to the front door. 'Can I see you again?' he asked as Kate opened the front door as quietly as she could.

'Yes,' she whispered. 'Definitely, definitely yes.' She kissed him again. 'If we'd stayed in the living room, we could have styled it out, but I don't really want to have to answer awkward questions from my son tonight. And I'm not sure I can just sit next to you and make polite conversation with him now I've stuck my hand in your trousers, either. Let's finish this soon.'

Harry moaned quietly as they kissed again. 'Very, very soon,' he said.

Kate giggled, but then swiftly shushed herself. 'I'll be thinking about *that* all night.'

'Me too.' Harry took her hand and pressed it against the fly of his jeans once more. 'You've given me *a lot* to think about.'

Kate pressed herself against Harry, trapping her hand against him and feeling more very definite stirrings. 'I can't believe Florence's baby's got such terrible timing. I'll be having words about that.'

'Goodnight, Kate,' Harry murmured. 'See you soon.'

'Goodnight, Harry,' Kate whispered. 'Now, quick, get out of here before Corey looks out of his bedroom window.'

As Harry left, Kate sagged against the door frame. She knew, without a doubt, she'd happily have had sex with Harry, had Corey not come home and put that prospect on ice. But there would be another time, she was sure. It was clear that he was as keen on her as she was on him. It was also clear, though, that new relationships were complicated, especially with children in the mix. At that thought, she realised she'd better send Sam a text and find out what was going on. After all, if there was going to be a new baby a little sooner than expected, she might be needed to help out.

37

Kate was still smiling as she cleared up the cafetière, and despite the fact that the coffee was well past its best, she poured out a cup to take up to bed, when her phone rang. So unaccustomed was she to actually using the phone to make or answer calls, she nearly dropped it onto the kitchen floor. Scrabbling to get hold of it, her heart leapt when she saw it was Sam, who she'd intended to text before she went to bed. It was a little soon, perhaps, for news of Florence and the baby, but then, as she knew from personal experience, these things didn't go by a stopwatch. Corey had been delivered so quickly she and Phil had barely made it to the hospital before his head had crowned, whereas Will had been a thirty-five hour labour and almost ended up in a C-section. Tom, after that, actually had been a Caesarean – but a planned one, this time.

'Hey,' she said, once she'd managed to locate the green button on screen. 'How are you and Florence doing? Corey told me you had to make a mad dash to the hospital.'

There was momentary silence on the line, and then Kate heard the drawing of a shaky breath. 'Sam?' she asked, a slow, rolling panic beginning in her stomach and rising up her throat. 'What is it? What's happened?'

Another breath, one with a definite shudder this time. Then what felt like an age before he spoke. 'Can you get here, Katie? To Magdalene Park Hospital?'

'Of course.' Kate jumped up from her seat, hastily thrusting aside the coffee cup as she did so. 'Tell me what's going on, Sam. Is Florence okay? Is the baby okay?'

'Oh Christ...' his voice trailed off again, and Kate's heart thumped, fearing the worst.

'Sam, what is it? Please, tell me.'

'Just come,' Sam's voice came eventually. 'I – we – need you.'

'I'll be there as soon as I can,' Kate said, forcing a calm she didn't feel into her voice. Her hands were shaking so badly, she could barely hold the phone. 'Can you tell me what's going on?'

Sam drew another shuddery breath that echoed down the phone line. 'It all happened so fast. I'll explain when you get here.'

'I'm leaving now.' Dashing back upstairs, she drew a deep breath before knocking on Corey's bedroom door. Corey was getting ready for bed, sliding his gangly frame into a T-shirt, hair still wet from the shower. She felt a rush of affection for her eldest, precious boy, and all of a sudden she remembered how over-whelming it was to become a parent. She had the instant, burning desire to gather all three of her children close, to have them back under one roof again. She couldn't imagine what Sam must be going through. Something was clearly very, very wrong.

'Sam's just rung me,' Kate said. 'He wants me to meet him over at Magdalene Park Hospital.'

Corey's face registered concern, then panic, and Kate cursed herself for her own shaky tone. 'What's wrong? Is it the baby?'

'I'm not quite sure, love. I'll know more when I get there.'

'Is Florence okay?' Corey walked up to Kate, and she pulled him close in a hug to fortify them both.

'I'll call you as soon as I know anything. Will you be all right for the rest of the night if I head over to the hospital to help out?'

'Sure.' Corey smiled, but Kate could see how upset he was at the news. 'Let me know if there's anything I can do.'

'I will. Thanks, love. And if anything comes up, or you're unsure about anything, call me.'

'Just go, Mum. I'll be fine. Uncle Sam and Aunt Florence need you.' As Kate released Corey from her embrace, she gave what she hoped was an encouraging smile.

'I'll speak to you soon.' Kissing him on the forehead, she headed swiftly back down the stairs.

Kate grabbed her handbag and a hoodie from the hooks by the front door, changed her shoes into a more practical pair of Converse, then checked that she had car and house keys before she pulled open the door and stepped out into the dusky summer night. Her hands were shaking so badly that she could barely hold the steering wheel. What if Florence, heaven forbid, had died? How would Sam cope with being a single father to a child only hours old? No, she couldn't think like that; she had to stay positive. Sam hadn't made much sense on the phone, understandably; she'd find out more when she got there.

As she sped the miles between Willowbury and the hospital in Taunton, Kate's mind flashed back to all three of her own births. At the time they had been shattering, physically and emotionally, but she and Phil had, despite the shell shock, got through those tough days with overwhelming love for the babies they'd created between them. Even though the marriage was over, she'd forever be grateful for the children. What if Florence never got the chance to be the mother she'd been so excited to be?

Pulling into the hospital car park a little time later, Kate barely remembered to lock her car before she was dashing through the doors, desperate to find Sam. She followed the signs to the maternity ward, and it was only then that she hesitated. Would they even let her in at this time? Were visiting hours for relations over? Thinking that the best course of action was to call Sam and let him know she was here, she was just swiping her phone to get to his number when she caught sight of him through the window of the sturdy double doors that led to the ward. Even from that distance, she could see the haunted look of his body language.

At a loss as to how to attract his attention, she was relieved when he looked over to the door. Hurrying to the button that released the door, he pulled it swiftly shut after him and joined her just outside in the corridor.

'Katie, thank Christ you're here,' he said, his voice marginally stronger than it had seemed on the phone.

For a moment, Kate was lost for words, so, reaching out, she enfolded Sam in the firmest hug she could muster. 'What happened? Where're Florence and the baby?'

As Sam broke away from her, he ran a weary hand over his eyes, which only looked marginally less haunted now that she was here with him. 'Florence went into labour this evening, about three hours after Corey came over,' he said. 'We'd been warned that because of the way the placenta was lying, it might happen. At first we thought it was just a false alarm, but we decided it was best to make a move when the contractions got to five minutes apart.'

'Sensible decision,' Kate said.

'Our daughter was born fairly quickly, but there was an issue with the placenta; it just wouldn't budge. And then...' He swallowed hard, obviously struggling to relive the frantic post-birth moments. 'Florence started bleeding. Badly. Christ, Katie, even flying patients to hospital like I do, I've never seen someone lose so much blood so quickly.' Sam was well used to the daily traumas of the emergency services, having served as a pilot in the Somerset Air Ambulance for the past three and a bit years. He'd often spoken of the ability to shut off and do the job, to put things into boxes while the medics tended to patients in flight, even if the trauma caught up with him afterwards, but this was different. This was very, very personal.

'Oh God, Sam,' Kate whispered. 'I'm so sorry.' She reached out and squeezed his hand. They'd paused in the corridor.

'They took her to theatre about an hour ago,' Sam continued. 'When someone came down to tell me how she was, they told me they'd had to give her a massive blood transfusion. They're still working on her.' He raked his hand impatiently over his eyes, although the tears hadn't yet spilt.

'And the baby?' Kate asked. 'Where is she?'

Sam, despite the horrors of the past few hours, managed a small smile. 'She's in the nursery. I was with her until I figured you were close to the hospital.'

'Can I see her?'

'Give me a minute and I'll check with the staff. Being as it's so late, they probably won't let you in, but I'll see what they say.'

Kate waited as Sam hurried off, hoping against hope that she'd be permitted through the security doors. She'd never seen Sam so shaken up, even when their brother, Aidan, had been at his worst after Helmand, and she ached to comfort him.

In a minute or two Sam was back, a midwife from the ward at his side.

'You can come in for a few minutes, if you're super quiet,' she said. Then, turning to Sam, 'There's a small visitors' room just off to the right down the corridor. I'll let you know when Florence comes back down from theatre.'

'Thanks, Claire.' Sam smiled briefly. 'I appreciate it.' He turned back to Kate. 'I'll go and get her.'

The midwife, Claire, walked with the two of them to the visitors'

room, and then headed back to the desk, which was situated immediately on the other side of the hall. Kate had the feeling that Sam
had called in a pretty big favour to get her through the security
door at this time of night, and was relieved.

In a few more moments, Sam was heading back down the
corridor with a snugly wrapped bundle in his arms. As they drew
closer, Kate stood, unable to wait to see her new niece.

'Oh, Sam...' Kate breathed. 'She's beautiful.'

Sam nodded, and then, finally, his face crumpled. 'What am I
going to do if Florence doesn't pull through, Katie?' he croaked. 'I
can't do this on my own.'

'You mustn't think like that,' Kate said, her heart thumping
wildly in her own chest at the same, horrible thought. 'She's in the
best place. They'll do everything they can.' She looked again at the
little newborn bundle in Sam's arms.

Sam nodded, and walked on shaky legs to the nearest comfy
chair. Kate moved a little closer to them, to get a longer look at
Sam's little daughter. Inhaling that exquisite newborn scent, she
was transported back to what it had been like to cradle her own
babies in that emotional time straight after they'd been born.

For a few minutes they sat there, drawing strength from each
other, trying to distract themselves from what Florence was going
through by focusing on the little bundle in Sam's arms. Seeing a
kettle tucked in the corner of the visitors' room, in a small kitchen
area, she was suddenly aware of just how late it was.

'Shall I make us a coffee?' Kate asked.

'Thanks,' Sam said, still not taking his eyes off the baby.

'It's okay,' Kate said softly. 'You won't drop her.'

Sam looked up and managed a small smile. 'It feels so different
to holding my nephews all those years ago.'

'It's bound to,' Kate said. 'She's yours. Yours and Florence's. And soon Florence is going to be demanding all the cuddles, so I'd make the most of them while you can.'

'I hope you're right, Katie,' Sam said, his voice cracking again. 'I really, really, hope you're right.'

As Kate walked over and flipped the switch on the kettle, she wished she felt as optimistic as she'd tried to sound. Just the thought of losing Florence was enough to make her stomach turn, and she couldn't begin to imagine how Sam would feel if the absolute worst happened. *Please God*, she thought as she went in search of coffee, *make this all be okay*.

A few minutes later, with two coffees made, Kate carefully put them down on the table in front of the chair where Sam was sitting. For a moment Kate took some time to watch the two of them, seeing the powerful bond that had taken hold of them both, and hoping against hope that Florence would soon be there to share it.

'Christ, it's at times like this I miss Dad,' Sam said quietly as she sat back down.

Kate's eyes burned as she thought about how pleased their father would have been to have had another grandchild, and his first granddaughter. 'I miss him too.' Leaning forward, she placed a hand on Sam's arm, trying to give, as well as find strength. She'd never been good with words, always afraid to say too much, and then ending up saying far too little. But somehow she knew she had to say something now. In the aching absence of their father, it was down to her, as the eldest sibling.

'He'd be so proud of you, Sam, if he could see you now.' She squeezed his arm gently, not wanting to wake the sleeping bundle in his arms. 'I mean, he always was, but what you've been through in the past few years... he'd have wanted so much to meet this little one.'

Sam blinked furiously and, mindful of the bundle in his arms, wiped his eyes with the back of one hand. 'I wish he was here, Katie. I just... I don't know what to do.'

Kate wrapped an arm around his shoulders. 'I wish I could tell you it was going to be all right, Sam, I really do,' she said, leaning into him and stroking his hair back from his face. 'You have to put your trust in the doctors. They'll have seen this so many times. You have to hope.'

'I know, but, Katie... I can't lose her.' He looked up at her, his eyes huge and scared in his tired face. He looked like the terrified boy he'd been so many years ago when he'd accidentally thrown their brother Aidan off the family see-saw and concussed him. 'I can't... she's everything. Katie, what am I going to do if... if...' He choked back another sob.

'It's not going to come to that,' Kate whispered. 'You, and Florence, and this little one will be back home before you know it.'

'But what if we aren't? What if I'm walking out of here with just the baby? What the hell am I going to do?' He was shaking so badly that Kate genuinely feared he was going to drop his daughter.

'Here, let me take her for a bit,' she said, gently trying to disentangle the baby from Sam's grip.

'No, let me keep her. What if she's all I have left of Florence?' Sam's trembling worsened, and Kate realised he was about a hair's breadth from a full-blown meltdown.

'Sam.' She knelt beside him so that he could see her more clearly. 'I promise I'm not going to take her away from you. Let me have her for a few minutes, just so you can have a break.'

Sam thought about that for a long moment, and then, with a shaky sigh, he handed the baby over. Kate gratefully took the little girl, holding her close.

'Go and stretch your legs in the corridor,' Kate said quietly. 'You don't have to go far.' She smoothed the sleeping baby's hair back from her little face and felt her heart contract at the thought that this little mite may not get to meet her mother. What if Sam was right, and he really did end up leaving hospital alone? Kate's heart pounded again at the prospect and she clutched her baby niece closer to her for comfort. The prospect of that was unthinkable.

39

After what seemed like hours, but was probably only a few minutes, Sam was returning to the visitors' room when a consultant popped her head around the door, then, catching sight of Sam down the corridor, approached him, just out of Kate's earshot. Torn between wanting to go to him and not wanting to disturb the baby in her arms, she saw the doctor turning towards Sam, so that her view of her brother's expression was obscured. Kate waited, panic rising, witnessing but unable to hear, what was being said. She could see Sam nodding, the tension in his body palpable, and the doctor reaching out a hand to touch his arm as she gave him the news.

Unable to bear it any longer, Kate wandered out of the nursery, still carrying Sam's new daughter.

'Florence's blood loss was extensive, but we managed to stabilise her and give her a transfusion. She was very poorly for quite a while,' the consultant was explaining as Kate reached them.

'Can I see her?' Sam asked.

The consultant nodded. 'They're bringing her down to the ward now. Do you want to come down to her bed?'

Sam, unable to speak, just nodded.

'You know how it is, Sam, doing what you do, so I'm not going to lie to you,' she continued, 'it wasn't looking good for quite a while, and Florence might need to stay with us for a few days, but she's over the worst now.'

Kate watched as Sam's jaw gritted hard, in an attempt not to lose control in front of the consultant. Eventually, he gave a tight, relieved smile. 'Thank you for all that you've done.'

'Go and wait for her,' the consultant said. 'She's still out for the count, but when she wakes up, I bet she'd love to meet her daughter.'

Sam nodded, and Kate drew closer as the consultant left.

'She's going to be all right, Katie,' Sam choked. 'She's going to be all right.'

Kate nodded, tiredness and relief overwhelming her as she saw the look of absolute relief on Sam's face, too. Just as she was about to reach out to him, the baby stirred in her arms and snuffled a little.

'I think you'd better have her back now,' Kate said softly. 'Florence'll be wanting to say hello to her daughter, and she'll be due a feed, too, soon.'

'And you ought to get home,' Sam said. 'I'm sorry to drag you out here in the middle of the night, and away from Corey.'

'Corey's crashed out at home.' Kate smiled. 'I think you knackered him out with the pizza and PlayStation.'

'He's a great kid,' Sam replied. 'And he seems really happy here. When did you say he was going back?'

'Not sure yet,' Kate said. 'He wasn't terribly happy staying with Phil, so I've said we'll see how it goes. I was actually thinking of getting Will and Tom down here for a bit, too. I miss them.'

'I bet,' Sam said. He leaned forward, mindful of the baby in his arms, and gave Kate a brief hug. 'I'd better go and wait for Florence to come down. I'll call you as soon as I can.'

'Send her my love when she wakes up,' Kate whispered. 'And I'll see you both – all – soon.' Reaching out a hand to stroke the head of Sam's tiny daughter, she smiled. 'You'll be all right now.'

'See you soon,' Sam replied. 'Oh, and how was your date with Harry?'

Kate blinked, exhaustion and the drama of the evening suddenly making dinner seem an awfully long time ago. 'It was fine,' she said, with some surprise. 'In fact, it was lovely.'

'Glad to hear it.' Sam gave her a tired smile.

Leaving Sam to wait for Florence, Kate made her way out of the security doors and, so tired, her feet felt as though they were guiding her back out of the hospital. As she began the drive through the winding, middle of the night dark lanes between Taunton and Willowbury, she mused on the extremes of the evening. Before midnight, all she'd been thinking about was making mad, passionate love to Harry in her single bed in her brother's house. The thrill of that encounter was still lingering in her bones and tantalising her senses. And yet, that had only, in the end, been part of a far more complicated picture. The tragic irony that Harry would never get to experience holding his newborn child in his arms, just as Sam had tonight, and the horror at the prospect that Florence had very nearly died giving birth to that child, was entirely too much to comprehend at this late hour.

She pulled into the parking space at the side of Bay Tree Terrace wearily, and even at half past three in the morning it was already getting light. The earthy, herby scent of the night stocks in the back gardens of Bay Tree Terrace reached her as she locked up the car, along with the heavy balsam smell of conifers in the woodlands beyond, stronger in the small hours. Creeping through the front door, she stopped briefly on her way to bed to check in on Corey, who was fast asleep. She decided not to wake him. Florence was out of danger now, and there was no point reliving the horrors of the night with him right now. As she padded into her own room, too tired to even brush her teeth, she stripped off quickly and pulled the covers over her head, exhaustion overcoming adrenaline, and she crashed out immediately.

40

The next morning, after a night spent regrettably but understandably alone, Harry opened up Vale Volumes to find his newest sales assistant already standing outside.

'I ought to pay you overtime!' Harry joked as he let Corey into the shop. 'I wasn't sure I'd see you after last night.' He immediately mentally kicked himself. Corey wasn't supposed to know he'd been hiding up in Kate's bedroom when he'd come back to break the news about Florence going into labour.

Corey smiled as he walked through the door of the shop, apparently not noticing Harry's slip-up. 'Oh, did Mum text you and tell you about Florence?'

'Um, yep,' Harry said, busying himself with rearranging the latest pile of commercial fiction releases on the table near the front of the shop. He didn't want to lie to Corey, but that had been a close one.

'Well, Mum dashed off to the hospital because Florence was really ill,' Corey replied. 'But thankfully, she seems to have got through it, and now I've got a new baby cousin.'

'Congratulations,' Harry said. 'Your aunt and uncle must be

thrilled.'

'From what Mum said, they were too scared to be thrilled last night, but hopefully now Florence is on the mend, they can be happy, too.'

'I'm sure they will be.' Harry paused before adding, 'Is your mum okay?'

Corey smiled. 'She's a bit knackered after spending most of last night in the hospital, but she seemed all right when I left this morning. She was still in bed when I left, but I told her I was off to work. That's when she told me Sam and Florence were okay. Don't think she'll be getting much work done on Uncle Aidan's house today, though!'

'Perhaps I'll take her round a coffee and a Danish later,' Harry said. 'That's if you don't mind keeping an eye on this place for half an hour.'

'You'd leave me alone?' Corey asked. 'Really? I mean, I haven't exactly been working here long.'

'If you're okay with that,' Harry said. 'You've really proved yourself. I think you can handle keeping an eye on a quiet old bookshop for half an hour. And if anything comes up, just call me, or pop next door and see Mariad in the next shop.'

'Thanks,' Corey said. 'It's cool that you trust me. I won't let you down.'

'I know,' Harry replied. 'You've done really well this week. It's a shame you have to go home soon or I'd offer you a weekend job. I could always do with an extra pair of hands, especially when the tourists come.'

'And you seem to, er, be getting on well with Mum,' Corey said carefully. 'I mean, she seemed really happy when I got home last night. It's nice to see her enjoying herself again.'

You have no idea, Harry thought.

'We had a good meal and it was a nice evening,' Harry said

discreetly. 'But I know she's going home at the end of the summer, too, so I'm not getting my hopes up about things getting too serious.'

'Why? Wouldn't you want that?' Corey said, and Harry noticed a defensive note in his voice.

'It's not that simple, Corey,' Harry said, calmly. 'You and your mum are only here for a few weeks more. No matter what I might want, that's the truth of it.'

'So you're not serious about her, then? You're just, like *having fun*?' The implication was obvious, and Corey's face began to flush. Harry realised he'd have to tread carefully. The boy might seem outwardly unfazed by his developing relationship with Kate, but that didn't mean he wasn't unnerved and possibly upset underneath.

'I'm not going to hurt her,' Harry said softly. 'I know she's had a difficult time over the past couple of years. We like each other. A lot. But there are things to think about.'

Corey's face was grim, and Harry wondered if he'd managed to say the right thing. This was such tricky territory. He and Corey had been getting on really well, and he was worried that, if he got it wrong now, Corey would feel alienated, which was the last thing he wanted.

'I get it,' Corey replied. 'It's like, just for the summer? Have a bit of fun and then move on?'

'Corey,' Harry said gently. 'Adult relationships can't just fit into little boxes like that; especially when there are children to think about, too.' As Corey seemed to baulk at the idea of being called a child, Harry rapidly continued, 'I mean, your mum's not daft, and neither am I. I promise you, you don't need to worry.'

Corey looked back at him, and just for a moment, Harry caught a glimpse of the hurt and insecurity the teenager obviously felt about things. He remembered, if only from back in the days when he was that age himself, that it was possible to feel extremes of emotion in the blink of an eye, and he could understand why Corey might be struggling.

'Look,' he said, 'how about you grab those copies of the new Jeffrey Archer from the stockroom. If we leave them there any longer, he'll probably have written another one by the time we remember to put them out! And while you're doing that, I'll make us a cup of tea.'

This proposition seemed to work. Corey smiled and apologised. 'I'm sorry, Harry,' he said. 'It's just a bit weird when I think about it, you know. And I'm glad Mum's happy, honestly.'

Breathing a sigh of relief that a teenage storm seemed to have been averted, Harry wondered if he ought to mention the conversation to Kate, the next time he saw her. He'd never dated anyone with teenage sons before, and he hoped he'd handled things properly. After all, despite what his body had been screaming at him last night in Kate's bedroom, it was still early days, and she was, to the best of his knowledge, going back to Cambridge at the end of the summer. But if a summer fling was all this was, why did the thought of Kate leaving fill him with more than a little bit of sadness? It had been a long time since he'd been in love with someone; could it be that he was falling for her?

There was no point in thinking that way. More than likely, he was just lonely and out of practise. Kate was a lovely, warm and attractive woman and he enjoyed spending time with her, but she was clearly cautious after her divorce. And no matter how well he got on with Corey, Kate had two other sons to consider, too. It was better to take each day as it came and not to get too hung up on what would happen once the summer was over. He was rooted in Somerset, and she had all of her significant connections in Cambridge. Even with high-speed rail links, it couldn't work... could it?

41

Kate woke on Saturday morning feeling groggy and disorientated. Usually, she was up with the birds, but after not getting back from the hospital until nearly four, she'd crashed into bed and slept late. She vaguely remembered Corey popping in before heading off to Vale Volumes, but she must have dropped right off again after that. Glancing at her phone on the bedside table, she realised it was nearly ten o'clock. While she was effectively her own boss on this decorating job, she hated getting up late, and cursed as she got out of bed, staggering to the shower and turning it on to its coldest setting in an attempt to blast away any lingering tiredness.

After she'd got dressed and before she made breakfast, she texted Sam to see how things were with Florence. To her surprise and relief, he video-called her back almost straight away.

'Hey,' she said once his camera came up on her screen. 'How are you doing? And, more importantly, how are Florence and the baby?'

'See for yourself,' Sam replied, panning his phone around. After a quick, flickering adjustment, Kate smiled widely to see her sister-in-law sitting up in bed, with her baby in her arms.

'Hey,' she said again. 'How are you feeling?'

'Like my undercarriage has been hit by a ten-tonne truck!' Florence said. 'But apart from that, not too bad.'

Kate winced. 'I hope you've got a decent cushion to sit on.'

'They've given me some good drugs,' Florence said, 'but I can't take them home with me, so I'm making the most of them while I can.'

'You do that,' Kate laughed. 'And how's the baby?'

Sam re-angled his phone so that Kate could get a better view of the family's newest addition.

'Can we introduce Mia Katherine Ellis to you?' Florence said softly. 'Safe and sound, and more than ready to come home.'

Kate's eyes prickled. 'I can't wait to see you all in person.'

'We thought Katherine might make a good middle name,' Sam's voice drifted from the other side of the phone. 'And guarantee a few decent Christmas presents from her Aunt Katie for the rest of her life!'

'Cheeky bugger,' Kate muttered, but she was truly touched. 'So, when can you come home?'

'Well, they want to make sure my haemoglobin levels are back up to where they should be, and that I can actually feed this child properly before they let us out, but with a bit of luck, I'll be home by the day after tomorrow,' Florence said. 'To be honest, even though I'm going to miss the painkillers, I'm dying to get out of here.'

Kate winced again. Perhaps she could blame the drugs Florence was on for the turn of phrase, but having seen the state Sam was in last night, it all felt a bit too recent. 'Well, let me know when you're due back and I'll make sure you've got some dinner to come home to.'

'Thanks, Katie.' Sam's face came back into view. 'And thanks for last night. I'm sorry I was freaking out so much.'

'It's completely understandable,' Kate said. 'Now, get off the call and help your wife with that beautiful baby.'

'I will. See you soon.'

And with that, they were gone. Kate smiled. It was good to see them looking so cheerful after the trauma of Mia's birth. They might still be running on adrenaline for a few days, but she felt sure they'd work through it. And at least, with Mia coming early, Kate could help out if she was needed.

As she made herself a cup of tea and contemplated breakfast, she smiled as she saw that, while she was making the tea, Harry had texted her:

I had a great time last night. Shame we had to leave it where we did. Hope all is well with Sam, Florence and the baby. Are you free for a coffee sometime this morning? My new employee is desperate for some responsibility! If you're feeling tired, I can bring Danish and caffeine to you... Hx

Bless Harry, she thought fondly. Although she wondered just how wise it was to leave Vale Volumes in the hands of a sixteen-year-old, even if he would be seventeen next month. Then, she rationalised, it was hardly likely that a fight was going to break out in a bookshop, was it? What was the worst that could go wrong for the sake of half an hour? Texting back a quick yes, she suggested he came over for about half past eleven, which would give her some time to get her head together and hopefully paint out the bags under her eyes, if not do any more on the house. *Was that allowed*, she thought? And then she realised that if Corey was working in Vale Volumes, he wouldn't be back home to interrupt them when Harry came over. Did that mean... she stopped those thoughts in their tracks.

The past twenty-four hours had been entirely too much of a

rollercoaster to throw any more complications into the mix. She and Harry would simply have coffee and cake, and she could fill him in on the events of the small hours of the morning: nothing more. After all, last night had only technically been their first date, and wasn't there some rule about going out seven times before sleeping with someone? She'd virtually got to third base in a single bed in her brother's house after having one dinner with the guy. *No*, she thought as she raced upstairs to her bedroom and dragged out her make-up bag; *I'm not going to rush into anything*.

42

'*Two* coffees? Got company?' Jack's eyes gleamed as he took Harry's order and started to make up the lattes.

Harry grinned. 'Just dropping in to see a friend who had a late night, that's all.'

'Anyone I know?'

'Maybe.'

'You old dog... you asked Kate out, didn't you? Was she high on gloss paint fumes when she said yes, or could she just not resist the smell of fusty old books?'

'We had a good dinner,' Harry said, 'and I thought she might like a cup of coffee while she carries on painting her brother's house.'

'Not breakfast in bed, then?' Jack raised an eyebrow suggestively.

Harry's expression must have given something more away than he'd intended, as Jack's eyebrow was joined by a smirk. 'There's definitely something you're not telling me, isn't there?'

'I don't kiss and tell,' Harry said briskly. 'And that milk's going to boil over if you don't watch what you're doing.'

Jack pulled the jug out from under the steamer just in time, and swiftly topped up the reusable coffee cups that Harry had brought in with him. He put them both in a cardboard takeaway tray and then handed Harry the bag with the Danish pastries. 'Enjoy.'

'I will. Thanks, Jack.'

'Pleasure's all mine. Keep me posted.' He gave Harry a wink, which Harry didn't dignify with a response.

A few minutes later, Harry knocked on the door of number one, Bay Tree Terrace. Kate answered swiftly. She still looked a little tired, but after last night that wasn't surprising.

'Hey,' she said, opening the door wider. 'You're a sight for very sore eyes.' She led him through to the living room, where he deposited the coffees and Danish pastries on the coffee table. As he straightened back up, Kate was standing close behind him. His heart thumped as she reached up on tiptoes and gave him a kiss on the mouth, and he could taste toothpaste and feel the warmth of that mouth. Treacherous thoughts began to creep into his mind about how things could have gone the night before.

'The last time we put coffee on that table it went cold,' he said as Kate moved away from him again.

'Can't let that happen again,' Kate teased. 'Anyway, it wouldn't be right to leave Corey in charge of the bookshop for too long. He is still only a trainee!'

'You're right, of course,' Harry said, still feeling a bit regretful. 'But I couldn't resist coming over to see you after our swift goodbye last night. How's Florence?'

Kate sat down on the sofa and took the cup of coffee that Harry had bought her out of the tray. After a long, reviving sip, she replied. 'Out of the woods, thank goodness. Baby Mia came quickly and poor Florence haemorrhaged. Sam was in bits by the time I got there.' She frowned at the memory. 'He's an air ambulance pilot so he sees a lot of medical drama every day, but it's different when it's your own family.'

'Of course,' Harry said gently. 'I can't imagine what he must have been through.'

'But thankfully Florence came out the other side and was wide awake and desperate to get home when I spoke to them this morning. And Mia's fine, too, so that's a weight off everyone's mind.'

'Long night for you, in the end, though,' Harry said, sipping his own coffee.

'It was a bit. I think I fell into bed just before four o'clock, so I'm feeling it a bit.'

'Seems like a good reason to take things easy today,' Harry said. 'Why don't you and Corey come over to dinner tonight? I'll cook something hearty and undemanding and we can all relax.'

Kate smiled. 'That sounds great. I'm sure Corey would appreciate that after a day on his feet in the shop, too.'

'Is there anything he, or you, don't eat?'

'He's a teenage boy and so will eat anything you put in front of him.' Kate took a bite of her Danish pastry. 'I'm allergic to prawns, though.'

'Noted.' Harry smiled at her. 'It'll be nice to relax a bit.'

Kate suddenly looked very uncertain, and Harry immediately sensed her unease.

'What's wrong?'

'Nothing... really. I think I'm just tired.'

Realising that this was only part of the story, Harry turned to face Kate on the sofa and shifted a little closer. 'Are you sure?'

Harry's heart tumbled in his chest as Kate's eyes filled with tears and she shook her head. 'It's stupid... after last night and everything... I haven't really had time to process what happened. What if Florence really *had* died on the operating table? Poor Sam would have been left alone with a baby only minutes old. I've never seen him look so scared.' She wiped her eyes furiously with the back of one hand. 'And yet, it's all worked out fine, so why am I thinking like that?'

Harry reached forward and enfolded her in a warm embrace. 'You're probably still in shock. It makes you replay things over and over again. And it all only happened a few hours ago. Give it time to sink in. And give yourself a break.'

As Kate snuggled into him, obviously drawing warmth and reassurance from his presence, Harry's emotions whirled around his brain. He felt so protective of this woman and her son, who'd come so randomly into his life, and yet the sadness of what he'd never had, and never would have, was also creeping up on him. Sam and Florence had welcomed a new life into their world and it had made them a family. That was a gift he had no hope of achieving, and no right to ask for. For the first time in a long time, the enormity of what had happened to him in his early twenties came crashing over him like a freezing cold wave on a beach in January. He couldn't help a shaky breath or two of his own. What the hell was he doing, getting involved so quickly with a woman who had troubles and a family of her own?

As if sensing his conflict, Kate drew back from him again and looked up into his eyes. Her own were red-rimmed with tiredness and tears, and Harry felt his heart turning over again. This was starting to feel like far more than a summer fling for him, and he wasn't sure how to proceed from here. Things had escalated emotionally so quickly in such a short space of time. And he hadn't even met her other two sons.

'Are *you* okay?' Kate asked gently. 'I mean, this must be stirring up a lot of memories for you, too.'

Harry smiled down at her. 'I won't lie and say that it hasn't, but it's not about me. I want to be a part of your life, Kate, whether that's as a friend on this side of the country when you come to visit your family here, or something more. I love spending time with you, and I want to get to know you much, much better. If you want the same thing, then that's wonderful.'

'I don't know what I want, Harry,' Kate said. 'I wish I did, but so much of my life is in flux right now. For the moment, I want to take each day as it comes, see how things go.'

'I understand,' said Harry. 'Things are a lot simpler for me than they are for you. There's just me, and the shop, and the odd weird author to contend with. I'm here, if you need me, if you want me to be, as whatever you need me to be.'

Kate smiled again. 'I appreciate that, Harry, I really do. You're a patient man.'

'I never used to be!' Harry laughed. 'But I learned to slow down and wait for the things and people that were worth waiting for. I suppose living in Willowbury's taught me that; it's worked its own peculiar brand of magic on me, and no mistake.'

'Careful,' Kate laughed, 'you're sounding like an old hippy. What would your former self say if he heard you talking like that?'

'He'd never believe his ears,' Harry said softly. Putting his coffee mug down on the table, he edged towards Kate. 'Now, I really ought to get back and relieve your son in the shop. May I kiss you before I go?'

Kate laughed. 'Well, since you asked so nicely...'

Kate's mouth tasted of coffee and the sweetness of the Danish, and as Harry's tongue explored, he felt the blood rushing southwards in a sharp, stinging reminder of where they'd nearly gone the night before. He'd never reacted quite so instantly to a woman, even when he'd been a sex-mad teenager. There was something about the way she tasted, the way her lips felt against his, that got him achingly hard in seconds.

As if she sensed this, Kate deepened the kiss, pulling him closer to her, almost on top of her as she sank down onto the oversized cushions of the sofa until his arms slid around her, and his hips pressed tantalisingly against hers, reminding him just how hard he was in his jeans and how thick two layers of denim seemed when you were turned on and fully clothed.

Just as they were coming up for air, a voice, surprised but definitely amused, came from the doorway.

'Well, I thought you were supposed to be painting walls while you stayed here, not snogging guys on my brand-new sofa!'

Springing apart from Kate, Harry drew in a sharp breath as he saw two other men, a couple of years younger than Kate by the looks of them, standing in the doorway of the living room.

'Aidan! Tom!' Kate sat up abruptly, running a hand through her hair to try to smooth it. 'What are you doing back so soon?'

'Got bored of all of the amazing food and scenery and thought we'd cut the holiday short,' one of the guys said. He glanced fondly in the other man's direction. 'Someone here was also getting jitters about the new production, as rehearsals officially start next week. Thought we'd get an earlier flight.'

Harry could see Kate's face flaming as she took all of this in.

'So aren't you going to introduce me to your friend?' the first man asked, grinning broadly.

'Of course,' Kate replied hurriedly, obviously trying to regain the upper hand. 'Harry, this is my brother, Aidan, and his husband, Tom.'

Harry smiled, deciding it was best to pretend as if he hadn't just been caught snogging on the sofa like a teenager. He stood up, thankful his shirt was now untucked, and wandered across the room. 'Nice to meet you.' Glancing back at Kate, he added, 'I'll, er, get back to the shop so Corey can have a tea break. See you about seven?'

'Sure,' Kate said. 'See you later.'

As Harry hurried from the house, the warm, knowing smiles of the two men who owned it seemed to follow behind him, and he wondered what kind of a ribbing Kate was now going to get from her brother and his husband.

43

Kate had, thankfully, despite Aidan's jibes to the contrary, made impressive headway with the redecoration of the house. She was pleased to see and hear her brother's expressions of pleasure over the quality of the job, and how right Tom had been with the colour combinations. It would only take a few more days' work now to finish off the skirting boards upstairs and the odd touch-up here and there, and the work would be done. She'd intended to stay for a little longer once Tom and Aidan came home to spend some time with them anyway, and she hoped she'd still be able to do so, even with Corey in tow. In fact, she wondered if now might be a good time to get Will and Tom over for a few days. Phil had been more than generous in his offer to have them for the whole summer, but after everything that happened with baby Mia and Florence, Kate felt a strong desire to see all three of her children. It would be a lovely opportunity for them to meet their new cousin, and, although it would be a bit of a squeeze, all four of them in Tom and Aidan's two spare rooms, seeing them would make up for it.

Over coffee, Kate had filled Tom and Aidan in on Corey's sudden appearance in Willowbury, too.

'Well, I'm not surprised he decided to push off down here really,' Aidan said as he reached for a chocolate digestive. 'He and Phil don't have a lot in common, do they?'

'I didn't have a lot of choice, leaving them with Phil,' Kate protested, stung by Aidan's directness. She knew, because of his experiences in Helmand Province as an army officer, and his subsequent discharge from the army on medical grounds, that the nature of his injuries sometimes made him more blunt than he realised, but she still felt jolted. 'It was hardly as though I could bring all three of them here with me for the whole summer. I'd never have got *anything* done.'

'I'm not criticising you, Kate,' Aidan said more gently. 'It was the best decision, and a pragmatic one. And despite Corey making a bad choice as to how he got here, he seems to have settled in okay from what you've said. Even got himself a summer job.'

Kate nodded. 'He was over the moon when Harry offered him the work experience.'

'You seemed pretty happy yourself when we came home,' Tom said wryly.

Kate's cheeks burned. 'It's nothing serious.'

'Kate,' Aidan chided, putting down his coffee cup, 'it doesn't matter if it is or not. After all of the shit Phil put you through, you deserve a little fun. And you looked like you were having it, too.'

'We were just kissing,' Kate said, but she could hear the defensive tone in her voice. 'We weren't about to make mad passionate love on your sofa!'

'I should hope not,' Aidan said. 'I mean, Tom and I haven't even christened it yet!'

'Gross!' Kate threw the remains of her biscuit at her brother.

'The feeling's mutual, sis.' Aidan laughed, catching the biscuit and swallowing it down. 'Just because you're having fun doesn't mean I want to walk in on it! And from what he said, you've already made plans for tonight, so don't let us coming home change that.'

'Well, as a matter of fact, he's invited me and Corey over to dinner tonight,' Kate replied.

'Lovely,' Tom said. 'I mean, I won't have the slide show ready for a day or two, so we can save the holiday snaps for another time. And Corey's happy to play gooseberry with you two, is he?'

'It's not like that,' Kate replied, aware even as she said it that it lacked credibility after what Aidan and Tom had walked in on. 'Besides, Corey and Harry get on really well, which is lovely to see.'

Aidan smiled. 'What, they're bonding already? Good work, sis!'

Kate didn't dignify that with a response. Her brothers had been hugely supportive, albeit from a distance, during the divorce, and a little good-natured teasing wasn't the end of the world. Even if it was a bit OTT, considering she was supposed to be going home soon. But as she thought about returning to Cambridge, she felt a pang of something that definitely wasn't homesickness, or relief to be going back there. Perhaps, as Harry had said earlier, Willowbury was working its peculiar magic on her, as well.

Changing the subject swiftly, she asked if Tom and Aidan would mind if Will and Tom came down to stay for a few days.

'Sure,' Aidan said. 'The more the merrier. You know how much I like seeing your kids – all of them. You must be missing them, after, what is it, nearly five weeks?'

Kate nodded. 'I am. It'll be great to have them back for a little while. Although squishing into your spare rooms will be almost as cosy as going back to Mum's annexe, which it seems I'm doomed to do when the summer's over.'

'Rather you than me!' Aidan laughed. He and their mother had never been close as adults, and although they maintained a reasonable relationship, the miles between them definitely helped, most of the time.

'She's going to visit again at some point, you know,' Kate said. 'After all, she'll want to meet the new baby.'

Aidan rolled his eyes. 'I'm not sure Sam and Florence'll be up to having her stay, and if she stays here both she and I will have to keep the booze flowing to keep the peace. You sure I can't convince you to hang about a bit longer in Willowbury, to mediate between us when she does come?'

Kate laughed. 'I never thought I'd see the day when you asked me to stick around! Aren't I just the boring old big sister who usually spoils all your fun?'

'Maybe you're mellowing with age.' Aidan grinned back at her. 'Or I'm just well pleased with the paint job. Either way, stay as long as you want, sis, and yes, get the other two boys down as well. You're all welcome.'

As Kate, feeling revitalised after her coffee and also much happier after her chat with Aidan and Tom, went to put a bit more work into the upstairs skirting boards, she reflected on what Aidan had said. She'd been getting on so well with Sam and Florence over the holiday, and there was no doubt that she was loving the change of scene that Willowbury offered. It was lovely to see Aidan looking so refreshed and relaxed after their trip, and having her other two sons here for a few days would be the icing on the cake. And then, of course, there was her deepening attachment to Harry, too. A thought crossed her mind before she could stop it, having contemplated all this. What if she *could* stay? Not just for the summer, but make her own home here in Willowbury? But was that just the summer air clouding her judgement? She'd probably feel differently when she had three boys to wrangle, and the new school year loomed, anyway. After all, despite her change in circumstances, she still had three children to consider. And didn't everyone feel that way during a good holiday?

That evening, Kate was getting ready to go out when Corey put his head around the door.

'Hey,' she said, catching sight of his reflection in the Cheval mirror in the spare room. 'Are you nearly ready?'

Corey fixed his eyes steadfastly on the carpet in front of him. 'Er, do you mind if I don't go with you to Harry's tonight?'

Kate turned around to face him. 'Why?' she replied, chucking her hairbrush down onto the bed. 'What's up?'

'I'm just a bit knackered from work, that's all,' Corey said. 'I fancy an early night.'

'Is everything okay?' Kate moved towards her son, who was still hovering in the doorway.

Corey glanced up at her. 'Fine,' he muttered, before looking away again.

'Corey...'

'I said I'm fine.' He raised his eyes again. 'Sorry, Mum. I'm really tired, honestly.'

'Look, if you're not okay with me seeing Harry, can we talk about it?' Kate said gently. 'I don't want you to feel uncomfortable.'

'It's a bit weird,' Corey conceded. 'I mean, all I've ever known is you and Dad being together, and then you weren't, and we were okay, me, you and my brothers, weren't we?'

'We were. We *are*,' Kate amended quickly. 'And me having a date or two with Harry won't change that. I promise. Besides, we're going back home at the end of the summer, and finding a whole new place to live. This isn't forever.'

'Would you want it to be?' Corey said. 'You seem really happy here.'

Kate smiled, taken back to her train of thought after her chat with Aidan that afternoon. 'I'm on holiday, Corey. Sure, I'm working on this house, but this isn't reality, is it? It's just a bit for fun for the summer.'

Corey looked at her for a moment longer before giving her a brief smile and heading back to his room. Kate, still unsure if she'd really got to the bottom of what was bothering him, decided it was best just to wait for him to elucidate further in his own time. Also, Corey had always been close to his uncles; perhaps Aidan would be able to work out what else was on his mind. *Sometimes*, she thought, *finding the balance between when to push a teenager to talk and when to back off and let them come to you is really tricky*. She felt as though the tightrope she walked with her boys' feelings and emotions was becoming higher and trickier with every step she took.

She'd phoned Phil earlier, too, and he'd agreed to get the boys over to Willowbury in a couple of days' time, to meet their new cousin and spend some time with her. She'd then been surprised to get a call from her mother, who said she'd drive the boys over to Somerset, as she was really keen to meet her new granddaughter. The ever-practical Selina had already booked a room at the Travellers' Rest, so as not to overcrowd the new parents, and to avoid even more of a squeeze at Tom and Aidan's, so it looked as though Aidan's desire to have Kate as a mediator when their mother visited was happening. Kate thought how nice it was going to be to have everyone together to celebrate baby Mia's arrival, and found herself smiling as she put the finishing touches to her mascara.

A little while later, she took a deep breath and knocked on the door of Harry's flat, which could be reached from a separate entrance to the shop behind the street. As she waited for him to open the door, she felt another ridiculous nervous tingling in her stomach. With no Corey there as chaperone, what might Harry expect of her? What might she expect of *him*?

Fortunately, she didn't have long to wait, as Harry opened the door before she'd finished knocking. He was casually but well dressed in a dark blue cotton shirt, unbuttoned at the neck, and lighter blue jeans. His sleeves were rolled up to show lightly tanned forearms and a white mark where his watch had been. Kate had to suppress the urge to grab his wrist and plant a kiss on it.

'Hi.' Harry smiled. 'Corey couldn't make it?' He leaned forward and kissed her on the cheek as he said this, and she smelt the tantalisingly expensive scent of a lemon and sandalwood aftershave which made her senses reel. She breathed in to try to steady herself, but it didn't help much.

'He sends his apologies,' Kate replied. 'I think it's going to take him a while to acclimatise to doing a full working day, no matter how much he enjoys it.'

'He's working very hard,' Harry said as they walked back up the stairs to his flat. 'I wasn't expecting him to work Saturdays as well, but he seemed keen to be at the shop this morning. I'll miss him when you both go back to Cambridge.'

'We'll miss you too,' Kate said. She couldn't bring herself to articulate the turmoil she'd been in, thinking about where and how she was going to spend the rest of her life. That was a talk for another time.

'Well, I took what you said about seafood to heart and steered clear of it,' Harry grinned over his shoulder as he led her to the large, airy kitchen of his flat, which opened out to a small balcony overlooking the back street. More picturesque than it sounded, the early evening sun was warming the stone of the buildings behind, and Kate could see the undulating green landscape of the Mendip Hills rolling away into the distance. There seemed to be nowhere in Willowbury that didn't have the most gorgeous view of the county of Somerset. Cambridge, though undoubtedly beautiful, was a totally different and much flatter landscape. She was determined to get out and explore the countryside at least once before she went back home.

'Even though you're in the centre of town, it feels so peaceful,' Kate said, as she turned back to where Harry was standing. He was looking at her intently, and she felt another flutter of nerves. 'What?' she teased, trying to hide how she felt.

'The sunlight suits you,' Harry said.

'Oh, bugger off.' Kate laughed, trying to hide her embarrassment. 'When you get to my age, candlelight is the favourable option, believe me!'

'I'm three years older than you, don't forget,' Harry countered, moving towards her. He turned her back around so that they were both looking out over the rooftops and towards the hills again. Kate found herself leaning into Harry, who'd slid his hands around her waist, and as he dipped his head to kiss her neck, she arched her back in pleasure.

'Is it wrong of me to be a little bit pleased that we're on our own this evening?' Harry murmured.

Kate smiled. 'I'm prepared to overlook it if you keep doing that.' Tingles of pleasure were rippling up and down her spine as Harry continued to kiss her neck, and the evening sun felt warm on her skin. Turning back around to face him, she pulled him towards her, so that her back was against the wall of the small balcony. As her lips met his in a deep, warm, sweet kiss, she felt her body responding more and more to his touch. Holiday fling or not, as her brain became fuzzy and addled with sensation, they had so much crackling between them, she'd never forget it.

Harry's body was pressing into hers, and whereas before she'd had to cut things short, Kate knew that this time, if they wanted it, they had all the time in the world. That didn't seem to register with her hands, though, as they travelled southward to run over Harry's jeans-clad behind, pulling herself even closer to him so their hips touched and there was no doubt just how aroused he was.

'Can dinner wait?' Kate asked. 'I feel like we have some unfinished business from the other night.'

'Business?' Harry's rumble of laughter was almost lost in another kiss. 'Is that what I am to you?'

Kate smiled back into the kiss. 'Oh no,' she said softly. 'Tonight you're all pleasure.'

As they broke apart, Harry took her hand. 'I know you know where the bedroom is, but hopefully this time will be a whole lot more fun than having to play nurse.'

They padded across the floor and back into the corridor, and as Kate walked through the door of Harry's tidy, comfortable bedroom, she paused. 'I want you to know that I am very, very okay with this,' she said softly. 'In fact, if we don't get into that bed soon, I'm going to explode with frustration.'

Harry grinned. 'No pressure or anything, then!' His smile turned into something entirely more thoughtful. 'And for the record, I feel exactly the same way. I've been hard pressed to keep my mind, and other things, off you since last night.'

'Glad to hear it.' Kate padded across the floorboards of Harry's room, but hesitated when she got to the bed. She breathed in the clean, fresh scent of his cotton bedding, underpinned by the smell of freshly cut grass that was drifting in from the communal gardens of the flats in the street behind and felt an absolute sense of rightness; that whatever the future held, being here with Harry, in this room, right now, was the most important thing.

'If I remember correctly,' she began as Harry joined her, 'we were snogging like teenagers the last time we went near a bed.'

'I remember it *so* well,' Harry murmured. 'Would you like to pick up where we left off?'

In answer, Kate sat down on the bed, kicked off her shoes and swung her legs up onto the white embroidered duvet. 'Come here,' she said gently, feeling her stomach flutter as Harry did just that.

And just like that they were a gloriously erotic jumble of wandering hands and pressing limbs, exploratory lips and tangled denim as they revelled, uninterrupted, in picking up just where they'd left off. Kate felt the wonderful, pressing weight of Harry's body on top of hers as they kissed and began to tentatively explore each other. She gasped as one of Harry's warm hands slid under the material of her top to caress the bare skin of her waist, and then crept upwards to stroke the underside of her breast through her bra, running a firm but gentle thumb over a peaking nipple that sprang up to his touch almost instantly.

'I don't remember much about being a teenager, but I think that counts as second base,' Kate said, trying to keep a metaphorical foot on the seabed as the warmth of Harry's hands kept stroking her further from shore. She could feel the heat growing in her belly even though she was still fully clothed, and when Harry paused to shift position slightly, she took the chance to slip her shirt over her head. Thanking God she'd worn her best underwear, she felt a burst of confidence as Harry's eyes widened at the sight of her pale skin contrasted with the black bra he'd been feeling moments ago.

'Well, if you insist.' Harry smiled, unbuttoning his own shirt to reveal an attractively proportioned chest with a smattering of darkish hair. As their torsos touched, Kate felt another surge of desire. It had been a long time since she'd been to bed with someone, but even allowing for that, Harry seemed to be awakening something long dormant within her. The comfortable, familiar motions of sex in marriage had become so commonplace that this all felt like incredibly new territory. So much so that when Harry reached around to undo the clasp on her bra, she jumped.

'Sorry,' Harry murmured, 'too soon?'

Kate laughed. 'Not at all... it's just no one's tried to take my bra off for bloody years!' The laugh soon became a sigh when Harry's mouth replaced his fingers and she once again arched her back towards him.

In the end, they spent quite a long time half-clothed, both relishing the sensation of taking things slowly, exploring every new area of exposed skin and checking in with each other as they did so. It was a sexy, leisurely experience, and one that was quite unlike anything Kate had ever felt before. While she was melting with desire inside, it felt as though, in these moments, there was all the time in the world.

Eventually, though, they'd shed the rest of their clothing and were tumbling under the bed linen, throwing off the duvet as the room, warmed by the sun all day, was deliciously comfortable. Kate, worried that after such a long fallow period, she might be a little out of practise, found herself throwing caution to the winds and exploring Harry, and letting herself be explored, with an excitement and an assurance that grew with every caress. After three children and a long marriage, she thought she was long past the waves of excitement that washed over her as Harry kissed, touched and explored every inch of her, until she was thrilled, breathless and desperate to feel him inside her. And, on the edge and more than ready for him, he obliged, slowly at first and then, as they found their own momentum, moving together towards a shared, throbbing undoing. As she broke, and Harry followed a moment after, she found herself looking into those dark, depths-of-the-sea blue eyes, and wanting to drown herself in them for always.

A little later, when they'd both regained their breath and were lying side by side wrapped in the sheets, Kate propped herself on one elbow and looked down at Harry again.

'My holiday romances as a teenager were *nothing* like this,' she said playfully, trying to hide how jolted she'd been by their intimacy. 'You haven't made it very easy for me to go home when the summer's over.'

Harry smiled. 'I wish you didn't have to go.' Then a look of apology crossed his face, which had been hitherto relaxed and sated by their lovemaking. 'Sorry, I didn't mean to make you feel bad by saying that, but it *is* true. I'll miss you, Kate.'

'I'll miss you, too,' Kate said quietly. She suddenly remembered how it felt, many, many years ago, to have said goodbye to a boyfriend whose parents were moving far away from the village she'd grown up in. The pain, as a teenager in the throes of first love, had felt unbearable. They'd seen each other once a month for a year afterwards, and the thrill of meeting up and then the agony of saying goodbye at the train station every time were equal in measure. Knowing that she was going to have to say goodbye to Harry at the end of the summer was reminding her of those intense teenage times, and she was unsettled by it. Surely she was old enough to enjoy this for what it was, and not torture herself with fantasies about what might have been?

'Penny for them,' Harry said gently, clearly noticing the faraway look on her face.

Kate smiled down at him. 'Just thinking about how much I've enjoyed getting to know you, and how much I don't want to go back to Cambridge when the holidays are over.'

'Funny,' Harry replied, pulling her down towards him for a kiss. 'I won't miss you at all. Not one little bit!'

'Charming!' Kate's smile grew wider. 'Well, I suppose I could try to remind you just how much you *will* miss me when I'm gone.' Sliding a little further down the bed, she set about proving him wrong.

45

After a while, both Harry and Kate decided they'd worked up enough of an appetite to have the dinner that Harry had prepared. Mercifully, the lasagne only took half an hour to warm through in the oven, and since both were eating it ravenously, neither worried about the pleasurable and extremely tasty excess of garlic in the garlic bread. That, and a few glasses of a very robust red, left them both feeling even more relaxed. So much so that when Kate looked at her watch, she was amazed to see that it was nearly midnight.

'I'd better get off,' she said reluctantly. 'Tom and Aidan are likely to be waiting up like my surrogate parents, just to make sure you haven't abducted me.'

'I'm looking forward to meeting them properly, and not just having to dash off,' Harry said. 'From what you've told me about them, they're quite a pair.'

'Like you wouldn't believe,' Kate said. After they'd finally got out of bed, she'd spent some time that evening filling Harry in on how Aidan and Tom had met during the Willowbury Dramatical Spectacular Christmas play a couple of years ago; the same production that had brought Sam and Florence together, too. Aidan's coming out had been a bit of a surprise to both Sam and Kate, but they'd both been delighted when Aidan and Tom had decided, a few months after Sam and Florence had got married, to tie the knot themselves.

'I think it took me a week to get over the hangover from their wedding!' Kate laughed. 'And although I never thought of Aidan as the – er – *flamboyant* type, he certainly let his creative side out at the wedding. I've never seen so many pink flamingo shaped balloons in one place in my life.' She paused. 'Although it was really sweet that some of his army mates set up a guard of honour for them outside the registry office. Tom, despite being head over heels in love with my brother, was thoroughly overexcited by that, although, to be fair, if I'd had a guard of honour like them at my wedding, I might have reconsidered which bloke to marry!' She could have sounded bitter at this, but, to her surprise, her voice was light and a whole lot more carefree. It was amazing what great sex and a really good meal could do to lift your mood.

'Sounds like quite a party,' Harry said. 'My older brother's wedding was an altogether more *sensible* affair. And for sensible read a bridezilla in my sister-in-law who even had a seating plan for the church. Definitely no fun allowed there.'

'Sounds, er, *different*,' Kate said. 'Of course, three teenage boys and a free bar meant that, despite my admittedly far from best efforts, I was stonkingly hung-over the next day, and Corey had a few glasses of champagne and then threw up all over the en suite in the Travelodge, and guess who had to clear *that* up? To be fair to him, though, I don't think he's touched a drop since, that I know of.'

'And your other two boys?' Harry asked, topping up their glasses with the last of the wine.

Kate's voice softened. 'Both hardy, sturdy, stoical things who seem to take everything in their stride. Will's about to start his GCSEs and Tom's happy so long as he's within stretching distance of an Xbox or a football. They seem to have handled the divorce a whole lot better than Corey did; but I suppose he was more aware of just how fragile I was when it all came out about Phil and Jennifer. I tried to hide it from the boys, but it was difficult to pretend everything was normal when you've just found out your husband, no matter how much you might be bored with him yourself, has gone and fallen in love with someone else.' She shook her head. 'But that's water under the bridge now, and I can tell you for sure, now it's all done and dusted, I wouldn't have it any other way.'

'I'm glad,' Harry said. 'Or I'd be seriously questioning this whole evening.'

'And on that note, I'd better get home,' Kate said, draining her glass. She stood up from the table, thinking she should feel more drunk but, given the gargantuan helping of lasagne and garlic bread Harry had served her, she felt remarkably steady on her feet.

'Can I walk you back?' Harry asked. 'I'd hate to think of you out on the mean streets of Willowbury without a chaperone.'

'That would be lovely, kind sir.' Kate smiled. And in a short time, they were taking a walk through the town, towards Tom and Aidan's front door. The moon overhead was bright, but the sky was still a warm grey, and the honey-coloured stone buildings had retained much of the heat of the day. There wasn't a whisper of a breeze in the air, and the stillness brought with it faraway calls of those enjoying a final drink outside the pub and heading off home for the night.

They reached Bay Tree Terrace, and Kate's attention was drawn to the sorry looking third house on the row, which had lain deserted and unloved for a long time. In all the time she'd been at Tom and Aidan's, she hadn't seen anyone, not even the postal workers, going near the place, and she wondered who it belonged to. Obviously, someone who had enough money to live elsewhere and not bother too much about it, from the dust and smears on the windowsill and the peeling paint on the front door. She wondered if Sam or Aidan knew what the story of the place was.

'Well, this is me,' she said as they walked up to the path that led to the front door of number one. She paused, still relishing the feeling of Harry's hand in hers. 'Thank you for a wonderful evening, Harry.'

Harry smiled in the moonlight, the crows' feet around his eyes shadowing slightly and making his eyes seem an even deeper blue. 'It was a pleasure. And I'd love to see you again before you head back to Cambridgeshire.'

'I'd like that, too,' Kate murmured. She only needed to step slightly on tiptoes to kiss him again, because of the height of the borrowed sandals from Florence. 'Tom and Will are coming to stay the day after tomorrow, and I'm not quite sure how long they'll be here for, whether they'll stay until we all have to go home, or whether Phil's having them back for the last week of the holidays, but I'm sure there'll be a chance or two for us to get together before we all have to go back to the *real world*.'

Harry suddenly looked concerned, and perhaps a little deflated. 'I don't want to get in the way while all of your sons are here,' he said, running his hands down her arms to hold her hands. 'And all this talk of the *real world* reminds me that, at the end of the summer holidays you're going to be heading out of here.' Suddenly serious, he gazed down at her. 'Kate... you can ignore me if I'm getting too heavy too quickly, but I really do want to see you again. And again. And at this point, I'd even consider commuting to Cambridge on a Sunday just to spend a couple of hours with you. I know you're not looking for anything serious right now, and I totally respect that, but I thought it was only fair to tell you that I don't do one-night stands.'

Kate's heart started to beat so quickly that she was frightened it was going to burst from her chest. 'Surely that's just the wine and the sex talking?' she said, trying to make light of Harry's words.

Harry smiled down at her, and in addition to her heart thumping madly, the curve of his mouth made her knees wobble. Really, all these jokes about being a teenager in love were one thing, but the actual sensations were something else.

'If I might make an observation,' he said, after a careful pause, 'you have every right to feel more confident. I mean every word of what I've just said, and if it meant spending even five minutes with you before having to turn around and head back here, I'd happily do three hours across country and back on a regular basis.' He shook his head ruefully before adding, 'But I said I wasn't going to get heavy, so you can ignore that, if you want.'

In answer, Kate reached up on tiptoes and gave him a long, lingering kiss. When they were still within a whisper of each other, she replied, 'You're sweet.' It was her turn to smile. 'And, although I could happily spend the whole night out here on the doorstep with you, I'm sure I can feel Aidan's stare from behind the curtains, so I'd better get in there and face the inquisition.' She couldn't resist kissing him again, though. 'Goodnight, Harry, and thank you.'

As they parted, Kate paused on the doorstep and watched Harry loping off towards the High Street again and kept smiling. It was such a strange feeling, she held a hand to her cheek to feel it. How was it possible that, in such a short time, she could feel so alive again? Putting it down to the weird Willowbury air, which must, she figured, be saturated with all kinds of bizarre substances, mystical and otherwise, she pushed open the front door and prepared to face Aidan and Tom.

46

Kate wasn't sure if she had felt disappointed or relieved when neither Tom nor Aidan were in evidence downstairs when she'd got back last night. She wasn't a great talker about her emotions, and although a friendly ear would have been a nice thing, it also might have confused her even more. She'd grabbed a pint glass of water, brushed her teeth, poked her head around Corey's bedroom door, relieved that he was asleep, even if he'd dropped off with his phone in his hand, and then she'd crashed out, sleeping better than she had in a very long time despite the few glasses of red wine. In fact, she hadn't woken up until gone eight. Sunday had been spent chilling with Aidan, Tom and Corey, and checking in with Sam and Florence, who were hoping to bring baby Mia home the next day. It turned out to be one of those lazy, family days, and just what Kate needed to slow down and process everything that had happened in the weeks she'd now been in Willowbury. She also needed to get the spare rooms ready for Tom and Will's visit, although since they were bringing sleeping bags and airbeds, there wasn't a great deal to do. They would be arriving late afternoon Monday, and Kate couldn't wait to see them.

Monday morning came, after another good night's sleep, and when she wandered down to the kitchen, she found a note from Tom and Aidan saying that, since there was 'bugger all except your crappy muesli' in for breakfast, they'd gone to the Cosy Coffee Shop for the Full English and she was welcome to join them when she 'eventually dragged herself out of bed'.

Kate grinned. Even on paper, Aidan could make her laugh. He'd always had the ability to make her cry tears of helpless laughter, and it was something she really missed now that they lived so far apart. Perhaps she would join them for breakfast, and see if Corey fancied a fry-up, too. Being a teenage boy, he had the appetite of a ravenous Labrador, and she was sure he'd say yes.

Abandoning the coffee she was making, she headed back upstairs to the spare room that Corey had claimed as his own. Distracted momentarily by her phone, which pinged with a message just as she pushed open Corey's door, she smiled as she saw Harry's name flashing up on the screen with a thank you and lots of kisses for Saturday night. Glancing up only as she entered the room, she was surprised to see Corey's bed made and the curtains open. He'd obviously headed out to Vale Volumes already, or maybe he'd just gone for a walk. *Oh well*, Kate thought. Perhaps she'd get him a take-out sausage sandwich and a coffee and drop them into the shop on her way back from breakfast with Aidan and Tom.

Heading into the café twenty minutes later, she immediately caught sight of her brother and his husband at a corner table, both of them reading a newspaper each and enjoying a coffee. Tom saw her first and waved her over.

'Couldn't resist the lure of a proper breakfast, then?' Aidan teased as she sat down. 'I mean, with all the work you've done on the house since we've been away, I'd have thought you'd have been starting your day with something a little more substantial than that rabbit food in the cupboard.'

'Unlike you, brother dear, I can't just eat and drink what I want any more,' Kate said, 'but since you're offering a more decent breakfast, I figured I'd take you up on it.'

'Harry didn't offer to make one for you, then?' Aidan waggled an eyebrow at her.

'I didn't want to leave you babysitting Corey in your own house all night,' Kate said, before realising she'd effectively walked into the knowing smiles that both Tom and Aidan now gave her.

'So how was your, er, *night*?' Aidan asked. 'You were pretty late home.'

'Who are you, Dad?' Kate shot back, and then felt the familiar dull pain of remembrance laced with love at the memory of their late father, who'd been such a quiet, reserved and gentle presence in their lives.

'Oh, no judgement.' Aidan grinned. 'You're entitled to a bit of fun. I just never saw you as the holiday romance type.'

Kate blushed, despite her best efforts not to. 'It's not like that.'

'Really?' Aidan broke off as Jack came over to the table with two plates of his famed Willowbury Warmer Full English breakfast. Kate swiftly requested another plateful, surprisingly hungry, and a takeaway sausage sandwich and coffee for Corey.

When Jack had walked away again, Aidan returned to the interrogation. 'So if it's not a holiday fling, what is it then?'

'To be absolutely honest, Aidan, I'm not sure.' Kate leaned back in her chair and fell quiet for a moment. 'I like Harry a lot. But he's here, and it looks like I'm going back to the annexe at Mum's soon to try to get on with the rest of my life. It doesn't add up, really, does it?'

'Do you want it to, though?' Aidan asked. 'I mean, you were going to meet someone else after Phil at some point. And there's something to be said for getting back on the horse after a fall. That doesn't mean you have to buy the horse, stable it and put it out to stud for the rest of your life, does it?'

'That's a crap metaphor for a girl who loved ponies.' Kate laughed. 'And I doubt Harry would take kindly to the idea I was just using him for practise or, er, *stud purposes*!'

'He's a bloke, isn't he?' Aidan grinned more widely. 'And you're not exactly undateable, sis.'

'Thanks,' Kate said dryly.

'I think what my darling husband is trying to say is that perhaps you don't have to keep thinking about the big, complicated, future stuff,' Tom interjected. 'If you like spending time with Harry, then just enjoy it for what it is. Think about what happens later, well... later.'

Kate thanked Jack as he returned to the table with coffee and a plate of breakfast, and a sausage butty wrapped in layers of grease-proof paper. Tucking in hungrily, she relished the decadence of a breakfast not cooked by herself. 'I know I should just take things as they come, but it's so hard after being married for so much of my life. I mean, after Phil, I never imagined I'd sleep with anyone ever again, and here I am, flinging out my inhibitions while basically homeless, and in a fairly precarious position job wise until word gets out about my new business. It's all freaking me out, to be honest.'

'But you've enjoyed spending some time here, and meeting Harry is a bonus?' Aidan asked. 'I mean, we've been saying for ages that you should come and stay. I know it's been a bit of a working holiday, but you have had a good time, haven't you?'

'Yes, definitely,' Kate said between mouthfuls. 'In fact, if I had the nerve, I'd...'

'You'd what?'

'Oh, it's a stupid idea,' Kate muttered. 'And there's no way you'd want me and the boys upping sticks to this part of the world, anyway.'

Aidan put his knife and fork down and regarded Kate intently. 'And why would I not want that?'

'Well, you and I... we've never been what you'd call close, have we? I mean, you and Sam were thick as thieves as kids, and as I said at the weekend, I was just the boring older sister who spoiled all your fun. You wouldn't really want me hanging about, getting in the way, even now, would you?'

Aidan regarded her levelly. 'I'd love it if you and the boys were closer. If being on tour in the military taught me anything, it's how important family and friends really are. And whether you decide to stay in Cambridge or do move somewhere else, I'm here for you.' He shifted his gaze to Tom, who was also smiling in Kate's direction. 'We both are. Although I might draw the line if you try to bring Mum to live with you!'

'Fair enough,' Kate said, touched beyond words at Aidan's admission. 'She's dead set on seeing out her days in her house, anyway, and to be honest, through sheer force of will she'll probably outlive us all!' Realising, too late, that this might not have been the most tactful of things to say to a brother who very nearly lost his life in an IED explosion in Afghanistan, she flushed uncomfortably. 'Sorry,' she said. 'It's not that I forget what happened to you, but seeing you happy and settled, it's easy to put it in the background these days.'

'As it should be,' Aidan said gently. 'You can't live your life looking back, Kate, and you can't be afraid to take risks sometimes. Can't you just trust your own instincts for once?'

Kate shook her head and gave a hollow laugh. 'It's not that easy to trust again after the man you married walks out to be with another woman. Something like that makes you super wary about everything, believe me.'

'So wary you throw your knickers at a bookshop owner's bedroom wall?' Aidan's eyes were twinkling.

'Well, okay, perhaps I have been a little bit more reckless than I usually am, but that's probably because I don't see being here as permanent – I mean, it was a six-week working holiday I'd planned, not an up-sticks-and-start-a-new-life kind of adventure. But the longer I'm here, the more I keep wondering what the hell I've got to go back to Cambridge for, apart from Mum, of course.'

'What about the kids?' Tom interjected. 'How do you think they'd feel about moving so far away from where they grew up?'

'That's the big thing that worries me,' Kate said. 'I think Corey'd move tomorrow, but Will and Tom are trickier. The rail links are really good, though, and they'd still be able to see their mates when they went to stay with Phil.'

'Would you really think about moving here?' Aidan asked. 'I mean, if you hadn't met Harry, would you still be thinking that way?'

'This might sound like bollocks, but it's not really about Harry,' Kate said, taking a bite of doorstep toast, dripping with locally sourced butter. 'I have felt happier being here, doing the decorating job, than I have in years. You and Sam both said Willowbury has an effect on people.' She paused. 'I think it's having an effect on me, too. It's healing me, even though I thought I *was* healed, after everything that happened. I feel peaceful here, but excited about the future, too. And let's face it, if I'm going to be a painter and decorator, I can do that just as well here as I can in Cambridge.'

Aidan nicked Kate's other slice of toast and grinned at her. 'Well, whatever you decide, we're here for you,' he said, looking fondly over at Tom. 'And if you were a bit closer, you could share the inevitable babysitting duties we're bound to get once Sam and Florence get desperate for some alone time again!'

'Very true,' Kate agreed. 'But not a word about this to Corey, okay? I'm not even sure it's what I want anyway, and if I'm going to make decisions, I need to think really carefully first. I can't go off half-cocked and mess it all up. It's not like I can just say "fuck it" and just stay here, is it? There'd be a hell of a lot to organise.'

'That's the Kate I know,' Aidan teased. 'Risk averse to the last. I figured she was hiding inside there somewhere. And we promise; not a word until you're ready to sort things out properly.'

'I'd better get going,' Kate said. 'Your house won't paint itself, and I've got a butty to deliver.' She went to get her purse out, but Tom waved it away.

'We'll get this,' he said. 'You can shout us when you've moved here.'

Kate smiled. 'Thanks.'

As she left, she yet again marvelled at just how happy and settled both of her brothers now were. *Perhaps there really was something magical in the air in Willowbury*, she thought as she headed down the High Street to Vale Volumes to deliver Corey's sandwich and coffee. She hoped his boss wouldn't mind his young employee snacking on work time. Had she known just what she was going to find when she got to the bookshop, she wouldn't have been so relaxed.

47

Harry glanced at the clock on the bookshop's wall yet again and felt another prickle of anxiety laced with impatience. Corey had been punctual to a fault since he'd been working at Vale Volumes, and Harry wished, today of all days, that the boy had been on time. He looked at the till roll again and shook his head. It was no good. No matter how many times he totted up the takings from yesterday and compared it with the total on the receipt from cashing up, the two figures wouldn't match.

Most likely it was an admin error; Corey had learned how to use the till very quickly, but even the most technologically savvy people made mistakes with unfamiliar devices. A major discrepancy, like keying in an extra couple of zeros on a transaction, would be explainable, but this was an odd amount that the takings were down, almost as if someone had just pocketed some cash instead of putting it in the till.

That Corey hadn't turned up yet was a further worry. Perhaps he'd had enough of the job, decided to grab some money and then just duck out? But everything Harry had seen of the boy since he'd been working at the shop contradicted that idea. Corey obviously loved working at Vale Volumes and didn't seem the dishonest type. He had been through a troubled time lately, with Kate's divorce and his subsequent running away, and his insecurities about Harry being part of Kate's life. What if Harry had misjudged the boy? Put too much trust in him because of his own growing attachment to Kate?

As if summoned by his emotions, Harry looked up when the bell over the front door tinkled to see Kate standing in the shop.

'Hi.' She was smiling, and Harry's heart lurched.

'Hi,' he replied, wondering exactly how to broach the subject of the till receipt and her no-show of a son. 'How are you?'

'I'm great, thanks.' She was still smiling. 'I just brought some breakfast in for Corey, if the boss is happy for him to eat it.' She glanced around the shop. 'Is he out the back? Have you got him hefting boxes of stock? If not, please feel free to work him hard!'

'Um...' Harry heard the hesitation in his voice and hated it. Nicola had always said he was afraid of confrontation, and it had irritated the hell out of her. 'I'm sorry to say he's not here. He hasn't shown up for work yet.'

As Harry told her this, the colour drained from Kate's face. 'What? Why didn't you call me and let me know?'

'I wanted to give him half an hour or so before I rang. You know what teenagers are like. He could have overslept and been on his way, for all I know. I didn't want to worry you.' The words came out in a rush, and Harry could see they were making no difference to Kate. Obviously reliving the moment when she'd found out Corey had gone AWOL from his father's house, she'd put the package and the coffee cup down on the counter and was gripping the mahogany top for dear life.

'Didn't want to worry me?' she repeated. 'Harry... he got up before I did this morning, left the house and now I have absolutely no idea where he is.'

'Have you called him this morning?' Harry could see the fear in Kate's face, which was swiftly replaced by irritation.

'I didn't think I had to,' Kate snapped. 'I thought he was here in the shop with you. He loves working here, so I figured he'd just got an early start and had forgotten to let me know.'

'I'm afraid not.' Harry dithered for a moment longer, debating whether or not to tell Kate about the missing cash from yesterday, but that information might well prove to be important, if indeed Corey had taken some money and was now regretting it.

'Look, Kate,' he began, coming out from behind the counter so he could reach out for her. 'There's something else you should know.'

'What is it?' Kate asked. 'I thought you said you hadn't seen him.'

'I haven't,' Harry replied. 'But the till's seventy-three pounds out from yesterday. I wouldn't have mentioned it, but it's an odd amount to be down. Corey was on his own for a fair bit when I came over to see you...'

'Are you suggesting that my son's a thief?' Kate's voice began to rise. 'Because I can assure you, he's about the most honest person you're ever likely to meet.'

'I'm not suggesting anything,' Harry said. 'But you have to admit, the discrepancy in the takings and his not showing up this morning could be linked.'

'I can't believe I'm hearing this,' Kate said, her eyes suddenly seeming harder and a whole lot more defensive than they ever had before. A lioness protecting her cub, Harry realised he'd gone about this all wrong.

'I'm sorry, Kate,' Harry said. 'I'm sure there's a perfectly reasonable explanation for the money.'

'I don't care about that right now, Harry,' Kate snapped. She was looking down at her phone, her trembling hands trying to get the fingerprint recognition to work so she could call Corey. 'I just need to know where my son is.'

'I understand,' Harry said.

'I doubt that,' Kate snapped. 'Or there's no way you'd have conflated those two things.' As the phone paused before trying to connect, she turned her back on Harry and started to walk back out of the shop. Just as she got to the door, her shoulders visibly tensed further, and she cut off the phone in frustration. Harry correctly assumed it had clicked through to Corey's voicemail, or maybe Corey was in one of the many mobile black spots that Willowbury had.

'Kate...' he called again. 'Let me help. I'll shut up shop for a bit and help you find him.'

'What, so you can question him about the missing cash? I don't think so.' Kate didn't even turn around to address this to him. 'I've got to go,' she said, and with that, she hurried from the shop.

Damn. Harry was kicking himself. He should never have mentioned the missing money. Kate, quite rightly, had sprung to Corey's defence, and now he wasn't sure how to remedy the situation or the more pressing issue that was Corey's disappearance. But if the boy didn't have anything to do with the missing money, why the hell hadn't he shown up this morning? One thing was certain; standing here like a lemon in the shop wasn't helping to find him. Leaving a note for Joan, who was due into work at eleven and thankfully had her own set of keys, he decided that he'd try to find Corey himself, despite what Kate had said. Perhaps he could sort the situation out without making it even worse, and then Kate might speak to him again. The question was, where was a quiet, bookish lad like Corey likely to be in a place like Willowbury? Racking his brains as he locked the shop door, he suddenly had an idea.

48

As Harry headed down the High Street, he hoped his hunch was right. When he'd first met Corey, he'd been impressed by how mature, self-possessed and sensible the lad had seemed; he just wasn't the type to go off the rails in a town he didn't know. If he could intercept Corey, and gently advise him to ring Kate to let her know he was fine, it would save a lot of bother. Although how he'd do that without sounding like a class one twat, and an interfering one at that, he had no idea. He wondered how he'd have reacted at Corey's age if some random bloke his mum knew had come up to him and started suggesting he phone home; not well, he concluded.

At least it was a sunny day. Trawling about in a rainstorm wouldn't have been much fun, and this part of the country was infamous for its wet weather as much as its sunshine. He glanced in the shop doorways as he passed them, but there was no sign of Corey browsing the shelves. Something told him that Corey wasn't just idly bunking off work, either. He simply didn't seem the type not to turn up when he'd committed to something. Just to be sure, though, Harry even poked his head through the door of the Travellers' Rest pub, but the bar was empty except for old Jim, the eighty-five-year-old handyman, enjoying a very early half of stout alongside his coffee. But, Harry reasoned, at that age, Jim was entitled to have whatever breakfast he chose.

Heading further up the High Street, with Willowbury Hill looming at the top, Harry hoped his earlier hunch would prove to be correct. He took a sharp left. The benefit of having been a slightly geeky, bookish teenager himself once was that he had a decent idea where Corey might have ended up, especially since he'd noticed that, when he thought no one was looking, Corey had been spending a lot of time in the Transport section of Vale Volumes, and the boy always seemed to have a notebook tucked into the back pocket of his jeans. Harry would put good money that he knew what was written there, too.

As his destination came into view, Harry wondered what on earth he was going to say to Corey if, indeed, he did find him here. He knew from the conversations he'd had with the teenager that he was still extremely torn up about his parents' divorce; indeed, what child wouldn't be? Perhaps he'd taken badly to the idea of Kate staying so late at Harry's place on Saturday night and didn't want to face Harry at work this morning out of embarrassment? That seemed more likely than the unpalatable theory he'd blundered into with Kate about money missing from the till, on reflection. Corey, as he knew from his earlier conversations with him, was bound to be feeling all kinds of emotions about his mum going on a date.

Just as he was approaching the place he suspected Corey was, the Bristol to Penzance express train whooshed through, and the welcome breeze on such a humid summer's day cooled him down a bit.

Willowbury station itself was a modern one, and rather plain and functional. Essentially, it was an unmanned slab of concrete next to the line with a ticket machine and a rain shelter. There were enough commuters to Taunton and Bristol to warrant the line reopening several years back, and it had certainly brought wealth back to an area that might otherwise have suffered the decline a lot of English tourist towns over the years had. Over the railway line was the passenger foot-bridge to the other platform, and there, standing on the bridge, looking towards Bristol, with his back towards where Harry had emerged onto the platform, was Corey. Harry felt a wave of relief wash over him. He instinctively grabbed his phone to call Kate, but just before he did, he paused. Perhaps he could sort this out himself, and in some way make amends to Kate for their terse exchange this morning.

Carefully, mindful that the teenager might not welcome the intrusion, Harry began to climb the steps to the bridge. As he neared the top of it, Corey, who was standing hunched over the side of the bridge, head down, glanced back at him. Harry almost pulled his phone out again and called Kate, as he saw the look on Corey's face. He wasn't sure he had the correct skill set to manage a teenage meltdown.

'What do you want?' Corey asked as Harry approached him. The boy had a mixture of irritation and something Harry couldn't quite identify written all over his features.

'Your mum's been into the shop looking for you,' Harry said calmly. 'And when I told her that you hadn't come in this morning, she was concerned you'd get yourself lost or something.' Carefully, he drew closer to Corey, who, gratifyingly, didn't move from his position.

Corey said nothing, obviously not wanting to divulge the reasons he hadn't turned up to Vale Volumes. Harry didn't quite know where to go from there. He leaned over the side of the bridge, about two feet from Corey, so as not to crowd him.

'The Bristol train's due in about four minutes,' Harry said, after a moment or two's silence. 'I saw the Penzance one going through just now.'

'How do you know?' Corey gazed back down the track.

'The shop's so close to the back of the line, I've learned to distinguish the different sound of a northbound and a southbound train,' Harry replied. 'But then I was a bit of a trainspotter in my younger days.'

Corey snorted. 'You're taking the piss, right?'

Harry shook his head. 'About which bit?'

'Oh, I don't know.' Corey still had his gaze fixed on the track. 'Doesn't matter, actually.'

'That doesn't sound like you,' Harry said.

'And what the hell would you know about what I sound like?' Corey snapped. 'You don't know anything about me.'

Careful, Harry thought. Corey was obviously upset about something, and he didn't want to exacerbate those emotions. 'I know you're a thoughtful, kind person who's really been there for his mum over the past couple of years,' Harry said gently. 'Your mum's told me how much that's meant to her, especially when she's been feeling low.'

'She still buggered off and left us all with Dad and his new woman for the summer, though, didn't she?' Corey retorted. 'She didn't even think about what we wanted.'

'Are you sure that's what you're really cross about?' Harry asked gently. 'I mean, you seemed pretty happy yesterday at work, and happy to be here in Willowbury where it's just you and your mum for a bit.'

'I was,' Corey conceded. 'But things change, don't they? That's what Mum kept saying to me, when she and Dad split up. And now they're changing again.'

Harry took a step back as he saw Corey's shoulders tensing again in an effort not to lose control of what was left of the hold on his emotions. He took a deep breath, and decided to take a risk.

'Is it bothering you?' Harry said gently. 'That your mum and I are spending some time together?'

'That's a pretty lame euphemism,' Corey said. 'Can't you just tell it like it is?'

'Corey.' Harry put his hands out on the handrail of the bridge, waiting to feel the vibration in the metal when the Bristol-bound train began to approach. It helped to anchor him a little more to what was an increasingly odd situation for him to be in. 'Whatever happens with Kate and me, whatever this is, I promise you, I have no bad intentions towards her, or you. I meant what I said the other day. We're both pretty cautious people. I want you to know that I would never hurt your mother. Although she's pretty pissed off with me at the moment,' he added, almost as an afterthought.

'Oh yeah?' Corey asked, a flare of interest in his eyes. 'And why's that, then? What have you done?'

Harry paused. The last thing he wanted to do was to accuse Corey of stealing, having so thoroughly botched things up on that score with Kate. 'Oh, nothing much,' he said vaguely. 'But she's going to be pleased that you haven't done a runner again.'

'I might be pissed off, but I'm not stupid,' Corey muttered, a brief smile lifting at the corner of his mouth. 'I mean, if I mess up, she'll try and send me back to Dad's, and that's the last place I want to be.' He paused. 'But, Harry, there is something I probably should have told you...'

Harry mentally braced himself for the worst. Was Corey going to confess to stealing the cash from the till? He wasn't quite sure how to respond, if he did.

'What's that, then?' he replied, after a heartbeat, and realising that Corey was waiting for him to speak.

'I messed up at the shop and forgot to let you know before I left.'

Corey was looking over the track again, unwilling to meet Harry's eyes. 'That's, er, kind of why I ducked out of dinner with you and Mum on Saturday.'

'What happened?' Harry asked gently.

'While you were taking that cup of coffee over to Mum, I rang up a cash payment on the till for about seventy pounds' worth of books. It was a group of kids who came in, and they said they'd saved up some birthday money to get all of the Artemis Bane books in the series, as well as few other bits and pieces, stationery and stuff like that. They asked if we had any more copies of the new Artemis book, and I knew we had a couple in the stockroom.' Corey paused and shook his head.

'Go on,' Harry said, beginning to suspect where this was going.

'I scanned in the copy they'd brought over from the New Releases table, and then scanned it in two more times before I went to look for the other copies in the back room. I know some of the bar codes on the books can be a bit weird and I didn't want to look like a tit in front of the kids. When I came back, they'd all run off out of the shop with the books and everything else they'd brought to the till.' Corey hung his head. 'I tried to cancel the sale, but I couldn't remember how to do it, and then I felt really, really stupid for falling for such an obvious scam. So as well as messing up the till, I lost you money in stolen stock, too.'

'Oh, Corey.' Harry ached to put a hand on the boy's shoulder, but mindful that he still didn't know him that well, no matter how much he liked him, he held back. 'These things happen. And I'd left you in sole charge of the shop, too. It's not your fault.'

Corey sniffed and brushed a hand over his eyes. 'Dad would have gone ballistic,' he said. 'He's always going on about how I've got no common sense, and I let people walk all over me. That I'm too soft for my own good.'

'I'm not your dad,' Harry said simply. 'And I also don't have much experience with talking to teenagers, so I'm kind of struggling about what to say here, except that it can happen to the best of us. When I first took over the bookshop, it took me about a month to figure out how to work the till. I can't blame you for making a mistake in your first couple of weeks, can I?'

'Are you going to sack me?'

Harry grinned as Corey looked up at him from underneath his fringe, suddenly so vulnerable and uncertain. 'Not today, no. And next time, you'll know better than to trust a gaggle of teenagers, won't you? See the cash upfront; that's the way to go in that situation. And if something like this happens again, just tell me.'

'So I can come back, then?'

'Of course.' Harry gestured. 'I'll even walk back with you, if you want me to.'

'Hadn't you better go and make peace with Mum?'

Harry grinned ruefully. 'I don't think she's going to have calmed down yet.'

'Why? What did you actually do?'

It was Harry's turn to feel uncomfortable and caught out, and Corey must have clocked the shift in his body language, as he suddenly put two and two together. 'You knew I had something to do with the till problem, didn't you?'

Harry nodded. 'And I got the wrong end of the stick, and thought that you...'

'That I'd nicked the cash,' Corey said. Then, inexplicably, he grinned. 'Seriously, Harry? I'm a frigging trainspotter who reads Artemis Bane novels! Did you honestly think I'd have the balls to steal?'

Harry, unnerved by the boy's reaction, began to laugh. 'That's not how I expected you to react.'

'And I'm guessing Mum went off the deep end when you mentioned this to her?' Corey said.

Harry nodded. 'Quite rightly, too. I should have known that there would be a more rational explanation. I should have stopped to think about it, but your mum came into the shop just as I'd realised the cash was missing, and so I jumped to entirely the wrong conclusion. She, understandably, was not best pleased.'

'To be fair, it *was* my fault, even if I didn't steal the money,' Corey said. 'And you weren't to blame for jumping on the idea that your new employee was responsible. After all, you barely know me, and you offered me the job.'

'And you've given me no reason to doubt you,' Harry said. 'Except, perhaps, not turning up this morning.'

Corey dropped his gaze. 'I'm sorry,' he said. 'I should have just told you what happened.'

'Shall we just say it's water under the bridge?' Harry said as they started to walk back to the platform. 'Or trains?' The Bristol-bound express thundered underneath them.

'I'd like that,' Corey said. 'And I promise it won't happen again.'

'But even if it does, as I said, just tell me,' Harry said. 'Oh and, I don't mean to get heavy here, but you should call your mother. She's going out of her mind with worry, and I think that's far more important than her being cross with me.'

'Fair enough.' Corey grinned. 'Do you want me to put in a good word for you?'

'I'm not sure if any words, good or otherwise, would help,' Harry confessed. 'I mean, I should have known better than to say anything until I'd thought things through, shouldn't I?'

'She'll come around,' Corey said. 'And I'm hoping she'll be so pleased to see me, she'll forget to ask why I went in the first place. It was embarrassing enough telling you, let alone Mum.'

'Your secret's safe with me,' Harry said. He felt relieved, and happy that he'd been able to talk Corey round. He only hoped that when Kate had calmed down, she'd see her way to forgiving his own misinformed judgements about Corey's trustworthiness, as well. He kicked himself again for jumping to conclusions.

As they walked back in the direction of the town, and after Corey had sent Kate a text, telling her where he'd been, Harry thought again about how much he'd missed out on by not being able to have children, biological or otherwise. He wondered, though, if it would have been quite so easy to have talked Corey back down from his emotions if he'd had actual parental responsibility for him. The waters got muddied when you were dealing with your own kids, he knew that, if not from direct experience. He could only imagine what Kate would have to say to Corey when they were face to face again, and hoped that he himself had helped rather than hindered that conversation.

49

The gut-loosening panic about where her eldest son might be was a sensation that Kate did not want to get used to. She also knew she'd bitten off Harry's head in fear about where Corey might have got to this time, but what did he expect, practically accusing Corey of theft? She paced the living room, hoping against hope that Tom and Aidan, who'd sprung into action when she'd gone back to the Cosy Coffee Shop and told them what had happened, would find Corey and bring him home before she went through the roof with worry.

Was it always going to be like this from now on with her eldest son, she wondered? Was the flight response going to be what he chose when things got difficult for him? And how much of that was her and Phil's fault for the early acrimony of their separation and divorce? Things were more settled now, to be sure, but trauma left its scars, especially on young, developing minds. Guilt, that familiar, ebbing and flowing emotion, washed over her yet again as she thought about the past couple of years. She knew she still thought about it all too much; and that she wasn't alone in the disintegration of the marriage, but it was all too easy to spiral down if she wasn't careful. Especially now she was considering uprooting her children and bringing them to an entirely new place. What the hell was she thinking? Could it really work? Or would all three of her sons resent her for that decision, in the end?

Tom and Aidan had suggested that she go back to the house, in case Corey showed up of his own accord, and, since they knew Willowbury far better than she did, they assured her that they'd find him if he hadn't already come home. But the feeling of having to wait, of being helpless, was gnawing away at her, reminding her unbearably of the hours she'd been waiting when Corey had absconded from Phil's place and ended up in Willowbury. She kept compulsively checking her phone, making sure the volume was switched up, ringing Corey's number over and over again, and then cursing that she might be tying up the line when he was trying to call her. Eventually, she collapsed back onto the sofa and tried to fight off the pain that threatened to overwhelm her brain and her lungs as her breath grew short and the adrenaline flooded her body over and over again.

She had no idea how long she sat there, but the phone finally pinged with a text, which took her sharply out of the spiral. Hands trembling, she scanned the brief message from Corey and then decided she needed to speak to him. He wasn't just going to get away with texting her and then moving on.

'Corey?'

'Hey, Mum.'

His voice sounded reassuringly normal. Kate drew a long, shuddering breath. 'Where are you?'

'Chill, Mum, I'm on my way to Harry's shop for work.'

At the mention of Harry's name, on top of everything else, Kate's composure almost slipped completely.

'You weren't there when I popped in earlier.'

'I, er, went for a walk.'

Kate knew there was more to it than that, but over the phone wasn't the time to discuss it.

'Did you fall in a black hole, or trip over a ley line or something? We've been worried sick about you. You can't just walk out and not let anyone know where you're going.'

'I know. I'm sorry.' Corey's voice sounded shakier. 'I promise I'll tell you everything when I get home after work.'

'You don't have to go in, you know.'

Corey paused before answering. 'Yes, I do. I can't let Harry down.'

'You don't owe Harry anything,' Kate said. 'In fact, if anything, he owes *you* an apology.'

'It's not what you think, Mum,' Corey protested. 'And go easy on Harry, will you?'

'Did he tell you to say that?'

'No. But I know you're pissed off with him, and you don't need to be. He's a cool guy.'

'I'm glad you think so,' Kate said grudgingly. 'So, what are you going to tell him when he asks why you didn't turn up to work this morning?'

'Gotta go, Mum, the line's breaking up. I'll see you later.'

'The line sounds fine to me.'

'What? Can't hear you. Laters!' And he was gone.

Kate let out a long sigh. She was perceptive enough to know that it had probably been Harry who'd found Corey, or her son wouldn't have sounded half so chipper about facing the music at Vale Volumes. She was wildly curious about how that conversation had gone, but, given that neither Corey nor Harry were particularly prone to confiding in other people, perhaps she'd never really know.

Just as she was musing on this, the front door opened and in came Tom and Aidan.

'He rang me,' Kate called to them as they hurried to the living room. 'He's on his way to Vale Volumes as we speak.'

'We know,' Tom said. 'We passed them on the High Street. It took all of my well documented tact and diplomacy to stop Aidan from weighing in on your behalf and letting Harry have it for accusing Corey of theft.'

Aidan looked sheepish. 'I wish I could say Tom's exaggerating, but I was fully prepared to have a strong word or two, at least.'

'But you figured you'd keep your cred with your nephew and hopefully you didn't do or say anything daft?' Kate's upward inflection was pure big sister, and she knew it, but it did still work occasionally with her brothers.

'Absolutely.' Aidan grinned. 'Besides, Corey and Harry looked pretty chummy walking back to the bookshop, so I figured they'd worked out the whole missing money thing.'

'I'm sure we'll all find out at some point.' Kate smiled back. 'Thanks, you two, for rushing out to look. I appreciate it.'

'What are family for?' Aidan smiled. 'Speaking of which, I noticed that Sam's car was back in the driveway. Shall I nip round and see if they're up to visitors? We still haven't met our new niece.'

'Why don't you text them first before you descend on them?' Kate said. 'The first few days at home with a new baby can be overwhelming, and they didn't have the easiest time of it. Not to mention that, with Mum, Will and Tom arriving later, they might like a bit of time to settle in before we all go round there.'

'Fair enough,' Aidan said. 'And it'll give me some time to go and grab an organic, corn-fed onesie or something equally ethical from the High Street for Mia, and perhaps some supplies for the new parents, too.' He glanced at Tom. 'Want to come back out with me?'

'I've got lines to learn,' Tom said. 'Rehearsals start soon and I don't want to be the one who cocks up in front of Bristol's best theatre director.'

'You'll be brilliant,' Aidan said warmly. 'But fair enough. I'll see you both in a bit.' Kissing Tom, and waving a hand vaguely in Kate's direction, he sauntered back out of the front door.

'I can't believe how well he looks,' Kate said, when the front door had closed again. 'Married life obviously agrees with him. Although I never thought I'd see the day, after everything he's been through.'

'He doesn't talk much about it,' Tom said carefully. 'But the longer we're together, the more he opens up.' He shook his head. 'Makes you really appreciate the little, day to day things. Every moment is precious.' He could have sounded like the ultimate luvvy as he said that, but Kate recognised the sincerity and the love in his voice.

'He's lucky to have you,' she said.

'I'm just as lucky,' Tom replied. 'My choices weren't always so good. Aidan's restored my trust in a lot of ways, too.'

Kate considered that word, *trust*, and how it had shockingly changed everything between her and Phil once it had gone. She'd been beginning to trust Harry, too, until his error of judgement this morning. But was that really enough of a reason to push him away? Corey had obviously worked out his differences with him, so couldn't she? Or was she just looking for an excuse to walk away? To head back to Cambridge and not look back? She felt even more confused.

'Aidan meant it, you know.' Tom's voice intruded, but kindly, into her thoughts. 'He'd love it if you and your boys moved closer. He's pretty much resigned to not having kids of his own, not because we couldn't adopt but because he's still very much aware of his own recovery and isn't sure if he'll ever be in a place where we'll be able to have our own. He'd love to be a bigger part of all his nephews' lives. He might joke about and take the piss, but he loves you all, a lot.'

Isn't that what it all comes down to in the end, Kate thought. *Love?*

She smiled at Tom. 'I'm so glad you're part of the family now.' Reaching out, she gave her brother-in-law a hug. 'And you're right.'

'About what?'

'Everything,' she replied, knowing how cryptic she sounded. 'Now, I'd better crack on with the last of that painting in the hall-way, or I won't have earned my money here.' Smiling at Tom, she headed back upstairs to finish the job.

50

Having received a text from Sam and Florence that they'd love to have visitors in the early evening, Aidan, Tom and Kate had wrapped a huge pile of new baby presents for both parents and Mia by the time they were due to pop next door. Kate had also jumped online and arranged for a week's worth of prepared, nutritious meals to be delivered the next day. She remembered all too well how much 'food you can eat with one hand' was a hugely useful thing from having her own children. That situation of soothing or feeding a newborn with one arm while trying to get some food into yourself was one that was still vivid in her mind, and no matter how capable Florence might be proving with a new baby, every little really did help.

She still hadn't cleared the air with Harry, but since Corey was still at Vale Volumes, and presumably would be until closing time, she figured that the issue was at least partly resolved. She was dithering about sending him a text to test the water, but in all honesty, she wasn't sure what to say. She still wasn't all right with Harry's accusation, no matter how hesitant he'd been about articulating it to her, and she didn't know how to word a text to that effect, but also make it clear that she'd calmed down a little now Corey had been located, presumably by Harry himself.

Putting all thoughts of Harry aside for the moment, though, after all, her family should be her priority this evening, she checked in with her other two sons by text to see how far away they were. Then, when Corey texted her and said he'd be home just after six thirty, she let him know she'd be heading next door with Tom and Aidan, and his two brothers and grandmother, who would all have arrived by then. If he wanted cake and celebrations he was welcome to come over and join them when he got back. She had a feeling that, despite his disappearing act that morning, Corey would be over like a shot.

She was buzzing with excitement by the time Will had texted her to say they'd reached Willowbury, and when her mother's red Mercedes had come into view, and was turning into the parking spaces by the terraces, she was already out there, ready to welcome them.

As her mother carefully pulled up alongside Kate's Volvo, Kate flung open the front passenger door before her middle son, Will, could open it himself, and barely waited for him to get out before she was wrapping him in a massive cuddle.

'Get off, Mum!' Will said good-naturedly as he wiped off the huge kiss she put on his cheek.

Laughing, feeling an incredible sense of lightness now that all of her sons were here, she opened the back door nearest to her and did the same to Tom, who grinned and pushed her away playfully. 'Where's Corey?' Tom idolised his eldest brother, and had clearly missed him.

'He's at work, but he'll be home about half six.'

'At work?' Selina had got out of the car now and was heading to the boot so the boys could get their stuff out. Kate gave her mother a slightly gentler hug and kiss.

'Yeah,' Kate said, realising too late that she'd called Bay Tree Terrace home, probably for the first time, even though it wasn't *her* home. 'He's been working in the local bookshop – the owner offered him some work experience while he was staying here.'

'If I'd been you, I'd have packed him straight back to his father's for pulling a trick like that,' Selina said as she pushed her overnight bag out of the way, so the boys could get to theirs in the boot. 'He should have known better than to make everyone worry.'

'It's fine, Mum, honestly,' Kate said hurriedly, not wanting to start this visit on a sour note. 'And you're all here now, to see baby Mia and unwind for a few days, which is great.'

'Can I kip in the lounge, Mum?' Tom asked as they headed to the house. 'Will farts in his sleep.'

'Do not!' Will punched his brother on the arm and Tom tried not to wince.

'We'll see what Uncle Aidan and Tom have to say,' Kate said. 'Just fling your stuff in the bedroom at the end of the landing for now, and we'll sort it later.'

After a quick cup of tea, Selina headed off to book into the Travellers' Rest, and Kate found herself slipping easily back into the role of referee-cum-parent with her two younger sons. As they alternated between showing her their holiday photos on their mobiles and arguing about which sleeping bag belonged to whom, before declaring they were 'starving' because Gran had only made them a sandwich for the trip and that was 'hours' ago, Kate relished being reunited with them. It would be a squeeze the next few days, but it was worth it to have her boys back with her. She couldn't wait for Corey to come home, too, and then she felt she'd be able to truly relax. Somewhere in the back of her mind, the unfinished business with Harry niggled, but now wasn't the time to worry about that. Spending time with her two sons was all that mattered.

51

'Seriously, Harry, don't worry about it. Once Mum sees you and I are cool, she'll stop being stressy.'

Harry knew that the doubt was written all over his face, despite Corey's breezy assurances. 'Really?'

'Sure.' Corey grinned. 'She likes you. *Really.* She'll get over it.'

'I'm not so sure.'

They were clearing up for the day, straightening up books and making sure nothing had been left around the shop, especially in the Children's section. It was amazing how many beloved cuddly toys, comforters and other trinkets were left in Vale Volumes once children got immersed in the many choices on the shelves in the corner of the shop. Harry kept a little basket tucked under the counter to store any found property and tried to update the shop's Facebook and Instagram feeds with any finds in an attempt to reunite them with their owners. Most of the time, they did find their way home.

'Well, as I see it, you've got two choices,' Corey said.

'Which are?'

'Come back with me and have a word, apologise for jumping to conclusions and hope she forgives you, or spend the time until we all go back home hiding from her.'

'Neither sounds particularly preferable.' Harry grinned ruefully back at Corey and couldn't help wondering when he'd started taking advice about his love life from a sixteen-year-old.

'Well, it's up to you,' Corey said. 'But for what it's worth, Mum doesn't hold grudges. And once she sees that you and I are cool, I bet she'll get over being pissed off with you.'

'I'm glad you have such faith,' Harry replied.

Corey stopped straightening books and turned back to face Harry. 'What's the worst that can happen?'

'She brains me with a can of gloss paint? Shoves a paintbrush where the sun doesn't shine?'

'I'll make sure she's unarmed.' Corey's grin was infectious, and Harry found himself agreeing to walk back to Bay Tree Terrace after closing. At least he'd know, once and for all, whether he'd burned his bridges with Kate.

As they made their way there, just after six-fifteen on a warm, sunny Willowbury evening, Harry really hoped that Corey was right. He'd hate for things to finish with Kate this way. He really did want to be part of her life or, if not, then to say goodbye on a good note rather than a sour one.

'Oh, I meant to say, Mum's next door at my Uncle Sam and Aunt Florence's,' Corey said as they approached the houses. 'They're having a bit of a get-together and some party food.'

'I probably shouldn't intrude, then,' Harry said. He felt a stab of disappointment that he wouldn't be able to clear the air with Kate tonight, but Corey shook his head.

'Mum won't mind. No time like the present.'

Despite his gut screaming at him that intruding on a family celebration wouldn't exactly be the right way to make amends, Harry found himself swept up in Corey's optimism, and before he knew it, he was heading up the garden path to number two, Bay Tree Terrace. If it all went tits up, and Kate didn't want to see him, then at least he could make a swift getaway, he figured.

Corey knocked at the door, and within moments it was opened by none other than Kate herself. If she was shocked to see him hovering behind Corey on the doorstep, she did a good job of hiding it. 'All right, Mum?' Corey asked, sounding as normal as if he hadn't gone AWOL, been accused of theft and then been trying to matchmake his own mother.

'You and I will be having a chat later,' Kate said, clearly unwilling to enter into a parental discussion during a family party; much less in front of Harry.

'I brought Harry to see you,' Corey continued. 'That okay?'

'Well, we are in the middle of something right now,' Kate said. 'Aunt Florence is playing pass the parcel with baby Mia and Tom and Aidan are about to have their first spat over who gets to hold her first. My mother's due any minute from the Travellers' Rest where she's staying, and my two other sons are already here. It's a bit of a tribe out in the garden.' Despite her evident coolness towards Harry, he noticed the pleasure from having all of her children back with her in her eyes.

'Well, I'll go and wind up my brothers and meet my new cousin, then,' Corey said, 'and leave you two to it.' He gave his mother a knowing look and scooted past her and inside the house.

'Subtle,' Kate muttered. She turned back to Harry. 'Well?'

Harry swallowed. She wasn't going to make this easy for him; it was clear from her body language that she hadn't forgiven him for their conversation earlier.

'I'm so sorry, Kate,' Harry said. 'I should never have jumped to conclusions about Corey's honesty; especially without talking to him first. I was stupid, and I didn't think, and I'd hate for you to go back home without us having cleared the air.'

'You're right,' Kate said. 'You didn't think, and you did jump to conclusions.' She paused, then smiled. 'But I accept your apology. Your timing was lousy, but I couldn't definitively say that I would have reacted any differently. In fact, if Corey hadn't dragged you here this evening, I'd probably have texted you to tell you the same thing, anyway.' She took a step forward and reached out a hand to take one of Harry's, and he felt the jolt of electricity between them, as well as a huge sense of relief.

Harry took her hand and then pulled her closer, and their lips met in a slow, sweet kiss. 'That's a relief,' he said softly as they parted again. 'Corey doesn't need to protect me from flying paint cans, then.'

Kate looked quizzical for a moment, and then laughed. 'Not today, Harry, not today.'

As they broke apart, she gestured to the front door. 'Do you want to come and join us? There's plenty of party food and cake!'

'I wouldn't want to gate-crash a family celebration,' Harry said.

'No, honestly, come in and say hello if you like,' Kate replied. 'If nothing else, it saves you cooking your own tea tonight!'

Harry, buoyed up by the reconciliation with Kate, found himself being pulled through the hallway and into a kitchen that opened up into the garden by way of elegant French windows. With his hand firmly in hers, relief and happiness coursed through him. He suddenly knew, with a flash of recognition through his heart and mind, that he was falling in love with her, and he definitely didn't want her to go back to Cambridge without knowing that. But how and when to tell her was another matter completely. After all, he'd nearly buggered things up completely this morning, and he didn't want to make that mistake again, not with something that to him felt so vital, so important.

As they wandered through the kitchen and out onto the decking that was in the first part of the garden, Harry saw the family gathering and felt a lurch in his stomach for entirely different reasons. There were Florence and Sam, the proud, knackered parents, sitting on the comfy-looking garden sofa, while Kate's brother, Aidan, and his husband, Tom, one of whom was holding a tiny bundle in his arms, chatted amiably. Corey was lounging in another wooden patio chair, with a glass of Coke already in his hand and a plate of food in his lap. Two younger boys, obviously Will and Tom, were kicking a ball around at the bottom of the lawn, and trying to get Aidan to join them.

On seeing this contented family sight, Harry's hand instinctively tightened in Kate's before he could stop it. It wasn't as if he hadn't attended lots of these kinds of gatherings over the years, as various friends and family had married and had children, but there was something so loaded with significance about this one; so many people connected to Kate, and absolutely unconnected to him. And they'd all been through so much, both separately and together. He suddenly felt as though all of the years since his infertility diagnosis had rolled away, and he was slapped in the face with the realisation of just what had been denied him.

'It's all right,' Kate murmured, mistaking Harry's sudden change of mood for apprehension about seeing her family. 'They're an easy-going bunch; they won't give you the third degree.'

Harry swallowed hard, heart hammering in his chest. Despite the airy summer evening, he began to struggle for breath, and he felt a cold, creeping hand clawing at his throat in a horrible reminder of the panic attacks he hadn't had for a long time; at least not since he'd moved to Willowbury.

Kate, obviously noticing his sudden change of demeanour, stopped in her tracks and turned back to him, a quizzical yet concerned look on her face. 'Are you okay, Harry?'

Her voice, so gentle and concerned, made his eyes sting. He shook his head. 'I'm so sorry, Kate,' he said. 'I can't do this.' He knew he was trembling, and he quickly withdrew his hand from hers, full of shame and self-loathing, and that frustration that always seemed to follow hand in hand with an attack. 'I've got to go.' He shook his head and tried to make eye contact with her, attempting to ground himself, but his eyes started to swim.

'Let me drive you back home,' Kate said, the concern written all over her face now. 'You're in no state to walk back like this.'

'No, honestly, I'll be fine. I'll... I'll give you a ring.' He couldn't stay there any longer. Feeling as though he was going to black out, he bolted through the house and out of the front door, remembering just in time to pull it shut as he left. As he stared fixedly at the pavement in front of him, focusing on putting one foot in front of the other without throwing up or passing out, he somehow made it home.

52

Kate stared after Harry as he literally bolted back through Sam and Florence's house and her jaw dropped. Of all the things that could have happened, this *volte face* was something she hadn't seen coming; although, perhaps she should have. Being confronted with her entire family would be intimidating for anyone, let alone for someone with such a complicated history. Frozen to the spot, she dithered about what to do. Her mother was due back at Bay Tree Terrace any minute, and her sons were all together for the first time in weeks. But she felt instinctively that Harry shouldn't be left all alone after the way he'd reacted. What was the right decision?

'Was it something you said?' asked Aidan, trying to make light of what could have been a pretty awkward situation, had it not taken place in front of her own family. He wandered over to where Kate stood on the decking, baby Mia still protectively cradled in his arms.

'I'm not sure,' Kate said. 'One minute he was fine, and coming to meet you all, and the next he just bolted.'

Mia stirred in Aidan's arms, and for a second Kate hoped against hope that Aidan would eventually go on to have his own children. He'd always been such a natural with them, and from the way he kept glancing down at this latest addition to the family, he was clearly smitten with her. As Mia woke fully and began the familiar gesture that meant she was hungry, Aidan walked with Kate back to the others and passed the baby gently back to Florence.

'I think it's time she came back to you.' Aidan smiled.

'She's super hungry since we came home from hospital.' Florence smiled, and, glancing at Sam, added, 'Can you grab me a glass of water? A big one.'

'Sure.' Sam smiled back. 'Anything else while I'm in the kitchen?' As Florence shook her head, Kate followed Sam back through to the house.

'That was some freak out just now,' Sam said as he reached for a pint glass from the top cupboard. 'What was it all about?'

Kate shook her head. 'Ordinarily I'd tell you, you know that, but I'm only half sure myself.' She paused. 'What do you think I should do?'

'He looked pretty shaken up, Katie,' Sam said as he filled the glass full of water and took a gulp out of it himself before refilling it to take back out to Florence. 'If I were you, I'd get after him. We can all keep an eye on the boys.'

'Are you sure?' Kate asked. 'And I can't just walk out on my boys, not to mention Mum.'

'Go after him,' Sam said. 'You know you'll be worrying all evening if you don't. And the boys are fine. I can handle Mum, too.'

Kate was torn. 'But we're supposed to be celebrating you, Florence and Mia coming home. I can't just run out after some bloke.'

Sam regarded her levelly. 'Most of the time I'd agree,' he said, 'but something really got to him, Katie. I don't think you should have let him leave on his own. We'll still be here when you get back.' Sam yawned suddenly. 'And if that's the middle of the night, you can walk Mia up and down the garden until she goes to sleep; give Florence and me a break!'

'Fair enough.' Kate smiled. 'I'd better get going then.'

As she walked quickly back through the front door and hurried towards Harry's place, her mind was racing. Had Harry even got home, she wondered? Taking a deep, calming breath, she began to retrace the steps from Bay Tree Terrace to Vale Volumes, hoping against hope that she'd find Harry somewhere along the route and that he was all right.

53

When Harry opened the door, Kate immediately knew that all right was the last thing he was. He looked worse than he had when he'd had the flu, and, despite the fact that he gave a brief smile when he opened the door, his hands shook when he closed it behind her. Feeling a sense of relief that he had, at least, made it home and, more reassuringly, let her into the house, his appearance still concerned her. Whether he would let her into his headspace was another matter, too. He had once, when they'd been painting the shop, but whether he would again, in this state, was debatable.

'I'm sorry I ran out on you and your family,' he said. He was leaning against the wall in the hallway that went one way, on the ground floor, to the back of the shop, and the other way, via a staircase, to Harry's living space above. Kate remembered the last time she'd been here, and where she and Harry had swiftly ended up. This time, though, she felt an entirely different set of emotions as she looked at him.

'I thought I could do it,' he was saying, almost to himself. 'I thought, after all these years, that I'd be able to stand there, smile and be part of a family like yours.' He slid down the wall and slumped on the bottom step of the staircase.

Kate swiftly moved to sit next to Harry and this time, she didn't hesitate. Pulling his head down to her shoulder, just as she would have done for one of her sons, she cradled him in her arms, stroking his hair and holding tightly as he trembled, the waves of the panic attack still washing over him.

'It's all right,' she murmured. 'I'm here. It's all right, Harry.'

'No,' he said, so quietly that she could barely hear him. 'It's not all right, Kate. *I'm* not all right. I thought I was, but it's still the same. I'm damaged, useless. And seeing you all so happy, celebrating the one thing I could never give anyone else, brought it all crashing down around me again. Now, instead of celebrating Mia's new little life, and catching up with the sons you haven't seen in weeks, you're here, trying to put this useless, hopeless bloke back together again.' He brought his left palm up and smacked it hard against his forehead, once, twice, three times, until Kate took hold of it and laced his fingers through her own.

Kate wasn't afraid of what she saw in Harry; her own experiences with her younger brother, Aidan, had equipped her well for the mental trauma that panic and anxiety could bring. She'd talked Aidan down a few times during his rehabilitation after the horrors he'd faced when his platoon had been blown up in a roadside bomb in Helmand Province, and she'd never forget the haunted expression on his face as he relived the tragedy, over and over again in his waking and sleeping hours. While the reason for Harry's distress was vastly different, the symptoms were similar, and Kate knew that she needed to let the panic attack run its course before he'd be calm again.

'It's all right,' Kate said again, holding him not so tightly as to restrict him but closely enough to reassure him. 'You haven't done anything wrong. I'm here.' She focused on her own breathing, trying to transmit the rhythm to Harry, whose shakes were starting to subside as they sat there. He was gripping her hand, their fingers still entwined, and it seemed to anchor him to the moment, to allow him to escape out from the head loop that was playing over and over again.

It felt like an age that she sat there with Harry, saying nothing but trying to transmit reassurance through her physical presence. He'd lapsed into silence, apart from the odd shaky breath, but he seemed to draw strength from having her there beside him.

Eventually, Kate's knees were growing stiff, and she made a move.

'I think we should get you upstairs and somewhere more comfortable.' Standing creakily, she was relieved when he, too, stood up.

'It's all right,' he said softly. 'I can take it from here on my own.'

'Are you sure?' Kate didn't want to leave him.

Harry smiled. 'I'm not about to do anything stupid. Well, *more* stupid.'

'Having a panic attack isn't stupid,' Kate said. 'It can happen to anyone. Okay, making it from Bay Tree Terrace to here at the speed you did while having a panic attack, well, I can't work out if *that's* stupid or some world record, but you can't get stuck in a spiral about it now.'

They both stood, slightly awkwardly, at the bottom of the stairs, until Harry gave Kate a brief smile. 'I mustn't keep you from your family. Honestly, Kate, I'm completely okay with how this works now. It's just been a while since I've had one as bad as this but I'll be fine.'

'If you're sure,' Kate said, a note of doubt in her voice. She knew it was equally important to be guided by the person when it came to panic attacks, and not to crowd them, and she didn't want to invade Harry's space if that wasn't what he wanted.

'I'm sure.' Harry put his hands on Kate's shoulders before drawing her to him in a tight hug. 'You've done more than enough already.'

For a long, delicious moment, Kate luxuriated in the warmth of the hug. It felt so right to be here, in his arms. Their chemistry had always crackled, and now she'd seen how vulnerable he could be, a layer of protectiveness and compassion, a deeper understanding, had been added to that attraction. But he was right; the family were waiting back at Bay Tree Terrace for her.

'Call me tomorrow?' Kate said as they broke apart again. 'Or any time before then if you need me.'

'I'm fine, Kate, I promise.' Harry drew her to him, and placed a gentle kiss on her lips. 'It's nothing that hasn't happened before; it just crept up on me, when I thought I was going to be all right.' He shook his head. 'I've been around so many babies and children over the years, I can't think what the trigger was this time.'

'It's been a mad few weeks,' Kate said. 'I'm not sure if I'm coming or going, half the time; you must be exhausted too after being ill. Perhaps you just need to take a deep breath – metaphorically speaking – and think about what you want, and how you feel.'

'Very wise.' Harry gave a shaky laugh. 'But if I told you that I think I already know the answer to both of those questions, and she's standing right in front of me, what would you say?'

Kate smiled up at Harry, experiencing a flutter in her stomach that she'd grown accustomed to when she was with him. 'I'd say go and relax for the night, and we'll talk about this another time.'

'Fair enough.' Harry kissed her one more time before turning to the stairs.

'You'll be okay walking back by yourself?'

'Of course. Take care, Harry.'

As Kate watched Harry ascend the stairs to his flat, she tried to untangle the complex, knotted skein of emotions that being with him evoked in her. She knew she was beginning to let herself feel again, after such a long time of being too afraid to make that leap. The question was, was it the right thing to do, given her current living arrangements, his clearly fragile issues and three growing sons to consider? Shaking her head in bewilderment as she wandered back out of Harry's door, she set off home to spend some time with Mia, Sam, Florence and the rest of the family. Perhaps just being there with them this evening would give her the clarity she finally needed about just what to do with the rest of her life.

54

'Everything okay?' Florence asked as, twenty minutes later, Kate walked back out into the garden of Florence and Sam's house.

Kate smiled at her sister-in-law. 'Yes, I think so.'

Sam, Aidan and Tom had retreated inside with Corey, Will and Tom to play the latest *Call of Duty* on Sam's PlayStation, to continue the game Sam and Corey had started before Mia's somewhat precipitous arrival. The sounds of various guns and explosions drifted out of the living room as they played, but they weren't loud enough to wake Mia, who was snoozing peacefully in the Moses basket next to the garden sofa. Selina was indoors making a cup of tea, and had thankfully refrained from asking too many questions when Kate had walked back into the house. Kate knew they'd come later, though.

'It never ceases to amaze me that two guys who used to be in the armed forces can spend so much time shooting imaginary insurgents in a video game,' Kate observed as she poured herself a glass of wine from the bottle in the ice bucket on the picnic table. 'You'd have thought they'd have seen enough of the real thing.'

'Aidan told Sam it was kind of cathartic,' Florence said. 'And they're both so competitive, they can't stand the thought of their nephews continually kicking their arses!'

'That sounds more accurate.' Kate laughed. 'Aidan and Sam were horrendously competitive as kids, even though they loved each other so much. The times I had to mediate between them, even in card games.' Kate took a sip of her wine. 'I don't think Sam ever really got over it when Aidan beat his one hundred metres school record two years after Sam had set it. He still brings it up at family gatherings.'

'He's always been a bit of a perfectionist, hasn't he?' Florence mused. 'I hope he doesn't turn into a super competitive dad when this one's old enough to notice.'

'He'll be fine,' Kate said, 'although he'll probably go into training for the parents' races at Sports Day!' She looked thoughtful. 'You're going to be great at this, you know.'

Florence smiled. 'Don't. My hormones are shot to pieces as it is. The sight of a new baby giraffe at Bristol Zoo's Wild Place on *BBC Points West* finished me off at lunchtime!'

'They'll soon settle down,' Kate said, smiling too. 'Although, having said that, I still can't watch any films involving children or animals in danger – even *Home Alone* can catch me if I'm having an off day!'

'Great!' Florence rolled her eyes. 'So what you're saying is I'm basically going to be a basket case for the rest of my life.'

'That's exactly what I'm saying. But you'll get used to it,' Kate said.

'So, er, am I allowed to ask what freaked Harry out?'

Kate paused, wondering if she should disclose Harry's situation to Florence, who was, admittedly, trustworthy and an all-round lovely person. It wasn't her confidence to give, but it felt weird not to tell her.

'He's got some complex history around having kids,' Kate said, hoping to keep it vague. 'And being here this afternoon triggered his anxiety. He was much better when I left him, though.'

'So... is it serious between you guys?' Florence asked. 'I mean, staying in touch when you go home serious, or is this just for the summer?'

Kate took another sip of her wine before she answered. 'Honestly, Florence? I just don't know.' She leaned back on the garden sofa, staring up at the rapidly darkening sky. 'I really, really like him. He's clever, funny, actually seems to want to listen to what I have to say, and, most importantly, I feel like I can trust him.'

'And you obviously fancy the pants off him,' Florence added wryly. 'Aidan said you got home the other night with the biggest smile on your face, and he reckoned you hadn't just played chess all evening!'

'Bloody gossipy little brothers,' Kate grumbled good-naturedly. 'I didn't even know he was still awake when I got home. I know he just wants to see me fixed up again, but I don't know if that's what I want.'

'Well, who says you have to decide?' Florence said. 'I know you're not used to taking things as they come, but perhaps it's time just to go with the flow and see where it takes you.'

'That's just it.' Kate sighed. 'So much has changed over the past couple of years, and I don't know which way to jump now. I mean, should I just chuck all of my cards up in the air and say fuck it, move to Willowbury and take a risk that Harry and I might become something more permanent, thus potentially incurring the wrath of two of my sons, who haven't a clue what's been going on this summer, and probably won't take kindly to being moved away from their dad and all their friends, or do I just go back to Cambridge and an annexe in Mum's garden that's too small for me and three boys, and watch my bank balance getting smaller as house prices spiral away from me?'

Kate looked at Florence, who was regarding her thoughtfully. 'What?'

'Well, who says a move here has to be about whether or not something will happen with Harry?' she said after a pause. 'I mean, you've been saying all summer how nice it is that the three of you, Sam, Aidan and yourself, are all enjoying each other's company. Can't the move be about what *you* want, rather than worrying about what your boys might *not* want? Or what Harry *might* want? Isn't that the question you should be asking yourself? After all, in a few years, the boys will be off to university, or starting their grown-up lives in other ways; don't you think maybe you're allowed to do something just for you, and forget everything or everyone else?'

Kate shook her head. 'You talk a lot of sense for a woman who's just had a baby.'

'Thanks,' Florence said wryly. 'Think about it, though. Isn't it time you decided what was best for *you*?'

'If I promise I'll try, can I have another glass of wine?' Kate replied.

'Feel free.' Florence sighed. 'I'm on a booze ban for a bit longer, anyway, so you might as well have my share.'

'With pleasure,' Kate said. As she got up and went to top up her glass, she glanced over the garden wall at the empty, unloved house on Bay Tree Terrace that adjoined Sam and Florence's place and rounded off the dwellings.

'Do you know who owns that place?' she asked, taking a sip from her newly replenished glass.

Florence shook her head. 'No one's lived there since I've been here. I reckon someone around here would know, though. Why do you ask?'

'Oh, you know, just curious,' Kate said. 'It would make someone a good project.'

'*Someone?*' Florence asked, that wry note in her voice again. 'Would that someone be you, by any chance?'

'It's probably not big enough for me and the boys, anyway,' Kate replied hastily. 'I mean, you've only got the three bedrooms upstairs, haven't you?'

'Yeah, but I reckon that house is bigger,' Florence said. 'It's got three windows at the back, see, and we've only got two. Wouldn't surprise me if there was a box room or something you could use as a bedroom if you wanted to.'

Kate looked again. 'You're right,' she said, feeling a sudden fizz of excitement, before quashing it again. After all, the house wasn't even on the market. 'But it's all pie in the sky, really. I mean, for all we know, it's just being left as an investment, and the owners are waiting for the market to rise high enough to sell it.'

'True enough,' Florence replied, 'although, to be honest, the railway station's been open a few years now, so any commuter related property bounce will have happened already. Whoever does own it might be open to selling. But it would need a lot of work. Are you sure you'd be up for a project like that?'

Kate laughed. 'Steady on. I was just thinking out loud. Next time, I'll try to do it more quietly.'

'It would be nice, though.' Florence sounded a little dreamy now, which Kate put down to post-partum sleep deprivation. 'Imagine, the three of you all living on Bay Tree Terrace.'

Kate shook her head. 'I'm not sure if that's a dream or a nightmare! Aidan might well argue the latter.'

'Well, it's worth the thought,' Florence said. 'And if it means you get to spend a bit more time with Harry as a by-product of that, then all the better, right?'

'Let's just keep our feet on the ground, shall we?' Kate said, although inside, her mind was whirring. What if that house was achievable? Would she really take the plunge and move to Willowbury? Deciding that, after the day she'd had, now really wasn't the time to start thinking too deeply, she sat back on the garden sofa, drank her wine, and tried to relax.

55

A little the worse for wear after another glass of wine, but safe in the knowledge that she'd told the boys to come back to Aidan and Tom's place before ten o'clock, which was their 'holiday' bedtime, Kate rather unsteadily hopped over the dividing wall between the two houses on Bay Tree Terrace but paused before she put her key in the front door of Aidan and Tom's place. Curiosity, and that persistent itch of an idea that was just dying to be scratched made her mooch back out onto the pavement in front of the whole terrace and take a closer look at number three.

It certainly looks in a sorry state, she thought as she ambled up the cracked, weed-riven pathway to the front door with the paint peeling off it. The downstairs windows were grimy although none were broken, but it made it difficult to see, in what was left of the evening light, what the inside of the place might be like. Glancing behind her, to make sure no one was passing by to wonder what she was up to, she stepped off the garden path and put her hands and eyes up to the dirty front window, trying to get a glimpse of what lay behind the glass. It was difficult to make much out, but what she did see wasn't exactly an edifying sight. Faded wallpaper, with a pattern last in vogue in the 1980s, lined the walls of the front room, and looked rather unpleasantly nicotine-stained, unless that was just time and age or, even worse, damp. There was an equally grimy patterned carpet, the swirls of which Kate could just make out in the dying light, but no furniture. Next to the decidedly 1930s beige tiled fireplace was a dull brass coal scuttle, shoved wonkily to one side as if someone had decided that there was very little point in removing it, but nothing else graced the room. It looked as though it hadn't had a foot set in it for a very, very long time.

The dimensions were good, though. Florence and Sam's place, being mid-terrace, was a little more regularly shaped, with decent sized rooms, but Kate's impression was that this house on the side of the terrace might be slightly bigger. She knew there was an extension on the back, too, which was two storeys and perhaps added a fourth bedroom. A fourth bedroom, with three sons of her own, would be perfect. A flicker of excitement began to kindle in her stomach and her mind. How hard could it be to find out who owned this place in a small town like Willowbury, after all? Everyone seemed to know everyone around here, and she was sure someone would know. What if they could be persuaded to sell?

Shaking her head, she tried to ground her thoughts and her emotions again. She'd had a lot to drink and she hadn't even seen inside the place, except through the grubby front window. It could all be a pipe dream. And there was no guarantee that whoever owned it would want to sell, anyway. Glancing at her watch, she turned to walk back down the garden path and back to the house where she *was* currently living. As she did so, her phone buzzed with a text. Feeling mellow from the wine, she swiped the notification without paying much attention to the sender.

Her heart started to thump painfully in her chest, and that old, familiar sick feeling began to rise as it hadn't for nearly six months now; she really wished she'd ignored the message. Slumping down on the low wall that separated the unlived in, unloved house on Bay Tree Terrace from the other two, she swallowed down the bile that had shot up into her mouth at the name and message on the screen. Although she knew the conversation she was being asked to have was going to happen at some point, she really, really couldn't deal with it right now. She stood back up, on slightly shaky legs, and walked back to Tom and Aidan's house. The message had been from Jennifer, Phil's new partner, and had simply read:

Can you call me when you get a moment. I'd like to discuss the plans for the new baby.

* * *

After a night spent tossing and turning, Kate threw back her bedclothes in frustration. Was it too early to call Jennifer? She glanced at her watch. It was six thirty. Probably, she conceded grimly.

Time had done much to dull the anger and the pain that she'd first felt when Phil had come clean about his affair, but that didn't mean she was ready to have regular contact with Jennifer. Where necessary, and for the sake of her children, she'd communicated with her, and she'd often found herself thinking that, had circumstances been different, she might even have considered being friends with her. But circumstances weren't different. Jennifer would always be the woman that Phil fell in love with to replace her. That would always be the inescapable, inalienable truth, no matter how many years passed, and how much internal peace she tried to make.

Realising that no one in the house was going to be stirring for a while, with Corey and Will crashed out in the bedroom upstairs, and Tom, true to his word, still fast asleep on the sofa, Kate decided

to take herself off for an early walk to clear her head before she
made the call. Unable to face breakfast, she dressed quickly and
headed out of the house.

At six thirty in the morning, the High Street was, unsurprisingly, empty. Wandering up the incline in the direction of Willowbury Hill, hoping that a brisk stroll would clear the cobwebs, not
just from the sleepless night over the text but also from the wine,
Kate found herself looking up at the front window of Harry's flat as
she passed Vale Volumes. She wondered how he'd slept. Perhaps
when she'd spoken to Jennifer, she'd give him a call, too. God
knows she might need cheering up after that, although given
Harry's state of mind yesterday, perhaps they'd be cheering each
other up.

The slope of Willowbury Hill was a welcome distraction from
her thoughts as she began the ascent to the summit, from which,
she'd been reliably informed, she'd be able to see the whole of
Somerset laid out before her. The sun had risen a fair bit earlier,
and its comforting warmth soothed her body, if not her mind.
Approaching the top, she slowed her pace, looking around her to
take in the view, which truly was spectacular. Miles and miles of
patchwork fields spread away from the hill, embroidered with
hedgerows and clumps of trees. To the west lay the majestic trio of
outcrops, one on land, Brent Knoll, rising unevenly from the grassy
ocean of the Somerset Levels, and two more, Steep Holm and Flat
Holm islands, literally rising from the Bristol Channel, with Wales
dim and blueish grey beyond. A little turn and she saw the outline
of the Quantock Hills. The sense of standing on an ancient island,
with the other landmarks scattered around, was immense, and, in
the weirdness of her life at this present time, a timely visual
metaphor that choosing isolation was a lonely path to tread. She
knew she'd never truly be alone so long as she had her siblings and
her sons, but being with Harry this summer had reminded her just

how much she missed the companionship and passion of someone she... someone she...

'Hey,' a voice came from behind her. She started as a shadow fell across her own. 'I saw you from the window as you went past the shop. Not that I'm stalking you, or anything, but you looked a bit like you needed a chat.'

Kate's eyes suddenly, inexplicably, burned. She shook her head. 'I'm fine, honestly.' But even as the words came out, she knew she didn't believe them.

'Kate.' Harry's voice was soft and gentle, and as welcome as the sun that was now warming her face. Taking a deep breath, she was just about to turn around, to look at him standing behind her, when his right hand settled on her shoulder. She luxuriated in the contact for a long, delicious moment, marvelling once again how just that simple touch could both excite and reassure her. Leaning into him, she relaxed her body as he drew up behind her, until his arms were around her, and they were both looking out over the seemingly endless view, out to the sea and beyond.

'This place was meant to have been an island once,' Harry murmured into her ear. 'And legend has it that King Arthur came here to be healed. Perhaps it's time for both of us to get better.'

'Arthur's spouse played around on him, too, didn't she?' Kate's voice, while intended to be light, caught in a sob as she spoke.

Harry's arms tightened around her and he rested his head on her shoulder. 'I know it'll never really go away,' he began, 'but I want to be in your life to help you live the rest of it, to show you that you deserve all the love I can give you, if you'll have me.'

'I know you do.' She looked down at the vibrant green grass beneath her feet. 'It's just... there will always be things I'll have to deal with, even now Phil and I are divorced.'

'Do you want to talk about it?' Harry's breath against her ear made Kate's senses reel, despite her tumult of emotions.

'Not right now,' Kate said. 'But I will, I promise. I need to phone Phil's new partner and I'm just quietly freaking out about it.'

'Is it the boys?'

Kate shook her head. 'Something else.'

They lapsed into silence again, and Kate turned round. She noticed Harry's untucked white shirt, undone at the neck and rolled to the forearms, the dark blue jeans and smart trainers. He was back in control after yesterday and, oddly, looked all the more at peace for it.

'Are *you* all right?' she asked softly.

Harry smiled. 'Yes. Yes, I really am. I can't pretend there won't be times when I'm not, but I can deal with them.' He broke his gaze from hers and looked out over the vista once more. 'I've learned, especially since I've been living in Willowbury, that being happy, being contented isn't a goal... it's a series of moments made all the more sweet by the journey. Being sad, or hurt, or angry are all parts of that journey, too.'

Kate smiled. 'You sound like a right old hippy again.'

In answer, Harry, dropped his gaze, and his lips to hers in a sweet, gentle kiss. 'I don't care,' he murmured. 'Being here in this moment with you is what matters.'

Kate's lips responded immediately to Harry's, deepening the kiss, and her knees had virtually given way. After everything that had happened over the past few weeks, and despite the call she was going to have to make when she got down the hill again, she felt at peace in Harry's arms, even with the intense physical excitement that always rose in her when she kissed him.

After a little while, they broke the kiss again but stayed close. His embrace felt solid, reassuring and real. And at that moment, she knew for sure what she'd been skirting around pretty much since the moment she'd spilled coffee on him weeks ago. She was falling completely and utterly head over heels in love with him.

And, although her residual conflict over the end of her marriage and her ex-husband's new life would never really go away, it would, perhaps, just sit in the background a little more easily as time went on. Especially if this new chapter of her life, or at least what she was hoping would be a new chapter, could have Harry in it.

She took a step back and looked up at Harry once again. 'I want to tell you something,' she said softly. 'But I don't expect you to do anything about it, if you don't want to. I've learned the hard way not to ignore emotions, and what they're telling me, and I don't want to end up doing the same this time.'

'Okay.' Harry smiled gently. 'Then tell me.'

Kate took a deep breath. 'This summer has been the happiest I've had for a long time. In spite of all of the ups and downs, I've come to realise a few things. And one of those things is that I'm falling in love with you, Harry.' She shook her head. 'I'm not saying that to put any kind of pressure on you, and what I have to tell you next might make you run about a thousand miles in the opposite direction, but it did cross my mind that perhaps I might want to spend some more time in Willowbury, if I can.'

Harry's look of surprise was swiftly followed by one of excitement, which, even before he spoke, reassured Kate. 'Wow. I mean... wow!' He ran his hands down her arms until he was holding her hands. 'And there I was, worrying about pressuring *you*.'

Kate laughed shakily. 'I have no idea if it's practical or not, and the house I want isn't even on the market, but one step at a time.'

'And you're falling in love with me?' Harry said wonderingly, as if the first part of her confession had only just sunk in. 'With me?'

Kate's laugh turned to a hiccup as she nodded. 'I am, Harry.'

'Oh God, Kate...' Harry pulled her close. 'I didn't want to pressure you by telling you that I felt exactly the same, but since you said it first...' He trailed off tantalisingly, pulling back again to look into her eyes. She noticed, not for the first time, how deeply, darkly blue they were. 'I'm falling in love with you too. And if my hands weren't shaking so badly right now, I'd be trying to find a sappy track by Foreigner on my phone to underline the bloody point.'

Kate laughed again. 'I'll hold you to that, the next time we're back at yours.'

They embraced again, both shaking rather more now than they had been at the start of their conversation.

'Come back now if you like,' Harry said huskily. 'No time like the present. And the shop doesn't open until nine o'clock.'

Kate shook her head. 'Much as I'd love to, I'd better make this call, and then I really should discuss the possibility of moving here with my sons.'

'I don't envy you,' Harry said. 'Of all the conversations to have, that's right up there on the list of tricky ones.'

'I know,' Kate said. 'But I honestly do think it could work for us. And they'll still be able to spend lots of time back with their dad who has a house big enough to accommodate them without them having to cram in together. Even with the new baby.'

Kate felt Harry stiffen in surprise, but then he just as quickly relaxed. 'So that's what you've got to make your call about, I presume?'

'Yup.' Kate, despite herself, smiled. 'Can't say I envy him the sleepless nights and nappy changes.' Then, realising what she'd said, especially after Harry's stressful event yesterday, she shook her head. 'I'm sorry, Harry, that was insensitive.'

Harry, to her relief, smiled back. 'I don't expect you to pussy-foot around the subject, Kate, especially not if you and I are going to be spending more time together. I can't live my life trying to avoid it, after all. And as I said, I know there will be moments like yesterday when I struggle, when something triggers a response like that, but it's part of me, it's who I am. And I'm at peace with that.'

Kate leaned up and kissed him again. 'I really am falling in love with you, you know.'

'And I with you. Now let's get off this hill, shall we, and get a coffee.'

Nodding, hand in hand with Harry, Kate headed back down to Willowbury, feeling more than ready to face Jennifer, Corey, his brothers and whatever else was going to be thrown her way.

56

After a coffee with Harry from the Cosy Coffee Shop, and a croissant for breakfast, Kate decided it was now a reasonable time to call Jennifer back. It was coming up to eight thirty, after all. It was likely that the boys would be stirring too, and she needed to make sure she was on hand for when they did. They might all be getting older, but she still wanted to spend as much time with them as she could. Fortunately, the conversation with Jennifer turned out to be not half as awkward as she'd been anticipating. Perhaps it was just that she, Kate, felt a whole lot more settled after coming to her own decisions about the next stages of her life, and as she ended the call, she felt lighter. Jennifer had been guarded, but her excitement had shone through and, to her surprise, Kate found herself feeling pleased for the other woman, if not a little smug that Phil would be the one facing sleepless nights all over again. She definitely felt as though her time for all that had well and truly passed and was glad.

'Everything okay, Mum?' Corey asked as he came downstairs showered and ready to begin work at Vale Volumes.

'Yeah,' Kate said. 'Yes, actually, it really is.' She paused, wondering if now was the time to bring Corey into the conversation about her potential future plans. 'Have you got a minute?'

'I think so,' Corey replied. 'Harry's not expecting me in until ten today, so if it turns into more than a minute, can you drive me to the shop?'

'Sure. Can you go and get your brothers for me, too?'

Corey nodded and, within a couple of minutes, all three of her sons were seated at the kitchen table. Tom and Will were still in their pyjamas, but were, at least, awake.

'So, what's on your mind, Mum?' Corey said.

Kate looked at her eldest son, who, in these few short weeks already seemed happier, more relaxed and more confident. *Was it to do with being here?* she thought. She felt suddenly nervous about discussing her plans with them all.

'Well, I was thinking about what happens after the holidays,' she began. 'And the more I think about it, the more I think I'd like to make some changes to how things are at the moment. After all, even though Gran's offered us her annexe, it's hardly big enough for you all and me, and I reckon we'd all go nuts within weeks.'

'Okay,' Corey said carefully. 'So, what is the alternative plan?'

'Yeah, Mum, what are you thinking?' Tom piped up, his face a mixture of excitement and concern.

'Well...' Kate looked down at her hands, prolonging the moment for as long as she could. 'How would you all feel about moving here, to Willowbury?'

'Are you serious?' Corey said. 'I mean, is this because of Harry?'

'Who's Harry?' Will asked.

'No!' Kate said quickly. 'Harry's just a friend—'

'*Friend?* Yeah right!' Corey smirked.

'Anyway,' Kate went on hurriedly. 'It's more that I've really liked being closer to your uncles and aunt while we've been here. And I feel settled.' She paused, searching the boys' faces for a reaction, but they were listening carefully to her, not giving anything away. 'And I'm not going to up sticks after knowing some guy for six weeks, anyway. I should hope you know me better than that.'

'Fair enough,' Will said. 'But it would suck, being on the other side of the country from my mates.'

'I know,' Kate said. 'And I wouldn't do anything without talking it through with you all first. It's just that...' She trailed off as the reality of her decision, not just for herself but for her sons, really hit home. 'I could never afford a house like we had in Cambridge when Dad and I were still together. Here, there's a chance we could have something better, and the chance to do some new things. And I know how much you've liked being here when we've visited. This week, before we have to go back to Gran's, we've got a real chance to explore, and see if this is the kind of place we feel we can live. What do you think?'

'You're not going to, like, make any decisions right away are you, Mum?' Will asked. 'I mean, we *are* going to go back home at the end of the summer, aren't we?'

'Of course,' Kate said. 'But we can't stay at Gran's forever; the annexe just isn't big enough. Here, we've got the chance to find somewhere we really like, and we'll also be closer to your uncles. A lot closer,' Kate said unguardedly.

'What?' Corey looked quizzical.

'Oh, nothing,' Kate replied hastily. 'It's just a pie in the sky idea at the moment anyway. I need to do some more thinking first.'

'And we'll get to stay with Dad as much as we want, too?' Tom said.

Kate smiled. 'I'm sure your dad and I will be able to work something out that suits all of us.'

'Look, Mum.' Corey's voice became very serious. Kate heard in it the same tone she used to use when she wanted to speak for herself and her brothers, as the eldest. 'Do what you want to do. We'll all be fine, honestly. If moving here's what feels right, then just do it. It's about time you did something to make you happy, instead of worrying about everyone else.'

Kate looked at all three of her boys in turn, and wasn't surprised that her younger two were looking decidedly less happy about this potential life decision than their brother. But then, she reasoned, this was a hell of a bombshell to drop on them when she hadn't seen them for a lot of the summer. Kate's throat constricted. 'Thank you,' she said quietly. 'That means a lot, Corey, it really does. But I promise I'm not going to make any mad decisions without fully considering you all first. This has to be something that works for all of us.'

'Cool.' Corey got up from the table. 'I'd better get to the bookshop. If I jog, I'll just about make it on time.'

Kate was encouraged by Corey's acceptance of the proposal, but something told her she'd have a way to go to convince her other two sons. Although, as Will got up, he turned back to her and grinned. 'It *is* pretty nice here,' he said. 'And you seem miles happier than you've been in ages, Mum. I'm not saying I'm, like, *cool* about it—' he rolled his eyes at Corey as his older brother slapped him on the back of the head on the way out to get ready for work, 'but as long as I could still see my mates, maybe it wouldn't be totally lame.'

'Even if we do decide to do this, it'll take time to get schools and things sorted, anyway,' Kate said. 'I'm not going to drag you here kicking and screaming overnight, I promise.'

Tom, who'd been fairly quiet throughout the conversation, looked up at Kate from where he was still sitting at the kitchen table. 'Can we stay with Dad if we want to?'

Kate felt her heart lurch. 'Would that be what you really wanted, love?'

Tom shrugged, fingers picking at a bit of loose varnish on the tabletop. 'I dunno.'

'There's a lot to think about for all of us,' Kate replied. She stood up from the table and went over to Tom, putting an arm around his shoulders. 'I know you've been through a lot, these past couple of years. That's why I wanted to talk to you all, to see how you might feel about this.'

Tom leaned into her for a moment, before he got up and gave her a smile. 'Uncle Aidan's a better footballer than Dad... maybe it wouldn't be *that* bad.'

Realising that her youngest son was making quite a concession, she smiled back at him. 'Maybe it wouldn't,' she said softly, as Tom wandered off to get dressed.

57

Corey was happily rearranging the 'Thrillers' section of Vale Volumes when Harry decided that it was time to take his newest employee out to lunch. Since Corey's 'official' work experience stint was coming to an end soon, Harry figured it warranted some sort of reward. He'd grown to like having Corey around, and if things didn't work out in the way Kate had hinted back on Willowbury Hill, he'd miss the boy when he went back to Cambridge.

'Fancy a bite to eat?' Harry asked as he ambled down the shop, ostensibly to inspect Corey's handiwork with the shelves.

'Sure,' Corey said, stepping back from the shelf. 'Did you want me to nip out and grab you something, boss?'

'I thought I'd treat you today, since you'll be going home at the end of next week,' Harry said. He didn't know quite how much of her plans Kate had shared with Corey, so he tried to act as though he was none the wiser about Kate's possible relocation to Willowbury.

'Chill, Harry,' Corey replied, giving Harry a grin. 'Mum's already told me we might be moving here, so you *can* talk about it if you want to.'

Harry shook his head. 'Why do I always feel as if you're one step ahead of me?'

'Your age, boss,' Corey said wryly.

'Do you still want a job or not?' Harry grinned back. 'So, about that lunch...'

* * *

A little while later, they were munching on Somerset Brie and grape baguettes and sipping lattes in the window of the Cosy Coffee Shop. Harry, who was a more seasoned coffee drinker, walked up to the counter to get another one. Jack Winter was in conversation with another customer, so he waited patiently. While Jack was making his cappuccino, they chatted idly, until Jack interjected suddenly.

'I know what I meant to tell you,' he said as he frothed the milk for the top of Harry's coffee, 'if Kate's looking for another decorating job before she goes back home, I might be able to point her in the right direction.'

'Oh yeah?' Harry replied. He wasn't sure, given Kate's time-frame, that she'd be in the market for another job, but it might be worth mentioning to her, just in case. After all, if it meant she hung around in Willowbury a little bit longer...

'There's a bloke who bought a house a couple of streets from here a few years ago as an investment who's now looking to sell. Needs the money for some other development he's got. He was in here the other day asking if we knew of anyone who could spruce it up for him. Make it look presentable for the estate agent's pictures. I thought Kate might be up for the job, if she's got time. I've no idea if it's just a quick lick of paint or something more involved, though, so it might not be a goer for her.'

Harry's mind began to race. 'Any idea what his name is?'

Jack looked quizzical. 'Chris... something, I think. I'll see if I can find out. Do you have Kate's number, in case he comes back in?'

'Let me have a word with her first,' Harry said, uncomfortable at the notion of just handing over Kate's personal mobile number for Jack to give to someone at random. 'I'm seeing her later, so I'll let her know, see if she's interested.'

'Okay,' Jack said. 'But I know he was keen to get the ball rolling, so don't get all distracted and forget to mention it.' He winked at Harry. 'I know that's a possibility as far as you and Kate are concerned.'

'Very funny,' Harry muttered as Jack handed him his coffee. Chances were, Kate wouldn't have time to do another job before the end of the summer, but he owed it to her to pass on Jack's message, just in case, and it would give him a reason to ask her out for a drink later, after all.

58

Kate, having done the final 'snagging' of the work at Tom and Aidan's house, was at a loss as to what to do with herself for once. She'd spent the past five weeks scraping, painting, sanding and repainting the walls of this happy terraced house, and now, finally satisfied that she'd done the best job she could, she could relax a little. Aidan had already paid her agreed fee, and so she was free to do what she wanted for a week or so before she had to go back to Cambridge.

The trouble was, she was so unaccustomed to having the time to do what she wanted, she didn't quite know what to do. She should be setting up a website, getting Aidan to write her first testimonial and putting the word out there about her new business, but she felt in a strange sort of limbo. In truth, she still couldn't start any of that until she knew exactly who she was aiming to attract with this new business; clientele in familiar, cosy Cambridge, or willing new customers in Willowbury?

Walking aimlessly through to Corey's room, she flipped idly through his copy of Artemis Bane's newest novel in the Redcliffe Trilogy. The blurb on the back made it seem like pretty standard

Young Adult fiction fare; a continuation of the story about the young, vulnerable hero, thrust suddenly into a world he doesn't understand, who has to fight against seemingly insurmountable odds to gain a foothold into a new existence, complete with complex first love and the inevitable heartache that it brings. Although she smirked at the predictable premise, she was soon drawn back into the story of the young man, Malcolm, and his trials and tribulations, and found herself captivated by the strength and clarity of Artemis Bane's writing. Much as she hated to admit it, she could see exactly why he was a multi-million selling international star.

Aidan and Tom had taken Will and Tom out to Bristol for the afternoon for an impromptu trip to walk Clifton Suspension Bridge and to explore the cave tunnels in the Avon Gorge, and Kate, being nervous both of heights and enclosed spaces, had decided not to go with them. They were planning on taking the boys out to eat before they came home, too, which meant that she had an uninterrupted afternoon and some of the evening ahead of her. Selina was next door with Sam and Florence. She'd cleaned their house from top to bottom and had now gone to the supermarket to get in some provisions. Kate had laughed at Sam's text, which he'd sent her when their mother had been elbow deep in washing up, which explained that, while he was grateful for the help, their mother had a way of making him feel completely useless. Kate, grinning, had told him to suck it up and be pleased he'd have a spotless house for a while. Selina was going back that afternoon, anyway, being reluctant to spend too much time away from home.

As the minutes ticked by, Kate forgot all about the world outside the book, and the fact that, while looking for the snags in her work, she had decided to put a final coat of paint on the hall skirting boards, as she was drawn further and further into Malcolm's story. When Malcolm was thrown headfirst into dangerous challenges, having lost everything of his old life except his memories, she found herself reflecting on how hard it was to start again, at any age.

Perhaps now really was the time to take the plunge in her own life. She'd broached the subject with the boys, who, while cautious, hadn't vetoed the idea outright, Harry was clearly ecstatic at the possibility of having her move closer and Sam and Aidan were also more than happy for her to move here, if she decided to. She'd come to Willowbury for a break from the traumas of the last few years, to get some breathing space before she, like Malcolm, started again. Why couldn't she just do it? What was she so afraid of?

She pondered, for a long time, exactly what was holding her back. Phil had hurt her deeply when he'd fallen in love with Jennifer, even though she knew things hadn't been right between them for years. She'd had the thought, more than once, that she'd wait for the boys to leave home and then leave Phil. The irony was that he'd got there before her. And, really, after two years, that was all it was. If he hadn't made the move, ended the marriage, would she still be sharing that bed with him, wondering how her life had come to this?

And yet. Phil had been security, stability; barring the end. Now she was on her own, making decisions for the boys and herself. Did another relationship fit into that life? Would it ever fit in? Just as she was finishing the penultimate chapter of Artemis Bane's novel, she received a text from Harry:

Are you busy tonight? I have some news that might interest you! H x

Texting back a quick, positive response, she wondered what he had to tell her, but before she could think much further, the phone flashed up Phil's number in a call.

'Hi,' she said, answering her phone.

'Hi, Kate,' Phil replied. She was still so attuned to the tone of his voice, she knew immediately that something was bothering him; you didn't stay married to someone for sixteen years without being able to recognise nuances like that.

'Everything okay?' she said.

'You tell me.'

Kate drew a breath. 'What's that supposed to mean?'

'I spoke to Tom earlier. He said you've been talking to them about making a move to the West Country. Were you planning on letting me know at any point?'

'It's an idea I'm throwing around at the moment, Phil, that's all. Nothing's been decided. After all, I've got Mum's annexe to go back to. And school's starting again soon, too.'

'Well, that's a relief,' Phil replied. 'After all, I'd like to think that you'd speak to me if you were seriously planning on taking my sons halfway across the country away from me.'

'Of course I would!' Kate replied. 'As I said, it's just an idea. I spoke to them this morning to see how they *might* feel about *possibly* moving closer to their uncles. I wouldn't make that kind of decision on the fly, without thinking carefully about it first. And talking to you, of course.'

'I'm glad to hear it,' Phil said. 'The way Tom told it, you'd basically decided that was what was going to happen. He didn't seem hugely impressed.'

'Look,' Kate said, forcing a patience into her voice that she was rapidly starting to lose. 'When have you ever known me to make a decision without thinking things through? Of course I'm not going to just move the boys here without talking to them, and you. But you have to understand that I need to draw some lines under everything that's happened over the past couple of years. Moving here, to be closer to most of my family, is something I'm considering.'

'It's quite a revenge tactic, Kate, moving our sons all that way away from me.' Phil didn't sound angry, Kate realised, rather more hurt.

Kate leaned back against the kitchen counter, suddenly feeling more than a little light-headed. 'It's not about revenge, Phil. You know that. If I was into that, I'd have made life far more difficult for you when we split. But I didn't, did I? You and Jennifer have had the chance to make a fresh start, set up your new home; why shouldn't I have the chance to do the same?'

'No one's saying you can't do that.' Phil sighed. 'But do you have to do it quite so far away? The boys'll hate being uprooted from their friends, their sports teams, their school. You're not being fair to them.'

Kate let out a long sigh. 'Don't you think I've thought about all that since I've been here? This isn't just some pie in the sky idea, Phil. I've got family here, family who've kept me going over the past couple of years. I think a move here could be a really good thing for us.'

There was a silence on the end of the line.

'Look,' Kate said, wanting to finish this up as calmly as she could, and not wanting to go over old ground. 'As I said, I haven't made any decisions yet, and if I do decide to move, I'm going to need your support. I've no intention of just uprooting the boys from their home on a whim. If, and I mean *if*, I do this, they'll need to know that you're going to be there for them, too. Can you do that?'

'Of course I can!' Phil said. 'They're my sons, and I want what's best for all of them. But, Kate...'

'What?'

'I know you. And this kind of decision-making isn't your style. You've always been so rooted in Cambridge. As someone who still cares very much for you, and our boys, please don't jump into anything that you might regret.'

Kate smiled, despite herself. 'Perhaps it's time I did a little more jumping, Phil. Things are different now.'

'Just be careful, Kate,' Phil warned as they ended the call. 'I know I have no right to say that, but I don't want to see you doing something you'll regret.'

'I know,' Kate said softly. 'And don't worry. I'll keep you posted about my wild and wacky plans, for the sake of the kids.'

As she ended the call, Kate reflected on the implications of a move to Willowbury. She knew it couldn't just be about what she wanted; her boys had to come first. But even in the short time they'd been here, she could see the good the change of scenery was doing them, and the increased contact with her brothers and their families. Going back to Cambridge was the safe thing, the sensible thing, but was it time to take some risks? If she didn't, would she end up regretting it? Or was a move to Willowbury going to be a huge mistake?

59

Despite his earlier reservations, Harry was buzzing with excitement when he brought the drinks out to the table on the front flagstones outside the Travellers' Rest. Kate picked up on this and smiled.

'What are you looking so pleased with yourself about?' she said, taking the glass of rosé wine he'd bought her.

Harry grinned. 'I was talking to Jack earlier. He mentioned that he might have found another decorating job in Willowbury, if you've got time before you go back.'

Kate swallowed her wine a little too quickly, and coughed. When she'd recovered her composure, she shook her head. 'I'm not sure I'll have time for another one! Doing your shop as well as Aidan's house was a push, and I'm going back to Cambridge next week.'

'Well, if you change your mind, Jack said to leave your number at the coffee shop and he'd pass it on,' Harry said. 'I've no idea if it's a big job or a small one, but it might be good for your portfolio. You've already got some great shots for your website, when you set it up, but it's good to give prospective clients as much of a visual as possible, especially as a new business.'

Just as he was taking another sip of his pint of cider, Harry's phone buzzed with a text. Kate saw him glance down and give a smile.

'It's Jack,' he said as he swiped and read. 'That guy came back into the coffee shop this afternoon and left his number. Did you want it?'

Kate felt her brow furrow. 'I honestly don't know,' she said. Then, after a moment more thought, 'I suppose there's no harm in talking to him. If it's a small job, I could probably squeeze it in before I have to go back. The boys are going back to Phil's at the weekend anyway. I was planning on going back with them, but a day or two more won't hurt, if it's money in the bank.'

Harry swiftly forwarded her the text from Jack and she stored the number in her phone's memory. 'Shall I call him now?'

'If you want to,' Harry said. 'Might be worth finding out what he wants.'

Before she could change her mind, Kate pressed the green button. After a few rings, the phone was picked up. 'This is Chris Charlton,' came the voice on the other end of the line, cool and businesslike.

'Er, hi,' she said. 'This is Kate Harris. Jack from the coffee shop passed on your number to me about some redecorating work. Is this a good time to talk?'

'I'd love to,' Chris replied. 'But I'm up to my ears in lime plaster at the moment. Can we meet at the house tomorrow morning and you can take a good look, see if you'd like the job?'

'Okay,' Kate said. 'Is eight o'clock too early? I've got my sons with me at the moment and we're off out for the day after that.'

'Eight's fine. Can I give you the address?'

'Absolutely,' Kate said. She scrabbled with her other hand in her bag for a pen and a scrap of paper.

'Right. So it's on the edge of Willowbury town centre, on the main road towards Bridgwater. As you head out of the town, you'll see a row of three terraced houses on the right-hand side, used to be railway workers' cottages, all red brick. The house is the last one on the right, number three.'

All this, to Kate was sounding heart thuddingly familiar. 'I think I know where you mean,' she said, feeling slightly breathless.

'Great,' Chris said. 'I'll meet you there in the morning. Oh, you'll need the road name as well, won't you?'

'Yes,' said Kate faintly. 'Of course.'

'Sorry,' said Chris. 'Should have mentioned that first. It's Bay Tree Terrace.'

60

The next morning, after battling with the twin sensations of excitement and trepidation, Kate got out of bed early and got ready to meet Chris Charlton at the last house on Bay Tree Terrace. She wasn't quite sure what she was going to say to him, after all. When she'd found out that he was the one who owned the house she'd been fantasising about, she was suddenly thrust into a tailspin of ideas, some half-baked and some rather more down to earth. What if...? Shaking her head, she remembered what Harry had said as they'd walked home from the pub last night. *There's no harm in just taking a look.*

That was true, but her agenda in doing so was suddenly very, very muddled. What she'd thought was going to be a possible job offer, to slap a bit of paint on some walls prior to a house sale, was suddenly far more complex. Should she mention to Chris that she'd been imagining buying this very house? Or would he just laugh in her face, and ask her to wait until it was up on the market officially? Was it too early to take a chance on her future, having literally just raised the possibility of moving to Willowbury with her sons? She was so confused. There would be other houses for sale in this area, of course, but the idea of buying the third house on Bay Tree Terrace had such a pleasing symmetry to it that she couldn't stop wondering *what if...*?

It was coming up to eight o'clock. Kate, far too strung out to eat breakfast, put her teacup in the sink and then headed out the front door. Sam, who was on his way out, too, caught her on the way past the middle house.

'Where are you off to?' he said, obviously clocking the odd expression on her face.

'You wouldn't believe me if I told you,' Kate said.

'Try me.' Sam fell into step beside her.

'How about right here?' Kate said, pausing at the rusted gate that led through to the front door of number three.

'What?' Sam stopped dead in his tracks. 'Why here?'

'The guy who owns it wants it redecorated.' Kate paused, then added, 'Before putting it on the market.'

Sam's jaw dropped. 'That's, er, some timing.'

'Isn't it?' Kate's hand on the gate began to shake. 'I mean, me having a pie in the sky idea after a couple of glasses of wine is one thing, but this changes everything. Makes it a bit more *real*, doesn't it?'

'Are you going to come clean about your, er, *pie in the sky idea* to this guy?'

'God, Sam, I don't know.' Suddenly the reality of it all hit Kate like a cider apple falling from a tree. 'I mean, truthfully, this changes nothing, does it?'

'Or it changes everything.' Sam gave a yawn. 'Sorry. It's not you. Mia was awake for most of last night. Florence has got her in our bed now, both of them sleeping it off.'

'So I can't rely on you for any sensible advice, then, in your current sleep deprived state?' Kate smiled wryly at her brother.

'Maybe not. But don't rush into anything, Katie. Yes, this could be a sign from the universe, and in Willowbury there are plenty of people who believe in that sort of thing, but the hard facts are a little more difficult to ignore. You need to think this through, for you and the boys. And even for Phil.'

'I know.' Kate saw a silver BMW estate pulling up to the kerb. A tall, lean guy wearing a plaid shirt got out, slammed the door and locked the car before heading towards them.

'Hi,' he said as he approached. 'I'm Chris. Kate?'

'That's right,' Kate replied. 'And this is my brother, Sam, who lives next door.'

Chris smiled at Sam. 'Yeah, I know Sam – we were in the town's production of "Much Ado About Christmas" a couple of years back.'

'Much against my better judgement!' Sam laughed at the memory. 'Although it all turned out okay in the end. Chris played Don John to my Benedick... it was an experience, all right.'

'At least you didn't end up getting dunked in a barrel of cider!' Chris grinned.

'True.' Directing his attention back to Kate again, Sam added, 'Not that I can offer any constructive help, but do you want me to come and take a look at the house with you?'

Kate shook her head. 'You go and grab what you need to from the shops and get back to Florence and Mia. I'll see you later.'

'Okay.' He turned back to Chris. 'Nice to see you again.'

'You too. Shall we?' Chris asked. Kate nodded, and he continued talking as they neared the front door. 'It had the central heating done, and the damp proofing when I bought it a couple of years ago but I wasn't really thinking too much about décor.' He glanced back at her as he opened the front door, which squeaked when it moved. 'The plan was to hang on to it until the market rose, but I've got a bigger project on the go, and I really need a cash injection, so it's time to get it ready to sell.'

'I see,' Kate said. As she stepped through the front door after Chris, despite her best intentions, she felt a frisson of excitement. But it was too soon for that. She needed proof that this could be what she'd daydreamed about. Or proof, indeed, that it could never be.

As they walked through the ground floor, Kate noticed the rather more generous dimensions of the place compared to the two other houses on the terrace. Her observations about an extension had largely been correct, and although it had obviously been done over twenty years ago, it had been a sympathetic addition. The kitchen, like Florence and Sam's, was at the back, and there was a small room off to one side of it with a window overlooking the back garden.

'It's got great space,' Kate said. 'When, er, were you thinking about getting it up on the market?'

'As soon as possible,' Chris replied. 'The place my wife and I are working on right now has some serious issues, and we need to get them sorted before we get any further. It's a shame, really, but something has to give.'

Looking at the state of the place, Kate knew almost immediately that she wouldn't have time to tackle a project this big before she went back to Cambridge. Gazing up at the ceilings, which had Artex swirls all over them, she turned back to Chris.

'I'm afraid this is too big a job, even if it was just a couple of coats of paint that you wanted, for me to get done before I go home,' she said.

'Fair enough,' Chris replied. 'I've got a local guy coming round this afternoon to take a look, but Jack seemed keen for you to get first refusal.'

'That was kind of him.' Kate smiled. It was another example of small-town spirit that appealed to her about Willowbury.

'Well, if you're sure, then I'd better get back,' Chris said. 'I've got a ton more lime plaster to mix and spread before today's over.'

It's now or never, Kate thought. 'Look, Chris...'

'Yeah?'

'I like this place. A lot. I'm not promising anything, but do you think you could give me an idea of what you're planning on selling for?'

Chris looked surprised. 'Well... in its current condition, or with the decorating done?'

Kate grinned. 'I think you and I both know that a paint job adds value, which is fine. But, and as I said, I'm not promising anything, if the price was right, and you were looking to move it quickly... I might be interested in buying.'

'You clearly get on better with your brother than I do with mine, if you're thinking of moving next door!' Chris laughed. 'But each to their own. I need to get a valuer in, but I can let you know when I have, if that's a serious proposal.'

'To be honest, I'm not sure if it is, right now,' Kate conceded. 'I've got three sons to consider, and a lot of thinking to do. But I'd like to keep my options open.'

'Fair enough.' Chris glanced at his watch. 'I'll be in touch.' He shook his head.

As they headed back out of the house, Kate's knees started to shake. This could be the beginning of something very exciting, very terrifying, or both.

That evening, Kate flopped down onto the sofa in Aidan and Tom's living room and wondered if she would ever get up again. She and the boys had hired some mountain bikes and had spent most of the day cycling the paths that criss-crossed the hills around Willow-bury, discovering the trails that led to secluded woodland spots, perfect for the picnic Kate had packed to take with them after she'd got back from looking at number three. The boys were sprawled around the living room, loose limbed as Labradors and utterly knackered, and were still talking about the 'Wall of Death' trail that ran through the beech and oak woodland on the other side of Willowbury Hill. Kate, genuinely afraid she was going to fly off her bike and break her neck, had taken things rather more steadily as all three boys had raced ahead. Harry had given Corey the day off, and it was wonderful to have all three of them outside in the open air, just having fun again, even if the speeds they tackled the trail made her very nervous.

Kate hadn't yet mentioned going to see the house on the end of the terrace; every time she'd thought about it during the day, she'd bottled out, not wanting to change the mood. But now, as she tried to relax on the sofa, she realised it was time to broach the subject. Replete from a dinner at the pub on the way back, the boys seemed amenable and relaxed.

'Did you have a good time today?' she asked Tom as he stretched out across the living room floor, lazily reaching for his phone.

'It was cool,' Tom said. 'Would have been better to have had my own bike, but the ones we hired weren't bad.'

'Perhaps next time we can do it on our own bikes,' Kate said.

Noticing a slightly reticent tone in her voice, all three boys swivelled their gaze towards their mother. 'What?' She laughed. 'Was it something I said?'

Corey, ever the natural spokesman for the brothers, broke the silence first. 'We've been thinking about what you said, Mum.'

'Oh yeah?' Kate laughed nervously. 'What's that, then?'

'About us moving here.'

'Look,' Kate began, 'I told you. I haven't made any decisions about anything, yet, and I wouldn't do it without talking to you all first, seeing what you think. It's been a lovely day... let's not start rowing.'

'It's all right, Mum,' Will interjected. 'We know all that. But we had a bit of a chance to think about what you said to us, and... well, we just want you to know... we're cool with whatever you decide.'

Kate's eyes filled with tears at the sincerity in her middle son's voice. 'That means a lot. Thank you.' She looked at her three sons, each in turn. 'Where's this come from, then?'

Will shrugged. 'We like it here. And we know you do, too.'

'But that's not the same as coming to live here, is it?'

'Well,' Tom said, picking up from his brother swiftly, 'it's not like, with Dad still being back home, we'd never see anyone again. Or like you're going to make us come to live here tomorrow, is it?'

'No,' Kate conceded. 'Even if I had found somewhere to live.'

Which, she thought quickly, *technically I haven't, yet*; pipe dreams didn't count. 'It would take a few months to get everything in place.'

'So we're still, like, going back to school in September, then?' Will said.

Kate grinned. 'Yup. 'Fraid so.' She looked again at her sons. 'But thank you, boys. What you've said means a lot. And I promise, no big decisions without consulting you first.'

At that moment, Kate's phone rang, and with an excited lurch, she saw Chris Charlton's name flashing up on screen. Jumping up from the sofa, she wandered through to the kitchen.

'Wow,' she said as she answered. 'I wasn't expecting to hear back from you so quickly.'

'I've got a good contact in the local estate agency,' Chris said. 'And I wanted to come back to you as quickly as I could. After all, if you decide it's not for you, I need to get it listed.'

'So what's the verdict?'

As Chris told her the figure he had in mind, Kate sank onto one of the kitchen chairs. 'I see,' she said softly. 'I'll be in touch. Thank you.' Ending the call, she couldn't work out if things had just got a whole lot simpler, or even more complicated.

Much later that evening, after the boys had gone to bed, Kate came downstairs after making sure all three of them had sleeping bags and enough space, and weren't about to punch each other's lights out. True to her word, she'd levelled with them immediately about Chris's phone call, and while they seemed shocked, they had again reminded her that they would be okay, whatever her decision was. As she entered the living room again, she found Aidan, who'd been round to see Sam and Florence earlier, sitting on the sofa watching *News at Ten*. Flumping down next to him, she let out a long sigh.

'So what gives, sis?' Aidan, eyes still fixed on the news, asked gently.

'What do you mean?'

'You've been on edge all evening. Want to tell me why?'

Kate sighed. 'Chris Charlton, the guy who owns the house at the end of Bay Tree Terrace, rang earlier let me know the price he wants to sell it for.'

'Oh yeah?' Aidan raised an eyebrow. 'And?'

'And... I *could* afford it.' She put her head briefly in her hands, before looking back up at her brother.

'You could... but do you want to?'

Kate shook her head. 'Now that it's real... I just don't know. There's a part of me that's jumping for joy. I mean, buying that house would be the answer to one set of problems, but am I letting myself in for even more? The boys have said they're okay with it, but are they really?'

'They'll adapt,' Aidan said gently. 'They're such good kids. You'll probably get a hard time for a while, but they've said themselves that they like it here.'

'But new schools, having to make new friends... a whole new house that at the moment's in shit order...?'

'People move across the country all the time,' Aidan said. 'Most of them, I'm sure, work it out in the end. And it's not as if you're moving somewhere you don't know anyone else. I'm here, Sam's here... Harry's here.'

At the mention of Harry's name, Kate's heart jumped. 'True,' she conceded. 'And with Phil still back in Cambridge, they'll be able to keep in touch with their mates.'

'And, to be fair, even if you do buy number three, the annexe at Mum's is going to be home for you for a little while. That place needs some serious work!'

'Fair point,' Kate said. 'When did you end up being the one who talked all the sense, out of the three of us?'

Aidan grinned. 'Someone has to pick up your slack, big sis. You can't be the sensible one all the time.'

'Phil's going to need keeping in the loop, too,' Kate said, 'if I do decide to go ahead with this.'

'Absolutely,' Aidan said. 'In spite of everything, you're going to need his help if you do. After all, doing up that house means weekends and free time over here.'

Kate again felt a huge flutter of nerves. 'I'm quite scared, actually.'

Aidan put an arm around her shoulders. 'Don't be. You've got all of us here to help.'

'Thanks,' Kate replied. 'You sound just like Dad.'

Aidan laughed a little. 'Who'd have thought I'd ever sound like a father?'

'Maybe one day you'll find out what that's like for real,' Kate said.

Aidan shook his head. 'I don't think so. It's great being an uncle, but I'm not sure I'm cut out for being a parent, even if Mia does make me feel broody. Besides, if Tom ends up touring with this play, or the next one, I'd quite like to be able to drop everything and go with him. Couldn't do that if I had a kid to worry about.' He glanced down at his lap, where Lucifer the cat was curled up, content to have his real owner back. 'And you can always feed this lump if we do go on tour.'

Kate shook her head. 'Providing you leave me a pair of thick gloves and a very long spoon! He doesn't like me at all.' As if he understood, Lucifer opened one brilliant green eye and regarded Kate with disdain.

'Yes, I think cats are about all the responsibility I can handle for the time being.' Aidan ruffled Lucifer under the chin and the cat stretched voluptuously.

'Fair enough,' Kate said. 'But never say never. You might find yourself wanting the nappy changes and the sleepless nights eventually.'

'You make it sound so appealing!' Aidan laughed. He paused, then looked thoughtful. 'You should probably sleep on it before you make any serious decisions about that house.'

Kate nodded. 'Definitely. I'm knackered. And I need to show the boys the house before I commit to anything.'

'What about Harry?' Aidan asked. 'Have you told him what's going on?'

Kate shook her head. 'Not yet.' She paused. 'I know it sounds weird, but I kind of want to set this in motion for myself before I tell him for sure.'

Aidan turned towards Kate on the sofa. 'It's not admitting weakness to acknowledge that seeing more of Harry is a good reason to be here.'

'I know.' Kate sighed. 'I just don't want to tempt fate. I mean, a holiday fling is one thing, but what happens when I'm literally just down the road? What if we decide we should have just called it a day when this house was done?'

'Then you'll be grown-ups about it, and walk away as friends,' Aidan said. 'I mean, come on, sis, I know you've been out of the dating game for bloody years, but you're not eighteen any more. You can handle it, whatever happens.'

'Thanks,' Kate said dryly.

Suddenly, Aidan yawned. 'Well, I'm off to bed. If you're still up when Tom gets back from his rehearsal, can you tell him there's a pasty in the fridge if he wants it?'

'How domesticated!' Kate teased.

Aidan grinned again. 'Everything changes, sis,' he said, ruffling her hair as he got up off the sofa. 'And with a bit of luck, it's all for the better.'

Long after Aidan had gone to bed, Kate was still sitting on the sofa. She hoped, with every bit of her being, that Aidan's last words were right. Suddenly, despite everything she'd said to Aidan, she picked up her phone.

'Hey,' she said softly when the call was answered. 'It's me.'

The voice on the end was sleepy, understandably, seeing as it was nearly midnight. 'Yes, everything's fine,' she said. Then she took a deep breath. 'I just thought you should know something.' She settled back against the comfy cushions of the sofa. 'Harry,' she said gently. 'Don't get excited, but I have a very strong feeling that Willowbury wasn't just for the summer.'

EPILOGUE
NINE MONTHS LATER

'Oh, thank goodness, the weather's going to hold,' Kate said as she checked the BBC weather app on her phone. 'I don't think we could have held this party indoors, now that everyone who was invited has decided to turn up!' Even Lorna, Kate's former next-door neighbour and close friend in Cambridge, who very rarely ventured out of the county unless she had to, had booked a room at the Avalon Rise Bed and Breakfast, so she could come to the housewarming party. She'd actually visited a couple of times while Kate had been renovating, and had eventually conceded that she could see the point in an upheaval to such a beautiful place.

Harry looked up from his laptop, where he was trying to make sense of the latest stock spreadsheet for Vale Volumes. 'We'd have managed,' he said mildly. Kate's middle son, Will, had settled well into his GCSE in Business Studies, despite the change of schools halfway through the year, and had been creating a searchable database for the bookshop as part of his coursework. Harry, unfortunately, still had yet to be able to make head or tail of it without his assistance, but that was more down to Harry's capacity for understanding it than Will's lack of skill in building it in the first place.

The renovations on number three, Bay Tree Terrace had been completed a month ago, and Kate had finally been persuaded that she could relax a little. Tom and Will had enrolled at Willowbury Academy after the Easter holiday and, despite some early reservations, had settled in well. They still spent every other weekend at Phil's place, and had bonded well with their new half-sister, who had been born a few months back. Although it was a long way to trek, they enjoyed the chance to spend time back in their old haunts. Tom had joined a local football team recently, which might mean fewer visits to Phil, but Kate was sure, like everything, it could all be worked out. Phil, despite his initial reservations about Kate's move, had eventually been persuaded that it was for the best.

Corey was in the Sixth Form at the academy and was working for Harry at the weekends. He'd settled well in Willowbury, was seeing the girl he'd met at Artemis Bane's book launch and was preparing to sit his AS Level exams. He was tickled to be taking English Literature with Florence's maternity cover teacher, and was jokingly looking forward to Florence's return to the classroom the following September, when, she'd assured him, there would be absolutely no favouritism.

Life was good. Harry was still living in his flat above the shop, but he was spending more and more time at Bay Tree Terrace. Kate was more than okay with his presence, and the two younger boys had taken to him well. Corey, of course, had gone from strength to strength, both in his usefulness in the bookshop and in his relationship with Harry. Both were more than happy with the way things were.

The party that afternoon was partly a celebration of the completion of the work on the house; Kate had taken hundreds of pictures of the renovations process, and they were proudly showcased on the website that Will had built for her, also as part of his coursework; this time for Computing. Work was coming in faster than she could commit to it, but she was loving the opportunity to make people's décor dreams a reality. It was also an unofficial naming ceremony for little Mia, who had grown into a feisty but sunny character and, despite Harry's early trauma at meeting her, she had been instrumental in cementing Harry's place in Kate's family. So much so that, after a little thought, Harry had agreed to be a kind of non-religious godparent to her, which had led Kate to joke that there really was no escape from the family, even if he wanted to.

Kate and Harry had been growing ever closer, but they were happy to let their relationship evolve at a slow, steady pace after the rush of the summer they'd spent together. This had allowed them both to really take their time, and for Harry to come to terms with the fact that, in dating Kate, he was also becoming part of her extended family. Kate's mother, Selina, had decided that she quite liked the view from Kate's well-appointed spare bedroom on the ground floor and was becoming a regular visitor to Willowbury. Kate was pretty sure that, eventually, her mother would end up living in the town permanently. Although Kate was sure that Aidan would have a word or two to say about this. Even he couldn't dispute the good sense of having their mother where they could keep a better eye on her. Selina had already planted some new roses in Kate's garden, which were just beginning to flower. Spending time at Bay Tree Terrace had done wonders for Selina's relationship with not just her own children, but her grandchildren, too, and Kate couldn't see her wanting to give that up in a hurry.

'It's all quite a change from where we were last summer, isn't it?' Harry said as he stood up from the kitchen table.

'It certainly is,' Kate agreed, putting her phone down on the counter and allowing Harry to pull her closer to him. 'And although I never would have imagined it this time last year, I wouldn't have it any other way.'

ACKNOWLEDGMENTS

As ever, a huge thank you to all at Boldwood Books, especially Sarah Ritherdon, who is a wonderful editor and who 'gets' it, every time I write a book. To Nia, Amanda and Claire for continuing to support this career of mine in such important, empowering ways. To Cecily Blench and Shirley Khan for being excellent copy and proof editors, respectively. Thank you, all, for everything you do!

Also, thanks to my brilliant agent, Sara Keane, who encourages and curbs my process in equal measure. Thanks also to the extremely supportive members of the Romantic Novelists' Association, locally and nationally, who provide endless banter, support and laughs. May we all be able to meet again in person soon! Special thanks to Teresa F. Morgan for the regular writerly chats and inspiration sessions over coffee.

To the usual friends and family for bearing with me through another book – I am so, so grateful. Nick, Flora and Roseanna, your understanding is something I will never take for granted, and I love you all for it.

A special shout out to Pippa Strachan, perinatal educator, for the help and advice on traumatic births and protocols, to ensure I was putting Florence and Sam through just enough.

To the *Horrible Histories* team, who made writing during a pandemic a bearable experience by keeping all of the family entertained with HH, *Ghosts* and *Yonderland*. You helped more than you will ever know, not least in giving me a style model for Harry

Sinclair, who bears more than a passing physical resemblance to Ben Willbond!

Finally, to you, my readers, for seeing Willowbury through another book. I am so, so grateful to each and every one of you for taking a chance on my novels. I hope you enjoyed the ride!

MORE FROM FAY KEENAN

We hope you enjoyed reading *Just for the Summer*. If you did, please leave a review.

If you'd like to gift a copy, this book is also available as an ebook, digital audio download and audiobook CD.

Sign up to Fay Keenan's mailing list for news, competitions and updates on future books.

http://bit.ly/FayKeenanNewsletter

Explore the Willowbury series.

ABOUT THE AUTHOR

Fay Keenan is the author of the bestselling *Little Somerby* series of novels. She has led writing workshops with Bristol University and has been a visiting speaker in schools. She is a full-time teacher and lives in Somerset.

Visit Fay's website: https://faykeenan.com/

Follow Fay on social media:

facebook.com/faykeenanauthor
twitter.com/faykeenan
instagram.com/faykeenan
bookbub.com/authors/fay-keenan

Boldwœd

Boldwood Books is an award-winning fiction publishing company seeking out the best stories from around the world.

Find out more at www.boldwoodbooks.com

Join our reader community for brilliant books, competitions and offers!

Follow us
@BoldwoodBooks
@BookandTonic

Sign up to our weekly deals newsletter

https://bit.ly/BoldwoodBNewsletter